The Second Mrs. Ringling

By Ellen Brosnahan

Jan,
I hope you enjoy this three-ring circus!
Ellen

Copyright © 2022 Ellen Brosnahan
Print Edition

All rights reserved. No part of this publication may be reproduced, distributed, or transmitted in any form or by any means, including photocopying, recording, or other electronic or mechanical methods, without the prior written permission of the publisher, except in the case of brief quotations embodied in critical reviews and certain other noncommercial uses permitted by copyright law.

This book is a work of fiction. Places, names, characters and events are either products of the author's imagination or used fictitiously. Any resemblance to actual events, locations, or persons, living or dead, is purely coincidental and not intended by the author.

Chapter One

THE DECEMBER MORNING light seeped through the window and nudged Emily awake. She stretched her arms toward the ceiling of her bedroom, then stared up at the crystal chandelier that hung above her.

It's my wedding day.

Her eyes scanned the room as if she were taking inventory—the dressing table laden with perfume bottles and jars of her creams and lotions, the burled armoire, the damask chaise longue where she'd often curled up with the latest issue of *The New Yorker*. *How strange—my last time awakening here at the Barclay.* She'd loved living here, loved her stylish apartment, loved her independence. But today was a new day and her housemaid would soon be packing it all up, some destined for Florida, some to be brought to John's Park Avenue apartment.

I'm getting married!

She sat up in bed, propping her pillows up behind her, and held out her left hand to examine the ring on her finger. *It really is a showstopper.* The emerald encircled by diamonds was almost too large for her small hand, but, as her friend Sophie had said when she first saw the ring, "There is no such thing as too many jewels."

And it suits the man who put it on my finger. He's a bit of a showstopper himself. She tipped her hand so the ring could catch the light. *Was John a showstopper?* He was not attractive in the usual sense, as he was many years her senior, a barrel-chested man with a fleshy face. But yes, she had been attracted to him from the moment they met, drawn to the force of his personality, to his larger—than-life presence in any room. *By this afternoon, I will be his wife.*

Her mind wandered back to her first wedding day, thirteen years ago.

On that warm June morning, her mother had see-sawed from teary-eyed laments about "losing my *Liebchen*" to issuing directives with the authority of a battlefield commandant. "Girls, stop all of the giggling and calm yourselves," she scolded Emily's younger sisters, as Olga and Louise erupted in fits of giggles while preparing for the wedding ceremony.

The sisters had been in a frenzy as they dressed in their finery, twirling about in their matching rose dresses, pinning on their picture hats over their freshly curled hair, and drifting from one bedroom to another in their peau de soie slippers. Emily found their silliness contagious, but refrained from joining in. She was a grown woman now, not a giddy girl, and by the end of the day she would be a married woman. She bit the inside of her cheeks to keep from snickering as Louise, the youngest, spun around so quickly that she lost her balance, falling onto Emily's bed.

"*Das ist alles!*" Mama cried, but she covered her mouth to hide her smile. "You girls are like chickens running around." She shooed them out of the room and, patting her reddening cheeks with a handkerchief, turned to Emily. "You look so beautiful, my dear daughter."

Emily recalled staring at herself in the Cheval mirror. *Is that really me?* She could hardly find herself in the reflection. Perspiration trickled down her back inside the voluminous dress of heavy brocade layered with a French lace. Even her blond hair was invisible, swathed in a lacy Juliet cap that anchored the long veil to her head.

She tugged at the ruffles at the neckline. "Mama, I'm so hot!"

"Don't fret, *Liebchen*. You look beautiful." She gave her daughter a kiss on the cheek, then examined her own reflection in the mirror. Straightening her wide-brimmed hat, she added, "Come. Papa is waiting."

Emily allowed herself to be led downstairs, where her father, in his morning coat, paced across the parlor floor. He cleared his throat as she approached him.

"How do I look, Papa?" *Was that a glimmer of a tear in his eye?*

"Beautiful, but we are going to be late. Ladies, into the car!" He whisked his wife and daughters into the waiting automobile, and they were driven to the German Presbyterian Church just blocks away, the same church where she had been baptized as an infant.

TODAY'S WEDDING WILL not be like that one. Today she would not be weighed down by a massive gown, carrying a bouquet the size of a bushel basket, withering in the oppressive heat of summer. Her vison would not be obscured through filmy tulle and, unlike when she met Charles at the altar thirteen years ago, she would be able to see her groom clearly, to look into his eyes.

At the age of nineteen, she had barely known the handsome Charles, well into his thirties, but he was intelligent and worldly-wise, and her father insisted that he was a good match. "He will be an excellent provider and he is German. Like we are," Papa had said. So, when he proposed to her in her parents' parlor, Emily had not hesitated to say yes.

She and Charles began their life together in a Riverside Drive apartment in New York, but business always seemed to take precedence for Charles. Emily was often alone, as Charles traveled to Europe to build up his imports company. She was hardly surprised when he announced he was leaving her for another woman, but he was generous in providing for her. On her own and with a sizable inheritance from her parents, Emily took charge of her finances and investments, insuring herself a comfortable life as an unmarried woman.

THIS TIME, PAPA and Mama are not here to advise me. And I'm not so dewy-eyed anymore. But am I any wiser today? For days, she had told herself that it was natural to have misgivings. Any bride-to-be would, especially when the romance had intensified in just a matter of months.

She threw back the bedcovers and stood. The chauffeur would be arriving in two hours to drive her across the Hudson.

Stop second-guessing yourself, Emily. Today is your wedding day.

From the very first day she accepted his proposal, John had pushed for an elaborate wedding. "Darling, how about the ballroom at the Waldorf? It's large enough to accommodate hundreds of well-wishers, and I want to show you off to the world."

The thought of an assembly of onlookers, mostly John's business associates she had never met, filled Emily with dread. "John, let's keep this simple. If we invite all of New York City, I will not have you to myself on our day. Please, let's keep our ceremony out of the public eye so we can focus on one another."

"But I want the world to know I'm the luckiest man alive to have found you." He clasped her hands and brought them to his lips.

"You are a sweet man. But a big event, a public spectacle—I don't want that." She wondered if she had chosen her words wisely. Perhaps a public spectacle was exactly what he wanted. She continued. "Let's keep our wedding simple and dignified. Please. Don't ask me to share you with others on our day. We can always throw a big party at some future date."

When John finally acquiesced, Emily threw her arms around his neck. "Thank you, my darling." She had prevailed, but she was struck by John's propensity for lavish extravagance. As the acclaimed Circus King, he seemed to bask in the limelight, while she preferred to go about life unimpeded by the scrutiny of others.

He moved in a stratum of celebrity and affluence that she had not encountered before. Yes, she herself was a wealthy woman, but John? In casual conversations, he referred to his railroads, his oil wells, his flotilla of automobiles and dropped the names of people who made the headlines of the financial pages. But wasn't that part of his appeal? Life with John Ringling was sure to be an adventure beyond compare.

Of course, it had seemed odd that he had borrowed money from her, but she had taken him at his word that the need for some liquid cash was just a temporary anomaly. Wasn't he promising her a life of unparalleled privilege and extravagance?

Emily dressed in a Chanel suit of ivory tweed and assessed her appearance in the mirror. *No grandiose bouquet, no gown encrusted with beads, but classic and elegant. This is who I want to be.*

And although John had given in to her wish to avoid a grandiose affair, she too had compromised. Any city clerk's office would have sufficed for her, but a few days after his plans for a Waldorf wedding were quashed, John insisted that they be married by his friend, Mayor Frank Hague of Jersey City.

"Jersey City?" she had asked. "Why there?" New Jersey, her childhood home, held little appeal for her and she'd considered herself a New Yorker for years.

"Frank's an old friend. We go way back. And the Office of the Mayor certainly has more ambiance than some dreary courthouse. Tex Rickard, my partner with Madison Square Garden, is setting it all up."

Had she met this Tex person? And wasn't Hague the man they called the Sphinx of Jersey City? So, John was managing to get his business connections involved anyway. But she went along. It seemed important to John. Jersey City it would be.

She added a slouchy velvet cloche to her ensemble and then tucked a few last-minute items into her travelling case. What had made her insist that they arrive separately, telling John it was bad luck to see his bride before the ceremony? Whatever old superstition she had dredged up, she was glad of her decision to ride alone, to imagine her future, on her way to meet her dashing groom, John Ringling.

Outside, the chauffeur was waiting for her and soon the car left the sunny streets of the city and headed into the depths of the Holland Tunnel. Darkness surrounded her as they sped along underneath the Hudson, but her thoughts were on what awaited her on the other side. *Just John and me, two clear-eyed adults who have fallen in love, beginning a future together.*

JOHN, DRESSED IN a double-breasted black pinstripe with a stephanotis pinned to his lapel, was waiting for her outside the Mayor's Office. "Here you are!" he said as she disembarked from the elevator. The sparkle Emily saw in his eyes quelled any apprehension she felt. *He truly loves me. And I love him.*

He reached out for her hands and broke into a smile. "How did I ever get to be so lucky, Emily, to have you as my beautiful bride. My heart is doing flip-flops at the sight of you."

"I feel the same way, John. It's magical." She squeezed his hands, savoring the devotion she found in his gaze.

"Come, Frank is waiting." He opened the door marked "Office of the Mayor" and led her in. He set down the dove gray fedora he'd been holding and kissed her. With a flourish, he pulled an arrangement of white roses from a florist box sitting on a table. "A bouquet for my bride."

But I didn't want a bouquet. And this one is enormous. Emily held her tongue. She knew John meant well, and what harm was there in carrying this bundle of flowers. "Lovely, darling. Thank you." She held them to her nose to inhale the perfume.

She and John were ushered into Hague's private office by an assistant. Hague stood and reached out to take Emily's hand. "So here is your beautiful bride I've heard so much about." Turning, Hague clapped John on the back. "You old rascal you! Guess they can teach an old dog new tricks."

John slid his arm around Emily's waist and guffawed. "I'm one lucky son of a gun, Frank."

The two men bantered back and forth about politics and a recent boxing match at Madison square Garden as Emily stood silent.

"Still think you made a big mistake putting your museum in a Florida jungle instead of Jersey City." The Mayor crossed his arms and shook his head.

"You're not still holding a grudge, are you, Frank? You've got to come to Sarasota and see the museum I've built down there. You'll see why I made the decision, even though your Jersey City offer was a sweet one." John squeezed Emily's shoulder. "We'd love to have you visit, wouldn't we, Emily?"

She smiled without opening her lips. "Well, I haven't seen it myself yet, John." *Would they ever stop talking about business? Hadn't they come here to get married?*

"Soon, dear. You're sure to be dazzled by what Mable and I accomplished." John pulled her in to him in a brief hug. "Say, Frank, let's get on with things. I came here to marry this gorgeous girl."

"Sure, sure. No witnesses with you?"

"No, just my bride and me. Emily wanted to keep things simple."

"Simple it is. Let me get two witnesses and we'll get this done." The Mayor called in a secretary and an assistant from the outer office and when they assembled, he peered through his glasses at the book in his hands and read in a monotone.

"Do you, John, take this woman…"

"Do you, Emily, take this man…"

The words washed over Emily and in a minute or two, they were married. *Husband and wife.*

John wrapped his arms around her and kissed her. Leaning his forehead on hers, he looked into her eyes. "You've made me a happy man, today, Emily. I love you, my beautiful wife."

She swallowed a lump in her throat. "And I love you, my husband." *This bear of a man, from this day forward.* She blinked and clung to John's arms as a newsreel-style image rolled across her mind's eye. *John as a daredevil barnstormer, and I the daring wing walker, teetering high above the real world, putting my future into his hands. I don't know where my life with John will lead me, but it is sure to be a lively escapade.*

Chapter Two

EMILY HAD NOT expected the gaggle of reporters gathered on the steps of the Mayor's Office after the ceremony, but apparently Frank Hague alerted them. He steered John and Emily so that they faced the photographers, hissed, "Smile," and then bellowed, "Gentlemen, I present Mr. John Ringling and his new bride Emily."

John tipped his gray fedora and threw out his chest while linking his arm through Emily's. He whispered into her ear, "This will be in all the papers tomorrow." She smiled on cue but could not avoid blinking as the flashbulbs popped and reporters shouted out questions.

Hague stepped forward and shooed the newsmen off the steps. "Let 'em through, let 'em through. You've got your pictures." Turning to John, he reached out to shake his hand. "Can't keep these fellas away, you know, John."

John shrugged. "Comes with the territory." Leading Emily to the waiting limousine, he remarked, "You'll get used to this kind of thing."

Would she? Would it now be considered *de riguer*?

She couldn't imagine that her comings and goings would be of interest to anyone. But she'd never been Mrs. Ringling before.

"ONCE WE GET settled on my rail car the *Jomar* and we depart for Florida, we'll pop the champagne and celebrate, just the two of us," John said when they settled into the back of the limousine. "Just wait until you experience it!" He patted her hand, then lit a cigar. "It's no doubt the most luxurious private rail car in the country."

"So you've mentioned. I'm thrilled to see it, darling." This was just one more element to John's level of affluence. While she had routinely travelled by rail in private Pullman suites, dining in the well-appointed dining cars, she had no experience with a private car with all the accoutrements of a luxurious home. Emily turned toward the window, losing herself in thought as John continued detailing *Jomar*'s features. The wealth, the privilege, the connections to the movers and shakers of industry and politics, this was all part of her world now. It was both breath-taking and daunting at the same time.

Heading back to New York, the limousine once again entered the Holland Tunnel. Emily clenched her jaw in the darkness, as she considered the river rushing over them. She closed her eyes and put herself back to the summer, when she and Sophie had, on a whim, decided to travel to Europe.

"Dahling," her friend Sophie had suggested over luncheon salads at the Waldorf Astoria, "Let's sail abroad. Some shopping in Paris, then on to Amsterdam." She signaled to the white-jacketed waiter hovering nearby, tapped on the rim of her goblet, and mouthed, "Another, please." Turning to Emily, she continued. "New York is so dreary these days, and the heat is oppressive. And on top of all that, aren't you tired of only being served tonic water? Imagine the wines and cocktails we could enjoy abroad. Besides, I'm hearing there are many eligible aristocrats there, debonair men with royal titles. You've been a woman alone for a while now. And you're barely past thirty. Maybe you'll meet some dashing duke!"

Emily stirred her club soda with a swizzle stick. "A dashing duke? Is that what I need?" She chuckled at Sophie's suggestion. "I'd say I'm fumbling along rather well without a man!"

"You certainly are! As am I. But maybe a little romance could add just a bit of spark to our lives." Sophie raised and lowered her eyebrows coquettishly.

Emily sipped her drink. She had been so young, so sheltered when she'd married Charles. She assumed she would be married forever, but then he'd left her early in their marriage. Since then, she struggled to establish herself in New York society where people tended to make inaccurate presumptions about a divorcee. It was Sophie, another divorcee, who recognized Emily's plight and befriended her when others gossiped behind her back.

Sophie pressed on. "New York is dull these days and everyone is so gloomy."

Should she go? What was stopping her? The last few years had been overwhelming. After the divorce, she was forced to address a barrage of decisions, personal and financial. Lawyers, accountants, business colleagues, all pulled at her in opposite directions. She'd remained steady, making each decision with a clear-headedness that seemed to surprise those men who'd expected her to fall apart. Maybe it was time to embrace life wholeheartedly—to meet new people, to travel, to experience the freedom that her wealth afforded her.

"Nothing in this world can be counted on, dear," continued Sophie, "but life goes on. Let the world take notice of your charm and vivacity." Sophie reached out to grasp her friend's hand. "Think about it, Emily. This could be the lark you need."

Emily twisted her mouth into a tentative smile. A lark, as Sophie called it, might be just the thing.

"Yes, I'll do it."

"Hurrah! I'll make the arrangements." Sophie raised her glass in triumph. "What an adventure we'll have!"

She and Sophie booked a transatlantic voyage—

Paris, then off to visit an acquaintance of Sophie's in Amsterdam. The Dutch city charmed Emily with its romantic canals, vibrant flower markets, and cobblestone streets. High society from all over the continent flocked to the cafes and night clubs, and yes, titled barons appeared at every soiree she attended. Emily was caught up in a whirl of new faces.

On the Fourth of July, Emily and Sophie joined a group of expats to celebrate. The ballroom of the Hotel Krasnapolsky was festooned in red, white, and blue bunting, and centerpieces featuring the Stars and Stripes decorated every table. Duke Ellington's lively band sent the entire crowd to the dance floor and the beautifully *avant garde* Josephine Baker performed her famous burlesque. Emily, wearing a newly purchased Schiaparelli gown of ivory silk, was enthralled.

She sipped her chilled martini as she scanned the room, "Sophie, you were so right about escaping tedious old New York for some summer enchantment across the pond. Who would have expected all this glamour, all of these stars?" Just across the room stood Florenz Ziegfeld, downing a cocktail and with Eddie Cantor, W.C. Fields, and a man she didn't recognize.

Sophie, elegant in a jade green chiffon confection that pooled around her ankles, smirked at her friend. "May I just say, 'I told you so'? And don't look now, but you're getting some attention from Mr. John." She discreetly tipped her head, adorned with a brocade turban she'd purchased in Paris, toward the cluster of tuxedoed entertainers that had caught Emily's eye.

"Mr. John? Not sure I know him."

"Well, you should. He's the very tall man in the center of the circle there. He's John Ringling, you know, the circus tycoon. He's quite a charmer, I hear. And a recent widower. Lost his wife last summer, I think. Lots of money, lots of glamourous friends. Big personality." Sophie waggled her fingers toward the group and called out, "Hello, Flo, darling. It's been ages. Will you introduce us to your friends?"

The men approached, introductions were made, and Sophie and Ziegfeld caught up on old times. Emily smiled at each of the gentlemen, wondering how on earth Sophie knew Florenz Ziegfeld. While she knew plenty of New York City's upper class, she generally didn't socialize with the show business set.

John reached out and touched her arm. "Emily, pleased to meet you. I'm sure you're bored with all this vaudeville talk. What have you enjoyed about Amsterdam?"

Looking upward into his face, Emily was taken by the sparkle in his eyes, as if what she was about to say was of utmost importance. "Oh, the bicycles, I think! Imagine all those bicycles in New York! Why, people would be crashing into each other left and right!"

He erupted in laughter. "Brilliant! Just what I have wondered."

More light banter continued, and before long, Emily was in his arms on the dance floor, John leading her gracefully among the other dancers to the mellow sounds of "Mood Indigo". Basking in the warmth of John's attention in this glamourous ballroom so far from home was as heady as fine champagne.

✧ ✧ ✧

SUDDENLY THE AUTOMOBILE emerged from the tunnel and bright sunshine streamed into the windows, rousing Emily from her reverie. She turned to John, and he stroked her cheek with his finger. "What are you thinking, my love? You look a million miles away."

She held his hand and kissed it. "I was far away, in Amsterdam, on the night we met. It was magical, wasn't it?" She beamed at him. *This is my husband. Is this really possible?*

"It was magical. And may we have many more magical moments in our future together."

PENN STATION WAS bustling with travelers, but as John and Emily made their way along the platform, a man in a shabby gray overcoat nudged another and announced, "There's Ringling himself! That's his train car!" Others turned to gape at them, and Emily felt as if a spotlight had been aimed at her, but she pressed her lips together and allowed John to lead them through the throng of passengers.

"Here we are, Emily! My *Jomar*!" John waved his arms with a flourish toward a train car, bottle green with gold embellishments, just ahead of them.

Emily was initially struck by its size as it extended along the platform. "Window after window! And this entire car is yours!" She could not help exclaiming as they approached the steps where a uniformed butler awaited them.

John tucked her hand into his and smiled. "Yes, darling. Over eighty-three feet long. Built especially for me and Mable. Hence the name. *Jo* for John, *Ma* for Mable, and *R* for Ringling." He nodded to the butler. "Robert, this is my new bride, Emily."

The butler's face remained impassive as he muttered a perfunctory "Hello," then stepped aside so Emily and John could enter the car. Inside, Emily drank in her surroundings as she shrugged off her coat and John handed it along with his topcoat to Robert.

"Come, dear, let me show you everything." No feature was omitted from John's descriptions of every room—the inlaid mahogany, the Tiffany shades on every lamp, the lush tapestry on the dining chairs, and the large tub in his bathroom. "It's like stepping into a jewel case, isn't it?"

"It is, truly." She ran her hands along the tufted burgundy velvet of the wall.

"And you are just the sparkling gem to set this place aglow." He encircled her in his arms. "You've made me a happy man today, Emily."

Leaning into John's chest, Emily sorted through her feelings. She felt disoriented, as if she were looking down at herself from high above, as if she were in a theater balcony, watching a play unfold on a stage. *The lap of luxury.* She had always known privilege and wealth. But this kind of wealth, this extravagance, was new to her. Would she become accustomed to it all? What would Mama and Papa say? They had provided a comfortable life for their daughters, but they strictly avoided any glimmer of ostentation. Would they disapprove of John's lavish way of life? But why should anyone disapprove? John had earned his wealth through hard work and shrewd decision-making. Why not enjoy the fruits of his labor?

And then there was Mabel. Even the car itself bore her name and her presence emanated from every inch of the interior. John could not describe any facet of the car without including Mable's name—Mable's brass beds, her French crystal, her imported fabrics. Emily told herself not to be petty. After all, Mable had been an integral part of the car's design. And she could be an integral part of redecorating it at some future date.

For now, she'd simply take it all in and enjoy the ride. She lifted her face towards John's and kissed him. "It's all so wonderful, my darling."

The train whistle sounded and the car, attached to the string of passenger cars, lurched forward and began its rhythmic chugging along.

John released her from his embrace. "Come, let's sit in the observation room and toast to our future as we watch the landscape glide past. The train will stop along the way, but we will never have to disembark. We've all we could want right here. Next stop, Florida."

Chapter Three

FOR MONTHS, EMILY had listened to John wax on about the grandeur of Ca d'Zan, his estate on the bay of Sarasota and fashioned after a Venetian palazzo. She'd been exhausted from the long train ride, but John seemed invigorated as they stepped from the train and into the waiting Rolls Royce, his chauffeur Frank piling their luggage onto a delivery lorry. The car made its way down a dark road to an elaborately designed gate house, then through the wrought iron gate embellished with vines and the letter R.

At the end of a long driveway, the house, lights glimmering in every window, came into view. Emily's breath caught in her throat. Ca d'Zan! It was grand, imposing, and larger than she imagined. *Like a foreign castle, not a place to live.* Before she could comment, the car came to a stop. As Frank opened the Rolls' door, John sighed, "At last! Home!" and guided Emily from the car and through the main doors. "Ca d'Zan awaits you, my dear."

As soon as Emily plucked off her gloves, unpinned

her hat and handed them and her fox cape to the waiting housekeeper whom John introduced as Martha, John, nearly bouncing on his toes in anticipation, insisted on giving her a tour. "Come along, my dear. I'm sure you're dying to see every inch of my Ca d'Zan."

What she was really dying for was a soak in a warm bath and a cocktail. After hours of riding along the rails, her equilibrium felt off-kilter and a headache threatened. But Emily flashed a brilliant smile at her new husband, clutched his arm, and said, "Oh, yes. Lead the way, my darling."

He began by pointing to the wall near the door. "We'll start right here in the reception. Take a look at these sconces. Once hung in the Astor place. And that tapestry, too. Yes, bought them for a song." He preened, hands on hips, then pointed out a set of six gilded throne chairs scattered around the foyer. "Mable and I got those beauties for pennies on the dollar. They're from the New Jersey estate of George Gould, the big railroad man. Poor chap died of a fever after visiting King Tut's tomb, and his estate was sold at a rock bottom price."

As tired as she was, Emily murmured appropriate compliments as she took stock of everything in the home, the gilt-encrusted furniture, the travertine marble, the elaborate Delft bird cage. It was more than she ever imagined—more lavish, more ornate. Mable and she certainly had a different aesthetic. *A bird cage? That needs to be removed. So many dreary antiques… so passé.*

"See here, Emily. This portrait is Marianna of Austria, seventeenth century, done by Juan Buatista Martinez del Mazo. Are you familiar with him?"

"I'm afraid not." She pretended to study the painting for a moment. Why would John want a portrait of Austrian royalty in his Venetian style home?

He pulled a cigar from his jacket and lit it. "No, of course, understandable. But it's quite a treasure actually. You'll soon learn the provenance of every piece. It's all catalogued." He patted her arm, then steered her toward two Flemish tapestries flanking the front door.

She stroked one, then brushed dust off her fingertips. *Musty old things.* The whole place could use some livening. With just a bit of work, she could transform Ca d'Zan into an *au courant* showplace. Art deco sofas, black enamel tables, sleek lines.

Before Emily could mentally transform the décor of the foyer, John whisked her into the parlor. "We call this the Court. See the painting on the ceiling? Called *The Winged Lion of Venice.* But before I describe everything in here, you must see the ceiling in ballroom." He cupped her elbow and led her to an adjoining room. "You're going to love it!"

In the ballroom, John tipped Emily's chin upward with his fingers. "Behold! Nothing like it in the entire world. Each of these twenty-two paintings were done in

New York by Willy Pogany, whose done set designs for the Met Opera and murals for William Hearst. Flo knows him and introduced us. What do you think?"

Emily stared at the coffered ceiling, each section featuring a vignette of dancers from around the world. John was right; she had not seen anything like this. "It's beguiling, John. There is a fresh, almost whimsical quality to each one." So far, this was the first aspect of the home that had caught her fancy.

John grinned and patted her hand. "I knew you'd like it. But let me show you the best one." Using his cigar as a pointer, he directed Emily's gaze to one of the pairs of dancers. "See! It's Mable and me, fox-trotting! Aren't we a delightful pair!" He drew in on his cigar, staring at the ceiling.

Emily took in the depiction of John and Mable, then glanced at John, whose eyes remained on the image of him and his deceased wife. *He's gone back in time. And I am not a part of that time.* She felt discomfited, as if she had intruded on an intimate moment, and stepped back to return to the parlor. There, she looked up again, *at The Wnged Lion*. The animal seemed to be smirking down at her, a trespasser in Mable's dominion. *What am I doing here? How will this ever be my home?*

John joined her, interrupting her thoughts. "Ah, here you are, Emily. Come. There's more to see." His tour continued through the dining room, the solarium, and his private bar, rhapsodizing as he went. As he was pointing out the Otis elevator—"the first one installed in a private home"—, Emily sighed. "An elevator! My goodness. You've thought of everything. It's all so much to take in, my darling. But can we save the rest of the tour for when I am not quite so tired, so that I can truly appreciate every detail?"

John paused and caressed the cheek of his new wife. "You do look exhausted. How thoughtless of me! Let's get you upstairs so that you can refresh a bit. We'll have some light supper, and tomorrow I'll continue to show you all our treasures. Wait until you see what's upstairs."

"Really, John, I couldn't eat a thing. The lunch we had on the *Jomar* was sumptuous. Please allow me to retire early. Tomorrow, after a good night's rest, I'll be eager to see everything." She smiled weakly and rubbed her temple. "I just need a good night's sleep." Looking up the marble stairs, she hesitated. "But where have the servants put my trunk? I'm not sure…"

"Emily, I'm sorry. It has been a bit of a whirlwind, hasn't it? I've allowed my enthusiasm for Ca d'Zan to get the best of me tonight, I'm afraid." He pulled her toward him and kissed her forehead, trailing his fingers through her hair. Releasing her, he stepped toward the kitchen door. "Martha," he called out, and the middle-aged woman who had met them at the door appeared, her hands clasped over her white apron, her eyes on her employer. Her graying hair was pulled away from her face and knotted at the nape of her neck and she wore an expression of long-suffering obedience. Emily took stock of her. *So grim and drab, and not cheerful like my gals at the Barclay.*

"Mrs. Emily would like to get settled. Can you show her upstairs?"

"Yes, sir. I've taken the liberty to settle her in the guest room next to Mrs. Mable's room. I hope that's acceptable."

"Perfect, Martha. Please show Mrs. Emily upstairs." Patting Emily on the arm, he added, "Goodnight, darling. Sleep well." Then he headed into the tap room.

Martha turned toward Emily, her reptilian eyes cold. "This way, Miss."

As the housekeeper led the way up the alabaster stairs, Emily's mind swirled in confusion. She was sure that she detected a sneer on the face of this woman. And was she being led to the guest room next to Miss Mable's room? Mable was dead! She was *Mrs.* Ringling now, not some guest. And why hadn't John objected? Entering the room she'd been assigned, she could barely contain her rancor as Martha pointed out the closet and said, "I've had the upstairs girl unpack for you." A hodgepodge of gowns and dresses, shoes and hats were crammed into a too-small space as if she were a weekend partyer who'd brought too many changes of clothes.

"Martha, this is unacceptable. My gowns are being ruined in this crush. I'll need additional space." Emily shook her head and scowled as she sifted through the jumble of dresses. Her Schiaparelli, her Chanel had been mashed into this miniscule closet.

"Yes, miss," replied Martha in a weary tone.

"And you may call me Mrs. Ringling. Now, if you would be so kind as to draw me a bath."

Yes, Mrs. Ringling." Martha scuttled into the bathroom. While the water ran in the tub, Emily surveyed the bedroom. Facing the front courtyard, it was small, about half the size of her room at the Barclay. Pink roses and green ivy climbed up the wallpaper. Filling most of the space were a mirrored armoire and a bed covered in a lacy pink counterpane, A dainty dressing table and its twee chair stood between the closet and the bathroom doors. It was unfathomable that she was expected to keep all her cosmetics and perfumes on this tiny table. And what about her jewelry? Sitting on the chair, Emily had to bend down to see her reflection in the mirror. She tugged off the gold earrings she wore and clenched her fist around them. Ridiculous! Why, it was like living inside of a fancy chocolate box! This should not be where the mistress of the house was supposed to live. And where was John's room? Angrily, she kicked off her pumps, aiming them toward the closet. They landed with a thud just as Martha emerged from the bathroom.

Your bath is ready, Missus. Towels are on the rack." Martha eyed the discarded shoes and bent to pick them up, her back to Emily in a silent rebuke.

"Martha, where is Mable's room?"

"Right through that door," she pointed to the corner of the room. "Mrs. Mable's sisters and her mother often stayed in this room when they visited. They liked it well enough."

Such an insolent tone! When they visited? Well, she was not visiting. She was Mrs. John Ringling, not some overnight guest. Emily clenched her jaw but managed to calmly say "Thank you. That will be all." Martha nodded and left the room, closing the door silently behind her.

With Martha out of the way, Emily opened the door leading to Mable's sanctuary. First, she came upon a luxurious bathroom with a marble tub tucked into an alcove. Delicately painted floral patterns accented the cupboards above the mirrored closet doors lining the room. Yes, this was what she expected, not that pokey little space she'd been allotted. Opening one of the closet doors, Emily was chagrined to find Mable's garments hanging there. In another cupboard, she found shelves lined with shoes—brown suede brogues, black peau de soie pumps, a navy blue buckled style, all made for feet much smaller than Emily's. It was as if Mable would return at any moment. Why? She'd been dead for nearly two years, for heaven's sake. Glancing around, she noted

Mable's hairbrush and comb still waiting for her on a dressing table, and a limp linen garden frock hanging on a dress form. It was past time for these things to be packed away. Crossing through the next door, Emily entered the boudoir, furnished with a French rococo suite gilded with golden cherubs. She assessed its contents. A bit gaudy, but clearly expensive. She supposed it would do for the time being. She opened the armoire to find Mable's peignoirs, still heavy with a cloying perfume that Emily couldn't name. More to pack up. She noted the French doors that led to a terrace and opened them to allow a cool breeze to swirl through the room.

She'd have to broach this carefully with John. But this suite *would* be hers, not Mable's any longer. She opened another door, this one leading into John's room, and scanned it quickly. Surely, he wanted his new bride near him at night. They were newlyweds, weren't they? She could make sure that he wouldn't want his bride so far away. She smiled to herself and retraced her steps back to the guest room. One night in here, and that would be that. She entered the little pink tiled bathroom, undressed, and sank into the tub. *Mrs. Ringling,* she told herself, *tomorrow you will find your place as the lady of the house.*

Chapter Four

SLEEP DID NOT come easily.

As she tossed and turned in this unfamiliar room, she once again considered what had drawn her to John.

He was not the handsomest of men, but a striking figure nonetheless—tall and impeccably dressed. John was witty, knew everyone of importance, and showered her with attention. His voice boomed, his laugh was hearty and infectious, and he sprinkled references to his oil holdings, his Pierce Arrows and Rolls Royces, his railroad interests into any conversation. He was a man of consequence, and he'd disarmed her, charmed her. In Amsterdam and then in New York, he took her to lovely places, never resisting the urge to hold her in his arms on the dance floor. And wherever they went, the song "Them There Eyes" seemed to follow them, providing the romantic musical score to their love story.

> *"I fell in love with you the first time I looked into them*
> *there eyes*
> *And you have a certain lil cute way of flirtin' with them*

there eyes
They make me feel so happy, they make me feel so blue
I'm fallin', no stallin' in a great big way for you"

How many times had John stared into her eyes and sang these words to her? It had all been intoxicating and she had thrown caution to the winds.

✧ ✧ ✧

EMILY LEFT HER bed and, stepping to the window, she drew back the curtains, revealing a sky filled with a million stars, so unlike the sky of the city.

Yes, there had been warning signs. When he spoke of Mable endlessly, she had simply just chalked that up to some lingering grief. After all, he was entitled to mourn a spouse of so many years, wasn't he? Then he'd proposed, promising her a life of excitement and glamour, a Park Avenue apartment and a mansion in a Floridian paradise, surrounded by elegance and art. How could she resist? She was quite fond of him. It would be a good match.

So here you are, Emily.

And so, in the morning, Emily left her assigned room and, peering over from the mezzanine, spied John gazing out at terrace windows. She was ready. She descended the stairs, crossed the vast room he called The Court, and stood next to him. "Good morning, John. Such a lovely view. I can see why you love it so."

He turned toward her. "I trust you slept well in your first night at Ca d'Zan, my dear. You look beautiful this morning... like a breath of fresh air." His eyes drank in her perfectly coiffed hair, her fashionable morning frock in a delicate pattern of blues and grays and he reached for her and gave her a peck on the cheek. He took a cigar out of is breast pocket, twirling it absent-mindedly.

"Truthfully, John, I didn't sleep very well." She sighed and examined her wedding ring, twisting it around her finger, then focused on his face. "This is difficult..." she hesitated, furrowing her brow.

"What is it? What can I do to make you happy?" Returning the cigar to the pocket of his linen shirt, he leaned forward, cocking his head to the side.

"John, I'm your wife, am I not?" She became aware of the scrapings of chairs, the clinking of silverware and china being laid out for their meal in the room just beyond them. Was Martha in there listening? But no, she could hear her issuing orders to the cook into the kitchen. Her eyes bore into John's.

"My goodness, yes! You've made me so happy, my dear." He grasped both of her hands and squeezed them. He searched her face for clues to explain her discomfort.

"But I've been relegated to a guest room, and a small one at that. Shouldn't I, as your wife, be in the suite of rooms next to yours?" She raised an eyebrow, biting her lower lip.

He flinched. "Mable's rooms?" he asked, his voice tremulous.

"John darling, Mable is no longer here. We are husband and wife now. I know you still grieve, and I will try every day to bring joy back into your life, but I am your wife now." She lowered her head, focusing on the floor. Had she hurt him? Made him angry? She held her breath as she awaited his response. A few seconds of silence passed. What had she done? Pushed too hard? But this was absurd! She was not some house guest.

John sighed and lifted her chin gently so he could look down into her eyes. "I've hurt you, Emily, and for this I am deeply sorry. I didn't think..." His eyes, hooded by thick eyebrows specked with gray, were etched with sadness, glassy with unshed tears. He shook his head and pursed his lips.

Relief washed over Emily. He wasn't not angry; simply sad. Good. "I love you, my darling. I want to make you happy. Let's put your dark days behind you." She reached up to hold his face between her palms and kissed him deeply.

"Oh, Emily. I've been thoughtless. Please forgive me." He held her in a tight embrace, and Emily, her head tucked under his chin, nuzzled into his chest, inhaling the scent of cigar and bay rum from his crisply ironed shirt.

"Shall I tell Martha to pack up Mable's things?" she

asked quietly, holding her breath for his answer.

"Of course. It's time." She detected a tone of regret in his voice, but a note of determination also. A blend of relief and victory washed over her. He wanted to please her; she knew he did.

Emily untangled herself from his embrace. "You know, my dear, my being right next door to you will have its advantages." She flashed an impish grin and batted her eyelashes comically like a silent screen actress.

A smile blossomed on his cheeks as he threw back his head in guffaw. "Oh, Emily, you make me young again! You and 'them there eyes.'" He swatted playfully at her bottom. "I'll let Martha know that we would like the task completed immediately."

"Now don't trouble yourself with that, John. I'm sure you have plenty of business to attend to. After breakfast I will happily speak to Martha." Emily cooed. It was time for her to understand just whom she was dealing with.

Chapter Five

AFTER BREAKFAST, JOHN said to Emily, "I know you've been eager to view the art collection Mable and I have acquired for our museum. I need to attend to some business in my office, but then, you and I can take a walk to see everything. Shall we say, around eleven o'clock?"

"My, yes. How thrilling to see it at last! And I'll see to having my things moved into my suite."

Together they ascended the majestic stairway, and when they reached the landing, he gave her a peck on the cheek.

"Off to my hideaway," he pointed to a narrow flight of stairs in a corner near the elevator.

"How clever of you to tuck your office out of the way, John. It must be so quiet and private."

"And it's got a spectacular view of the bay! Mabel and I planned Ca d'Zan down to every last detail," he said, climbing the steps that led directly to his office door.

Mabel again. I've seen Mable in every nook and cranny

of the house. Emily crossed the hallway and entered the suite that would now become hers, not Mable's. She rang the annunciator, then pulled open closet doors and bureau drawers, revealing all of Mable's belongings.

Martha arrived and scanned the room, tight-lipped at the upheaval. "Yes, ma'am?"

"Martha, all of the former Mrs. Ringling's things need to be removed. Please have everything boxed up. Then, all of my things need to be carefully brought in here and put away."

"I see." Martha crossed her arms. "And where shall we store Mrs. Ringling's things?"

"The *former* Mrs. Ringling. And I have no idea where you should put everything. An attic perhaps? That's not my concern. But I would like to get settled in here as quickly as possible. So please take care of this immediately." Her tone was crisp. *Martha will soon learn that I am the mistress of Ca d'Zan.*

"Yes, ma'am. I'll send Sadie up."

In a few minutes, a housemaid appeared, a scrawny girl with straw-colored hair twisted into a bun.

"I'm Sadie, ma'am. Martha sent me up." Sadie blinked and twisted the hem of her apron with her hands.

She looks like a frightened rabbit! While Emily wished to quell Martha's thinly veiled insolence, this child needed a different approach. "Come. Let me show you what needs to be done." Emily led the girl into the dressing room, explained the task, and retreated into the boudoir.

While Sadie worked in the dressing room, emptying the closets and folding Mable's garments into piles, Emily oversaw things from a chaise longue. With one eye on Sadie's progress, one eye on the *Vanity Fair* in her lap, she considering how she might approach John about updating the art collection. Gloomy Italian Madonnas, old Flemish hunting scenes, saints ascending, gold encrusted tabernacles and chalices… she'd heard about it all, and it sounded so timeworn. Perhaps she could plant a germ of an idea into John's head once she'd seen it. Could he sell some of this off, and acquire some Picasso? Henri Matisse? Maybe devote a wing to more lively contemporary works?

Her thoughts interrupted by the crunching of gravel and the purr of a motorcar outside, she peered out to see a black Pierce Arrow arrive at the front entrance. A uniformed driver got out and opened the passenger door, and a stout woman dressed in a tan duster and matching driving bonnet emerged. Who was she? Were they expecting a guest? Then, the light dawned. Must be Edith, Charles' widow. She's probably used to popping in unannounced.

She listened while the woman instructed the driver to wait, and then heard the door chime that echoed through the house. Emily quietly stepped into the hall, peering down from the mezzanine. Martha scurried toward the door, and Emily heard the woman's booming voice echo through the main floor.

"Where is John? Please tell him I'm here, Martha."

"Yes, Mrs. Charles. Please come in." But Martha's words were unnecessary, as Edith strode into the parlor, took off her coat and draped it over a chair. Martha headed up the stairs, and Emily continued to observe the guest, who was now making her way through the room, picking up an *objet d'art* and examining it, then setting it down and moving on to another. Emily assessed her long navy-blue skirt, her nondescript white blouse, her gray hair gathered into a tired pompadour. Old, older than John. Too old to care about fashion. She considered going down and introducing herself but decided to wait until John summoned her. This mezzanine provided an undetected lookout. She smiled to herself, amused by her bit of mischief.

John entered the room, holding out both hands. "Edith, how good to see you! I planned to telephone you today."

Edith leaned forward to accept John's perfunctory embrace and each managed to avoid contact as they kissed near the cheeks of the other. She sunk into on a small sofa and John took a chair facing her.

"So, you are married, John. I could hardly believe the

news when I received your telegram. I suppose my well wishes are in order." She daubed the corners of her eyes and shook her head. From above, Emily gripped the balustrade, cocking her head to better hear the conversation. She wished she could see more than the sides of their faces. Was Edith here to congratulate or chastise? Her voice sounds cheerless, not cheery.

And who was that lurking near the pillar in the corner. *Martha! Eavesdropping!*

"I expected that you would be rather surprised, Edith, but I'm quite happy. You should know that." He crossed his arms over his chest, leaning back in the chair.

She sat straighter in her seat. "I must say, I feel it is my duty to express my concern about you, with darling Mable so recently passed. Just who is this woman who has ensnared you?"

John leaned forward, hands on his knees. "Ensnared? Really, Edith! Perhaps when you meet Emily, you will see that I have ensnared her!"

"Hmmph. It's all so sudden, John. You and Mable were together for so many happy years. She was my dearest friend. How could you abandon her memories?" Her voice trembled.

"Edith, as a widow yourself, you must know that my heart aches for my Mable every day, as yours does for Charles. But I must continue my life, to take off the shackles of grief and to live again. Emily has a vibrancy that has been life changing. And I believe that she, as a beautiful and charming wife at my side, will be a true asset to all of my ventures. I hope you will give her a chance."

Edith's gaze drifted around the room, and her eyes settled on the portrait of Mable that hung on the wall. She covered lips with her fingertips and her shoulders slumped, then she turned to look back at John. "My dear brother-in-law, I want what is best for you, but I mourn for my dear friend every day. I do not want to see someone take advantage of your loneliness. You must protect yourself. And protect Mable's legacy."

He held up a palm. "Let me set your mind at ease. I believe Emily is upstairs. Let me go and get her, so you can see for yourself what a fine woman she is. I know she will be so happy to meet you." John stood and headed for the stairs, and Emily ducked back into her suite, unseen. This sanctimonious crone thought she was some hussy, out for John's money! How dare she make these insinuations? *Edith, my dear old girl, just who do you assume I am?*

When John rapped on the door and invited Emily downstairs, she feigned surprise and delight. Gliding into the parlor on John's arm, she beamed her best smile and reached out to clasp Edith's hand. "Edith, how divine to meet you at last! Welcome to our home! John has told me so much about you and how thrilled I am to know that you live right next door. Should we have some tea? Coffee? Let me call Martha." She sat down in the tapestry chair that John had told her was Mable's favorite and threw an arm languorously across its back.

Edith smiled weakly and shook her head. "Nothing for me, thank you. I really must be going soon. But I wanted to issue this invitation." She opened her handbag and produced an ivory vellum envelope and held it out to Emily. "I've taken the liberty to plan a soiree in your honor."

"Why, how kind," Emily said, "But shall I open it? It's addressed to John Ringling, not me."

"Please do," said Edith, and Emily carefully opened the envelope and slid the invitation from it. *Why was her name missing? An Oversight? Or deliberate?* "Look, John! A party to celebrate our nuptials. Edith, this is a lovely gesture." But a lovelier gesture would have included both her name and his. She reached forward to touch Edith's arm.

"Well, I feel I must, as John's closest living relative, offer my hospitality." She sniffed, her eyes leaden with the weight of familial obligation.

No kindness here, just duty, Emily noted. She stood up, walked around to the back of John's chair, placing her hands on his shoulders. She leaned over him as he scanned the invitation she'd handed him. "We're honored, aren't we, darling?"

"Without question. Very fine of you, Edith. It will give everyone the opportunity to meet Emily." He grasped his wife's hand and kissed it. "Emily, now you can begin to put faces with all of the names I've mentioned. Won't that be grand?"

"Oh, my yes. Now Edith, you must let me know if I can help you in any way. I wouldn't want you to tax yourself too much for our benefit." Emily said, wrinkling her brow.

Edith stood, collecting her coat and hat. "Thank you, but that won't be necessary. My staff... and I have my daughter Hester... she will aid me in the preparations. I'll be on my way now. Nice to meet you, Emily. We'll see you at the party." She nodded curtly at the newlyweds and hurried toward the door. Before she could be summoned, Martha appeared and stood at the door to open it for Edith.

"Good day, Mrs. Charles," she said, but Edith ignored her and headed for her automobile.

AND SO, ONE week later, the party.

Emily, after careful consideration, chose her ivory satin Schiaparelli, the one she'd worn the night she'd first met John in Amsterdam last summer. It was smashing, truly, with its simple yet sinuous design and plunging back. As she sat at her dressing table applying her lipstick, John tapped on the door. "Come in," she called.

Dressed in an impeccably tailored tuxedo and at six feet four inches tall, he made an impressive figure. "You look so handsome." She capped her lipstick. "So irresistibly distinguished."

He reached out to her, and she stood to grasp his hand. "And you are a vision. I recall the first time I saw you in this gown. It was love at first sight." He gently spun her around. "And doesn't your new jewelry make you even lovelier." He kissed the inside of her wrist, just below the sparkling cuff that matched the brooch at her shoulder and the adornments in her blonde waves. "The car is ready whenever you are, darling."

"Then on with the show." She gathered her velvet cape, catching a glimpse of herself in the mirror as she passed. She nodded in satisfaction. Time to meet Sarasota.

✧ ✧ ✧

JOHN SETTLED EMILY into the front seat of his green Rolls Royce, and they headed down the long driveway. "So warm for January." Emily, leaned back into the supple leather upholstery. "And funny that we are driving through one Ringling property to turn into the property of other Ringlings next door."

"These warm nights are just one of the reasons I love Sarasota. And I do love owning such a lush property. You know, my late brother Charlie was a bit jealous after

Mable and I build Ca d'Zan, so he built his place just north of us. Edith had it decorated by Marshall Field and Company in Chicago. Lots of antiques, but the typical stuff, not like ours. Their place is nice, but doesn't hold a candle to mine, as you'll soon see."

Asa the passed through the gates of Ca d'Zan, Emily asked, "Now tell me, John, who will I meet at the party tonight?"

"Well, I suspect that Edith has invited just about everyone who is important in Sarasota. First, her daughter Hester, of course. Married a fellow named Charles Sanford after her husband Lancaster died during the war. Then, The Gumpertzes, you've heard me talk about Sam, surely. Manages the circus."

"Wasn't he the one who was on board your yacht when it sunk?"

"Yes, he was the one. So irresponsible! Then John Caples, railroad man. Mayor Edwards, no doubt, and Stanley Field. And others, of course."

"Not just the men, John. The wives too, I assume?"

"Oh, to be sure. Can't have a party without the women, could we? Hmmm… Sara Field, Ellen Caples, …" he glanced over at his wife. "But you will be the most beautiful woman there, Emily."

"Thank you, John. That's a lovely thing to say."

Driving down the shell-covered lane, they reached the porte cochere of the stately marble mansion, its windows glowing with lights. Other vehicles were parked on the lawn, and the melodious blend of voices and music greeted them as a porter opened the doors of the Rolls. John cupped Emily's elbow and they stepped toward the open door.

Edith, in a severe-looking black bombazine gown, greeted them. "Here you are. We've all been waiting." She proffered a tight-lipped smile as Emily removed her velvet cape and handed it to the maid waiting to carry it away. "Come in, and I'll announce you to everyone."

Entering the expansive living room, Emily took note of Edith's penchant for British country houses. She recognized a Sheraton sideboard and several intricately inlaid chests and tables, just like the ones she had seen in an upstate New York home of an acquaintance, perhaps a decade ago. A grand fireplace of sienna marble that matched the floors was centered across from the main entrance and on either side, doors opened to the terrace. From the adjoining music room, a tuxedoed pianist played Beethoven's *Moonlight Sonata*. Some guests were seated on dainty Hepplewhite settees arranged for conversations. Others mingled in small clusters. She stifled a flinch from the chill of John's hand on her bare back and faced the throng of people gathered there. *Smile serenely, Emily*, she reminded herself as one by one, people spotted her and John, and hushed their conversations. Emily felt their eyes, some curious, some critical, boring into her.

"Ladies and gentlemen," Edith announced, "May I present our guest of honor, my brother-in-law John Ringling and..." she cleared her throat, "his wife Emily."

Did her name stick in Edith's craw? Or the word "wife"? She'd never felt so much like I was on display. Should she curtsey? Pirouette? Blow kisses? She tamped down a smirk threatening to escape her lips. *Be kind,* she reminded herself. John is an important man, and they're naturally interested. She gazed up at her husband, who was beaming and waving a greeting.

"Here's to the happy couple," a man shouted from the crowd, and a smattering of "Here, here" and applause followed. Several men came forward to shake John's hand or slap him on the shoulder. "Well done, old boy," one gray-haired gentleman barked, his gin nearly sloshing over the sides of his crystal tumbler. Emily stood stiff as a mannequin at John's side as he soaked up the accolades and greetings.

"Dear, please introduce me to your friends." She squeezed his arm gently. He blinked down at her.

It's as if he's forgotten I'm here.

As he rattled off the names, Emily rewarded each of the men with a smile and a "How nice to meet you." Their reactions varied; two of the men seemed to leer at her, another one, solely interested in speaking to John, barely glanced her way. One man, scanning her from head to toe, turned to John and said, "Quite a looker you have here." As if she was a new horse for the circus. Or a new motorcar to add to his fleet. But John, basking in the attention, chuckled and said," Yes, Emily is a beauty, isn't she?"

A woman dressed in a mauve gown entered the circle, interrupting the men's conversation. "Uncle John, let me rescue Emily from all of you gentlemen. Emily, I'm Hester, Edith's daughter." She reached out, her gloved fingers clutching Emily's hand. A collection of bracelets studded with an array of gemstones snaked up her elbow-length gray kid gloves. Her curls tumbled out from under a sparkling tiara, and she wore a hopeful, friendly expression.

Leading Emily away from the knot of men, Hester said, "I've been so looking forward to meeting you, Emily, and I must apologize for not coming to call. My two sons have been recovering from colds, and I've been so busy." She twisted her long strand of pearls. "My, what a lovely gown you're wearing. Champagne?" She motioned to the silver tray in the hands of a nearby waiter.

Emily reached for a flute from the tray and took one sip, then another. She focused on her companion. "Thank you, Hester. Sarasota is quite a change for me." Might this woman become a friend? She looked about her age, seems kind enough.

Two women approached and stood in between Emily and Hester. One, swathed in sapphire blue taffeta, waved her cigarette holder at Emily. "So, you're the new bride. I'm Mrs. Sam Gumpertz, and Mable was one of my dearest friends." Her lips pursed, she scrutinized Emily's gown. "My goodness, you must be quite chilly. I've only seen that plunging back in magazines," she sniffed.

"Charmed to meet you, Mrs. Gumpertz. And I'm perfectly comfortable, thank you. I believe that John has spoken about your husband. He works for the circus, doesn't he?" Emily reached out her hand but allowed it to fall to her side when Mrs. Gumpertz made no move to accept it. Emily's eyes narrowed. Cold as ice. She'd remember her. Eyebrows raised, she turned toward the other woman in a svelte magenta crepe with bell sleeves that kept her hands out of sight. "May I have your name?"

"I am Mrs. A. E. Cummers, and I too was a dear friend of your... of Mable." She bit her lower lips and lowered her eyes, as if expressing condolences at a funeral. "We miss her so."

"I'm sure it was difficult to lose your friend," Emily soothed, then changed the subject. Did these women have first names? It seemed aloof to introduce oneself as Mrs. Sam, Mrs. A. E. Would she be Mrs. John?

"Edith has a lovely home, doesn't she? The chandelier is magnificent." She looked up at crystal-laden fixture hanging from the high ceiling. "Reminds me of the one in the Regina Hotel in Paris. Lovely place."

"Yes, but the Ringlings have been struck by such tragedy. Poor Charles only lived here briefly before he succumbed, and then Mable, stuck down at such a young age." Mrs. Gumpertz and Mrs. Cummers looked toward each other in commiseration.

Emily, suddenly tongue tied, grasped for a topic of conversation that would not center on Mable. *Mable is dead*, she wanted to shout. She was Mrs. Ringling now. An uncomfortable silence befell the group. Then Mrs. Cummers reached out and put her hand on Emily's arm. "Yes, tragedy has struck, but today is a new day. Emily, I'm pleased that you will now be taking over some of Mable's pursuits. Her rose garden is in dire need of a loving hand. You know, of course, that Mable was the first president of our Sarasota Garden Club." She turned to Hester and Mrs. Gumpertz, who nodded their heads in agreement.

"Mable was a wonder when it came to roses. And she worked tirelessly to beautify our Main Street," Mrs. Gumpertz chimed in.

"Yes, John has mentioned the rose garden. Of course, it's January, so I suppose no roses now..." she faltered. Roses? What had John told her about a rose garden? She searched her memory. Oh, yes, he pointed it out on the walk to the museum. Nothing blooming that she recalled.

"So," Mrs. Cummers continued, "have you made plans yet on how you'll restore the gardens? I believe that a major pruning is in order, probably soon. I've always favored her yellow floribundas. Or do you prefer the pink? Mable always preferred the pinks to the yellows." Her eyes glittered in anticipation, leaning forward to await Emily's response.

"I'm afraid I have no knowledge of gardens. In New York City, my roses only arrived when a florist delivered them!" Emily chuckled, but then realized that her joke had fallen flat.

Mrs. Gumpertz scowled. "The gardens at Ca d'Zan have tragically fallen into terrible neglect. Surely as John's wife you'll see to it that they are returned to their former glory, as Mable would have wished."

Emily could feel heat rising from her chest to her neck, up toward her cheeks, and her fingernails dug into her palms. *"As Mable would have wished?"* She had no interest in floribundas or any other plant. She was not at Ca'd'Zan to tend to a patch of dead bushes, to dig in the dirt. And she wouldn't be puttering around in the mud on Main Street either. The very idea.

She opened her mouth in retort, but Edith, standing near the piano, clapped her hands loudly. "Attention, everyone. My daughter Hester, who as you know is classically trained in opera, will now perform the aria from Verdi's *Rigoletto*. Please find a seat and enjoy this musical interlude."

Hester whispered to Emily, "I'll speak to you soon. I'm pleased you're here." Emily, mouth agape, watched as Hester walked toward the stage. An opera singer? Now that was a surprise.

John, carrying two flutes of champagne, appeared at her side. She drank what was left in the flute in her hand, then set it on a nearby table. John handed her the fresh stem. "Shall we be seated, darling? I trust you're enjoying getting to know some of the fine ladies of Sarasota."

Chapter Six

AS HER BOUDOIR filled with morning light, Emily forced herself to open her eyes. Sun streamed into the room and set the gold ornamentations on the bedstead aglow. How late had she slept? She rubbed her temples to relieve the dull headache that throbbed behind her eyes. Must have been the champagne. Or the company? Lying on her back, she allowed herself to relive the night and to ruminate over her first party in Sarasota.

Well, she had been on display, that was certain. But John seemed to bask in the attention. it was rather nice, all told. Hester was pleasant. And what a surprise that she has such a compelling operatic voice. And the dancing was lovely. But some of the other women... my goodness.

A kaleidoscope of unfriendly faces danced before her eyes. Mrs. Gumpertz, Mrs. Cummers, the mayor's wife... all billing and cooing over gardens. And so many probing questions: "How did you meet Mr. John?" "Where are your people from?" "Have you always lived in New York?" She smirked. And John, so oblivious to the stares, piloting her around from one little cluster to another…. the banking associates, the circus associates, the developers. Her cheeks ached from forcing a smile all evening. "Oh, you're developing Lido Key, how thrilling!" "You're active in the yacht club. How lovely." And this morning, they were all a blur. She did miss Sophie. Wouldn't it be fun to rehash the event with her? To gossip about the fashion? She imagined what Sophie, with her New York sensibilities, might say about Edith's dreary bombazine. Emily could just hear her scorning "widow's weeds." She would write her…

A light tapping on the door from John's room interrupted her thoughts, and before she could answer, John, freshly shaven and in brown trousers, a white shirt, and brown and white spectators, opened the door and peered in. "Ah, I see you're awake, Emily. Shall I ask Martha to bring you some breakfast? We have some splendid grapefruit, straight from Bee Ridge Farm." He sat on the edge of her bed and leaned forward to kiss her temple, brushing a lock of blond curls from her forehead.

"Some coffee would be divine, John. Gracious! Have I slept away the entire morning?" She sat up and reached for the chiffon robe draped at the foot of the bed. Sliding her arms into the sleeves, she leaned over to peer at the bedside clock.

"It's just after ten, and I'm sure you needed your rest. You were smashing last night, my darling." He kissed the back of her hand and grinned. "I was so proud to show you off!"

Show her off? She forced a chuckle. "Like a new tiger in the circus? Or a new yacht?"

"Not like that, Emily. But you're a beautiful woman and I am so proud to be your husband. Of course, you know that." He walked over to the annunciator and pressed the button to summon someone from the kitchen. "Now let's get you some coffee, and perhaps some toast, a bit of grapefruit. The sun is shining, and my business affairs can be put aside today. What shall we do to entertain you? I've been so busy since we arrived in Sarasota, and today is devoted to you." He guided her to her feet, then twirled her around the room in a gentle waltz.

A flicker of vertigo descended upon her. "No dancing before my coffee, John." She stopped and considered his suggestion, gazing out the window at the palm and banyan trees lining the drive. "Hmmm, Ca d'Zan is so lovely, but I've seen so little of Sarasota itself. Last night I was quite at sea when others spoke about Main Street, about the Lido Key, and so on. Perhaps a tour in the motorcar?" She didn't add, *This could get me out of my doldrums.* With everyone singing the praises of Sarasota, she had to see what all of the fuss is about.

"Of course. Why haven't we done this sooner? Have your coffee and get dressed. Then off to see the loveliest city in Florida!" John swept his arm skyward with a flourish.

Ever the showman. But she did love his enthusiasm. "Give me an hour, John, and I'll be ready."

EMILY, IN NAVY blue linen trousers, gray cashmere sweater, and a Hermes scarf knotted at her neck, headed outdoors when she heard the purr of an automobile. But instead of the Rolls that she expected to see waiting for her, John was behind the wheel of a royal blue Cadillac. As she approached, he got out of the car and opened the passenger door for her.

"No Rolls Royce today, John?" she asked, settling into her seat.

"Not today. You've already ridden in that motorcar, so I thought you'd enjoy this one. We'd better keep the windows closed, though. So much dust." Handling the gleaming hardwood gearshift, he eased the car down the long driveway and onto the road, heading south.

"This one is handsome, too. How many motorcars do you have, John?" Emily caressed the soft white leather seat.

"Oh, several," he answered vaguely. His eyes stayed focused on the empty road ahead. "That's the gulf to your right," he pointed out. "We call this area Sapphire Shores. Water is a marvelous blue today, isn't it?"

"Bluest I've ever seen. I've never driven a car, but I'd

love to. You'll teach me, won't you?" She leaned toward him, putting her hand on his knee. She imagined herself driving along the shore road, the fresh air tousling her hair. Freedom! But he only grunted in reply. Had Mable driven or was she content to be chauffeured around?

As they passed a few homes, John explained who lived in each one. "George Prime... the Arborgasts...the Thompsons..." Names she'd heard mentioned but couldn't place. All the homes, mostly standing alone amidst empty lots, seemed to be some version of a Spanish style, with tile roofs and stucco exteriors. Palm trees stood on the lawns and wispy pines stretched skyward. She was used to bricks and mortar surrounded by maples and oaks, or sidewalks.

"My heavens! Look at that home! Quite a brilliant shade of pink," Emily said.

"Oh, yes. Belongs to Charles Corrigan. Calls his home Nagirroc... Corrigan spelled backwards. Quite a successful businessman. Started with electric vehicles. Retired now. You may have met his wife Alice at the party."

Emily shook her head. "I don't recall, but who's to say? So many new faces. Has everyone built this style home?" She crinkled her nose. *It's like a foreign country, but a rather charming one.*

"Yes, most have," John answered. "You know, Mable's choices influenced some of the others. But none are as grand as Ca d'Zan."

Of course. Emily sighed and turned her attention to the water. "Will we be driving over there?" she pointed to the island in the distance. A pelican hovered over the water, then dove in to make a catch. Marvelous!

"We will, right across my Ringling Causeway." And he began his story, all about his part in the development of Lido Key, St. Armand Key, his building of the causeway, his donating it to the city, the opportunity to have President Harding wintering in Sarasota dashed by his untimely death in 1923. "He was set to have his winter home right here on Bird Key, right next to our causeway!" He shook his head. "We've had our successes, but a few disappointments as well. Yet, we always prevail!"

On St. Armand, they drove down a boulevard and around a circle, lined with stone statuary in a classical style, like the ones scattered around the Ca d'Zan property. As John waxed on about its beauty, Emily was surprised to notice signs of disrepair. The paint on the band shell in the circle's center was weathered and chipped and the lawn was untended. A group of children ran through the overgrowth, tossing a ball around. Even the wooden causeway had seemed rickety. And where was the bustling real estate popping up? She saw no signs of new construction. A smattering of Spanish style homes dotted the side streets, and sidewalks, once painted circus red, were chipped and weed-choked.

"John," she said, "Things look a bit in need of some attention. I'm sure since the crash there have been some setbacks."

He scowled, staring ahead at the causeway that lay before them, taking them back to the mainland. "Don't worry your pretty little head about that. I've been in business for decades. Development has slowed a bit due to the situation on Wall Street, but we're on the move. Sarasota is very desirable and folks from the North are flocking here. We'll take a spin down downtown and I'll show you the sights, then let's head home. How about afternoon cocktails on the terrace?"

Flocking here? She could see that it was not the case. At least not at the present. A small itch of apprehension pecked at her. Just what was John's financial situation? Surely it was not all smoke and mirrors, the work of a consummate showman.

As they drove back to the mainland, Emily kept her comments light, pointing out a heron or two, and a pair of sandhill cranes loping along the roadside. Yet her mind was calculating the prices of the failed investments she'd seen against the cost of the fleet of motorcars, the artwork that accumulated in John's museum, the apartment on Park Avenue, the upkeep of Ca d'Zan. *"Don't worry my pretty little head?"* Her head may have been pretty, but it was not empty. Just what did the future hold?

"May we see Main Street now?" she asked. "It will be nice to see where your Sarasotan friends do their shopping." She swiveled in her seat to look out the car's side window, hoping to spot some posh, up-market shops to explore.

"First, we'll take a look at my bank." On a corner where five streets came together, John pointed toward a two-story flat-iron style building, The Bank of Sarasota. "Handsome building, isn't it? My private office is upstairs."

"May we go in and see it?" To Emily, the building appeared commonplace, like several on street corners in New York, but she was curious about John's workplace. Owning a bank, even in these unsteady times, struck her as one more indication of the prosperity he exuded.

"Oh, not this time, dear. I'm sure the workings of a bank would bore you. Let's see the rest of Main Street."

Emily opened her mouth, then swallowed her retort. She wanted to remind him that she was well-versed in finances, had been managing her own money for years, but decided not to spark an argument.

They drove past lackluster commercial buildings, mostly one- or two-story structures. A smattering of automobiles and mud-spattered trucks were parked along the curb. Locals walked along the sidewalks—women in everyday dresses heading into a bakery, a pair of businessmen, deep in conversation, gesturing and pointing at a building under construction. Emily noted Kress's, a store that resembled Woolworth's in New York. The curved windows displayed brooms and mops, bolts of fabric, aprons, stockings, and an assortment of children's toys. John pointed out every business as if each was a jewel—a shoe emporium, a haberdashery, a tea shop—but none inspired her interest.

Emily sighed and slumped into her seat. She couldn't imagine where the women shopped for fashion. Excursions to New York or possibly Miami? She recalled Hester's mauve party ensemble—could it been made by a seamstress in her employ? She replayed the fashions on display at Edith's—the blue taffeta worn by Mrs. Gumpertz, a frothy chiffon by a dowager whose name she'd already forgotten. Certainly, they hadn't been shopping on Main Street. Nothing displayed in these windows appeared to meet her standards and she silently applauded her intuition regarding bringing her New York wardrobe to Sarasota.

As the tour continued, Emily murmured words of praise as John's running commentary droned on. A church or two, a courthouse, and, near the train station, the ten-story Sarasota Terrace Hotel—"My brother Charlie built that one." Then, he drove past his hotel, The John Ringling. "Used to be called El Vernona Hotel, owned by Burns. Just bought it from him when he ran into some financial reversals."

"Isn't Mr. Burns an associate of yours?" she asked. "Surely I've heard his name mentioned."

But John vaguely brushed off her question. "Things change in business. Now, isn't this a handsome hotel? It's considered the jewel on the bay."

"Hmmm, charming, but please fill me in on Mr. Burns. After all, we will undoubtedly cross paths with him and his wife in our social circle. I should be aware—"

John cut her off, holding up his hand like a stop sign. "Emily, why not drop it? I really don't want to tax you with details that will only confuse you." He reached over and patted her knee. "Now, take a look at the hotel. Lovely rooftop terraces, great for sunsets."

"John, are you worried about guests coming this season? What with the stock market and all? There was rather a commotion among my friends in the city—I mean in New York, who planned and then, well, had to cancel travel arrangements."

"Oh, my dear Emily." John forced a smile. "Hardly anything passes my attention when it comes to tourism and entertainment. Why don't you take in the sights and rest yourself assured that all is well thought through? Maybe we'll set an occasion for you to host a gala at my hotel. I'm sure you'll know just the flowers needed for the event."

Once again, Emily found herself swallowing a reply, wondering if the reference to flowers was supposed to be provocative. But now was not a good time to dig deeper into John's business dealings. After all, this was supposed to be a pleasant drive through the city.

Avoiding John's eyes, she appraised his John Ringling Hotel, finding it pretty enough, but dwarfed by the hotels of Palm Beach and Miami. Compared to Florida's East Coast, Sarasota looked raw, unpolished, a country cousin to those well-heeled cosmopolitan cities on the Atlantic. She recalled a winter getaway she'd taken to the lush new Breakers Hotel and the majestic Biltmore in Coral Gables, each resort resplendent with elegant dining rooms, lavishly appointed ballrooms, shops that featured designs from Paris and New York. As much as John boasted about his Sarasota, it was lacking. Instead of wide boulevards lined with posh shops and gracious homes under towering palms, the streets and neighborhoods here were merely sprinkled with spots of newly acquired affluence. It was disconcerting to observe more than a few uncompleted endeavors that blighted the landscape.

Emily eyed her husband as they headed north on Tamiami Trail, the shrub-lined road heading back to Ca d'Zan. His confidence, his boosterism suddenly seemed to border on braggadocio. She told herself not to overreact, but she was unable to tamp down the questions that presented themselves. His bank... how is it managing since the stock market crash? And his hotel? Are cash-strapped people wintering in Sarasota these days? And property development? The area across the causeway was less than robust. His name, his heart was everywhere, but what about his finances? Was the state of his affairs rockier than he let on? She thought back to the disagreement she and John had just a few days before their marriage, centering on those legal documents he'd wanted her to sign.

THE QUARREL HAD nearly caused the cancellation of their marriage.

John had arrived at her Barclay Hotel apartment with an enormous spray of yellow roses tucked into a Baccarat vase. "For my bride, my beautiful bride," he'd sing-songed, as he swept into the parlor overlooking the lights of 48th Street. What a dear, Emily thought, as she poured each of them a sherry. They spoke about their honeymoon to Florida, and then John nonchalantly pulled out a sheaf of papers from his pinstriped suit coat pocket. "Just some legal matters that I need you to sign." He spread the papers on the table and producing a fountain pen.

Emily leaned forward and picked up the papers. "What's this all about, my darling?" She frowned as she read, her manicured fingertips flipping through the pages. "These say I don't inherit anything if you should predecease me." She tilted her head at him. "John!

What's the meaning of this?"

"Now, Emily, it's just something my lawyer insisted upon. It's nothing important." He waved his hand dismissively and his eyes glanced towards the window.

"Not important!" she stood up. "It most certainly is! You're asking me to relinquish any claim on your estate after you die! My goodness, John. Is that the way you wish to treat me, your wife?" She felt her cheeks flush, and she took a deep breath to quell the stridency she detected in her voice. Was he serious?

"Dear, it's just that I need to protect my assets. Surely you can understand." He held out his hands in supplication.

"Like the way I protected my assets just two days ago when I wrote you a check for fifty thousand dollars? Fifty thousand dollars, John. Think of that. And I didn't hesitate, you know that. You asked me for a loan, and I acquiesced immediately. You didn't expect me to protect my assets, did you?" What had she been thinking, agreeing to the loan he'd asked for? She clutched her stomach as if that could quiet the rumble of regret that had formed.

"That's beside the point, Emily. Please calm down. This agreement refers to my many business holdings. The funds you loaned me is another matter, soon to be resolved. I've told you that you'd have your money returned to you in three months' time, didn't I? And I'm as good as my word. That loan has nothing to do with this legal agreement here." He stood, picked up the documents and handed them to her. "Just sign, and then we can have a fine dinner at the Stork Club. Count Basie is playing tonight." He reached for her, but she batted his hand away.

"No, John, I will not sign." She snatched the papers from him and tore them into tiny pieces that fluttered to the floor like confetti. "Now leave." She jutted out her chin and pointed to the door. "Right now!"

"You're making too much of this, Emily. I'm surprised at your childishness. Let's sit down and discuss this like adults." He massaged his temple, then held a palm out to her. "See reason."

"I am not a child, John, who can be manipulated with a dinner at the Stork Club. Go. Just go." She crossed her arms, then turned her back on him. He stood there for a moment, silently. Emily didn't turn around until she heard the click of the door closing. *So, he's gone. The conniving bastard.*

But the next day, he returned. Teary-eyed, he'd begged for forgiveness. And she had married him anyway.

✧ ✧ ✧

YES, I MARRIED him. And my knowledge of his finances is no clearer today than it had been in December.

Chapter Seven

EMILY FILLED HER days with reading magazines, scanning the newspapers—the gossipy *Sarasota Herald Tribune* and a day-old *Wall Street Journal* that John had delivered—, and corresponding with friends, while John was frequently holed up in his office or downtown at the bank. Hester had telephoned and mentioned getting together for a luncheon soon, but nothing had been scheduled. So, Emily wandered around the grounds, at first savoring the tranquility, then finding it tedious. Nothing in the home was of her choosing, and she felt unsettled, temporary.

In the East Ballroom, she eyed Mable's desk, a frilly piece of furniture in a French style that featured a large top for writing and several drawers. She felt longing for her grand mahogany desk back at the Barclay, all her correspondence and files organized. When she'd moved out after her marriage to John, she'd jammed folders into a leather valise and a box or two to be dealt with later. Perhaps this desk would serve her purposes.

She sat on the desk chair and pulled at the middle

drawer. Locked. As were the others. "Martha," she called to the housekeeper attending to a floral arrangement in the parlor, "Do you know where the keys are to this desk? I'd like them, please."

The housekeeper pursed her lips and furrowed her brow. "That's Mrs. Mable's desk, ma'am."

Emily bristled. She stood up to face her. "I assume you know where the keys are kept. In fact, I can read it all over your face. Bring them to me immediately."

Martha's eyes darted round the room as she poked her chin with her index finger. "But Mr. John... I'm not sure... I should confirm this with him."

Emily sighed heavily. "Nonsense. Martha, there is no need for you to speak to Mr. John. I'm the mistress of this house, and I've just told you to bring me the keys. I do not want to have to report your insolence to my husband. Now, get them." She crossed her arms and glared at the housekeeper.

"Very well." Martha set down the floral shears and walked toward the kitchen, retuning a moment later with a brass key ring. She reluctantly held them out to Emily who snatched them from her hand.

"Thank you. And don't just stand there hovering, waiting for the keys back." Emily held the key ring up and dangled it in front of her as though she were summoning a butler. She turned her back and sat at the desk once again. She heard Martha leave the room.

Curious to see if any of Mable's belongings were inside, she unlocked the middle drawer and slid it towards her to reveal a tidy arrangement of fountain pens, bottles of ink, stamps, sealing wax and a silver letter opener engraved with MR. Another drawer contained letters, including some from John to Mable that were tied together with a black velvet ribbon. She untied the ribbon, then slid one letter from its envelope. "My dearest Mable…" the letter began, and Emily's eyes quickly scanned the page to see if there were any secrets unlocked, any insights into the long marriage of her husband and his dead wife. But, no. Just an account of whom John had seen on a trip to New York, a mention of their art dealer. She stuffed the letter back in its envelope and retied the ribbon.

The other drawers held files, and Emily flipped through them. She tossed the one labelled "Garden Club" on the desk —*no reason to keep this dull business*—, but others caught her attention, one labelled Art Acquisitions, another, Ca d'Zan Furnishings. Inside were lists of items purchased, along with invoices and other documentation. Intrigued, she speculated on whether John realized that these have been locked in this desk all this time instead of safely tucked into his locked office. Promising herself to scrutinize them further, Emily slid the folders back into the drawer and locked it, just as Martha reappeared, fussing over another floral arrangement but surreptitiously glancing her way.

"Martha," Emily said, her voice stern, "I don't seem to recall summoning you. We all need to get used to new ways of doing things here. While I am working at my desk, I insist on privacy. Unless I ask, please refrain from busying yourself so near me while I'm tending to personal matters. It appears that you are snooping and I won't have it."

Martha reddened and shook her head vehemently. "Oh, no, Miss, I... I... am only seeing to the vases."

Emily scoffed. "The vases... oh, spare me. Well, from now on, see to the vases when I am not an arm's length away from them. I'm going upstairs for just a moment, and when I return, I trust the vases will have been attended to and you will have found work to do in another area of the house." Emily strode across the room towards the stairs, imagining Martha's indignant glare boring into her back.

When she returned from retrieving a valise of papers from her dressing room closet, Martha had disappeared, off to complete some other household task. Emily sorted through her files and letters, organizing them into the drawers. She had insisted that her financiers in New York send her weekly reports regarding her holdings, and, although the country was reeling under the economic downturn, her portfolio remained stable. Silently, she thanked her father for his wisdom, and for insisting that she be educated and involved in their personal finances. She'd heard more than a few tales of wives blissfully going along, then shocked and devastated to find themselves in financial ruin. The husband of one woman in her circle had leapt from their apartment window onto the pavement below, escaping his financial demise but leaving his wife penniless and devastated. This would never happen to her.

She was studying a broker's report she'd recently received when John walked into the parlor. "Hello, darling," she greeted him, setting the papers down on the desk. "Did your meeting at the bank go well?"

"Emily, what are you doing?" His tone was brittle, his mouth set in a hard line.

"I'm going over some of my correspondence," she replied, cocking her head to the side. She assessed his reaction, noting his surprise, his irritation, but refusing to acknowledge it. "Why? Is something wrong?" She spoke in a soothing voice that belied the exasperation stirring inside of her.

"You're at Mable's desk." Scowling, he approached her, then punctuated his statement with finger taps on the desk's surface. She'd expected this. With every small change she had suggested—disposing of the Delft bird cages in the parlor, reupholstering the worn green leather chairs in the breakfast room—he'd been adamant. He liked Ca d'Zan just the way it was, no matter that there were no more birds in the cages, and the leather was cracking with wear.

"I am." A part of her welcomed a confrontation. She leaned back in the chair, shaking her head slightly. "Must we have this conversation again, every time I utilize something that was once hers? It's becoming quite tiresome." She clenched her jaw and slapped her hands on the desk's edge, feeling her annoyance bubble up into a froth of anger.

"But…." He hesitated, then dropped his head and sighed, wilting under Emily's glare. "This desk was special to her. She …" He paused and clamped his mouth closed. Exhaling, he continued. "We can find you another desk."

Is there no end to his mooning around? The fun-loving life-of-the-party who wooed her had been replaced by this petulant man clinging to the past. She swore to herself that this would be the last time, the very last time that she would hear this.

"Another desk? And what, pray tell, shall we do with this one? Listen, John, everything in this house was special to her. The desk…" she stood up and pointed, "those silly Aesop Fable upholstered chairs, that screen she bought from the Goulds… everything! I understand! But I am your wife, and I will not treat this home like a museum. I live here." She recognized a shrillness in her voice but forged on. "Here. These were in the precious desk. Letters she kept from you." She thrust the beribboned stack of letters towards him. "I have listened to the sanctification of all things Mable for the last time. I'll dine in my room this evening."

Mouth agape, John took the letters, but before he could respond, Emily grabbed the keys off the desk, along with the documents she had been reading, and headed for the stairs. It was the second time that afternoon that she'd marched up the alabaster stairs in anger, and it felt invigorating.

Upstairs in her room, Emily hid the desk key in a hat box, all the while asking herself why she felt the need to be so secretive. Martha would not dare poke around in her papers. And even if she were so brazen, would she be able to decipher the legal verbiage, the financial ledgers they contained? But what about John? Would he, who held his own business dealings so close to his vest, delve into hers? Surely not!

She plucked a cigarette from the ivory box on her nightstand and inserted it into an ebony holder. Tossing a pale blue cashmere wrap over her shoulders, she stepped out onto the loggia, her mind whirling. After lighting her cigarette, she inhaled deeply, allowing the smoke to soothe her. Night fell over the estate until she could barely see the silhouettes of the palm trees that rustled in the breeze, so warm for a January evening. She peered up at the black velvet sky, mesmerized by the abundance of stars, never visible in New York or the other big cities she'd frequented. She and John had only been married for a few weeks, and her world felt upside down. But this is what she wanted, wasn't it?

She took herself back to Amsterdam where John had first asked her to dance. How surprising that this man of considerable stature was so light on his feet, waltzing her across the floor while keeping his deep brown eyes focused on hers. For the entire evening, he never left her side, engaging her in conversation, complimenting her on her intellect and beauty. Of course, she was flattered, and as he pursued her over the next several days, she became more and more intrigued by this man, so cultured and self-assured. How could she have fallen in love so quickly?

Then, in New York City, their courtship flourished—lavish bouquets delivered almost daily, romantic evenings at candle-lit tables in the chicest restaurants. In the midst of a city reeling from financial woes, John's optimism was infectious. He captivated her with his descriptions of Sarasota and Ca d'Zan. Imagine, a Venetian villa with one's own name on the gate! And one's own art museum! His marriage proposal promised her a new life, a life in paradise. Sharing all of this with this happy-go-lucky man seemed irresistible, and she hadn't hesitated to begin anew, away from the constant swirl of New York City society. The city, with its glamourous vibrancy, had served as a balm after her divorce. But as the years passed and then, as prosperity dwindled, the shiny patina had dulled for her.

She was past thirty. How delightful to see John look at her as if she were the breath of spring. John seemed besotted with her, and, oozing confidence and charm, had offered her new adventures and a new life in a tropical wonderland. She didn't want to regret her decision to marry him and to come to Ca'd'Zan, but she and he needed to come to a clearer understanding of how their marriage would go forward.

EMILY HEARD THE loggia door open. "May I join you?" John asked, his voice gentle.

She nodded. "Of course." She eyed him coolly, her emotions still raw and unsettled. He stepped forward, his dark eyes solemn.

"Emily, can we make amends? I love you." His hands gently held her shoulders, and he searched her face to discover her state of mind. Her anger, her indignation, already tamped down as she'd reflected on their courtship and marriage, seemed to melt away in the warm air. She blinked back a tear and reached to clasp his hands in hers.

"John, I love you too. My fervent wish is that we can make amends and live happily together." She allowed him to draw her close, and she leaned on his broad chest as he stroked her hair. His cocooning embrace, his murmured words of endearment, soothed her hurt, and she closed her eyes, allowing herself to savor the warmth of his devotion. Clearly, he loved her, in spite of his ties to Mable, but she could not continue living under the strain of this friction. After a moment, she leaned back to look up into his eyes. She would not squander this opportunity to settle her grievances.

"John, you must understand my feelings. I do not feel as if I belong here. I respect Mable, truly, but I am not she. I cannot live in her shadow." She spoke firmly, never flinching from his gaze. "I will not ask permission to use the items in this home, our home, for my own purposes."

John nodded. "Emily, Emily…" He stared into the dark landscape and his voice quivered as he continued. "I understand what you are saying, and if I've hurt you once again by my foolishness, I beg your forgiveness. I'm an old goat, in many ways, stuck in the past. I can only tell you that I will try to do better." Once again, he explored her eyes, beseeching her to forgive him.

Emily hesitated. She'd heard similar declarations in the past few weeks, but each had seemed short-lived. Just days before, she'd mentioned that she'd like to order new linens with her monogram to replace those with Mable's, and John had balked. "Foolishness. We have cupboards full of the finest Italian damasks, custom designed."

Emily had withdrawn her request, but each night, as she sank her head into satin pillowcases monogrammed with the letters MBR, she was reminded of who the true mistress of Ca d'Zan seemed to be.

Were they at the crossroads of a new understanding? She hoped so. But it wasn't just the issues of the desk or the monogrammed linens that unsettled her. It was the feeling of being shut out of what mattered, John's business. Now was her opportunity to address this as well. She recalled conversations with her father, when he'd insisted that his daughters be well-versed in the management of their wealth. His words, "Always question what's going on around you," never left her as she'd navigated alone for the past several years. She was not about to dismiss this simply because she had married again.

"John, it's not only the household items like the desk that have made me feel less than a wife, less than your life's partner." Her voice was gentle, but her eyes burned with determination. "I want to be your helpmeet, your partner in all things. And you've shut me out of learning about your business enterprises."

John flinched. "Business? But that's my…" he hesitated, his brows drawing together. He drew in a long breath, then expelled it slowly. His eyes strayed from hers, and, and he looked downward, as if the answer to this question could be found at his feet.

She clutched his elbow, willing him to listen. "Dear, I want you to trust me, to take me into your confidence. Can we not have a simple session in which you review your business interests with me? The circus? The hotel? The real estate?" She watched as he absorbed her remarks, her eyes scrutinizing his reaction. He'd tossed off her questions about business before, and she'd swallowed those dismissals, avoiding conflict. This time, she was not going to settle for another rebuff. She had to know what was going on, behind the façade of wealth and opulence.

"My dear," he fidgeted with his collar. "That's quite a shift that you're asking for. I've never…"

She stifled a rush of impatience threatening to overcome her voice. "It may be a shift, but I need to know that you trust me. Unlike many women, I've had a great deal of experience in handling my own portfolio. I'm Mrs. John Ringling, am I not? I have a right."

His gaze once again met hers. "Dearest, a right may be a strong term to use."

Her eyes flashed, and he seemed to recognize that this time, she would not be dissuaded. Before she could respond, he continued. "I suppose…" He cleared his throat. "If you wish."

He had relented. She squelched a smile that would reveal her sense of triumph, "I do wish. And let's not delay. Let's make a firm appointment in your office tomorrow. Shall we say ten o'clock?"

"My goodness, you sound just like an accountant." He brought her hand to his lips and kissed it. "But you're much too beautiful to be an accountant."

Her mouth curved upward into a smile and she raised an eyebrow playfully. "And you won't regret allowing me to learn about your business matters. You may discover that I'm quite clever in that regard." Her mind hummed with the questions she planned to ask. What were the capital outlays for the development of St. Armand? For the hotel? What were the average receipts for the circus compared to the expenses? How many bank customers are in arrears on loans?

"Emily, I have no doubt about how clever you are." His large eyes, moments ago revealing uncertainty, softened. "I do love you so."

They stood locked in another embrace, one now free of tension and hurt. They had reconciled, and Emily allowed contentment to wash over her twinges of apprehension.

"Shall we go in?" she whispered. "We should be sure to be rested before our ten-a.m. meeting." She gazed into John's eyes and traced his lips with her finger.

"My, yes," he said, his voice husky. Together they walked back into Emily's boudoir.

She tossed her wrap on a chair and then John led her to the connecting door to his room.

Chapter Eight

ARMED WITH A fountain pen and pad of paper, Emily headed up the narrow staircase that led directly to John's private office. She'd only entered a time or two, acquiescing to John's insistence that this place in Ca d'Zan was his alone. Tapping lightly on the door, she wondered why John always kept the door closed. It was not as if the house was brimming with people who might interrupt him.

From within, John called out, "You may come in," and Emily entered. She was struck once again by the room's vastness and its arresting view of the terrace and the bay. John sat behind his big Regency desk, its gleaming mahogany top edged in gold, its center base as thick as a tree trunk. Unlike the desk she used, this one emanated power and strength, like the man seated there. Behind the desk was a massive credenza flanked by tall bookcases. Leather-bound binders bearing labels that Emily could not read without stepping closer lined shelf after shelf that seemed to groan under their weight.

"Are you ready to begin, John?" She held up her pen

and paper. "I'm ready to learn."

"Is that a legal pad, darling?" John joked. "I hope this isn't a deposition."

"No, no, nothing like that. Sometimes I find that taking notes helps me recall facts and figures." His tone was irritatingly patronizing, but now was not the time to take offense. She forced a smile.

"No time like the present," he said, lighting a cigar he'd removed from the inlaid rosewood box at his fingertips. Rising, he drew another chair toward his desk, signaling for her to be seated. "Shall we begin with my circus? It's where it all started, of course." He sank back into the tufted leather chair and puffed on his cigar. Emily's eyes smarted, but she ignored the thick odor. Cigars were as much a part of John Ringling as his beloved Sarasota.

Emily uncapped her pen. "I'm curious. How many shows does the circus perform a year? And the operating expenses, they must be significant. How on earth do you keep track of it all and make a profit? That will be a good start to my questions."

"Well, Emily, those are good questions and I wish I could answer them briefly…" he shuffled through a stack of papers on his desk, then slid a few her way. He blew a smoke ring and eyed her as she studied what he'd given her.

A crease formed between her eyebrows and her lips

pressed together in concentration. A list of cities on the circus tour and their gate receipts... a list of employees, but no salaries given... a list of vendors owed... "John, I'm not sure how to interpret this. Perhaps you have a summary of income and expenses that you can show me." She set down the papers, recapped her pen and looked up at him expectantly.

She detected another whiff of condescension in his smile. "If it were only that simple. These..." he tapped on the stack of papers, "are just a sample of all the analysis and decisions that I make to keep my circus so successful. I thought this would give you an inkling of what goes into the Greatest Show on Earth. Summing it all up on a sheet of paper, well, I just can't do that, my dear." He gestured to the shelves that lined the wall. "All of these files, all of our records, are kept in here. Surely you have no interest in perusing every one of them."

She felt her cheeks flush and she struggled to keep her voice measured. "No, of course don't care to examine every piece of paper in your files. That is not my intent, as I believe you understand. I simply am curious about the state of your—our—finances. It seems like a legitimate request." She gripped the armrests on her chair to quell the trembling that had traveled to her fingers. Once again, she was being stonewalled. Was she really asking for too much?

She thought back on her interactions over finances.

When Charles had left her, she was determined to manage her own wealth and had found a financial advisor who respected her. So many times, he'd say, "Emily, let me weigh the pros and cons of something aloud, and then you can weigh in." Under his tutelage she'd learned to decipher balance sheets, bank documents, and stock reports. It had been empowering to be taken seriously, to be considered knowledgeable and astute. Yes, she and John were only newly married, so she understood some hesitancy on his part. But it was grating, insulting.

"Emily, darling, I ask that you trust me. My business dealings are complex, and I've always achieved success." He pointed to a framed *Time* magazine cover sitting on the credenza behind him. "Here I am! One of the top fifteen wealthiest men in the U.S. in '25! You see all we have here. Why are you fretting about this?" His hands fluttered in exasperation.

How could she explain how important this was to her? She closed her eyes for a moment and took a deep breath. "John, my father was a successful businessman, and since he did not have a son, he was adamant that we daughters understand the workings of his very profitable business. And so, my knowledge of the world of finance is undoubtedly deeper than most wives. And when my father passed away, I've had to rely on my own instincts, especially since the Crash. If God forbid something should happen to you…" she reached out to grip his hand.

He covered her hand with his. "Let me assure you, you have nothing to fear." He paused, then brightened. "You know, I bet you could learn more about the circus by seeing its winter home right here in town. We could go there this morning, in fact. What do you say? A VIP tour?" A grin widened across his face.

Emily hesitated. She recognized his deflection. But did she really want to scrutinize pages of bank records? Bills of lading? Employment rolls? She felt her determination wane. Maybe she could just keep her eyes sharp and her nose to the ground and sniff out any problems. And get to know some of John's associates, like that Gumpertz fellow.

Was she relenting too easily? Possibly, but for today, she would take another path to gaining the information she sought. "Okay, let's do it. I suppose that would give me a better feel for how the circus operates as a business. You know I've only been to a circus once, when I was a child."

"Emily, that's about to change. You've been missing out on one of life's most exhilarating experiences." He stood and guided her from her chair toward a photograph that sat on one of the bookshelves.

"Surely you know who this is," he said, but she shrugged at the photograph of an intense-looking man in white tights, walking a tightrope.

"Why, he was in all of the New York papers. Can't imagine that you could have missed it." He shook his head in dismay and Emily stifled a smile. It was impossible for John to imagine that the entire world didn't know about every act in his circus, yet very few of her New York set did. Night clubs, perhaps a Broadway play—that was their milieu.

"So, who is this gentleman?" she asked.

"The one and only Karl Wallenda. Booked him for the Garden in '28. What a performance! Usually there's a net below, but somehow, it never arrived. Didn't stop Karl. Performed up there with nerves of steel. Fifteen minutes of a standing ovation. Spectacular." John's eyes glowed as he recounted the tale. "Bet you'd like to meet him!"

"My, yes." Emily smiled. Married to the Circus King, meeting a circus performer. Life had taken her on a surprising path. "I'll freshen up, and I'll be ready in about fifteen minutes."

John gave her a peck on the cheek. "That's my girl."

They rode to the circus grounds, a former county fairground, in the Pierce Arrow, under pewter colored skies. When they got out of the car, a brisk breeze made Emily wish that she had worn a coat instead of simply putting a cardigan sweater over her skirt and blouse. Just where had the balmy breezes of the night before gone?

She crossed her arms against the chill as John led her through the iron gates that proclaimed that they were entering the Winter Quarters of the Greatest Show on Earth. The grounds weren't yet open to the public, but workers bustled about readying things for the tourists who would arrive later in the afternoon.

"Good morning, Mr. John. Good morning, Mr. John," each individual they encountered called out. Starstruck, several bowed in his presence while John nodded and tapped his bowler to one and all, greeting many by name.

"So, everyone knows you?" Emily asked. A new dimension of her husband emerged. She'd seen him as a prominent member of their social class, but here, he was not simply a successful businessman. He was royalty, fawned over by loyal subjects. Grizzled men in soiled jumpsuits, women in aprons and kerchiefs, tattooed performers both male and female, some in tawdry show clothes, all paid homage to Mr. John.

"Of course! These are my folks." John gestured with a cigar he'd pulled from his lapel pocket. Two women in dusty dungarees and muck boots stopped to gawp, and one put her hand up to conceal a comment made to the other. *So rude!* Emily threw back her shoulders and glared but they simply stared back. John, oblivious to the spectacle he and Emily were creating, steered her around, providing a running commentary on every aspect of the circus, interrupting himself with an anecdote, then adding another. The Big Top—"magnificent!", the Midway—"none like it anywhere", the center ring— "audiences are awestruck." "Those seats are packed every day." He pointed to the rows of red and white bleachers lining the field.

And so it went. Emily, her hands tucked into her sweater sleeves to keep them warm, took note of acrobats practicing in the ring, uncostumed clowns emerging from tiny cars at one end, a line of horses bearing equestriennes prancing about at the other. She had never imagined what went into producing a circus, never thought beyond the show itself. People came and went from all directions. Food handlers were busy in their wagons, and the jumble of smells, some cloyingly sweet, others pungent, made Emily's lips curl. A burly man in a paper cap leaned over the counter from inside a wagon painted with garish pictures of popcorn and hot dogs. "Mr. John, wanna try a dog?"

"Love to, Bud. How about you, Emily? Nothing like a circus dog!"

She winced and shook her head. "Oh, no. I couldn't." She had seen hot dogs peddled from dirty little carts by ageing immigrants on New York street corners, but couldn't imagine actually eating one. Even the term "hot dog" stuck in her throat.

He shrugged. "Suit yourself." The vendor behind the

counter handed him a steaming hot dog slathered in ketchup and onions and John took an enormous bite, then wiped his mouth with the back of his hand. "Perfect, Bud. Mmmm-mmm."

While John wolfed down his hot dog, Emily averted her eyes and scanned the vast property. She spotted a row of simple cottages, white with red roofs, in a distant corner of the lot. Laundry flapped from clothes lines, and children ran about. One woman swept the porch steps, another was bent over a washtub, scrubbing.

"Do people live over there?" she pointed.

"Sure do." John swallowed the last piece of bun and wiping his hands on his handkerchief. "Most of my circus families spend the winter there. See all those little kids? Probably part of the Wallenda brood. He's already training 'em for the high wires. Let's see the animals, then head over, maybe meet Karl and the missus."

They continued to make their way across the lot. The shouts of trainers and drivers, the pounding of hammers, the whinnies of horses and the screeching of monkeys permeated the air, a cacophony that struck Emily as unorganized and chaotic. Topping it off were the smells that assaulted her with every breath she took.

"It seems all so hectic." A gust of wind lifted her hair and she smoothed it back into place. Why hadn't she thought to wear a hat? Or at least a scarf? She tipped up the collar of her blouse to keep the wind from swirling down her neck.

"Hectic? Maybe. It's all organized and runs like a finely tuned clock." John's eyes brimmed with pride, and he threw his arms out expansively. "We truly are the Greatest Show on Earth! Tourists are flocking to Sarasota just to see our winter quarters and to take in some of the rehearsals. Wait until you see the crowds pour in later."

"Later? Will we be staying all day?" Dismay inched its way into her voice. She'd seen enough, she felt covered in grit from the hay and sawdust paths, and the clouds refused to let any warm sunshine break through. Strange-looking people milled around—a giant, several midgets—and they made her uncomfortable. She tried to avoid staring, but John chatted with each one of them, introducing her as if they were important people she should get to know. How could one possibly make money from this ragtag business, she wondered.

"Don't you want to?" John asked, a flicker of annoyance crossing his face. "We haven't even seen the menagerie yet." He grasped her elbow and pointed to a row of cages. "You've got to see my animals up close, Emily."

"Well, all right." She allowed herself to be led. At each cage, they stopped, and John detailed just where the creature had been acquired and how it was trained while Emily struggled to hold her breath against the stench. She'd never been fond of animals, and the menacing teeth and the massive paws of the lions and bears filled her with trepidation. "Do they ever escape? Has anyone been maimed by them?" she asked. Nearby, a lion roared mightily, and she jumped. It felt as if her heart would come out of her chest.

John rolled his eyes. "Nothing to worry about. Never happens. Glorious beasts, aren't they?" He chuckled when he noticed her panicked expression. "Now don't be silly, Emily. You're perfectly safe with me." He patted her shoulders, but his soothing only served to annoy Emily. She felt as if she were a small child having a nightmare, being humored by a parent. Nearby, a man led a line of elephants to a separate tent. The largest one dispensed a steaming pile of dung, and the next elephant in line trudged through it. Bile rose in Emily's throat, and she covered her mouth.

"Please, John." She wrapped her arms around herself to suppress the nausea that threatened to overtake her. "I'm not feeling well. May we leave? Maybe I can meet Mr. Wallenda another time."

John sighed. He opened his mouth to speak, then stopped himself. His unsaid words spoke volumes to Emily. Was he going to mention Mable's love of circus animals? That she appreciated the commotion of the circus? That she admired John's acumen at managing it all? So be it.

John finally spoke. His voice was cold. "If you wish

to leave, we can go." Silently they returned to the car and drove back to Ca d'Zan. Emily stared ruefully at the soil and scuffmarks on her Italian kidskin pumps. She planned to hand them to Martha for the trash as soon as she could change into another pair.

Chapter Nine

How many weeks had passed—six? seven?—since she and John had married and had arrived at Ca d'Zan? Emily's appointment book pages, once filled with all types of appointments, cocktail parties, and dinner engagements, were mostly empty, and with John constantly busy in his office or driving out to the circus lot or to the bank on some errand, she often passed the time on the terrace, staring at the bay, or at her newly claimed desk, responding to congratulatory notes from New York friends as well as John's acquaintances in Sarasota. Her marriage to John had been the talk of both towns, she knew, and she felt obligated to respond to their gushing best wishes with a level of exuberance that went beyond what she was feeling. Thankfully, on this day, her calendar was filled in with a luncheon at Hester's. 12:30.

Since the night of Edith's party, she had hoped to get to know Hester a bit more. While Hester's mother Edith had remained aloof, even when she'd come to Ca d'Zan to speak to John about business, Hester had telephoned a time or two, simply to see how Emily was faring in her new home. Unlike the other guests at the party who had seemed to be measuring her against some invisible Mable yardstick, Hester did not appear to have any motive besides friendship.

In the days following the party, Emily sparked dinner conversations with John by posing questions about Hester. John, ever garrulous when the topic was people and not his private affairs, had filled her in. While he showed no affection for his sister-in-law Edith, he spoke fondly of his niece. "A good girl, very pleasant," he'd said, sliding a bite of Florida grouper onto his fork, "unlike that mother of hers. Just a few years younger than you, darling, but nowhere near as lovely." Hester had not always stayed home and tended to family. She'd attended Northwestern University, then pursued a career in opera in Germany. She was busy with familial and philanthropic obligations, he explained. She had two sons, teenagers, the children of her first husband who'd perished in the war.

"Louis Lancaster, first husband's name. Poor chap," John had told her, "a gung-ho sort who felt it was his duty to serve. And look where it got him." He'd shaken his head in disgust. "Left our Hester bereft."

"I'd like to know her better," Emily said, and John nodded in agreement. In their brief encounter at the party, Emily had felt a kinship for Hester. At first, Hester had seemed bland and ordinary, but as they conversed, she recognized a depth to Hester—highly educated, a cultured world traveler—that was refreshing and interesting.

John's depictions of a refined, kind, and gracious person solidified Emily's interest. She learned that with two little boys to raise, Hester had moved to Sarasota, and her parents had built her a home adjacent to theirs. "Of course," John had scoffed, "Edith loved having her daughter so close. So, she could rule over her as well." Emily stored all this information away in her mind, constructing a cast of characters as if she were sorting out the plot of a novel. These Ringlings were a complex group and Emily was compelled to delve deeply into learning all she could about them, from their circus to their bayside mansions.

AT BREAKFAST, EMILY commented, "John, I'll be lunching at Hester's today. She's invited me to join her." She peered over her coffee cup at him. Would he be pleased?

"Splendid! Lovely that you two will have a chance for a nice tete-a-tete." He tossed his napkin on the table and stood. "I'll be busy all morning, telephoning and such, so that will keep you occupied." He absent-mindedly pecked her on the cheek, unaware that his remark had annoyed her. *"Keep her occupied"*? It was as if she were a pesky puppy or a whiny toddler who needed entertaining.

She held back a snide rejoinder. "Do you recommend I walk? Is there a path?" On the night of the gala, they'd gone by automobile, but that was in the evening. Perhaps the families had paved a trail through the shrubbery so that the Ringlings could visit one another without the use of a vehicle.

"Walk? Oh heavens, no. There's no path cut, and we wouldn't want you ruining another pair of shoes." He patted her arm and chuckled but stopped himself as her lips thinned in exasperation.

"Well, it's not as if I can hail a taxi. What do you suggest?" How she hated this, having to rely on him for a simple trip to the home next to theirs. In New York, she could simply alert her doorman, and he'd have a cab at her service in an instant.

"Martha," he called, and the servant entered the dining room immediately. Had she been hovering in the doorway? Emily had lived with servants for all her life, but none before Martha had made her feel as if she were being scrutinized and spied upon.

"Yes, Mr. Ringling?" she asked, bowing slightly.

"Have Frank ready the Pierce Arrow and be out front to take Mrs. Emily to Miss Hester's..." he turned to Emily. "What time shall you need the car, dear?"

"A few minutes before 12:30, say 12:25," she answered.

"Certainly, Mr. Ringling." Without even a glance at Emily, she left the room.

"That's how it's done, Emily. When you'd like to return, simply telephone and ask for Frank to return. Now enjoy your day." He smiled at her and began to walk away, but Emily had one more remark.

"It would be all so simple if only I could drive."

He did not turn around, but Emily was sure that he had heard her.

Emily, her back to the kitchen door, called softly, "Martha?" And as she's suspected she would, Martha appeared in an instant.

Emily turned toward her, narrowing her eyes. "It is apparent to me, Martha, that you do quite a bit of needless hovering to take in our private conversations. This is unacceptable and if it continues, I will call it to the attention of Mr. John. He, like I, values his privacy. I have observed this behavior of yours since my first day at Ca d'Zan, and while I first chalked it up to your inquisitiveness, it has crossed a line into intrusiveness."

Martha reddened, her eyes flickering with indignation. Before she spoke, Emily added, "I believe you understand me, don't you? Now if you or Sadie would draw a warm bath for me upstairs, I would appreciate it." She lifted her coffee cup to her lips.

"Yes, ma'am." Insolence edged Martha's tone, but

Emily ignored it. She had made her point. Martha would now be on her guard, no matter how resentful she might feel, or she would pay the consequences. Emily lingered at the table, imagining Martha upstairs, filling her tub and no doubt, cursing Emily silently. No matter. She was in charge, and Martha knew it.

WHAT DID SARASOTAN women wear to lunch, Emily wondered. Of course, this was just a get-together with Hester, no other ladies, so there would be little or no scrutiny. Hester had not struck her as particularly stylish, so Emily didn't want to appear to be shallowly absorbed with the latest fashions. She decided on a seafoam green frock that she'd worn last summer in Amsterdam. Its cowl collar and lily-shaped sleeves added interest to its simple lines, but it wasn't too showy. Adding a simple cloche in a deeper green, she eyed herself in the mirror with satisfaction. Understated, yet smart—just the look she was striving for.

Frank, in a rumpled gray suit and cap, arrived on time.

"Thank, you, Frank, for being so prompt," Emily remarked as she settled into the back seat.

Frank mumbled a "Yes, ma'am," as he turned the car toward the gate.

Emily, who was in the habit of making pleasant small talk with New York City drivers, asked, "Have you always lived in Florida?"

"No, ma'am." He offered no additional information.

So that's how this was going to be, she thought. Just like Martha, stone cold. She sighed and crossed her arms. She could return coldness with coldness, but it was tiresome. The ride continued in silence.

It was Emily's first opportunity to see the home in daylight, as it was obscured by trees from Ca'd'Zan. Unlike Ca d'Zan which adhered meticulously to a Venetian style, this one was, like Edith's, a curious but not unpleasant blend of Italian Renaissance and Spanish. Its white stucco façade under a red tiled roof shone brilliantly in the sunshine, and intricate wrought iron balconies, railings and window grilles told of its Mediterranean inspiration. Emily marveled at its size as she stepped out of the car. Several elite Fifth Avenue apartments could fit in this manse. Perhaps Hester's tastes were not quite as simple and unpretentious as she had imagined.

A maid wearing a crisp white apron and a pleasant smile greeted Emily at the door, and Hester soon appeared in the foyer. Wearing an unremarkable navy-blue dress and a simple pearl choker, Hester reached out to grasp both of Emily's hands.

"So happy to see you, Emily. Let's sit in the parlor, shall we? Luncheon will be ready soon." She turned to the maid. "Gloria, could you please serve us tea?"

The maid nodded. "Yes, ma'am," she replied, then disappeared down a hallway.

Hester and Emily stepped into a cavernous living room, sunlight streaming through French windows facing the bay as well as from clerestory windows just below the barreled ceiling. Emily stifled the urge to whisper as she might if she were visiting an ancient cathedral in Europe.

"You have a lovely home," Emily said as she sat on the tufted blue sofa Hester pointed toward.

"Thank you. Quite large for the four of us, but of course, Mother would have it no other way," she said. "We're connected via a covered walkway to the home she and my father built, and Mother wanted the two homes to complement each other. I did steer clear of her desire to furnish it with fine antiques, however. Two adolescent boys and Hepplewhite tables do not mix." She chuckled, her eyes crinkling in the corners.

Gloria appeared with a tea tray, and Emily gazed around the room as Hester poured steaming liquid into Limoges porcelain cups. Despite its vastness, the room seemed more inviting than Edith's antique-filled gallery or the curated museum-like ambiance of Ca d'Zan. Here, the sofas and chairs featured deep cushions that invited one to sink back for casual conversation. Solid looking tables held piles of books, and a Victrola and a stack of records sat on a table near a grand piano. Emily imagined a warm family scene, Hester reading a book on one sofa while her husband companionably read his newspaper in a nearby chair. The teenaged boys might be playing the Victrola nearby, and perhaps Hester would put down her book and help her boys practice their dance steps to Harry Richman's *Putting on the Ritz*.

"I can see that everything here reflects your interests and your tastes. That's what makes a home so special, isn't it?" Emily accepted a cup of tea from Hester and stirred in a spoonful of sugar. She searched the room for another topic of conversation. "I'm curious about your musical pursuits, Hester. Do you and your husband have the same preferences when it comes to music?"

"I'd say my husband's tastes are more eclectic than mine." After a back-and-forth about classical composers versus current ones, Hester batted away the subject. "So, Emily, what do you think of Sarasota?" Hester asked. "It's quite a far cry from New York." She sipped from her teacup. "Now don't feel you can't be honest with me. I won't take anything personally, and I'm really interested to know your impressions."

Emily led off with positive comments. "I'm enthralled with birds! Did you read *Swiss Family Robinson* as a child? It was one of my favorites, and I feel as if I've stepped into the pages, with so many exotic birds—herons, cranes—just everywhere I look." Emily sipped her tea, wondering if Hester would press her further on the topic.

"Oh, that was a favorite book of mine as well," Hester replied. "And I do love our birds. But I'm curious about what you have ~~you've~~ noticed about the city of Sarasota."

Before the conversation could continue, Gloria slipped into the room. "Mrs. Lancaster, your luncheon is ready."

"Thank you, Gloria. Come, Emily, I'll lead the way."

Emily assumed that they would be eating in the dining room, but Hester led her through one of the French doors and onto the patio. A circular table covered in cheery yellow linen had been set up. In the center stood a simple arrangement of palms and hibiscus. A large umbrella in a nearby stand shaded the table from the sun's rays.

"I hope this suits. Our dining room is rather large, and two people sitting at the table seems so formal. I thought we'd enjoy being out of doors on such a nice day."

"Absolutely." Emily settled into a chair. "This is lovely." She scanned the patio, surrounded on three sides by wings of the home. Steps led down to the water, sparkling in the sun. Sarasota was a breathtakingly beautiful place, there was no denying it. But was that enough for her? Were palm trees and pelicans sufficient to keep her content?

Gloria presented each of them with a salad of shrimp, eggs, and asparagus served on a bed of crisp romaine.

"Shrimp Louie! One of my favorites," Emily remarked.

Hester accepted a small pitcher from Gloria, then passed it to Emily so she could drizzle the creamy pink dressing over her salad. "Gloria has perfected it." She smiled at her maid, who smiled back.

Emily, perceiving a mutual fondness between Hester and Gloria, felt a wave of melancholy sweep over her. Back in New York, she'd enjoyed an easy relationship with her personal maid Jane and her housekeeper and cook Bessie, but John had insisted that she would no longer need them when she moved out of her Barclay apartment. Even in the City, he'd said, he employed plenty of help. Why continue to pay people they no longer needed? Reluctantly, she'd let them go, and here she felt constantly on her guard, under the watchful, critical eye of Martha.

She would not dwell on that now. She raised her eyebrows and grinned at her hostess. "I'm eager to taste this." Turning to Gloria, she added, "This is as pretty as a picture."

When Gloria had left the terrace, Emily and Hester focused on their lunch for a few minutes. Then Hester continued the conversation they'd begun inside. "So, Emily, tell me more of your thoughts about Sarasota?"

Emily reflected for a moment, laying down her fork. "It's very different from what I'm used to, and not like the other parts of Florida I've visited." She hesitated. Should she go on? Reveal more? "And being newly married is an adjustment, of course." She sipped from her water goblet, avoiding Hester's gaze.

Hester leaned forward. "I'm prying. I apologize. I don't mean to put you on the spot, dear."

"Oh, no! You're not prying!" Emily ran her finger down the side of her water goblet, tracing a path through the condensation, then returned Hester's gaze. "Sarasota is a lovely spot and John is so proud of all he—and your father as well—have accomplished here. The Ringlings seemed to have created an oasis here that I'm sure will continue to flourish." There. She'd come up with something to say. She added, "John has driven me around a bit and we visited the circus. Perhaps you could tell me what else I should see."

"Ah, Uncle John! I can imagine the tour he's given you," Hester chuckled. "Has he shown you the theater? Or the Sarasota Terrace Hotel?"

Emily shook her head. "No theaters that I recall, but perhaps we did drive past the hotel. John was more focused on the one with his name."

"Well, you and I must tour again. I'd love to show you the performance venues we've established her."

"That sounds lovely." The women returned their

attention to their salads, and Hester remarked, "You mentioned the adjustment to being newly married. I understand that. As you probably know, I was a widow, and remarried several years ago. I believe you met my husband Charles at my mother's party."

"Yes, a very nice man. We spoke only briefly. My, the name Charles is a popular one. Your father, your husband… and isn't one of your sons named Charles as well? How does one keep them all straight?" Emily threw her hands upward in mock despair.

Hester laughed. "Well, everyone called my father Charlie. And my son has a nickname, Larl. It's what his younger brother Stuart called him when he couldn't pronounce Charles. So, we manage." She continued. "Remarrying is taking a big leap, I know, Emily. And my Charles, he not only married me, but he took on two children as well. We've had many adjustments to make, but it's been so rewarding. I know that my uncle John is smitten with you, and I hope your marriage will be as happy as mine is."

"Thank you, Hester. You're very kind. John is a dear man," Emily said. Hester's words had warmed her. It had been weeks since she'd chatted freely with a friend, and she realized how lonely she'd become. She laid her hand on Hester's. "I'm so pleased to get to know you. I'm far away from my friends and my sisters, and it's lovely to talk to another woman."

The conversation flowed through a mélange of topics—Hester's long-ago opera career, their mutual love of European travel as well as modern art. The blue sky was gradually replaced by a frothy layer of clouds, and Emily glanced at her wristwatch. "Oh, my! I've been taking up your entire day! May I use your telephone to call the driver to come and drive me back?"

"It's been a pleasure to get to know you, Emily. But let's not call. I'll be happy to drive you." Hester said. "Let's finish our tea and then go we'll go."

Moments later, Emily followed Hester to the garage near the front of the home. Hester opened the door, commenting, "Wait just a moment, and then you can get in." Emily watched in admiration while Hester started the motor on her black roadster, backed it out, and expertly turned it around on the shell-covered driveway.

Getting into the car, Emily remarked, "You drive so effortlessly, Hester. I'm envious!"

Hester glanced at her. "You don't drive?"

"I'm afraid not. Almost no one does in New York. But I would love to know how. It must feel so free!" Emily held her hand out the window, waving it about in the breeze as they rode down the long drive. "I've mentioned wanting to learn to John, but he avoids the subject."

"Oh, men. He balked when Mable wanted to drive as well, but then relented, of course. I'd be happy to teach you," Hester said. Emily opened her mouth to object, but Hester held up a hand and continued. "I'd love to, really. And it would be much easier to teach you, a cautious woman, than my two teenage sons. That was a hair-raising experience!" She shook her head slightly and chuckled.

"I'd be so grateful," Emily replied, "but I hate to impose." Yet, she was already picturing herself behind the wheel, perhaps in a convertible, driving along the waterfront road, or into downtown Sarasota. Just an outing alone, even to a trip to Kress's or to the stationery store, filled her with anticipation. Could she learn? Why, of course she could. If Mable drove, then she would as well.

"We can begin tomorrow afternoon if you like," Hester said. "Why don't I come at around 2:00, and we'll have our first lesson." The car was now nearing the front door of Ca d' Zan and Hester slowed to a stop behind two other vehicles in the drive. "Hmm, looks like my mother and Sam Gumpertz are visiting Uncle John. Those are their automobiles, and that's Mother's driver." She pointed to a man leaning against one of the cars, smoking a cigarette.

Emily barely noticed. "Two o'clock tomorrow would be perfect, Hester. Everything today was divine. I'll be forever in your debt if you can manage to help me get behind the wheel. I'm thrilled that you're willing to take me on." She exited the roadster, then stood on the steps and waved as Hester drove away.

Slipping in through the front door, Emily looked around to see if John was entertaining Edith and Mr. Gumpertz in the parlor. She hoped that they wouldn't be staying long. Edith made her tense, and she was eager to tell John her news. The loneliness she'd felt this morning had lifted, replaced by buoyancy and good humor. She was just about to call out to John when she heard shouting. Was it coming from his office? She headed for the stairs to find out.

"That's outrageous! You cannot do this!" John was roaring, his voice carrying a rage she'd never imagined he could summon.

What on earth was going on? What were they arguing about? She tiptoed up the stairs as his outbursts continued. "I'll sue you, Edith! I swear I will! And Sam, how can you be party to this?" Her heart began to pound as she listened to her husband become more infuriated. He sounded frantic, almost desperate. Suing Edith? What had she done? And Gumpertz—how was he involved?

Emily halted at the top of the stairs, There, right in front of her stood Martha, arms crossed and leaning forward, clearly listening to the goings-on behind John's office door.

"Martha!" Emily hissed, and the housekeeper jumped

and spun around. Surprise and guilt were painted across her face, but she quickly replaced them with a cool expression. Emily's eyes blazed and she thrust her hand out, pointing down the stairs. "Go. Now." How dare Martha sneak around and make herself privy to private conversations? This was the limit. Martha, with a toss of her head and her shoulders thrown back, retreated downstairs.

Meanwhile, the dispute continued to erupt from inside the office. Emily stood frozen, now taking up the position that Martha had held only a moment ago. She grasped for possible scenarios that would bring John to this overwrought state. Was it concerning the circus? Or some familial matter that she was unaware of? Did it have something to do with their marriage? Her mind swirled with possibilities.

"Edith, so help me, you will rue this day," John bellowed, his voice trembling. His words were drowned out by Edith's strident recriminations. "You're running us into the ground, John, with all of your ill-advised investments. This will not continue. The discussion is over. Good day."

Hearing the office door open, Emily stepped out of sight as Edith bustled down the stairs, a meek-looking Gumpertz trundling behind her. Peering over the railing on the mezzanine, she watched the pair head for the front door, then heard it close behind them. Should she go in to John? The slamming of drawers, the smashing of a glass—was it a picture frame?—reverberated from the office. She imagined John pacing back and forth, slamming his fist into his hand, his face red with fury. She grasped the loggia railing, weighing what to do. Could she comfort John? Or was he too agitated to welcome her solace? And did she have solace to give? She had no idea what had occurred, so how could she be sympathetic? Perhaps it would be best to avoid the situation and wait for John to share it with her. That seemed the wisest course for now. And later, she would deal with Martha. Certainly, John would see why she needed to be dismissed.

She slipped into her boudoir. Peering out from behind the curtains, she watched Edith and Gumpertz shake hands in the driveway, as if completing a hard-fought business deal. Then they got into their respective autos and drove away. Unbidden, another notion wormed its way into Emily's mind. Had Hester known what was going on? Had she invited Emily to lunch simply to get her out of the way? No, that couldn't be. Just because Hester was Edith's daughter did not mean that they were colluding against her. It must have been simply a coincidence that the lunch coincided with whatever occurred in John's office. She shook her head, breathing deeply to steady her ragged breathing. She sat on the edge of her bed to stave off a wave of dizziness that had overcome her.

Could Hester have known? Surely not, surely not.

Chapter Ten

SHE COULDN'T HIDE in her room forever. As a loving wife, she must seek out John, gauge his mood, and listen compassionately to his troubles. She freshened her lipstick, slipped her lighter, cigarette holder, and a cigarette into her cardigan pocket, and left the room. Hesitating before rapping lightly on John's office door, she wondered just how he would respond to her. No answer.

Downstairs, she found him in his tap room, a space she'd rarely entered. Gripping a tumbler of bourbon, John was leaning on the bar's oversized handrail, staring vacantly at the Tiffany windows. If he had heard her enter, he did not acknowledge it.

"Hello, darling. I wondered where you were." She joined him at the handrail. When he turned to face her, she was jolted by his appearance. His eyes were vacant, his cheeks sallow. Tufts of hair stood upright along his forehead, and his unbuttoned shirt collar lie crumpled against his neck. The rage that Emily had heard behind his office door had dissipated, and what remained was a man morose and defeated. She placed her hand on his shoulder.

"John, I heard a bit of what occurred in your office today when I returned from Hester's. You're clearly upset. What is it?" She stroked his back, waiting for him to respond. Would he tell her? How serious was it? What had Edith meant by his ill-advised investments? She resisted the impulse to pepper him with questions and waited. He stared down into his glass, took a long drink, and ran his fingers through his hair, disheveling it further.

After a moment, he looked up at her, his eyes still lackluster. "It's none of your concern, Emily." Turning away, he reached for the bottle of bourbon, topped off his glass. "Would you care for a drink?"

"A drink? No thank you." Before he could lift his glass to his lips, she reached out and put her hand over the top of it. "John, look at me please." She leaned forward, her eyes focused on his. Impatience bubbled up inside of her, but she tamped it down, keeping her voice tender. "Do not shut me out, John. Whatever it is, it has had a grave impact on you. I heard your anger earlier; I see your unhappiness now. What is it?" She stroked his cheek, searching his eyes for clues.

"Leave me be, Emily." Shaking his head slowly, he removed her hand from his cheek and placed it on the bar. "I appreciate your concern, but you're meddling.

Now be a good girl and allow me to think in peace." He forced a thin smile and patted her hand. "Later on, you can fill me in on your day with Hester." He turned again to stare at the wall.

Meddling? Be a good girl? "You speak to me as if I were a child."

"I speak to you as a woman who has overstepped. This matter has nothing to do with you. Allow me my privacy." His eyes remained focused on his bourbon. He swirled it around, watching it catch the light.

She stepped back as if he had pushed her, and a bolt of anger extinguished the empathy she'd brought into the room. She thrust her chin forward as she spat out her words. "I have offered my concern and kindness, and you're dismissing me, as you've done before. Whatever has gone wrong, John, I have no doubt that it is a major blow to some area of your circus business. Avoid telling me as you wish, John, but your reticence speaks volumes."

John's eyes remained on his bourbon. Was she of no consequence to him? Was he expecting her to just slip away? Without considering the impact of the wounds she was about to inflict, she pulled her sharpest arrow from her quiver. "Perhaps Edith was right when she said you were running things into the ground."

Spinning around and slamming the taproom door as she left, she headed out to the terrace to calm her racing heart. Had Martha been listening again? Well, if so, she'd heard a heavy dose of rancor to amuse her.

She lit her cigarette and sat on the edge of a settee facing the water, drawing smoke into her lungs and exhaling slowly. Humiliation, anger, defiance, and uncertainty crowded her mind, each emotion jostling for attention, pushing the others out of the way. What had she done, marrying this man? Had she been blind to who he really was? She'd been flattered and amused by his attention—the flowers and the compliments—but had tread lightly, telling herself that she was too mature to be swept off her feet by roses and perfume.

And so here she was. Mrs. John Ringling. Had she made a colossal mistake? Or was John regretting his decision to marry her? What if he sent her packing back to New York, just weeks after their nuptials had splashed across the society pages of the *New York Times*? The humiliation of prying questions and fawning concern would be excruciating. *All right, Emily, you've made your bed. Fix this.* She plucked her cigarette from the holder and tossed it into the bay, then headed into the house.

Martha was busying herself in the parlor. "Mrs. Ringling, a word, please?"

Her. She'd almost forgotten their confrontation on the stairs. "What is it?" She crossed her arms.

Martha tucked a stray lock of hair behind her ear. "I know that you thought that I was listening in Mr. John's conversation earlier. So, I spoke to Mr. John to explain that I was just about to knock to see if he and his guests would like some refreshments when you came up behind me. He said he understood." She held her chin up as she spoke but picked at her fingernails uneasily.

"Is that so?" Emily rolled her eyes. Was there no end to this woman's conniving? "Unlike Mr. John, I do not believe you for one minute, and if it were up to me, your days at Ca d'Zan would be over. I'll defer to my husband ... this time." She stepped forward, her eyes just inches from Martha's. "Am I understood?"

Martha stepped back, continuing to fidget with her fingernails. "Yes."

This tiny bit of deference would have to do for now. "Where is Mr. John?"

"He... he's upstairs, in the game room."

Emily strode past her portraying a confidence she didn't feel. She must go to John and to settle things there. There would be time for Martha later.

Even more than the taproom, the third-floor game room was John's hideaway. She found him leaning over his billiards table, studying the placement of the balls while he held a cigar between his teeth. He made no move to acknowledge her, and she stood back for a few minutes, watching him concentrate on his game. He carefully aimed the cue stick and sent the balls careening around the table, one dropping into a pocket with a thunk.

"You do that very well. Is it difficult?" Her heart thudded inside her chest. Could they make amends? Or was this going to be their pattern... arguments followed by coldness, followed by escalating arguments? Or, worse... would he decide that life with her was untenable?

John studied his next shot. "I've had a lot of practice." Again, he pushed the stick forward, and again, balls scattered around the table.

She swallowed and stepped forward into his line of vision. "I should not have spoken so harshly, John. I apologize."

"Be careful where you put your fingers on the table's edge. I don't want the balls to smash into them." Again, he aimed the cue. The balls caroomed around the table and another dropped out of sight.

So, he was still angry. Or wounded. Or both. She had gone too far, tossing Edith's cruel words back at him. "Please, John. I said some terrible things, and I'm sorry." She swallowed a lump in her throat. Yes, he'd made her furious with his reticence, but her comment regarding Edith was beyond the pale. Could it be forgiven?

He put down the pool stick, rubbed out his cigar in a brass ashtray, and looked up. "Emily, let's sit down." He pointed to a sofa along the wall, and she followed him and perched on the edge of a cushion. Biting her lower lip and clasping her hands together on her lap, she waited for what he would have to say.

"My meeting with Edith and Sam is my business, not yours. You knew that, yet you persisted." He ran a hand down the side of his face, then rubbed the back of his neck. "I will tell you this. I've contacted my attorney in Tampa, and I expect all will be resolved. Until then, I have no wish to explain." He paused, placing a hand on her knee. "Lord, I hate quarreling with you."

She met his eyes with hers. "And I hate quarrelling as well. My intentions were—well, to comfort you, but then I began prying, I know. When you rebuffed me, I became angry. Can you forgive me for being so unkind?"

He reached for her. "Let's this episode behind us." Relief washed over her as his arms encircled her. "I love you, my darling. You have no idea how much sunshine and joy you've brought to my life." He kissed her hair, then her forehead, then her lips.

"I love you too." No more bickering, she vowed, leaning into him as he pulled her closer. Once again, lovemaking would be the balm that soothed their disputes. So be it.

But just what had occurred in his office? Should she be concerned? And would she ever find out?

Chapter Eleven

WHEN EMILY ENTERED the breakfast room, she found only one place set and a folded note on her saucer. John had scrawled, "Gone to Tampa for two or three days on business. Didn't want to wake you and I needed to get an early start. Love, John." She poured a cup of coffee from the urn on the sideboard and sat down. Stirring her coffee, she reread the note, then crumpled it in her hand. Of course, he'd known last evening when he mentioned Tampa attorneys that he'd be heading there. So why hadn't he told her? Shouldn't a wife be informed of the travels of her husband ahead of time? This wasn't simply reticence, it was slipperiness. Their reconciliation of yesterday now seemed hollow.

Martha appeared in the doorway. "Good morning, Mrs. Ringling. Would you like some eggs? Toast?"

Her voice, usually cold and brittle, now seemed unctuous to Emily's ears. Was she trying to butter her up? Her irritation with John now transferred to the housekeeper. "Nothing. I'll just have my coffee." She sipped from her cup. "And Martha?"

The housekeeper stopped in her tracks. "Yes, Ma'am."

"Since Mr. John will not be here for a day or two, I'll take my lunch on the terrace and my dinner in my room. I won't be having my meals in the large dining room, so this is an opportune time for you to polish the chandelier and the sconces in there. I've noticed they've been sorely neglected."

"Of course." Martha returned to the kitchen and Emily sneered at her retreating back. If she was going to have to live with those gaudy fixtures, they could at least be polished properly. That should keep Martha occupied for most of the day. She smoothed out the note from John, then tore it into minute pieces and left them on the table. Martha could clean that up as well.

Drinking her coffee, Emily mulled over yesterday's events. Hester's promise of driving lessons had seemed enthusiastic and sincere, and Emily was keen to learn. But, had Hester known of trouble brewing between her mother and John? Did it matter if she had? Could she and Hester forge a friendship when John and Edith were so at odds? The driving lesson was set for two o'clock, so Emily would have to wait until then to weigh the situation.

Meanwhile, how to spend the morning? Emily filled her coffee cup and took it to the solarium. At her desk, she took a key from her pocket and unlocked a drawer, withdrawing a stack of letters she needed to attend to. She'd been avoiding the most recent one from her sister Lena. Poor Lena, she thought as she slipped the letter from its envelope and reread it. Time after time, Lena's letters had been filled with calamities, mostly self-inflicted, in Emily's mind. This one was no different.

When Emily was living in New York, she had made it a point to see her three sisters often, inviting them to the city for theater outings, treating them to luncheons. The younger sisters, Louisa and Olga, had made successful matches to men from their hometown of East Orange. They were well provided for, had borne healthy, thriving children, and while their lives had lacked the luxury and glamour of Emily's, they were content. Not so with Lena. Ignoring the warnings from her parents as well as from Emily, Lena, at age eighteen, had obstinately married a man she'd known only a few weeks. "Too slick by halves," Papa had said after the dewy-eyed Lena had brought Lawrence, a traveling salesman of some sort, to the Haag home. Within a year, Lawrence abandoned her and their infant son Nicholas, and her parents, embarrassed but steadfast in their loyalty, had taken in Lena and her baby son. *Poor Papa and Mutti.* Emily was convinced that her sister had driven both parents into an early grave. Since their deaths, Lena and Nicholas were even more adrift, squandering what was left of her inheritance.

So, what was Emily to do about Lena? She absently twirled a lock of hair at her temple, turning the letter over in her hand. Lena was clearly fishing for an invitation to Florida, bemoaning the frigid temperatures in New Jersey, mentioning that Nicholas needed a "fresh start". Emily had no idea what Nicholas might need a "fresh start" from, but at aged eighteen, he showed no more direction than his mother had. Perhaps they should come to Ca d'Zan. Despite all Lena's failings, she was a dear soul, perpetually hoping for a silver lining in any misfortune that came her way, and Emily missed her effervescence. She smiled as she imagined her sister, mouth agape, squealing, "Golly, Em, this is the bees' knees!" at all the wonders of Ca d'Zan. What fun it would be to see it through her eyes. As for Nicholas, Lena had mentioned "idleness" and Emily sensed that anything might be improve his situation, where temptations for easy and unscrupulous schemes no doubt littered his path. Perhaps John could find him some work at the circus.

Using the telephone in the parlor, Emily asked the operator to connect her to Western Union, then dictated a message. "Hoping you and Nicholas will visit Ca d'Zan. Check train schedules. I will transfer funds for tickets. Love, Emily." There! Someday soon, her sister and nephew would be with her. As anticipation bubbled up inside her, she batted away any thought that John might object. He wanted to see her content and happy, didn't he? And wouldn't he love to sing the praises of his beloved Sarasota to a rapt new audience?

PROMPTLY AT TWO o'clock, Emily heard the "Ah—ooh—ga!" of an automobile klaxon signaling that Hester was waiting for her in the driveway.

"Hello!" Hester waved cheerily and greeted Emily with a broad smile. "Hop in the front seat, and we'll begin. You'll be a driver in no time."

Emily walked around the car. The possibility that Hester was somehow tied up in John and Edith's business conflict had nagged her all morning, even as she reminded herself that Hester had shown her nothing but kindness. Hester's greeting, so guileless and friendly, warmed Emily and a knot of anxiety between her shoulders untwisted. How could she have been so mistrustful? She would not erect a wall around herself, to ward off nonexistent insincerity.

Sliding into the front seat, she grinned at Hester. "I've so rarely ridden in the front of the car! You'll have to explain everything, I'm afraid."

Hester laughed and tapped on the steering wheel. "So, this is how you keep the car from veering into a ditch." Her gray eyes sparkled with humor.

"Well, maybe I knew that already. But tell me about the pedals." Emily, her unease dissolved, crouched down to study the floor, and Hester pointed out the brakes, the gas, and the clutch. Sitting upright, she said, "Show me and explain what you're doing," and as Hester went through the steps to put the car in motion, Emily concentrated on each part of the process. After a few demonstrations that took them up and down the driveway, Hester parked the car and said, "Now you have a go. Let's change places."

Could she do this? Emily's hands trembled as she settled into the driver's seat and gripped the wheel. She mumbled Hester's instructions under her breath, furrowing her brow. Hester had said she was supposed to feel something with her foot, but what? Could the sole of her shoe be too thick? The car lurched forward, jerking her and Hester forward, then backwards into the seat. The engine coughed, then died.

"Oh, dear! Have I broken something?" Emily put a clenched fist to her lips and turned to Hester.

"It happens to everyone. Just try again." Hester patted Emily's shoulder lightly.

Emily straightened in her seat and repeated what she'd memorized. "Ease off the clutch…" Again, the car juddered to a stop, whipping the women back and forth once again.

"I don't think I …" Emily began, clearing her throat and wiping at the beads of perspiration that had formed above her lips. "Guess I'm just meant to be a passenger."

But Hester interrupted. "This old car is cantankerous at times. Give it another go." She leaned back in the seat and placidly stared out the front window.

How could Hester be so unruffled? Wasn't she concerned about her car's motor being damaged? Emily shook her head, then tried again. And again, the gears protested, and the car lurched to a halt.

"Damn it!" Emily sputtered. She shook her head, rubbing her hair from her forehead. How could she be so inept? Why couldn't she do this? Even teenage boys could manage, but not she. Maybe she should simply thank Hester and go back into the house. She turned to her companion. "I am so sorry. I shouldn't have cursed."

But Hester waved her off with a smile. "Oh, I've uttered a curse now and then myself. I have sons, remember. Once more. Easy does it. Then shift." Her voice was calm, almost soothing.

Biting her lower lip in concentration, Emily followed the steps she'd been taught, then grinned triumphantly when this time the car rolled smoothly down the drive. "I think I have it! Let me stop and start again, just to see."

Hester offered a few reminders and Emily once again succeeded. "Well done, you!" Hester clapped her hands. "My goodness, you are such a quick study, Emily, and so deliberate and attentive. You should have seen Larl and Stuart, grinding the gears and then roaring down the lane, frightening me half out of my wits." She shook her head and shuddered. "Sons! I thought they'd bring me to my death before we even ventured out beyond the gates."

"I can imagine. Speaking of boys, one of my nephews may be visiting soon with his mother, my sister Lena." Emily stared straight ahead, concentrating on keeping the tires from encroaching on the lawn. Perhaps Nicholas might find companionship with Hester's boys, although her first inkling was that these young men would have little in common. She'd have to take stock of Nicholas in person before she suggested anything to Hester.

"Your sister and nephew here? How nice." Hester paused as they approached the gate to Ca d'Zan. "Now come to a stop just beyond the portico, my dear. You're about to venture out on the road."

"Will it be safe?"

"I believe so. We'll avoid the Tamiami Trail for now, and travel down Bayshore Road for a bit. I've no fears, Emily." Hester folded her hands in her lap serenely. "Just look for oncoming cars in either direction."

After looking north, then south, Emily pulled the car out onto the road outside of Ca d'Zan's main entrance. Gravel crunched under the tires as Emily pursed her lips and focused on the road ahead of her. John had taken her here, she recalled as they passed the pink house with the strange name, somebody's name spelled backwards.

"That's Nagirroc where the Corrigans live... another

Charles, and his wife Alice." Hester pointed. "And over there, the Lords. I believe you met them at Mother's party."

"Do you know everyone who lives along here?" Emily asked.

"I imagine I do." Hester sighed. "I'm sure that seems odd to you, coming from a city of millions of strangers."

"Odd, yes, but I imagine it's rather nice as well." Off in the distance, she noticed a cloud of dust swirling as another vehicle approached. "Oh, no! Looks like a truck! What shall I do?" Should she brake? Drive off the road? Her jaw tightened as the truck's rumble and the gray dust cloud loomed nearer.

"Not to worry. Just keep a bit off to the right, and slow down if you wish. He'll find plenty of room to go past us."

Emily stole a glance at Hester and then concentrated on easing the car gently to the right. Had she allowed enough room? Would he run into them? How could Hester be so unflappable? The truck rumbled by, its driver offering a salute as he continued on his way.

As the perceived danger passed, Emily loosened her grip on the wheel. "I guess that wasn't so bad, was it?" She exhaled. "I just realized I've been holding my breath." She felt both foolish and exhilarated.

Hester patted Emily's arm. "I'd say that you've done quite well, Emily." She pointed at a wide space on the road ahead. "You can safely turn around then and we can head back. You've been a prize pupil!"

A "Hurrah!" that sounded like a schoolgirl squeal burst from Emily's lips. She clapped her hand over her mouth to suppress a giggle and flashed a quick look at Hester. "I'm actually driving, aren't I?"

Her shoulders and forearms relaxed, and she flexed her fingers on the steering wheel. So, this is what it feels like to control a car! No wonder John loved his automobiles so much. When he had spoken about his Pierce Arrow, his Rolls Royce, or his Cadillac, her eyes had glazed over in boredom. Now she understood—driving put one in command, providing the ability to control one's environment by simply climbing into a car and traveling to another place altogether.

The drive back seemed to take but a moment, and as Emily parked near the main door of the house, she turned to Hester. "I can't thank you enough."

Hester waved her comments aside. "My pleasure. Let's get together some time soon." Each woman exited the car, and as Hester walked around to the driver's seat, Emily hugged her impulsively, taking both women by surprise.

"I'm in your debt, Hester," Emily called out as she headed into the house. Inside, she smiled to herself as she watched Hester drive down the lane. The thought of Lena's delight at seeing her behind the wheel of the car made her chuckle. And Nicholas—wouldn't he be impressed with his Auntie Emily? Of course, she'd need to practice just a bit more. John would surely be surprised at how quickly she'd learned, and wouldn't he be pleased that she could get around Sarasota on her own? Tomorrow, she'd go out to the garage to see all the Ringling vehicles and she'd choose the one most to her liking. Not that green Rolls Royce, of course. That one seemed to be John's favorite, and it was a bit too ostentatious anyway. Was there something is a shade of blue?

Chapter Twelve

EMILY STARED THROUGH the venetian blinds of the breakfast room, watching a gloomy rain pour down on the terrazzo tiles. Adding to her irritability was the telegram she'd received from John late last evening. "Still busy in Tampa. Home in a few days. Will advise." So cold, so terse. A telegram was meant to be short and simple, but this one was painfully so. During their courtship, just a few months ago, John had wooed her with effusive letters proclaiming his love, his desire to be with her forever. Where was that now? She had hoped to show him her driving skills, but that would have to wait as well. Should she simply take a car and go it alone? Not on a rainy day like this, but if the sun came out...

She sipped her coffee, absently running her finger along the slats of the blinds, then eyed her fingertip with disgust. Dust! When was the last time these had been cleaned? It was as if the slats were covered with fur. Another neglected task. Was this how it had always been at Ca d'Zan? John was fastidious about things that mattered to him, but was he oblivious to the maintenance of the less obvious features of the house? She would see to it that such slovenliness would end. Setting down her cup, she pushed the button of the annunciator once, then two more times.

Martha appeared. "Yes. Mrs. Ringling." Her voice was a monotone.

"Just look at these blinds, Martha!" Emily slid her finger along another slat. "Filthy!" She held up her finger. "Once again, I'm noticing a carelessness regarding the cleanliness of our home. I'm going to take a thorough look at every crevice of Ca d'Zan, and I'll make a list for you. It appears that regular maintenance may have gone by the wayside in recent months, but that is about to change." She brushed off her hands.

Martha's face was unmoving, her arms hanging stiffly at her side. "May I offer an explanation, Mrs. Ringling?"

"I can hardly imagine that there is a valid one but go ahead." Emily crossed her arms and scowled at the housekeeper.

Martha took a deep breath. "When Mrs. Ringling was alive—excuse me, the first Mrs. Ringling—we had an extensive staff—two parlor maids, an upstairs maid, two cooks, a laundress, and others."

Emily tapped her foot. "Go on."

"So, after her demise, Mr. Ringling let several of the workers go. It's very difficult for me and one maid to keep things up as I'm sure you'd like them. The blinds have been neglected, as you say." Martha hung her head.

Emily eyed Martha through narrowed eyes. Perhaps Martha had a point. She considered her former home on Riverside Drive. It was smaller than Ca d'Zan, and she and Charles had a staff of seven or eight in their employ. What was John thinking, reducing the staff so drastically? She vowed to speak to him as soon as he returned. Or perhaps, she would just go ahead and hire more staff. "I see. Well, I shall take that into consideration. Get to these blinds as soon as possible then."

"Yes, Mrs. Ringling." Martha turned toward the kitchen.

"And another thing. We shall be having houseguests soon, and I wish to view the various guest rooms before I decide where we shall accommodate our guests. Are all of the rooms open?"

"The keys to those that are seldom used are in a cabinet in the kitchen. I can open any door you wish, Ma'am."

"No, I'll do it myself. Just show me." Emily followed Martha into the kitchen.

Martha opened a cabinet and stepped back, her mouth pinched. "Here they are. All labeled."

Emily reached out to examine the rows of keys, some made of thick brass, others tiny, each one hanging on a hook from a black ribbon strung with a cardboard label. "Bedroom #5." "Bedroom #4." "Silver cabinet."

"Garage." Just how many rooms, how many cupboards and closets were under lock and key in Ca d'Zan? She lifted one labeled "Mr. R Office." Its existence gave her pause. Might she use it one day? Going in alone could be instructive. She reached for the keys to the mezzanine guest rooms.

"I'll return these when I'm finished." She looped the ribbons over her wrist and headed for the door.

UPSTAIRS, EMILY CONSIDERED her options. She expected Lena's telegram to arrive this morning, announcing her arrival date, and she was eager to show her sister and nephew the very best Ca d'Zan had to offer. Should Lena stay in the room right next to hers, the one that Martha had relegated to her on the night she first arrived? It was unacceptable for the mistress of the house, but for Lena? It would be nice to have her sister in the room adjoining hers, and Lena was sure to love the feminine touches—the flowery wallpaper, the lacy counterpane, the pink tiled bathroom. Yes, this room would suit Lena well.

Now, for Nicholas. He was nearly an adult now. What room would best suit a young man? She'd only given the guest rooms a cursory glance when John had first shown her around, but now a closer inspection was called for. One by one, Emily opened their doors to the rooms that lined the mezzanine and took stock of their interiors, all bearing the mark of Mable's aesthetic.

Lavishly painted walls and ceilings, elaborately carved beds and dressers, and heavy draperies, jabots and cornices now dust-laden and dreary, made Emily's lips curl in disdain. The last room she entered, at the far end of the hall, seemed the least like a museum, offering its guest a view of the bay. Martha would have to take down the heavy window dressings before her family's arrival, but this room would do.

Emily returned to the first floor and sat at her desk in the solarium. The downpour had dwindled to a trickle, but, under a slate gray sky, the white-fringed waves beat against the break wall and palm branches thrashed about. John often quoted his advertising campaign, "Spend the summer in Sarasota this winter" when he spoke of the Northerners flocking to his city. A day like this would not lure anyone.

Toying with a sliver letter opener, she imagined what her day might hold if she were still in New York living on her own rather than the wife of John Ringling. Would she have lunch plans? Perhaps she and Sophie would be meeting at the tearoom of Henri Bendel, gossiping about the New Yorkers whose names appeared in Walter Winchell's column. The weather in winter was less than ideal, but then again, her sumptuous mink coat would be just the thing to ward off the chill. After lunch, they'd wander through Bendel's. There, while she was seated on a tufted silk chair in the private dressing room,

Margo, her personal assistant, would present her the newest couture... Chanel, Jean Lanvin. Sophie, with her impeccable taste, would eye the designs, declaring, "Emily, you must have that!"

Staring out at the gray waters of Sarasota Bay, Emily transported herself back to her hometown... late afternoon cocktails at a friend's Park Avenue apartment, maybe a Broadway show—perhaps the new Gershwin musical, *Girl Crazy*—or a debutante ball for another friend's daughter. She'd traded all of that to marry John, to bask in his devotion and attention. Where was that devotion now? Could she reclaim it?

The doorbell chimed, and Martha opened the door to a uniformed Western Union man. After accepting the telegram and closing the door, she walked toward Emily. "For you, Mrs. Ringling."

Emily took the telegram from Martha and turned her back to her. Opening the telegram, she scanned its contents. "Nicholas and I arrive February 21, 3:30. Please meet us. Love, Lena." February 21? That was three days from now! How typical of Lena, just to drop everything and jump on the next rain. Emily hadn't expected her to arrive for at least a week or so. She set the telegram on the table, rereading it. Fortunately, she'd already decided on their living arrangements, but more needed to be done.

"Martha," she turned to speak to the housekeeper,

who had remained standing near the desk. For once, Emily was not put off by her hovering. She ticked off a list of tasks. "My sister and my nephew arrive on the first on the 3:30 train. You will need to clean the rooms I've selected for them… the guest room adjacent to mine, the room at the far end of the mezzanine. And take down those hideous window treatments in that room. Appropriate meals need to be served, and arrangements need to be made for Frank to drive me to the station to meet them."

Martha blinked. "Is that all?"

"Yes, for now." Emily waved the back of her hand toward Martha, dismissing her. She sank into her chair. Lena and Nicholas at Ca d'Zan! What a diversion! Life was never dull when Lena was around, and despite her sister's quirks, Emily admired her high spirits. And Nicholas! She hadn't seen him for months. He'd been such a darling little boy but had shown some surliness in his adolescence. No doubt he'd outgrown that by now.

But what about John? Would Lena and Nicholas arrive before she'd had an opportunity to speak to him about their visit? How would he react? She shrugged, tossing off this question. It wasn't her fault that he chose to stay away in Tampa for so long. And, she didn't even know how to reach him. If he phoned her, she could speak to him about it. If not, he would just have to be surprised and to take it in stride.

Chapter Thirteen

NOT SURPRISINGLY, THE train was late. Emily paced the platform, smoking one cigarette, then another, as she waited for the station announcement. Today's sky was bright blue, the air warm, the kind of day that weather-weary travelers anticipated when they made their way to Florida. She ignored Frank, parked nearby and leaning on the black Rolls, the largest in the fleet. She could have sent him alone to meet Lena and Nicholas, she supposed, but she was eager to welcome her sister and nephew. Finally, a rumble was heard off in the distance—the Seaboard Air Railroad, chugging into the station.

Disembarking passengers blinked in the sunshine as they stepped onto the platform. A few businessmen carrying briefcases donned their Fedoras and headed toward taxis. Two elderly women dressed in heavy coats and hats seemed mystified by their surroundings and stood at the bottom of the train steps, blocking the way until they were greeted by a younger woman who ushered them off to an awaiting car. A conductor then guided an old man down. Emily craned her neck to see who was behind him. Finally, Lena appeared, followed by Nicholas.

The sisters spotted each other at the same moment, and Lena shrieked and ran toward Emily. "We're here, Emily! We're here!" She threw her arms around her sister, rocking her back and forth.

Emily, aware of the curious stares by others on the platform, peeled herself from her sister's embrace. "So good to see you, too, Lena. Welcome to you both!" She smiled at Nicholas, standing behind his mother, but his face remained expressionless as he muttered a hello.

"Why don't you see to the luggage, Nicholas? Frank, our driver is just there." She pointed towards the Rolls and beckoned for Frank. Slipping her arm through Lena's, she led her to the car. "I'm delighted you're here."

The luggage was too much for the Rolls to hold, so Frank loaded what would fit before arranging for a lorry to follow them with Lena's trunk, and they set off. On the way, Emily explained that John was away on business, and painted a bright picture of her life in Sarasota. As they drove through the brick entrance bearing the name Ca d'Zan, Emily took pleasure in seeing her sister's eyes widen as she scanned the property. Even Nicholas, who'd been slouching in the corner of the passenger seat, sat up and stared out the car window.

"Swanky place you got here, Aunt Emily." When Frank stopped the Rolls at the front door, Nicholas bounded out of the car. "A swimming pool! Now that's swell." Arms akimbo, he surveyed the landscape, nodding in approval.

Martha met them at the door, introductions were made, and Frank recruited one of the handymen to help with the luggage. Emily showed Lena and Nicholas to the elevator—"An elevator! Right in your home!" Lena gushed—and escorted them to the rooms she'd selected for them.

Nicholas showed little interest in the furnishings of his guest room but swung open the French door to the terrace facing the Bay and peered at the water.

"I thought you'd enjoy the view, Nicholas." Emily stood behind him, her hands on his shoulders. "Look carefully and you may even see a dolphin."

He snorted. "I doubt that."

"Nevertheless, they're there." Emily turned to Lena. "Let's leave Nicholas to get settled, and I'll show you your room."

Emily sat on a chintz covered chair in the corner while Lena bustled about, pulling garments from her trunk, hanging some up in the closet, stuffing some in dresser drawers, tossing others aside. Lena chattered incessantly. "Such a pretty room—Where shall I put these hats?—Nicholas will love the swimming pool!—

Now where did you say John was?—Emily, you're so lucky to live here!" Emily hugged herself and smiled as her sister fluttered around the room. She felt transported back to their childhood home in East Orange when she and Lena had shared a bedroom, staying up past their bedtimes, whispering confidences and giggling. Ca d'Zan felt cozier, homier with her sister here with her.

"Lena, dear, I hate to leave you, but I must speak to Martha about dinner. Why not get settled and then come to the parlor around 6:00?" Emily stood. "We'll have cocktails. No Prohibition in this house."

"Thanks so much for inviting me and Nicholas. He's... well," she hesitated, twisting a garment in her hands, "having a difficult time."

"We'll talk later, dear." Emily hugged her sister, then opened the door to her adjoining suite. She freshened up her make-up, then went downstairs to look for Martha.

Martha was in the dining room, putting finishing touches on a centerpiece. The table was set for four, with a place setting at the head of the table—John's place.

"Martha, I don't expect Mr. Ringling to be here for dinner. You can remove his setting," Emily said.

"Beg your pardon, Mrs. Ringling. But he phoned this morning. Said to expect him." Martha kept her eyes on the blooms.

"He phoned? Why didn't you tell me?" Emily felt her cheeks redden. This was humiliating, a housekeeper knowing more about her husband's plans than she did. She'd been in the house all morning, available to speak to John. Why hadn't he chosen to speak to her? Or had he told Martha to relay a message?

Martha shrugged. "He didn't ask me to tell you, so I assumed…"

Emily cut her off. "The next time my husband telephones, you may assume that I wish to speak to him. And you will inform me of his calls." She picked up a goblet and held it up to the light. "And wash this crystal again. It's cloudy." She set it down and retreated to the parlor, then went out on the terrace where she paced back and forth until her breathing calmed. Had John deliberately avoided speaking to her? Or was this Martha's doing? Was she making too much of a small matter, or was this an indication of a deeper rift between her and her husband? She told herself to dismiss it, to focus on the joy of having Lena and Nicholas with her, and on the pleasure of John's return. She'd go inside and greet her husband with a smile. There was no need for pettiness.

Inside, she lit a cigarette, sat on a divan and waited, for John's arrival, for Lena to join her. And where was Nicholas? Was he still in his room, or had he gone outside, perhaps to take a better look at the pool? Within a few moments, the front door opened, and John entered.

"Darling!" Emily rose and went to him, her arms outstretched. "Martha just told me you'd be home for dinner. I'm so glad!" There, she hadn't complained, only offered a loving greeting.

He set down his suitcase and a thick briefcase, then laid his hat on a credenza. He took off his suitcoat, revealing a rumpled linen shirt. "Hello, dear." He sighed and hugged her lightly. "It's good to be home. I'm exhausted."

She looked into his eyes, noting dark circles under them. "Poor dear. Come in. I have news."

"Can't it wait? I'd really just like a drink and a hot bath." He rubbed his hand across the stubble on his cheek.

Before she could respond, the elevator door opened and Lena drifted the room. Her dress, a diaphanous pink chiffon better suited for a cocktail party than for a family dinner, wafted around her. "John, darling! I'm so glad you're back home. I've been dying to see you again! And you haven't met my Nicholas yet." She grasped his cheeks in her hands, then kissed each one.

"Lena?" John's brows arched. "I had no idea…" He looked to Emily.

Emily tucked her arm into his. "John, I haven't had a chance to tell you yet since you've been away. And, you haven't phoned me. Lena and Nicholas arrived on today's train. Isn't that wonderful!" She beamed at him, telegraphing him a message. *Be kind. Be happy to see her.* "Let's show her the taproom and pour ourselves a drink. Poor dear, I'm sure you could use one after that dreadfully long ride from Tampa."

John allowed himself to be led to the taproom, his hesitation covered over with Lena's enthusiastic chatter. "My goodness, John! Look at these lovely antiques! Wherever did you find such treasures? Emily has promised a thorough tour, but we've only just arrived."

At the taproom door, John stopped abruptly. "You must be Nicholas," he said to the young man hanging on the bar rail. On the bar sat a depleted bottle of John's special reserve bourbon.

"Yes sir, Uncle John." He brushed a lock of dark hair off his forehead and raised up a half-filled tumbler in a salute. "Hope you don't mind, sir, but I found your bar and spotted this bottle. Good hooch you got here!" He grinned sheepishly, then brought the glass to his lips.

Chapter Fourteen

LENA FLAPPED HER hands in front of her and stepped between her son and John. "Nicholas! Where are your manners? You should not have helped yourself to your uncle's bourbon!" She reached to take the glass out of his hands, but Nicholas laughed and held it high above his head.

"You can't reach it, Mama!" He waved the tumbler back and forth as Lena attempted to grab it.

"Stop it this instant, Nicholas." The words burst out of Emily's mouth before she could restrain herself. "How can you taunt your mother so?" *And how could Lena allow such disrespect?*

Stunned by the rebuke, Nicholas put the glass down, sloshing some of the liquor onto the bar. "Gee, Aunt Emily, I'm only teasing." He smirked at her. "Now you made me spill some."

Lena whispered a timid "Nicholas" and gave her son an imploring stare. Then she turned to Emily and John and shrugged. "He is so high-spirited."

John stepped forward and spoke through clenched

teeth. "Young man, your Aunt Emily and I are pleased to have you and your mother as guests in our home. But you've started off on the wrong foot, I'm afraid. I will expect to see you employ a respectful tone when speaking to your mother and your aunt. And in the future, you will need to seek my permission before you come into the tap room. Shall we shake hands and begin again?" He reached out to grasp the boy's hand.

Nicholas, redness creeping up his neck, accepted John's handshake but avoided making eye contact. "Sure, Uncle John. Didn't mean any offense."

John gave a crisp nod. "Now, let me pour drinks for the rest of us, and we can toast to a fine visit."

Lena plucked at the sleeves of her gown and blinked rapidly, her gaze darting from one face to the next. "My goodness! Well, my goodness! My!"

Emily's agitation at Nicholas simmered, but she tamped it down and turned her attention to her sister. She'd seen this kind of nervous disquiet before in Lena. Poor dear. Her life had had its share of ups and downs. She put her hand on her sister's shoulder and squeezed it gently. "John makes a smashing Rob Roy. Would you like one?"

Emily watched as John took over behind the bar, donning the persona of gracious host as he mixed drinks and handed them out. She caught his eye and gave him a warm smile, pursing her lips to send a kiss. How smoothly John had handled the awkwardness, despite his weariness. It was good to have him back home. And, Nicholas could benefit from the guidance of a man like John.

OVER A SIMPLE meal of chicken and vegetables, Lena continued to gush over her new surroundings while Nicholas took second helpings of everything. Although John looked haggard, he rose to the occasion with anecdotes about everything in the dining room. Even Nicholas chuckled at the story of the unfinished paintings on the ceiling.

John leaned back in his chair, folding his arms over his chest. "That pompous artist Robert Webb tried to charge me an exorbitant amount, and I refused to pay him. I told him, 'What I'm giving you is fair, and I won't go a nickel higher!' Then Webb took down his ladder, packed up his paints, and quit. No integrity, that one. Look, you'll see where the murals end abruptly." He pointed and shook his head.

Lena squinted at the ceiling. "Yes, there. Why I'd never notice. Good for you for sticking to your principles, John."

"Yeah, that's sticking to your guns." Nicholas set down his fork and, elbows on the table, he propped his head up with his hands.

"Nicholas, you can learn a lot from your Uncle

John." Lena's glance darted from son to brother-in-law.

Emily had heard the ceiling story before, and she wondered once again how Mr. Webb would tell it. Would he cast John in a different light, one of a man who was too cheap to pay his employees appropriately? But, for now, it was good to see John acting more like himself, regaling his guests with grand tales. Nicholas's coolness seemed to be thawing, and Lena was clearly enthralled.

After coffee and a few more stories, John placed his napkin on the table. "It's lovely, Lena and Nicholas, to see you. But I am sure you're exhausted from travel, as am I, and are eager to call it a night. Shall we? Emily, are you ready to retire upstairs?" He stood, signaling that the gathering was over. Amidst a flurry of "good nights", John led them all to the elevator, then linked his arm through Emily's and guided her into his suite.

Behind the closed door, John clasped Emily's hands in his. "Emily, we have much to talk about. But first, I need a warm bath and a cigar. Perhaps you'd like to change into something more comfortable, and then in thirty minutes or so, we can sit down and talk." His eyelids drooped with fatigue and his tone was bland, undecipherable. Was he angry about Lena and Nicholas? Was he planning to tell her what had transpired in Tampa? Or was he simply happy to be with her, home at Ca d'Zan?

She brought his hands to her lips and kissed them. "Of course, darling. You must be quite worn out. I'll leave you to your bath."

"Thank you." He unbuttoned his shirt and pulled it from his trousers as Emily slipped from the room into her own. When she returned thirty minutes later, John, in silk pajamas, was sprawled on his bed, sound asleep. She leaned over him, bringing the coverlet up to his shoulders. There would be no conversation this evening. But when?

WHY ON EARTH had she impulsively decided to invite Lena and Nicholas to Ca d'Zan? She and John had had no private time, and their conversations were brief and shallow. She'd hoped to talk about her driving, to bring up Martha's need for more household help, but an optimal time never presented itself. Additionally, her questions about his business dealings were shelved. Searching her husband's face and his demeanor for clues, Emily surmised that things had not gone well in Tampa. John appeared preoccupied, drifting away from the thread of conversations at mealtimes. His geniality, usually so exuberant, seemed forced. Of course, it was understandable that he might tune out Lena's incessant chattering. Did any thought enter Lena's mind without her sharing it? An innocuous comment about the weather could spark a monologue about cold days in

New Jersey or a time at the shore when it rained. Emily was accustomed to her sister's prattle but saw that when Lena began one of her stories, John's face closed down as if a shade had been pulled over a window.

Then there was Nicholas. He generally slept past noon, then expected a late breakfast even while lunch and dinner were in the works. He was untidy, leaving coffee cups and empty glasses throughout the parlor, despite his mother's continuous reminders. "Nicholas, please do not put your feet up on Aunt Emily's damask sofa," she'd whine, and he'd scowl and roll his eyes at her. "Ma, let up, why don't you?" he'd retort, making sure that John was out of earshot, and then he did as he pleased.

John's jaw seemed to clench every time he crossed paths with Nicholas or came upon some disorder he'd left in his wake. "Has this boy no consideration?" he'd seethed through gritted teeth at Emily, after finding a water ring on the top of the grand piano after Nicholas had carelessly left a glass there. Emily found herself defending her nephew—"John, he's just young"—but inwardly abhorred his recalcitrance.

Emily had hoped that Nicholas might find companionship with Hester's two boys, and she wangled an invitation for Nicholas to join Stuart and Larl for a tennis match on the Lancaster family courts. Nicholas balked but Emily persisted. He was back to Ca d'Zan in an hour, scoffing at the "nancy boys" who were "silly schoolkids" and "dull as dirt." Just what impression had Nicholas made on the Lancasters? Emily cringed, imagining Nicholas's brashness, and knew she would not push her nephew onto them again. So, Nicholas continued to loll around at the pool, to complain, to harangue his mother about why she'd insisted he'd come to this backwater place.

At the dinner table, Nicholas routinely devoured his meal in minutes, never taking his elbows off the table, and then left the room. By unspoken agreement, she and John had ceased trying to cajole him into conversation. It was simpler to have him out of their sight.

One evening, after a long-winded story from Lena about some former neighbors in East Orange, John excused himself. "Ladies, I believe I'll retreat upstairs and have a cigar in the billiards room." He stood, squeezing Emily's shoulders lightly before leaving the room. Is that where Nicholas had gone? She hoped not.

"So, anyway," Lena set down her coffee cup. "The Schultzes daughter Agnes married Caspar Rill." Emily's attention drifted from Lena's story. Maybe she and John should host a dinner party. She'd had little chance to get to know anyone in Sarasota, and...

Lena tapped Emily's arm. "Remember him, Emily?"

"No, I'm afraid..." Her words were interrupted from a door slam that reverberated throughout the house.

"Damn it, damn it to hell! Emily! Come up here at once to see what he's done!" Emily and Lena were already on their feet, as John continued to bellow from the third-floor mezzanine. Emily dashed up the stairs two at a time, leaving Lena behind.

Upstairs, John pointed toward the billiard room, almost hitting her as he thrust his arm out. Spittle sprayed from his mouth. "He's burned my table. It's ruined." He slammed a clenched fist into the palm of his other hand. "Damn him! The ingrate!"

Emily grasped his arm. "Let's see." Inside the room, John led her to his billiard table and pointed to a blackened circle marring the green felt. "There!" She reached out to touch the spot, smudging her fingertips with ash. Clearly, the fabric was destroyed, on this elaborate antique table that John treasured. Could it be repaired? Then she noticed the burled mahogany edge had also been charred.

"To top it off, he burned it with one of my own cigars. I didn't put this here; he did." He pointed to a butt perched precariously on the table's edge. "The gall! He could have burned down the entire house!" John's face was crimson.

Emily stroked John's arm but knew there were no words to soothe his anger. His billiard room, even more than his taproom, was his private retreat. His sanctuary had been violated, a cherished possession debased. How could Nicholas have been so cavalier about their property?

And where was he now, off somewhere so he didn't have to own up to his carelessness? She was her wit's end with this lad, tired of defending and excusing him.

"They've got to go, Emily. I can indulge Lena, but that idler is not to be borne. The cost of this repair will be exorbitant, if it's even possible to effect."

She plucked the cigar from the table's edge and deposited it in a nearby ashtray. "Now John, let's not be too hasty. I'll speak to …"

"No! Not another word on his behalf. Arrange for their transportation. I expect them to be gone in a week's time. Now, go. Leave me in peace." He pointed to the door.

Suddenly Emily's anger shifted from her nephew to her husband. How dare he speak to her this way? She began her retort, but the fierce expression on John's face held her words at bay.

"I find you to be excessively harsh, but I will do as you say. However, the matter of your disrespect to me will be addressed when you've calmed down." She strode to the door, slamming it on her way out.

EMILY FOUND NICHOLAS in his room, feet up on the bed, reading an automotive magazine. "Nicholas, your Uncle John is very upset with you, as well he should be."

She sat down on the edge of the bed.

Nicholas put down the magazine and eyed Emily sheepishly. "I guess it's about the little mark on billiard table. An accident. Sorry."

Emily fumed. "An accident? It was no accident that you helped yourself to your uncle's cigars, then set one on the table. We are fortunate that the entire house didn't catch fire." She wanted to take him by the shirt collar and shake him. "John has had enough. You and your mother must leave within the week."

Nicholas blanched. "Leave? You mean we're kicked out?" He stood up, thrusting his hands out as if presenting his apology on a platter. "Gee, Aunt Emily, I'm said I was sorry."

"I imagine you are sorry that you have to leave our home. But your remorse is too late, it appears. Now, I suggest you find your uncle and apologize to him, while I have the unfortunate task of speaking to your mother about this." Emily stood, noting that Nicholas's chin was quivering. Maybe he was repentant after all, but she knew that John would not relent.

Breaking the news to Lena was no easy task. Emily could only hold her sister in her arms as Lena wept. "You've been so kind… I know Nicholas is difficult… I don't know what's to become of that boy…" Emily made soothing sounds and stroked her sister's hair, but she too wondered what would become of Nicholas, and

Lena, for that matter. But now was not the time to offer advice.

"You'll come back and visit soon," Emily promised, all the while wondering if that day would ever come. Her irritation with John increased with Lena's every sob. "Tomorrow we'll make railroad arrangements for you."

NICHOLAS WAS SUBDUED, Lena watery-eyed, John coldly polite. While Emily had arranged for Lena and Nicholas's departure, her resentment at John's insistence that they return to New Jersey gnawed at her. In front of Lena and Nicholas, Emily feigned cheerfulness, but tension hovered over them at mealtimes and followed them into the parlor.

On Lena and Nicholas's last day, John informed Emily that he would be spending the day at the bank and drove off in the Pierce Arrow. Nicholas watched him head down the drive in the sleek green car and whistled. "Wish I had the dough for a car like that."

Emily refrained from suggesting that Nicholas find some work so he could earn money. She still was unclear about why he was adrift, and Lena had offered only vague references to "trouble at school" and "bad influences."

"Say, Nicholas, would you like to go for an automobile ride today? I can take drive you and your mother out to the key." At once she felt a twinge of regret for offering but pushed aside her misgivings. Even though she had only driven one day with Hester, she'd been competent. Even Hester had told her so!

Nicholas's reaction reinforced her decision. His face lit up and he reached out to pull her toward him a bear hug. "Yes! Yes!" Before she could change her mind, he was bounding up the stairs, like the exuberant little boy she used to know, shouting for his mother to come quickly. "We're going for a ride!"

She couldn't disappoint him now. Neither Martha nor the cook were in the kitchen when she went to the cabinet and found the key to the garage. She'd allow Nicholas to choose which automobile they'd use.

Chapter Fifteen

OUT AT THE garage, Emily, Lena, and Nicholas found the doors open. The black truck that Frank used to drive the cook into town to pick up groceries was gone, but several other vehicles were lined up in their parking bays. Nicholas, hands in his pockets, inspected each vehicle, squinting into the windows, while his mother and Emily stood by, watching him.

"Some fine autos here. This Rolls Silver Ghost is a jewel." He reached out to run a hand over its shiny chassis. "Which one will we ride in?"

"Well, Nicholas, why don't you choose a favorite?" Emily scanned the line of cars. She'd ridden in two or three of them, but there were a few she had not seen before. Why on earth did John own so many? But whatever Nicholas chose, a car was a car. She was confident that she could handle any one of them... gears, shifts, brakes.

Nicholas wound his way through the garage, and then gave a low whistle. "It's got to be this beauty. I've read about it—it's a '24 with a six-cylinder engine." He stroked the hood of an open-air Pierce Arrow with a burgundy finish. Emily hadn't noticed it before but approved of Nicholas's choice.

"An open car will be perfect for a glorious day like this one. Get in!"

Without opening the door, Nicholas hopped into the back seat while Lena and Emily settled in the front.

"What a thrill, Emily! Won't this be grand, Nicky?" Lena wriggled in her seat, tapping the palms of her hands together, and turned to grin at her son, spread out with his arms extended over the seat back.

Emily scrutinized the floor pedals. "Hush! I'm thinking!" She mouthed her recollection of Hester's instructions, then set to work starting the car. The gears ground, the car lurched, then stalled.

"Awww, Aunt Emily! Can't you get her rolling?" Nicholas scoffed.

"Quiet! I've got it." Emily drew in her lips in concentration and tried again. After two more tries and some guffaws from Nicholas, the car rolled out onto the driveway.

"Huzzah!" Lena cried and Nicholas applauded. Emily felt the knots in her shoulders release. The hard part was over. She drove the car slowly down the drive, out through the portico, and onto Bayshore Drive. The sun sparkled on the water; the breeze tousled her hair. She became the guide, pointing out mansions along the quiet road as if she was on friendly terms with their residents while Lena gushed enthusiastic remarks.

After a few unsuccessful gear shifts and a couple of stalls, Emily became more adept as she drove along. When they arrived at the Causeway, she repeated John's story about the first day he rode across to St. Armand's in his green car, and even Nicholas lowered his jaded façade. "Uncle John is quite a big cheese, isn't he?" Maybe this young man isn't so bad, Emily mused. After all, he'd never had the benefit of a father to guide him.

When they reached Lido Beach, Emily pulled the car to the edge of the road and stopped. "There's the Lido Pavilion! John built that too." She pointed at a white structure where sunbathers and swimmers milled around.

"Can I go take a look? I'm seeing some pretty girls down there." Nicholas had already leapt from the car before Emily could answer him. She shooed him away and he trotted down the walkway. Out from under his cloak of cynicism, he displayed a boyish charm that endeared him to Emily. Perhaps he's just in need of a strong male in his life. She'd speak to John again about taking Nicholas under his wing, maybe one day.

Lena reached out pat her sister's hand. "Thank you so much for this day, Emily. I know we've been a trial. You've been so kind. But I realize we can't continue to take advantage."

Emily wanted to object but reminded herself that

John was firm that Lena and Nicholas must go. She wouldn't promise what she couldn't deliver, but she told herself that later, she could convince John to acquiesce to a future visit. "Well, sister dear, it's been lovely to have you here, even with some difficulties. We'll have you again soon." The women sat side by side, staring toward the shoreline in companionable silence.

After a while, Nicholas came bounding back and climbed into the car. "Pretty spiffy place!"

"Yes, it's spiffy, as you say." After a few missteps, Emily started the car and headed back toward the Causeway.

"Say, Aunt Emily, how about if I drive?" Nicholas tapped her on the shoulder.

Emily glanced in the mirror. His hands gripped the back of her seat and his eyes glowed. Did he even know how to drive? "Oh, I don't think so, Nicholas. Not this time."

"Aw, please! We're leaving tomorrow, so I won't get an opportunity again. I've always dreamt of driving a Pierce. It'd be a once-in-a-lifetime chance. I've driven plenty of times, and I know what I'm doing." His voice rose. "I'd be so grateful, Aunt Emily."

Emily glanced at Lena. Wasn't she going to interject? But Lena's mouth was sealed shut and she looked up at Emily expectantly. Did she expect Emily to give in? Emily stared at the road ahead, weighing her decision. "I don't think…"

"Please, I promise you won't regret it." Nicholas took on a wheedling tone that reminded Emily of long ago, when he was a little boy begging for an ice cream cone.

Emily chewed her bottom lip. What could be the harm? If he only drove down Bayshore, there would be little danger, with almost no other vehicles on the road. Why couldn't she give this boy a moment of pleasure before she sent him packing? She could imagine him back in New Jersey, boasting about his delightful aunt and her open-air Pierce Arrow. A few minutes of excitement for him would cost her nothing. How could she begrudge him?

"All right, Nicholas. Let's get over the Causeway and onto Bayshore, and then I'll allow you to have a go."

"Hurray! Hurray! Thank you!" His shouts caused two pedestrians to turn and stare as they drove by.

In the mirror, Emily caught sight of her nephew raising his arms overhead and punching the sky, and warmth spread through her chest. "You're welcome."

After Emily navigated the Pierce Arrow to the quiet of Bayshore Road, she pulled the car over. "All right, Nicholas, get behind the wheel." Emily slid into the middle of the seat where she could coach Nicholas.

But before Emily could issue any directives, he was behind the wheel, smoothly putting the car in gear and guiding it down the road.

"When did you learn to drive?" Despite Nicholas's apparent experience behind the wheel, Emily sat forward, her nails digging into the palms of her hand.

Nicholas shrugged. "Aw, one of my school mates had a car, and he showed me what to do. Plus, I read a lot of automotive magazines." He placed an elbow casually on the door frame, steering the cart with one hand. "Nothing to it, really." He leaned over to look at his mother. "What do you think, Ma?"

Lena, her hands clasped together in her lap, offered a tentative smile. "Very nice."

"Now let's see how she handles with a bit of speed." He shifted gears, then put his foot on the gas pedal. Like a horse reacting to the sharp tips of spurs, the car lurched forward with a velocity that slammed the passengers back into their seats.

"Nicholas! Slow down this instant!" Emily gripped the dashboard. "And get both hands on the wheel!"

Nicholas hooted and glanced at his aunt. "Nothing to fret about, Aunt Emily. This beauty really can go!"

"I'm serious. Slow down!" Emily's eyes darted from Nicholas back to the road. She gasped. Only a few yards ahead a pair of sandhill cranes, like down pillows on stilts, their gray feathers blending in with the pebbly road, loped along, oblivious to the imminent danger. "Look out!" Every muscle in her body—arms, shoulder, legs—tightened. Those stupid birds! Shards of images swirled through her mind—the mangled bodies of her sister and nephew, the shiny chassis of the Pierce Arrow crushed. Why had she allowed Nicholas to drive? What utter foolishness! Her breath came in shallow bursts. Should she grab the wheel?

Before she could make a move, Nicholas jerked the wheel, just as the car sent one crane hurtling into the air, its feathers raining down. The jolt sent the car off the road. "Holy damn!" Nicholas shouted. "What the hell!" Both hands were steering now, but the car was going too fast for him to control its direction. It careened into a ditch, then out, toward a stand of palmetto bushes and palm trees.

If the car ran headlong into a tree, Emily knew they'd be killed. How could this be happening? She threw her arm sideways to protect Lena, who was shrieking and covering her face with her hands. Thick palmetto branches slashed the side of the car, and the shrill caw-caws of the injured bird's mate pierced the air. Nicholas yanked the steering wheel back to the left. The car scraped against the trunk of a palm tree, tearing a headlamp off the chassis. They bumped along the protruding roots until Nicholas managed to stop.

Nicholas sprang out of the car. "What the hell! What the hell!" He jammed his hands under his arms, rocking forward and back. "It was an accident! The damn bird!" His eyes were squeezed shut as he paced back and forth, kicking at the ground and sending tufts of grass into the air.

Emily struggled to slow down her breathing while next to her Lena whimpered.

"I've been hurt." Lena wiped her forehead and gasped at the sight of blood on her fingertips. "I think the branches cut my face."

Emily pulled a handkerchief out of her handbag and daubed at Lena's forehead. "Lena, you're going to be all right, dear. It's a small scratch. Can you open the car door?" Her words sounded calm, but her stomach was roiling. She had to exit the car before she vomited. Lena made no effort to move, but sat there with her fist in her mouth, shaking her head. Emily reached over to grasp the door handle, but opening the door was impossible. They'd have to get out on the driver's side. "Come, Lena." She put her arm over her sister's shoulder, and they slid out.

Lena wailed and clutched her chest. "I'm going to faint! We could have died! We could have died!" She held the handkerchief to her forehead and moaned.

Do not vomit. Do not vomit. Emily put her hands on the car and bent over, drawing in deep breaths. It was clear that she needed to take control. She stood straight, and clasped Lena's shoulders. "We are all right. We've had a frightening experience, but we are all right." She tipped her sister's chin up with a fingertip and looked deeply into her eyes. "Come now, Lena. Let's be brave."

Lena gulped and nodded at her sister. Her wails were reduced to whimpers, and she brushed the tears from her face. "All right."

"Good girl." Emily turned to Nicholas, still shouting epithets between ragged—. "Nicholas, let's see what the damage is." She grasped his elbow and led him to the front of the car, then to the side. Smears of blood dotted the now-dented front grille, but the hood seemed undamaged.

Nicholas bent to the ground to pick up the broken headlamp while Emily examined the scrapes on the chassis and the crumpled fender. "It was just an accident, Aunt Emily! An accident! It was the birds' fault. Please don't be angry." His examined the headlamp he held, shaking his head, and biting his lower lip.

"Hush! This isn't helping!" She held up her hand. "Take your mother and sit in the car. And for heaven's sake, calm yourselves." Her harsh tone relayed a confidence that she did not feel, but Nicholas and Lena did as they were told, quieting themselves and sliding aback into the car. But now what? Was the car drivable? Should the accident be reported to authorities? And what would John have to say? She considered what to do first. On the road, the distraught mate of the dead bird continued its plaintive shrieks, and Emily put her hands over her ears to concentrate. With any luck, the car could be driven back to Ca d'Zan. As for authorities, she saw no need for that. No one had been seriously injured, no other cars were involved, so no need to cause a stir. As for John... her stomach pitched.

"We're going to see if the car starts. I think it will." She slid into the driver's seat, willing her trembling hands to calm. Squaring her shoulders, she turned on the ignition. A sputter, then a purr arose from the engine. "Good. Now let's see if I can get her back on the road." From the corner of her eye, she could see Nicholas clutching his hands together in concentration while Lena held the handkerchief to her forehead, both of them focused on the landscape ahead.

"Easy does it, Aunt Emily." Had she not been so shaken, she might have laughed at her nephew's advice. *Easy does it.* If only he been taking it a bit easier. But there was blame on her shoulders as well. Why had she allowed him to drive? Still, the birds on the road could have happened to anyone. She shook her head. It was simply an unfortunate accident and there would be time to revisit the incident later. Now, she needed to get the car on the road and back into the garage.

Please, please. The car bumped forward along the uneven ground, and she eased it back onto the road. "Thank heavens!" She glanced toward her passengers. Both appeared calmer now. Nicholas wiped his eyes with the back of his hand and Lena wiped her nose with her handkerchief.

Emily fixed her eyes on the road, making sure there were no more cranes in their path, relieved that no other vehicles were around. Now what to do when they arrived back at Ca d'Zan? How would she explain the incident to John? Perhaps if she emphasized their escape from injury or death, he'd be so overcome with relief that he'd overlook the damage to one of his precious cars. Silently, she rehearsed what she might say. *"My goodness, John! The bird nearly caused our death!"* She'd fall into his arms, allow him to soothe her. All would be forgiven.

"When we get home, I'll speak to John alone. I'm sure you have some final packing to do. No sense all of us getting our heads chopped off!" She chuckled, but her laugh sounded hollow.

"But I can try to explain..." Nicholas began.

Emily shook her head firmly. "Absolutely not. I will handle this." An explanation from Nicholas would only enrage John. "Simply go to your rooms for the time being."

If you're sure, Emily," Lena said.

"I'm sure. I'll just park in the garage, and when he gets home, I will tell him in my own way what ...." She stopped mid-sentence. She had not considered that John might arrive home before they did, would see the open garage bay, would realize that she had driven the car without speaking to him first. Yet there he was, standing in front of the garage door, his fists at his hips. Was he cross or simply puzzled? As the car glided closer, Emily read the transformation on his face the instant that he spotted the dented grille and the missing headlamp. His mouth dropped open, and he thrust his chest forward. Before she could bring the car to a stop, he charged toward them. His eyes bulged, his face purpled as he slammed his palm on the hood of the car.

His shouts crackled with outrage. "Stop right here! Stop! Damn it to hell, Emily! What have you done? How could you have destroyed Mable's Pierce Arrow?"

Chapter Sixteen

MABLE'S PIERCE ARROW? Is this where his concern lies? Emily's remorse evaporated as she pinpointed the source of her husband's distress. Any concern for her, for Lena and Nicholas? No. Yet again, it was Mable. She stopped the car and got out, followed by Nicholas and Lena.

Her voice had a sharp edge. "You'll be relieved to know that none of us is badly injured, except for a scrape on Lena's forehead." She corralled Nicholas and Lena toward the house. "Just go on in. Lena, wash off your cut and lie down."

They began walking away, and then Nicholas spun around. "I couldn't help it, Uncle John. There were these birds…"

"Never mind now, Nicholas." She motioned for the door. Hadn't she told him to stay quiet? "Help your mother inside."

John erupted again, his face now inches from Emily's. "He was driving? You allowed him to take the wheel?" He grabbed her by the arms, but she slapped his hands away.

"John, unhand me. Yes, I allowed Nicholas to drive for a bit. He is perfectly capable, as am I. This was unavoidable." She crossed her arms. "Repairs can be made."

"Unavoidable? Repairs? Ha! I'm appalled by your reckless disregard for what I hold dear, Emily. Mable's Pierce Arrow—her pride and joy! How could you treat it so shabbily?" He grasped his head with his hands. His eyes swept over the car, then back to her, his lips curled in disgust as he shook his head. "This is unforgiveable."

Emily had heard enough. Mable again. Her monogrammed pillowcases, her gilt-encrusted walls, her engraved silverware, her fussy Rococo desk. And today, her Pierce Arrow. She jabbed her finger into John's chest, her eyes wide, her nostrils flaring. "What is unforgivable is you, John. You. Your indifference towards me, let alone for my family. Did you bother to hear an explanation? Did you happen to notice that Lena is bleeding?"

John opened his mouth to retort, but Emily pushed both of her hands into his chest, emphasizing each word with a thrust of her palms. "This is humiliating." She dropped her hands to her side and continued. "You clearly care more about for Mable's car than you do about me. It is unbearable." Brushing away tears, she turned her back to John and took a few steps down the driveway. She fought to keep her tears at bay, hugging her shoulders and breathing deeply. She needed to get away, to get hold of herself. Facing John again, she struggled to keep her voice from quivering. "I'll step out of your way. Tomorrow, I'll be on the train with Lena and Nicholas, and back in New York. You know where to reach me."

"Emily, I..." he began, but she waved him off, ignoring the look of anguish that crossed his face.

"There is nothing more to discuss right now. You've made your priorities clear." Spinning around, she spotted Martha standing on the front steps, watching the argument unfold. "Martha, see to it that my luggage is brought to my room immediately."

She swept past her. In her boudoir, she yanked clothing from her closet and replayed what transpired in the driveway... John's harsh words, his contempt. She would not subject herself to this any longer. Her heart thumped as she rummaged through her jewelry cases, sorting out what pieces to pack. New York would give her time to think. To reconsider. To map out a future, with or without John.

EMILY HAD BEEN in the Park Avenue apartment for almost a week, but still had not ventured out. Her emotions roller-coastered as she reexamined her decision to leave Ca d'Zan. Had it been the right thing to do? Was she too rash? Or was this her best course of action?

On the evening of the accident, a subdued John had come to her room to ask her to reconsider. She refused, and the following day, she boarded the train with Lena and Nicholas. Securing a private Pullman compartment for herself, she kept her sister at bay by feigning a migraine. When the train pulled into Grand Central Station two days later, she ushered Lena and Nicholas onto their connecting train bound for New Jersey, and then arranged for transport to the apartment.

"Mr. Ringling won't be joining me at this time," she'd said coolly. If the building concierge was surprised to see her, he did not display it. Her luggage was delivered, and the housekeeping staff was alerted to her arrival. She contacted no friends, not even Sophie, dreading their curiosity.

It was unsettling to find traces of Mable everywhere in this apartment, just as they were at Ca d'Zan. When Emily and John married, he'd urged her to give up her Barclay Hotel residence. His place on Park Avenue was larger, and there was no practical reason for two places in the city, especially since they'd be spending most of their time in Sarasota. She'd agreed, storing or selling off many of her contemporary pieces. Now she regretted that decision. As at Ca d'Zan, nothing reflected her taste or her past, while Mable's aura was ever-present, from the Rubens on the wall to the green silk chaise longue. How could Emily come to terms with the fate of her marriage to John when Mable shadowed her through every room?

Emily stared out the window, observing the bustling city below. Cabs moved like yellow beetles down the busy street, and neon signs beckoned passersby to restaurants. Shoppers and businessmen in heavy coats bustled along, shoulders hunched against the cold. After weeks of the soporific quiet and warmth of Ca d'Zan, Emily found comfort in the city's energy. Turning around to face the living room, her eyes were drawn to vases of yellow roses, one on a cocktail table, two standing on either end of a breakfront. John had sent them, along with notes that professed his love for her. She picked up fallen petals on the breakfront and crushed them between her fingers. A cloying scent enveloped her as she reread the cards: "My dearest Emily, please forgive me." "Darling Emily, please let us begin again. I am bereft without you."

"Begin again." She had not yet responded to his entreaties, but today she would. His contrition was genuine, wasn't it? Her mind drifted back to that long-ago day when she married Charles. In her bedroom, her mother was adjusting her veil when she offered Emily some advice. "Remember, *liebchen*, it is the woman who makes a marriage a success. A wife must always be willing to forgive and forget." A lump formed in Emily's throat. If only her mother were still alive, to provide counsel, to offer a shoulder to lean on. But Emily knew what her mother would advise. *Yes, Mama, I will.*

She would send a telegram, asking John to come to New York. In the city where she felt most at home, she would be waiting for him, and they could put their differences behind them and start fresh. With a new resolve, she picked up the telephone to call Western Union.

EMILY HAD ARRANGED a lunch with Sophie at the Rose Room of the Waldorf, and, in typical fashion, Sophie was late. Fiddling with the carnations in the vase on the table while she waited, Emily considered what she would reveal about her marriage.

It was Sophie who had introduced her to John, who had listened to Emily describe her feelings for him. Emily was brought back to the deck of the ocean liner *Ile de France* where she and Sophie sat on the deck drinking coffee after settling into their cabins. They had just departed from Europe after several whirlwind weeks in Amsterdam and Paris.

"I'M SO PLEASED we chose to return on the *Ile de France*. It's quite up to the minute, isn't it? Imagine, a shooting gallery, a gymnasium. Not that I'd ever use either one," Emily commented. "I'm enthralled with its modernity; so stylish." She waved a feather fan in front of her face, then set it on the table so that she could sip her espresso.

"My, yes. None of that outmoded old-world aesthetic. And the grand staircase, perfect for making an entrance, wouldn't you say?" Sophie smirked, inhaled her cigarette and pointed the long gold holder toward Emily. "On another topic, my friend, it seems John Ringling is completely smitten with you. Why, he's been showering you with attention ever since the night of the Fourth of July ball."

Emily shrugged and raised her eyebrows. "Yes, he has. I find him charming and rather captivating. He seems larger than life, doesn't he? So vibrant!"

"Oh, he's vibrant, all right. But Emily, are you sure you're not just intrigued with all of the trappings? He does talk quite a bit about his art collection, his Florida estate, his ties to glamorous show businesspeople. Is that's what's turning your head?"

Emily sipped from the demitasse, then gazed at the open waters in deep thought. "Sophie, I've spent quite a bit of time alone, even with good friends like you to fill my days. John has brought back some gaiety and adventure into my life."

"I see. Has he proposed?" Sophie leaned forward, searching Emily's face for clues. "Do tell!"

Emily blushed, barely smothering a smile. "Well, not quite. But I believe he will very soon, once we are reunited in New York. And if he does propose, my answer will be yes."

"Any trepidations? It's all rather sudden."

"Oh, a few. He's older by many years. And, there's Mable. She seems omnipresent. John talks about her all the time, which I suppose is to be expected after such a long marriage. But he's so attentive to me, and I believe I can turn his heart away from Mable."

"Oh, I agree, Emily. You're young, vivacious, and I'm sure it was stifling for him living with a woman in ill health. I'd say you're a breath of fresh air for Mr. John. Well, hurrah for you both!" Sophie gave her friend a peck on the cheek. "If you're happy, then I'm delighted for you."

"Thanks, Sophie." Emily sighed in contentment. "And I'll be eternally grateful that you urged me to take this trip."

✧ ✧ ✧

WOULD SOPHIE SENSE Emily's sadness? *I don't want to unwrap my feelings right now, to bring them to light.*

Just then, she spotted Sophie handing her fur to the maître d'. She arranged a bright smile and waved at her. Sophie strode forward and reached out to embrace Emily. "My, it's so wonderful to see you! You look marvelous!" The women clasped hands, beaming at one another.

Sophie slid onto a chair. "I didn't expect to see you

here in New York. The cold is frightful! Why ever would you leave your paradise of Florida in the dead of winter?" She shivered as if the frigid temperatures had permeated the restaurant. "Do tell!"

Emily knew that this would be her first hurdle, and she was prepared. She would not talk about the tension between her and John, about the isolation of Ca d'Zan, about the car accident. She smiled and tossed her hands in the air. "Oh, Ca d'Zan is so lovely, Sophie. It's a dream! But I'm afraid I had some business to attend to. So tiresome." She shrugged. "John was detained due to business in Florida, but he's hoping to join me." Emily propped her chin on her hands. "Now, you must tell me all the news of New York. I'm absolutely starved for gossip!"

Apparently satisfied with Emily's explanation, Sophie's eyes twinkled. "Well, where should I begin?" As the women sipped tea and nibbled on their salads, Sophie filled Emily in on the goings-on of their social set. One or two had been forced into bankruptcy, and remarkably, one or two seemed to be prospering. As for Sophie herself? Her family's land holdings in Europe had kept her in good stead. "But I admit I'm a bit bored." Sophie pulled a cigarette out of a gold case and clipped it into an ebony holder. "Being a divorcee is rather grim."

"My dear, you had no choice. Ralph..." Emily stopped herself. No need to dredge up all the pain

Sophie had suffered when Ralph abandoned her for a vapid young heiress. Emily too lit a cigarette, and under a haze of smoke, she scrutinized her friend. As always, Sophie was dressed stylishly, today in an elegant black Chanel suit. But Emily had seen this suit many times. It was far from new. Was Sophie's financial picture not as rosy as she claimed? When had Sophie's liquid brown eyes become etched with crow's feet? And when had her slender neck taken on a shadow of crepiness? Despite Sophie's devil-may-care manner, had the passage of time and new worries left their mark?

An unwelcome thought worked its way into Emily's mind. Sophie and she were nearly the same age. Was she a mirror image of her friend, with skin less taut than it once was, and lines blossoming at the corners of her mouth? Neither one of them was the dewy-eyed ingénue anymore. Yet, how different their lives had become. Sophie was alone, while Emily was married to John Ringling, who, despite his flaws, professed to love her. A man with wealth and culture, someone highly respected for his accomplishments.

And he chose me. Funny she hadn't considered that before. John could have just as easily pursued Sophie instead. Did Sophie ever wish she were in Emily's shoes?

Sophie interrupted Emily's thoughts. "I so envy you. As they say in the circus, you've grabbed the brass ring."

Had Sophie read her mind? "Yes, it appears I have,

and you will too, I'm sure of it." *The brass ring.* Yes, she had it in her hands. It was a bit tarnished, but she and John could surely polish it back to its original glow, with a little love and attention. Suddenly, she was eager for John's arrival. She would welcome him to their Park Avenue apartment, arms open wide, ready to reinvigorate their love.

She extinguished her cigarette. "Sophie, dear, have you time for some shopping at Bendel's?" She raised her eyebrows and smirked. "I may need to pick up something to beguile my Circus King."

"Sounds divine! Something to bring out the tiger in him? I'd love to help." Sophie signaled the waiter for the check, but when it arrived, Emily snatched it from his hands.

Chapter Seventeen

EMILY KEPT HERSELF busy preparing for John's arrival in New York, conferring with the cook about stocking the kitchen with John's favorites, and indulging in shopping sprees at Bergdorf's and Saks, where Emily had always enjoyed VIP treatment. Solicitous salespeople enticed her with their most recent offerings, and Emily found herself saying over and over, "Just bill my husband John Ringling," as she arranged for delivery to her new Park Avenue address.

On the evening of John's arrival, she dressed in a newly purchased ice-blue satin gown, sensuous and understated, and clipped a gem-encrusted barrette into her blonde waves. Champagne was chilling in a silver ice bucket, and John's Special Reserve bourbon sat on the sideboard. Waiting for the sound of the key in the lock, Emily paced through the apartment. Would she and John be able to reconcile, reigniting the attraction that they both felt in their courtship's early days be? Or would a continued tension hover over them? The scene in the driveway at Ca d' Zan still festered, but she was resolved to quash the strife in their marriage.

Emily had estimated John's arrival time, but an hour, then ninety minutes passed. Leaning her forehead on the window glass, she stared at the traffic below, as if she could determine which cab might deliver John to her door. Would all her preparations for a romantic evening be wasted? The sound of the champagne bottle shifting in the now-melted ice in the silver stand jarred her. She headed for the kitchen to get more ice just as the door opened in the foyer.

"Emily?" John called out. "Darling?"

She rushed toward him, and he caught her in his arms, kissing her hair, her neck, and then her lips. Emily embraced him, returning his ardor and stroking the back of his neck, then leaning back to look into his eyes.

"I've missed you, John. Welcome home." Her voice was husky as she put her hands on his cheeks to draw his lips back to hers. Worries and apprehension that had tormented her since she'd left Ca d'Zan drained away.

"Maybe I should take my coat off and come in." John playfully touched his forehead to hers but did not release his grasp. His brown eyes gazed into her blue ones. "I love you so, Emily. I've so missed Them There Eyes." He hummed the song that had underscored their romance while swaying back and forth with her in his arms.

Her eyelids fluttered. "And I you, my darling."

The evening was all Emily had hoped for. Nestled on

the sofa, she and John sipped drinks, shared caviar and an assortment of canapes, and rekindled their love for one another. They vowed to be more understanding, more devoted, more compassionate. They spoke of the early days of their romance; they caressed, until their passion carried them from the living room into the bedroom. The next morning, Emily awoke to the gentle snoring of her husband lying next to her. She smiled to herself when she spotted her new ice-blue gown in a tangle on the bedroom carpet. A good cleaner would be able to steam out the wrinkles, but better yet, it seemed that the wrinkles had been steamed out of her marriage.

Away from the trappings of Ca d'Zan, Emily relaxed, and when Sophie alerted others to their presence in the city, invitations poured in. John, content to dine at home after attending to business dealings during the day, went along good-naturedly, donning a tuxedo when it was called for. Emily found it thrilling to enter a party on the arm of the illustrious John Ringling. She basked in the admiration of her friends, and she could see that John relished the limelight as well. "You look ravishing," he'd whisper in her ear, as they stepped into a room full of café society New Yorkers. He often claimed that he'd never met a stranger, and even when he'd been reluctant to spend another evening out, he was soon delighting an audience of new acquaintances with circus stories or his travels through Europe.

ONE AFTERNOON. JOHN spent nearly an hour on the telephone while Emily, reclining on the bedroom chaise, flipped through magazines and the Times.

"Darling I have wonderful news!" John burst into the room. He reached toward her, grabbing the *Vogue* from her hands and tossing it aside, and kissed her. "Just wait until you hear." He strode around the room, hands on his hips.

"My goodness. Look at you! You're positively bursting. What is it?" Emily stood. John's joy was infectious, and she chuckled at the bounce in his step.

"Tonight, we're going out on the town, with Lulu Bohler. I believe we are ready to open the museum!"

Lulu Bohler? Who's that? Emily stopped herself from asking and tried to recall if she had heard that name before. *Opening the museum?* She knew little about John and Mable's art collection housed in a Uffizi-styled building on the Ca d'Zan property. John had shown her around on one of her first days at Ca d'Zan, and she was impressed with its grandeur and scope. But a fine art museum in Sarasota, Florida struck her as excessively grandiose and ostentatious, an affectation that seemed to shout, "Look at how wealthy and cultured we are!" And again, it was about Mable. She took a deep breath and forced a smile.

"Fill me in, John. And have I met Lulu Bohler?"

"Ah, Lulu is my art dealer. Real name is Julius. He's

a genius in the art world, knows his way all across galleries throughout Europe. He's got some new finds for us and hinted at ideas for our grand opening. You'll adore him. Dinner is at the Empire Room at seven. I'm sure you can be ready by then, my dear." He hugged her, then stepped back and thrust out his chest. "The John and Mable Museum of Art. Soon to be a reality!"

"Yes, imagine." Emily offered a tepid smile, hoping that John would not notice her lack of enthusiasm. Find out the details first, she chided herself.

EMILY HAD DINED in the Waldorf's Empire Room before, but she found its ornamentation garish and its atmosphere stifling. Dark green marble pillars etched in gold lined the room, and gloomy frescoes covered every wall. Humorless waiters glided among the tables covered in heavy brocades, presenting domed dishes with a dramatic flourish. She recalled John's desire to be married here, and she was thankful that she had persuaded him otherwise. The Jersey City Mayor's Office, without gaudy frills, had sufficed.

Following the maître d', John guided Emily, in a deep blue crepe de chine, towards the table where Lulu Bohler awaited them. He stood as they approached, revealing himself to be a man no taller than Emily. He puffed out his chest as he reached for and planted a kiss on Emily's hand as John made introductions. Emily tried not to crinkle her nose as she inhaled the cloying scent of the pomade that glistened through the perfectly lined tracks Lulu had combed through his black hair.

"Charmed to meet you, Frau Ringling." He offered a slight bow.

Had he actually clicked his heels? "*Bitte nenn mich Emily, Herr Bohler.*" Emily took a seat and John slid her chair forward.

"*Du sprichst Deutsch?*" Bohler's mouth fell open.

"*Absolut.*" Emily nodded, enjoying the surprise on Bohler's face. "My parents were born in Germany."

"Ah then you must delight in the German aesthetic of this glorious restaurant, designed after Neuschwanstein Castle in Bavaria." He scanned the room, nodding in appreciation. "You have a remarkable wife, John." Bohler tipped his hand in a salute.

John agreed. "Isn't she a beauty?" John patted Emily's hands, folded demurely on the table.

Emily lowered her eyes. *It's as if I'm a new procurement John has made for his art collection.*

After a few pleasantries and some grumbling about the prohibition of alcohol, the men entered into a conversation that did not include her. Sliding her finger along the rim of her glass, she studied Lulu. Why would a man nickname himself Lulu? Did this little man always shower John with compliments about his keen eye as an art collector? Surely John could see through this performance.

Bohler turned toward Emily. "Your husband was brilliant to add the *Eucharist* series. You know it, Emily?" He did not wait for a response, and once again addressed John. "What a coup to add these magnificent pieces to the collection." Bohler lifted his glass in a toast. "It is a privilege to know such a knowledgeable connoisseur as yourself."

John preened under Bohler's accolades. The two men reminisced about several other collaborative purchases—a Francesco Granacci, a unique Renaissance Madonna, a rare triptych from an Antwerp collection.

"But, Lulu, where is the catalog of my collection that you've been promising?" John's tone was cajoling, but Emily recognized a trace of impatience. She knew that when John issued a directive, he expected that it would be carried out. Maybe Bohler was falling out of favor with her husband, even after their long business association.

Emily watched a flush creep up Bohler's neck as he reached for his glass and took several gulps of his water.

"It is nearly completed, I assure you." Lulu studied the glass, then patted his mouth with his napkin. "But now I must tell you about a new piece that I believe will interest you. It will be just the acquisition that will make your opening the talk of the art world." He licked his lips, boring his eyes into John's.

John's eyes widened. "What is it?"

Bohler flicked an invisible speck of dust off his sleeve. "An El Greco, John. *The Crucifixion with Mary and Saint John.*"

John gasped and straightened in his chair. "El Greco? I must have it."

"I knew you would feel that way. So, I've already purchased it on your behalf." Lulu tossed his head back with a flourish.

John's eyes glowed. "Think of it. The *piece de resistance* of the collection."

Emily's eyes darted back and forth from her husband to the art dealer, and back again. How presumptuous for Lulu to authorize such a purchase without consulting John. Emily put her hand on John's arm, reminding both men of her presence at the table. An El Greco? What might this cost? Certainly, Bohler would profit from this immensely. Was this about helping John's museum rise in prominence, or Lulu's attempt to line his own pockets? She stifled the urge to voice her questions, even as they multiplied.

"Such a prestigious acquisition like this is something we'll have to consider, John." Had her heard her use the pronoun *we*? She beamed at her husband but saw in the faraway look in his eyes that he was already imagining the painting hanging on the walls of his museum. "But darling, I'm famished. Shall we look at the menus?"

Chapter Eighteen

WITHIN A FEW weeks, Emily found herself on the train back to Ca d'Zan. John had hoped to have his private railroad car delivered to New York to transport them back to Florida, but complications prevented him from doing so. Instead, he booked separate Pullman compartments for himself and Emily, and they remained secluded for much of the journey. "This way I won't disturb you when I'm working," he'd told her. But Emily knew that was simply a smokescreen. In fact, the past weeks had been filled with an underlying tension between John and her, each one consistently sought out private spaces, avoiding the festering discord that wearied them both.

Staring out the train window, Emily recalled the most recent spark that had ignited further disharmony in their marriage.

Just days after their dinner with Lulu, Emily breezed into the apartment, several shopping bags and a hatbox hanging from her arm. Dropping the packages on the foyer floor, she stripped off her cashmere gloves and shrugged off her coat, calling out, "John, I'm home." Then, she heard his voice in conversation. On the phone with Bohler again? The little man seemed to call daily, and after each conversation, John bubbled with anticipation about the arrival of the El Greco, on its way to Sarasota from Italy.

But when she heard the stern tenor of his voice, Emily moved toward the office door, adjacent to the foyer, to listen. "Do you realize who I am? Your insinuations that I am in arrears are highly insulting. You shall be paid, I can assure you. Please do not bother me again." Emily heard the jangle of the receiver being hung up.

"John?" Emily tapped on the door, then opened it to see him seated at his desk, rubbing his temple with his fingers. She walked behind his chair, leaning down to kiss him on the head. "How was your afternoon? I've had a lovely luncheon with Genevieve—you remember her from the dinner party at the Millers. Then we dipped into Bendel's, and I found the most cunning little hat. Would you like to see it?"

John tuned to look at her. "Not right now, dear. I'm sure it's very nice." He hesitated for a moment, and then exhaled loudly. "Could you sit down for a moment?"

Emily sank into a leather chair across from him. His eyes seemed glassy under the crease of his brow. Was he ill? "Something is troubling you, John. Tell me."

He offered a weak smile. "Oddly enough, it seems that I'm having some difficulties with obtaining the cash necessary to pay a creditor or two, and some of them are behaving in a completely inflexible manner. Of course, I have plenty of assets. I'm a very wealthy man, after all. But for the time being, I've had to postpone some reimbursements." He swallowed, then continued. "Do you have any idea what you've spent over the past several months, ordering merchandise by mail and adding more purchases since you've been in the city?" He picked up a stack of bills piled in front of him and shuffled through them. "Saks, Bendel's, some boutique named Chez Maurice. It's quite astounding. In fact, that was the manager of Bendel's on the phone right now." His voice trailed off and a frown carved itself into his face.

Emily froze. Her stylist at Bendel's typically fawned over her but today had seemed standoffish, even cold. How humiliating to be the object of a salesperson's scorn due to unpaid bills! And was John actually accusing her of over-indulgence, extravagance? All at once, heat rose in her chest and her shoulders stiffened. Through tightened lips, she said, "Are you implying that I'm the cause for your over-extension? That I've brought on your financial predicament?"

"Emily, no need to get upset. I'm simply pointing out that you've charged quite a bit recently, and it's difficult at this time to …"

She interrupted. "Charged quite a bit, you say? I've bought clothing, nothing more. And I dare say that you bask in the glow of having a well-dressed wife. Holding my arm as we enter a party or a restaurant, showing me off like I'm some newly acquired piece for your art collection." She crossed her arms. "And now you're chastised me for creating the image you so desire in a wife?"

"Calm down, my dear. Of course, I'm proud to have you, my beautiful wife, by my side, but these expenses…" He cleared his throat. "They're excessive, I'm afraid."

Excessive? She mentally inventoried what she'd recently purchased. A few gowns, several dresses for various occasions, the hats and shoes necessary to accessorize an ensemble. Nothing was excessive; everything was required of a woman in her social strata. She would not dignify his accusation with a justification.

Indignation roiled within her. Never had anyone—not her parents, not Charles—ever suggested that she was reckless with money. How dare John make such a claim, as if she were some gold-digger instead of a woman of means in her own right.

She stood, shooting her words at him as if firing bullets from a gun. "If we're talking about excesses, may I ask what you've paid Lulu Bohler recently, what you're spending on that dreadful El Greco. And what are you squandering on a museum with your name splashed all over it? Your scolding of me is demeaning. I won't listen to another word." She grabbed the pile of bills from his hands and flung them at him. As the papers fluttered around him, some landing on the desk, some on the floor, Emily left the room, slamming the door as she made her exit.

In the foyer once again, Emily scooped up her packages and took them into her dressing room. She sat on a tufted ottoman and opening the box that contained her new purchase, she lifted a velvety black slouch style hat from a nest of tissue paper. It was just the thing to complement a new red sheath, but now its charm was blemished by John's remarks.

Twirling the hat absently on her fingers, she replayed a comment that Genevieve had made at lunch. "How brilliant of you," she'd said, "to have access to all of those piles of circus money. Nicely done, my dear, to have snagged such a catch." Emily had not replied, chalking it up to Genevieve's bent toward cattiness. But now, she wondered if Genevieve voiced what was being said all over the city, behind her back. Of course, she could have paid for her purchases with her own funds. But why should she? She was the wife of John Ringling, and that entitled her to access to his funds. She should have taken umbrage with Genevieve right then and there. Imagine if she had declared to Genevieve that, in fact, John still owed her fifty thousand dollars she had lent him. That would set tongues wagging. Since their marriage, she had refrained from mentioning the loan to John, but now might be time to hold him accountable, to demand a reimbursement. How dare he criticize her, someone who had never in her life approached another person for a loan of any kind, while he enriched himself with her money. She tossed the hat on a shelf and stuffed the other unopened packages in the closet.

THE DAYS THAT had followed had been layered with tension. While she and John had not entered into further argument, they spoke only when necessary, keeping themselves occupied in separate rooms. Emily stifled the urge to demand repayment from John, while the tentacles of her grievance grew inside her. They continued to meet social obligations, and, vowing not to become the fodder for gossip about the strength of her marriage, Emily greeted friends and acquaintances with a well-practiced air of conviviality. John, ever the impresario, lost no opportunity to promote his museum, drinking in accolades and attention.

Emily found that dining out was a respite from mealtimes in the apartment that were devoid of all but the smallest pleasantries and often ended quickly as John scuttled back to his office under the pretext of "museum business." One evening he announced that a return to Ca d'Zan was imperative. "Please return with me, Emily. I know we've had our differences, but I do so want you by my side. Let's turn the page and move on."

Weary from living under the glare of New York society and maintaining a façade of the besotted wife of John Ringling, she agreed to go. At least at Ca d'Zan she could enjoy some solitude. Perhaps they could turn the page and open a happier chapter. "I'll go with you, John."

"Thank you, darling. I assure you that you won't regret it. You can't imagine how much I adore you." He rose from his seat at the dinner table and came to her. Taking her face into his hands, he kissed her. "I need you by my side, dearest."

She had not responded to his declaration of devotion. She supposed he meant to be sincere, but he'd made similar declarations in the past, but each of the affronts still gnawed at her. Moving on from each incident—his irritation over Mable's desk, his fury over Mable's car, his rebuke about her spending, and the matter of the unpaid loan—was like swallowing a stone. How many more would she have to take in?

As the train chugged its way south, Emily pressed her face to the window glass. She considered how her life in Sarasota might be different this time. She promised herself that she would find some interests of her own, would cultivate new friends. John had invited Lulu

Bohler to stay with them at Ca d'Zan, and Emily was keen to find a diversion. The thought of Lulu at their dinner table night after night, making pompous pronouncements about the art world while he slathered John with adulations, filled Emily with dread. The need for other dinner guests was clear. Who else could she bring into their dining room? Hester had been so warm and welcoming. She would be Emily's first link to making connections in Sarasota.

And after a while, maybe she could host a magnificent party. John would surely approve of another opportunity to tout his museum. As the train passed miles of farm fields and eventually wound its way through a greener landscape, Emily imagined fresh new versions of herself. By the time the train arrived in Sarasota, she had a strong grasp on what she would do to make a name for herself as an accomplished hostess and a woman of culture, and not as just some vapid gold-digger hanging on the arm of the Circus King.

Chapter Nineteen

A FEW WEEKS had gone by since John and Emily had returned to Ca d'Zan, and an uneasy peace had settled over them. Since John had invited Lulu Bohler to join them, there had been no private time for Emily and John to rekindle their affection, no opportunity to address the issues that had driven a wedge between them. Lulu was ever-present, spending hours holed up with John in his office while they worked on "museum business", or lounging around in the taproom, pouring himself glasses of bourbon and smoking John's cigars. Emily watched with amused cynicism as the two men seemed bent on flattering one another with unremitting praise.

"Lulu, you must stay in the tower room, the guest room reserved for my most favored guests."

"John, no other art collector has your vision, your exquisite taste."

Neither one of them displayed any skepticism regarding the constant shower of compliments, but Emily considered what each man's motives might be. Was Lulu in need of John's fame to bolster his prestige in the art world? Or was John in need of Lulu's professional reputation to augment the prestige of his museum? To Emily, it appeared to be a mutually exploitive relationship, one that each man was determined to propagate.

At mealtimes, Emily sat silently while Lulu and John reminisced about their art-buying trips through Europe. Their conversations bounced around her as if she were invisible, but Emily quietly attended to the tidbits they tossed around. One evening, when John boasted, "I've added four hundred pieces to my collection in just four years," Emily's astonishment caused her to tip over her water goblet. She had heard John's frequent chiding of Lulu regarding the completion of a catalog of the museum's contents, a task not yet completed. She wondered if Lulu's talent lay only with the spending of John's money and not with exacting task of chronicling the purchases.

On one occasion, after John had mentioned the lack of a catalog, Emily interjected a remark. "John, you're adamant that a catalog is the vital documentation the museum requires. Lulu, what is holding up the process?"

Lulu set down his fork and patted his mouth with his napkin. "My dear lady, you have no idea what this entails. The scholarly appraisals are a painstaking process. But I wouldn't expect you to comprehend the complexities." He turned his attention back to John.

Emily smoldered in silence. Had John not noticed Lulu's dismissal of her question? She eyed her husband, who had gone on to detailing a trip to Munich that he and Mable had taken several years before. "Remember, Lulu? She was so enamored with that rococo silver set that we had to buy it."

Lulu chuckled. "Ah, Frau Ringling, she had a keen eye for beauty and value, did she not?"

John sighed. "She surely did."

"I am Frau Ringling," Emily wanted to say. But she held her tongue, choosing instead to learn about the enormous value of the collection that resided here on the grounds of Ca d'Zan.

ONE MORNING, JOHN greeted Emily at the breakfast table with a kiss on her cheek and he swept his arm toward the sparkling bay just beyond the window. "Isn't it lovely to be back in beautiful Ca d'Zan? No snow or ice to worry about here!"

Emily sipped her coffee. "Yes, it's pretty. But I do enjoy some snow and the brisk air of New York. What are your plans for the day?"

John poured himself a cup of coffee from the urn on the sideboard, then filled a plate with eggs and bacon from the chafing dishes. "Lulu and I will be going through the museum. We'll have to decide where to hang the new acquisitions, especially the El Greco. I'm sure this would all be tedious for you." Sitting down, he snapped open his napkin and tucked it into his shirt collar, then dug his fork into his steaming plate of scrambled eggs.

Emily nibbled a piece of toast. Since she had returned to Florida, she and Hester had met for lunch on two or three occasions, and a tentative plan was set for later today. But, she could telephone Hester to rearrange that. While she had little interest in Baroque art and even less desire to listen to Lulu's pontificating and posturing, going through the museum could be instructive. She had not gleaned any details of the new acquisitions beyond the El Greco. As for the costs? She was in the dark. "I think, John, if you don't mind, I'll tag along with you and Lulu. It will be enlightening."

Before John could respond, Lulu joined them.

"Ah, Lulu! I was just telling John that I plan to walk through the museum with the two of you this morning. I have so much to learn." She peered at him over her coffee cup, taking note of the sideways glance he shot at John, as if he were gauging his reaction. John, his lips drawn tight, gave a small nod.

Lulu clasped his hands together, tilting his head to the side. "I hope we don't bore you with all of our talk about the art and the painstaking decisions about its placement. For the uninitiated, I fear it might be overwhelming."

Emily resisted the urge to snarl at the man's condescending tone. She kept her voice light. "I'll do my best to keep up. Let me know when you're ready to go."

After a short phone call to Hester, she retreated to her desk in the solarium where she unlocked a drawer and pulled out a thick folder she had only glanced at months before. In Mable's spidery handwriting, the label read "Art Acquisitions." She recalled wondering why this folder was not in John's office but considered that this might be a duplicate of one in his possession. Flipping through the pages, she studied the invoices and the documentation for several works—*Still Life with Parrots*, *Landscape with Hunters*, *Portrait of Anna Hofstreek*. She was unfamiliar with each of them or the artists who'd created them—Nicolas Maes, Adam Pynacker, Jan de Heem. But the values listed astounded her. These were only three of the works that John and Mable had acquired. Her mind reeled at the potential worth of the entire collection. The museum was more than a hobby or a diversion for John; it was a vast fortune. And it was time for her to get involved.

"I'D SAY IT was rather savvy of me to line up John Philips, the same man who worked on the Met Museum in New York and Grand Central Station, to design my museum," John said as the threesome entered the marble lobby. "Quite a genius when it comes to architecture, as you might imagine. He calls this an *enfilade* design, where one gallery flows into the next. Even though we were only open for one day last year, just to give the populace a small taste, we had over ten thousand visitors. And they were agog!" He took Emily's arm as she mentally calculated the amount of money ten thousand visitors, each paying a small fee, would generate. She had not considered that this museum could be more than a dilettante's pursuit, and its financial potential intrigued her.

John guided her to the first gallery. "Let's proceed, and I'll show you some of the best Baroque art in the world, all arranged in chronological order."

Emily had paid little attention to John's monologue on her first visit, but this time she zeroed in the specifics and peppered him with questions. "Why did you purchase this piece? What makes it valuable? Is the artist of any importance? Why?" At times, she jotted notes into a leather-bound notebook.

John beamed at her. "My dear, you're showing an immense interest today. I didn't think my collection was important to you." He patted her arm. "But I'm afraid we're getting off track. Jot your questions down, and we can discuss them later."

Lulu chimed in. "The little lady is quite eager to learn, I see." Then he turned to John. "But, John, let us return to the task at hand. Now that we are in the

Spanish gallery, where shall we display the El Greco?" His face took on a pensive air as he tapped his index finger to his lips. John, his hands clasped behind his back, strode into the center of the room and followed Lulu's gaze.

Emily's jaw clenched. Once again, she had been dismissed by this pompous little art dealer and John was oblivious to his behavior. "I have a thought." Emily walked in between them toward a wall filled with small works. "These pieces, "she waved her arm, "appear to be of little consequence. Some dismal landscapes that all resemble one another. Why not sell them off and allow the El Greco to hang here? This place of prominence seems wasted." She put a hand on her hip and raised her eyebrows quizzically at her husband.

"My dear Emily, I don't…'

Lulu interrupted John. "Frau Ringling, I don't believe you understand." He chuckled quietly as he quoted her. "'Dismal landscapes' you say. These are precious works. Important."

"Important?" She scowled. "How are they distinctive? Please enlighten me, Lulu." She pointed to one of the paintings. "If the El Greco is as fabulous as you say, this drab little nothing might be sold off in order to make room."

"Emily, let's not become distracted." John stepped toward her and reached for her arm. "Let's let Lulu make the recommendations for displaying the new piece. As for selling these," he shuddered and waved his hand at the wall, "that is something I would never consider."

"Why not?" She pulled her arm away from him. After studying the papers in Mable's folder, she'd realized the practicality of auctioning off some art to smooth out the financial difficulties John was facing. Even one unremarkable landscape would cover the bills at Bendel's. Why was he so hesitant?

"Because each and every item in this glorious museum represents a dream fulfilled." His eyes took on a faraway look. "You have no idea…"

Then Lulu added. "Frau Ringling, your husband and his departed wife scoured Europe for each piece in this museum. Surely you can appreciate his reluctance."

Her face reddened as if she had been slapped. "Of course. Thank you, Lulu, for clearing up this matter." Her voice dripped with sarcasm. "Whatever was I thinking, John, suggesting that even the most inconsequential memento of your beloved Mable might be disposed of?" She resisted the urge to leave the gallery and imagined the sound of her heels hammering the wood floors echoing the hammering of her heart. Instead, she remained. She would keep her thoughts to herself for now, knowing this conversation with John was not over. She would confront him about his finances, about his repayment of the fifty thousand dollars that he'd promised her.

The museum housed a fortune and there was no excuse for his failure to repay her loan, no excuse for his welshing on financial obligations. If John insisted on keeping every last piece, then he must open the doors for more than one day, to allow the museum to generate income. If the completion of a catalog was a hindrance, then John must insist that Lulu get it completed. As for Lulu, how dare he speak to her of John's departed wife? She would no longer suffer his intrusion into their lives. Lulu would have to go.

Chapter Twenty

LATER THAT EVENING, when each of them had retreated to their rooms to dress for dinner, Emily seized on the opportunity to speak to John alone. *Keep it light*, she reminded herself. She tapped on the door linking their rooms and entered before John could respond. She found him in front of his cheval mirror, buttoning a freshly ironed blue shirt. "Here, let me do that for you." Standing between him and the mirror, she finished the buttoning, then looked into his face and kissed him. "Would it be silly to say I've missed you?"

John put his arms around her waist and returned the kiss. "Missed me? I've been right here!"

"Yes, darling, but we've had no time to ourselves, with Lulu here. I may as well be a potted plant, for all the attention you've shown me. I was hoping for time together, just the two of us." She stroked his arms and looked into his eyes. "Can't you send Lulu away?"

John smiled at her but shook his head. "Ah, if only it were that simple, Emily. But I can't open the museum without the catalog, and Lulu is responsible for it." He removed his hands from around her waist and sat on the edge of the bed, slipping his feet into a pair of brogues. "Please understand, Emily."

She perched on a chair, keeping silent for a moment or two, reminding herself to speak gently. "To be frank, John, I do not understand. It appears to me that you can simply open the museum any time you wish, catalog or not. You said yourself that you had ten thousand visitors on the day you opened it last year. As for Lulu and the catalog, why can't he compile it elsewhere?"

"Well, that would be difficult." He looked up at her. "Say, do you know if Martha is preparing grouper this evening?"

Emily could feel heat rising in her chest, singeing the softness she'd promised herself she'd use. "John, I was speaking about Lulu, and I would appreciate your attention. Lulu certainly isn't working here, when all I observe him doing is toadying to you when he could be getting something accomplished." She knew that she had crossed a line, but the words had escaped before she could rein them in.

John's head snapped. "Toadying to me?"

"Perhaps I spoke too harshly, but surely you can see that yourself. All of his ingratiating talk about what a fine connoisseur of art you are, on and on. From my point of view, I see a man using you for his own gain, taking advantage of you." She swept a hand under a curl, flipping it behind her head.

John's face reddened and his eyes narrowed. "You don't realize, Emily, that beyond our business arrangement, Lulu and I have a years' long…'

She interrupted. "Oh, yes. Years' long." How tired she was of the nostalgia for his previous life. She rolled her eyes. "He's insufferable, slathering on so much flattery that you're coated with it. And you're blind to his insulting behavior towards me."

John's mouth dropped open. "Flattery? Do you take me for a fool, Emily? And insulting to you? You're imagining things." He scoffed and returned his attention to his shoelaces.

Emily's words were edged with steel. "John, I want Lulu to leave. Shall you send him away, or shall I?" She had not meant for this conversation to escalate into a quarrel, nor had she intended to issue an ultimatum. But here they were again, at odds with one another. It was as if a fire lay smoldering between them and John inevitably tossed match to it with his insensitivity.

John leaned back and, staring at the ceiling, took several deep breaths before he responded. Then he straightened and looked at her. "Once again, Emily, we're engaged in a squabble. And dinner and Lulu are waiting for us downstairs. Let's table this discussion. I promise you I will consider what you have said." He reached out his hand. "Can you agree to that for now?"

She hesitated. How she despised recriminations, ugly scenes! She was exhausted from living under a shroud of bitterness. "I'll agree for now, John. But just for now."

He kissed her hand. "Fine. Now let's enjoy our dinner."

HAD JOHN SENT Lulu on his way? Or did Lulu decide it was time to return to his wife and children? Either way, Emily was pleased when just a few days after the museum tour, Lulu bid them farewell, and she and John were finally alone at Ca d' Zan. Emily knew that she must seize the opportunity to approach John about her festering financial concerns. But when? It seemed that no time was right.

One late afternoon, Emily opened the door to John's office just wide enough to poke her head in. "Darling, it's such a lovely afternoon. Let's—"

He stopped tapping on the keys to his adding machine and, keeping his eyes on papers in front of him, signaled "one moment" with an index finger. Then he resumed entering more numbers while she waited. After a few moments, the clacking of the keys halted, and he looked up at her.

"Yes, dear?" His smile was tepid and his complexion washed out and pale under the light of the desk lamp.

"Darling, you look like you could use some glorious Florida sunshine. Come with me for drinks on the terrace."

He pinched the bridge of his nose and exhaled a weary sigh. "I'm awfully tied up right now."

She twisted her features into an exaggerated pout. "Please, pretty please, John."

He chuckled. "I guess I can't say no when you give me that look. I'll be ready in about an hour."

"See you then." She winked and closed the door.

ON THE TERRACE, Emily waited in a chair facing the bay. One hour had turned in to two, and the sun was lowering into the sky, streaking the clouds with amber and casting ever-changing hues of yellow and gold over the rippling water. Just what was keeping John? Impatience gnawed at her, muting the tranquil beauty that lie before her.

How many minutes, hours, days had she spent, sitting idly, waiting for him to steer the course of their days? Untethered to the life she had known, she longed for the firm grasp she once had on her own destiny. She ruminated while pelicans skimmed over the water in front of her, then plunged to scoop fish into their beaks. "*Was ist, ist.*" She heard her mother's oft-spoken words whenever she or her sisters complained about their fate. *The world is filled with women who would love to be in your shoes right now.* She couldn't help smiling when a manatee surfaced just a few feet from the terrace's edge and punctuated her thoughts by snuffling out a blast of air.

When John appeared, the sun was nearing the horizon. He carried two cocktails and wore a sheepish expression. "I lost track of the time, darling." Handing her a glass, he settled into the waiting chair and reached over to tap her glass with his. "Cheers, Emily." They sat in companionable silence for a few moments.

"Mother Nature puts on quite a show, doesn't she?" John placed his hand on Emily's lap, and she covered it with her own.

"Breathtaking." Emily glanced at him. The creases of worry that she'd seen on his face in the office had smoothed out, and the corners of his mouth were turned slightly upward. "It's nice to see you looking more relaxed."

He shrugged. "We live in interesting times. No rest for the weary, they say." He patted her knee. "Listen to me, just spouting clichés." More silence.

The sun disappeared as they finished their drinks. The bay breeze turned chilly. Emily shivered. "Shall we go in? I told Martha to serve dinner after the sun goes down." Hand in hand, they walked back to the house and into the dining room.

"Fried chicken and mashed potatoes! Martha, you know this is one of my favorites." John rubbed his hands in anticipation as Martha set the plates before them, then returned to the kitchen. He picked up a chicken leg and bit into it.

Emily wrinkled her nose. *Circus food.* She trimmed the coating from her chicken and speared a small piece. Once she had suggested a chicken dish that her mother had prepared, but John had rejected the idea. "Just give me good old fried chicken and I'm a happy man."

Emily moved morsels of meat around her plate. "John, it's nice to see you enjoying your meal. You're clearly working too hard and are bearing some tremendous burdens. I wish that you would share them with me."

John rubbed his hands on his napkin and reached for another chicken leg on the serving platter. "Emily, none of this is your concern. I've told you that many times."

She watched him continue eating. *Was ist, ist,* she told herself. *Was ist, ist.* She looked around the dining room, taking in its *trompe l'oeil* ceiling, its lavish silver chandelier and sconces. Surrounded by extravagance when bills went unpaid? *No.* she set down her fork and reminded herself to speak in soft tones. "Then, John, I must insist that you return the fifty thousand dollars I loaned you before we married. At the time you said I'd be repaid in three months. That time is long past."

John's eyes bulged and he pushed the palm of his hand toward her. "Hush!"

Hush? Emily spat out her words. "I will not hush,

John. How dare you—"

He leaned forward and hissed. "Not now. Do you think I want the help hovering around in the kitchen to overhear our conversation? Then, spreading tales all through Sarasota? Finish your dinner and we will continue this discussion in my office."

So, the help could listen in to his grandiose descriptions of his museum, but now he was calling for discretion? She tossed her napkin onto the table and rose. "I'll be waiting upstairs. Enjoy your chicken."

Would he actually follow through and invite her to his office? And if not, what recourse did she have? Not for the first time, she regretted the loan she had made. She'd wanted to please him, and he'd said it was just to smooth over a "rough patch." Rough patch indeed! Why hadn't she insisted on more details? And why had she not put the loan in writing? These funds, her possibly be lost forever. How could she have been such a fool? She was standing on the loggia, staring into the dark, when John entered the room and came up behind her.

He placed his hand on her shoulder. "Let's go into my office and talk."

Mutely, she followed him. He closed the office door behind them and offered her a chair. Instead of sitting behind the desk, he pulled another chair toward hers and sat facing her. He clasped her hands in his.

He kept his eyes on their hands while he spoke.

"Emily, when I asked you for the loan, I had every intention of returning your money quickly. But things have changed. Some of my business interests—the railroads, the oil, the real estate development—have not been as successful as I'd imagined. Surely you realize this is the case ever since the Crash."

"Of course, I—"

"Let me finish. I'm doing all I can to mitigate the situation, and I hope that you will stand by me patiently. I assure you that you will be repaid." His eyes searched hers as if looking for acquiescence.

Emily bit her lower lip. How could she not feel compassion for this man, nearly broken by the happenstances of events beyond his control? Sympathy engulfed her, but only for a moment. She resolved to be firm. "John, I see your predicament. But I insist you be forthright with me. By all appearances, you enjoy astounding wealth. This estate, the museum, the automobiles, the circus, the bank. The list goes on."

John turned his eyes toward his desk, laden with folders and loose papers. "As you can see, I'm working to put it all to rights. When will I repay you? I cannot be specific at the moment. It's my strongest desire to clear that up between us. And for you to expect me to detail every bit of business that I've been undertaking over the past months, well, that is impossible."

She persisted. "Can't you liquidate some of the art

that you've acquired? It seems to me that—"

He shook his head violently, tightening his grip of her hands. "No. That will not happen. I will not relinquish the art. I'm sorry that you do not respect it as I do, but do not ever ask that of me again. I beg you, as my wife, to respect my wishes and to trust in me."

Trust. Respect. Could she give him that? How, when she was left in the dark? But what choice did she have? She could not force him to reveal anything, no matter what demands or ultimatums she made. She wished to be John's valued partner, not simply the pretty wife hanging on his elbow. Wives had no standing when it came to financial decision making. Her mind whirled with rebuttals and demands, but she stopped herself hurling them at him. *Was ist, ist.*

She bowed her head and drew her hands from his grasp. "All right, John."

"Good girl." John stood and reached out his hands to guide her from her chair. Kissing her on her forehead, he murmured, "I love you, Emily."

She did not respond as she slipped out the door. She had lost this skirmish, but there would be others, and she would renew her arsenal before the next one.

WEEKS TURNED INTO months. Emily found the Sarasota summer to be unbearable, with its oppressive heat and humidity. Many Sarasotans headed north for the summer, including Hester, the only person she'd gotten to know well. When even the swimming pool offered little relief, she returned to New York for several weeks. Although she relished time in the city she loved, the shadow of the Depression was unavoidable. Several of her favorite shops were boarded up and grizzled men appeared on every street corner, asking for handouts. One afternoon, from the window of her taxi, she observed a line of bedraggled women and children outside a Fifth Avenue church.

"What's going on there?" she asked the driver.

"Soup kitchen, ma'am."

On Fifth Avenue? She shook her head in disbelief, then reminded herself of the stories she'd heard of acquaintances who had suddenly left the city, no forwarding addresses. It was all dreadful, but here Emily felt more like herself, the vivacious and popular Emily Haag Buck, and not merely an appendage of John Ringling. But when summer waned and the air tuned cool, Emily, swayed by John's loving telegrams and his declarations of loneliness without her, returned to Ca d'Zan. She reminded herself that she was a married woman, after all, and her place was with her husband.

BACK AT CA d'Zan, John was attentive and affectionate at first, but within days, old habits resurfaced. John barely spoke with her at mealtimes, and her attempts at conversation landed flat. Business associates came and went, but when Emily chanced to be present when Martha greeted them at the door, the visitors offered her few pleasantries before John appeared and whisked them upstairs to his office. In the evenings, John frequently drove to his bank office and often did not return until long after she had gone to bed.

But at least Hester had returned. Catching up over lunch at the Sarasota Terrace Hotel, Emily could not tamp her envy when Hester described her summer.

Hester's eyes shone with merriment as she described her Wisconsin escapades. "You've probably never heard of the Wisconsin Dells, but it's just a short jaunt from Baraboo. It's a joy to return to where we Ringlings grew up. We went boating almost every day. Charles and the boys insist on climbing the bluffs above the river, and then jumping into the water below. One day, I shocked them all, climbing up a bluff and then plunging in myself."

"You didn't!" Emily laughed, as if on cue, all the while hollowed out by Hester's joy. When had she felt such gladness herself? She had almost forgotten what true happiness looked like until she saw it radiating from Hester's face.

Hester waved her hand towards Emily. "Enough about me. How was your time in New York?"

"Oh, fine. Saw some old friends. But, my goodness,

there is hardship on every corner. So terrible to see men begging on the street." Emily lowered her eyes and busied herself with spearing a tomato from her salad. "John has been so busy and distracted these days, so I wanted to let him work in peace."

Hester began to reply, but when Emily looked up at her, Hester hesitated. "Yes... I'm sure he's busy."

"Hester, I'd really like to host a dinner party now that autumn is here. I've barely gotten to know people and I wonder if you could help him decide whom to invite." How had that idea popped up into her mind? But immediately she knew that it was a good one. A way to make her mark on Sarasota.

With silver tongs, Hester plucked a sugar cube from a crystal bowl and dropped it into her iced tea. "Have you spoken to John?"

"Funny thing, no. I just this instant arrived at the idea. What do you think?" Emily propped her chin on her fist, waiting for Hester's reply. Studying her friend's face, she detected a reluctance. "What is it, Hester? I see your hesitancy."

Hester reddened. "Emily, I..." She took a sip of her iced tea. "I just think you should speak to John first. I'm not privy to Uncle John's business dealings, but Mother has shared some things. Things are difficult for everyone right now—you know, with the Crash and all—so maybe John would prefer to decide whom to entertain."

Reaching out her hand to grasp Emily's, she continued. "I think a party sounds like a wonderful plan, and I'd love to help. But a guest list ... that could be awkward."

Emily removed her hands from Hester's and placed both on her lap, clasping them together to keep them from trembling. Hester was too kind to say it, but it was clear now that some of John's business alliances were foundering. And Hester knew what Emily did not. "I see." She arranged her face into an amused smirk. "Men will be men, I suppose. Business can be ruthless. I'll definitely run my ideas past John."

Relief washed over Hester's face and she brightened. "Wonderful."

Chapter Twenty-One

THERE WOULD BE no party.

After concocting the idea at the luncheon with Hester, Emily mulled over party plans. Presenting a *fait accompli* to John could make it more difficult for him to refuse. Now that November wasn't too far away, she considered a Thanksgiving theme. Cornucopias as centerpieces, perhaps. And a cosmopolitan menu. Duck l'orange? That seemed autumnal. She wondered if any local orchestra knew the latest dance numbers. She'd invite Sophie, who'd been dying to visit, as well as a few other New Yorkers. John's dour mood would surely be lifted if he was able to show off the grandeur of Ca d'Zan. By assuring him that she would bear the burden of planning, she was confident that she could convince him that a party was long overdue.

One afternoon, Sam Gumpertz arrived shortly after lunch to meet with John, and Emily busied herself at her solarium desk, composing a guest list and drawing sketches of tablescapes. Two hours passed, and eventually, Sam came down the stairs and headed for the door.

"Hello, Sam. Did your meeting go well?" Emily stood and walked toward him.

Sam startled. "Hello, Emily. I- I didn't see you." His tie askew and his jacket draped over his shoulder, he shifted a bulging leather portfolio from under one arm to the other. "Nice to see you again." Without answering her question, he reached for the door handle and made his exit.

Shrugging off Sam's abrupt departure, Emily headed upstairs. With notebook in hand, she tapped on John's office door, then opened it. "Darling, you and Sam have been meeting for hours. Let me come in and take your mind off business for a few moments."

John looked up, but he appeared so lost in thought that it seemed his gaze traveled right through her. She walked over to stand behind him. Encircling his shoulders with her arms, she leaned down and nuzzled his neck. Then, planting a kiss on the top of his head, she whispered, "May I sit?"

"Of course. But I…" he replied.

"John, I have the most outstanding idea." Taking a seat on a chair across from him, her voice bubbled as she opened her notebook. "And I've worked out almost all of the details. You won't have to lift a finger."

He closed his eyes and rolled his shoulders, then lifted his eyelids slightly. "What is it?"

"A party! We have yet to throw one of the famous Ca

d'Zan galas, and it's high time we did. I'm thinking an autumnal theme, and I've already chosen a couple of possible dates. And scads of plans for everything."

John leaned back into his leather chair and placed the palms of his hands on his desk. "No. No party."

It was as if he had jabbed her enthusiasm with a sharp pin and expelled all her excitement. "No? Why ever not? Look, I've got it all planned. All you'll need to do is be the charming host."

He shook his head. "Clearly you can see the strain I'm under right now. A party is out of the question." He folded his arms across his chest. "I'm in no mood for frivolity, Emily."

When had he become so negative? She tipped her head to the side, staring into his eyes. Where had his spark gone? When had his smile been permanently replaced with a thin grim line of lips pressed together? Where was the confident man who had been boasting about opening his museum for all to see? "But, John, this will no doubt be good for business as well, inviting your associates. Impressing them al with the splendor of Ca d'Zan, giving them an evening of entertainment that will be the talk of the town."

John snorted. "Some of these business associates are hounding me like a pack of wolves. Emily, this is not possible. I see you're disappointed, and maybe we can revisit this at another time. But not now."

His unyielding tone told Emily not to argue. She took in his slumped shoulders, his dull expression. How could she spar with a man who appeared so broken, so downcast? She scooped up her notebook and stood. "I see, John. I'm disappointed that you feel this way, but I'll not bother you any longer."

HESTER NEVER MENTIONED the party, and for that, Emily was grateful. Although they got together often, they navigated their conversations around the topic of Ringling family business. When Hester invited Emily to join her with other friends, she chose those unconnected to Ringling affairs. Emily tried to decipher the workings of John's dealings, but it was a muddle. Once, when Hester made an offhand remark regarding the rift between John and Owen Burns, Emily had nodded knowingly, hoping that Hester would mention details. But Hester scrupulously avoided gossip, leaving Emily in the dark.

The Sarasota Herald offered a few clues, and Emily made a point to scour the pages to determine the links between prominent Sarasotans. She knew that banks across the country were in an upheaval. Were John's bank board members, like Ralph Caples and A.E. Cumner, maintaining a smooth working relationship with one another? Was the bank in danger of failing? And Gumpertz? And Edith? Why were they and John on such thin ice?

HERBERT HOOVER PROCLAIMED November 26, 1931, as Thanksgiving Day, and Hester and Charles invited John and Emily to join them for their traditional family dinner. Edith would be there, too, of course, but Emily counted on the distraction of the young boys at the table—Hester's teenage sons and six-year-old James, the son of Hester's brother Robert and his wife Virginia, who were visiting from Chicago.

Emily chose a knit suit in deep green, accented with a Hermes scarf, for the occasion. She was surprised when Hester greeted her and John at the door, dressed in a simple tweed skirt and tailored blouse covered with a cotton cobbler's apron.

"Emily and John, do come in! How nice you look." Hester tucked a stand of hair behind her ear. "I suppose you didn't expect to see me in an apron. But I didn't want Gloria to be apart from her family on a holiday and I love to cook, so…" She gestured toward the kitchen.

Charles joined them in the foyer. "John, you'd better come with me before Hester puts you to work cutting up vegetables or something. Why don't you join me and Robert on the terrace with the boys? We'll leave the cooking to the women." He hugged his wife's shoulders and pecked her cheek. "This woman is a whirling dervish in the kitchen. Wait until you taste her sweet potatoes,

Emily!"

"Sounds like a fine idea, Charles." John allowed Charles to lead him outside. Emily could hear the clamoring of "Hello, Uncle John" from the boys.

"You'll meet Robert later but come with me." Hester took Emily's hand and led her into the kitchen. "Mother, Virginia, I've brought reinforcements. Emily, this is my sister-in-law, Virginia." She pointed toward a woman slicing carrots.

"So nice to meet you." Emily smiled. "Hello, Edith." She nodded toward John's sister-in-law, who barely looked up from stirring something on the stove to acknowledge Emily.

Virginia waved a knife at her. "Nice to meet you, too, Emily. Hester speaks so fondly of you." She, too, was wearing an apron, and the sleeves of her dress were rolled up.

"My, everything smells delicious in here." Emily inhaled the aromas wafting around the kitchen. "Hester, I never knew you cooked."

"Well, I don't often, but Mother taught me the basics when I was a girl, didn't you, Mother?" Hester wiped her hands on her apron and patted Edith's shoulder. "We Wisconsin girls know how to put on a feast!"

Edith's expression softened. "Yes, we do. Now, hand me that cinnamon and I'll stir it into the applesauce."

"Edith, are you making applesauce?" Emily walked

toward the stove and peered into the pot. "My goodness! My mother did also. Tell me, do you use nutmeg? Mama always did. And allspice. She taught me and my sisters and I'd forgotten how much I loved it. I can't wait to taste this."

"Really?" Edith raised an eyebrow at Emily. "I didn't take you for a woman who knew her way around a kitchen."

Emily shrugged. "I suppose I could say the same about you, Edith. I don't suppose any of us do much cooking these days. But, mmm, you should taste my plum *kuchen*. We would say *kostlich*!" She rolled her eyes toward the ceiling. "My mouth waters just thinking about it."

Edith's cheeks pinked with pleasure. Could Emily's love of applesauce have won her over? "Say, Hester, do you have a spare apron? And Edith, would it be rude to ask if I may I stir the applesauce for you? I haven't had the pleasure in years."

Hester set down her rolling pin, pulled an apron from a drawer and tossed it at Emily. "Here you go. Mama, let Emily take over while you help me form the dinner rolls."

A hint of a smile crept onto Edith's face and she handed Emily the spoon. "Don't add too much nutmeg. Just a pinch."

As Emily stirred, she absorbed the doings around her.

The women moved in a well-choreographed dance, Hester rolling dough, Edith patting it into biscuit-sized clumps and lining them up onto a baking sheet, Virginia chop-chop-chopping through carrots, now celery. The sweet fragrance of apples mingled with the savory aroma of the roasting turkey along with the bustle of activity brought her back to the Haag kitchen in New Jersey so long ago, when her mother was directing her three sisters and her as they prepared a holiday feast. A lump formed in her throat. Life had taken her so far away from those days. How could she be homesick, after so many years had passed?

HESTER SERVED DINNER in the dining room, enlisting her boys Larl and Stuart to carry the platters and bowls to the table. As if he were part of a Norman Rockwell illustration, Charles rolled up his sleeves and carved the turkey with much flourish, as his stepsons and his brother-in-law Robert tossed good-natured barbs his way. Edith led the family in a blessing, and then the family passed the dishes—roast turkey, cornbread stuffing, gravy, sweet potatoes, glazed carrots, applesauce, warm biscuits, creamed celery—around the table. The clatter of silverware on Hester's Spode china, the murmurs of appreciation as food was tasted, the easy flow of conversation harmonized with the savory aromas and flavors of the meal. Emily ate quietly, surprised at the sudden onset of melancholy and loneliness engulfing her. She could almost see herself and her three sisters, dressed in starched dresses, enormous bows pinned to their braids, as her mother brought platters of German specialties to the table and her father led them in a blessing. "*Komm Herr Jesus, Sei unser gast.*"

"Uncle John, do your clown song!" Stuart's words were muffled by a mouthful of potatoes.

Hester shook her head at her son. "My goodness, Stuart! Where are your manners?"

"Can't fault the boy for his hearty appetite, Hester." John's face became rubber-like, his features arranged in an exaggerated grin. In a stentorian voice, while gesticulating wildly, he bellowed out,

Du, du, liegst mir am Herzen,
Du, du, liegst mir im Sinn.
Du, du, machst mir viel Schmerzen,
Weißt nicht, wie gut ich dir bin.
Du, du, du, du weißt nicht, wie gut ich dir bin

Emily's spine straightened and she set down her fork. John's song resounding around the dining room was one from her childhood. Yes, it was a familiar folk tune, but how strange that he had included it in his clown act years ago. Pierced by nostalgia, she mouthed the familiar words as he sang.

John's performance ended and his facial expression

returned to normal. Stuart and Larl howled with laughter and little Jimmy glanced from one cousin to another, then to John. In a tremulous whisper, Jimmy asked, "Mommy, is Uncle John a clown?"

An explosion of laughter burst forth from the entire family, and Jimmy stuck out his bottom lip. He lowered his eyes to study his hands on his lap.

"I can be a clown, Jimmy. A clown is just a person in a costume, you know. Did I startle you?" He spoke gently and Jimmy looked up at him. The creases between Jimmy's eyes smoothed.

"Say, young man, what's that I see behind your ear? Come over here and let me see." John gestured to the little boy.

Robert smiled at his son. "Go ahead. Better have Uncle John take a look."

Jimmy left his chair to walk around the table.

John reached behind the boy's ear. "What's this? A nickel? Did you know you had a nickel hiding behind your ear?" John's eyes widened in surprise as he handed the little boy the nickel.

Jimmy gasped. "I didn't put it there, honest. Can I keep it?"

"Of course! We'd better check your other ear." John extracted another nickel, holding it up with exaggerated fanfare. "You must have magic in your ears, lad!"

Jimmy studied the two coins as if they were a pirate's

treasure and then rubbed behind each ear. Eyes wide, he gazed into his uncle's face. "I never knew you could find magic nickels behind my ears."

Emily couldn't help but smile as she observed the family members. She had not seen this side of John before. Publicly, John displayed a confident geniality, but at home, he often withdrew into remoteness. His willingness to mug for his nephews and his tenderness with the little one was endearing. Even the coolness between him and Edith seemed to have thawed. This version of John, the one so relaxed, so at peace with himself, was the man she loved.

HER MEMORY DRIFTED back to one evening in July of 1930 when her feelings for John had deepened. Walking along the banks of the Herengracht Canal in Amsterdam, John had told her his story—not one that featured him as the world's greatest showman, but one of a Wisconsin boy with six older brothers who together began a little circus.

"As the youngest boy, I had to do what I could to impress my big brothers. I wanted to do more than drive a wagon. So, I smeared on the greasepaint, and they added my clown act to our circus. It ended up that I was pretty good at being a clown." He chuckled and stared off into the canal, remembering.

"Eventually I wasn't simply the little brother of no

consequence. As the years went on, I traveled to Europe to find acts. I've had plenty of good fortune, Emily, but I'm still a farm boy from Wisconsin at heart." He shrugged his shoulders and gave her a sheepish glance.

As Emily listened to his story of humble beginnings, she saw a man who, despite all his wealth and acclaim, never took his standing in the world for granted. So many in Emily's circle were affected and jaded, and she was tired of their cynicism. John marveled at his own good fortune, was thrilled beyond measure with all he had attained. She linked her arm through his. "Your story is so admirable, John."

What others may have dismissed as braggadocio, she recognized as his genuine delight at the adventures of life. In his eyes, she saw warmth and optimism. And she fell in love.

✧ ✧ ✧

AT THE END of the meal, Charles enlisted his stepsons to clear the table and urged Hester and the other women to gather in the parlor.

John concurred. "We men will have the dishes done in no time." Expertly balancing several plates on his arms, he joined the others and headed toward the kitchen.

Virginia linked arms with Emily and led her to a sofa. "Emily, it's nice to have a chance to chat with you.

Hester speaks so highly of you. Tell me, how do you find life in Florida?"

"Hester is a dear." There was that question again: How was she finding Sarasota? She supposed that Virginia was simply making conversation, but Emily found her a bit too cloying, a bit too eager. She avoided the questions and changed the subject. "Your Jimmy is adorable and so bright. He must be such a joy to you and Robert. Is he in school?"

"Yes, he's in kindergarten." Virginia's eyes shone. "He's already reading a bit."

"Marvelous!"

Virginia continued her description of Jimmy's precociousness, allowing Emily to feign interest while she mulled over her feelings.

What were her sisters doing today? Had they gathered for Thanksgiving without her, assuming that she would not accept an invitation even if they'd offered one? It had been months since she'd seen Lena, Louise, or Olga. When had she last joined them on a holiday? Not last year—she and John were in a whirl right before their marriage. While she interjected appropriate comments of "My goodness!" and "How charming!" into Virginia's monologue, the old melody of "*Du, du, liegst mir am Herzen*" ribboned itself through her mind. Now amongst a gathering of Ringlings, she began to plan for a family Christmas away from Ca d'Zan.

WHEN JOHN AND Emily returned to Ca d'Zan, John suggested a nightcap in the tap room.

Emily agreed. "I'd love one, but not the tap room. It's cozier in the parlor." While he headed off to mix the drinks, Emily turned on lamps and, taking off her pumps, she settled herself into a brocade sofa, tucking her feet underneath her.

John soon joined her, handing her a Rob Roy and sitting at the other end of the sofa, throwing his arm across its back. "Wonderful dinner, wasn't it?" He raised his glass towards her in a toast. "I just wish that Hester and Charles would serve some decent liquor. I know it's difficult to get these days, but..." He shook his head and sipped his whiskey. "Thank goodness I had the foresight to stock up."

"It was a wonderful dinner." Emily stirred her swizzle stick in her drink. "All of those traditional dishes. The applesauce was almost as good as my mother's. And John, those young boys adore you. With your nickel trick, Jimmy now worships you."

"Well, that old stunt never fails with a new audience." John's eyes twinkled. "Stuart and Larl always fell for that one, too. I never visited them without a few nickels tucked into my pocket."

They sat in silence until Emily spoke, running her finger around the rim of her glass. "The whole day had me thinking about my sisters, wondering how they were spending the holiday."

John did not reply, and Emily continued. "I was thinking, I haven't been with my family for a holiday in ages. Last year we were swept up with wedding plans, then our honeymoon." She glanced up. Was he listening? His eyes had a soft, faraway look. Perhaps he was reliving the events of the day.

"John." She tapped his hand draped over the sofa's back and he turned his gaze toward her. "I want to go back to New York. Spend the Christmas holidays with my sisters in New Jersey or have them to our place in the city."

"Emily, that's just not practical. Business needs to be attended to right now. Out of the question. We can have a lovely Christmas here, just the two of us."

Emily set her drink down on the side table. "Sarasota is no place to be on Christmas. Palm trees instead of holly and evergreens? And I miss my family. And my city. Please, John. Can't you work while in New York?"

"I must be here, Emily. The museum, the bank—that work must be done from here. It's coming to the end of the fiscal year and books must be settled." The twinkle that had been in his eyes was replaced by steeliness. "Why can't you immerse yourself in the beauty of Ca d'Zan and create a beautiful Christmas here? Mable used to decorate—"

Emily spat out her words. "I'm not Mable. I have no

interest in decorating Mable's house for Christmas." She crossed her arms and bit her lower lip. Once again, Mable was right in the room between them. Could he not see how alone she felt here? She had no history, no connections in this place. Warm tears welled up in her eyes. She had no appetite for more quarrels, but neither did she have an appetite for more lonely days at Ca d'Zan. She took a deep breath. "All right. You can't leave. I understand. But while you're busy working, I am here isolated from family and friends that are precious to me."

"But Emily, you knew that when you married me." He, too, crossed his arms and shook his head.

"I did not know that I'd be all but deserted by you because your all-consuming business. I didn't know how wretchedly lonely I'd feel." The tears were now trickling down her cheeks and she wiped them away with the back of her hand.

"My goodness, Emily, no need for crying. You're being dramatic. Nothing seems to please you. We live in this beautiful paradise, an escape from the cold and brutal New York winters. Priceless works of art surround you. I'm working day and night to maintain these luxuries. And your sister and nephew spent weeks here, with a disastrous result, I might add. I just don't understand your unhappiness." He slapped the back of the sofa to emphasize his words.

"I've just expressed my sadness and I'm being dramatic?" She stood. "As for your working day and night, perhaps if you had accepted my suggestion to meet with my advisors in New York, or sell off some of your art, you may not be in the predicament you find yourself. I see that yet another conversation with you is going nowhere."

John stood as well, pointing his finger at her. "I have no need of your sources interfering into my business. And I will not sell any of my art. This remains my business, not yours." He turned his back to her, clenching his hands into fists. Then he turned to face her again, dropping his now-open palms to his side. "I spoke harshly, but I simply cannot countenance your interference and complaints."

She drew in a deep breath, then expelled it slowly. "Let's agree to this. I'll spend the next month in New York. You can stay here without me, focusing on your work. Perhaps you can find the opportunity to join me up North for Christmas."

His eyes, less fiery now, stared into hers. He grasped her elbows. "Is that really what you want to do?"

Emily blinked away her tears. She sensed resignation in his voice, and she imagined that her absence would be welcome. Was he telling himself that he might be better off without her constant prying? "Yes. It will be best for both of us."

"All right. I suppose that would be best." He kissed her cheek. "I'll be there with you for Christmas. And we'll ring in the New Year together."

She managed a smile she did not feel. "I'll be waiting for you."

John pulled her into a hug. "Darling, just be patient. 1932 will be a better year for us all."

Chapter Twenty-Two

ONCE SETTLED INTO the Park Avenue apartment, Emily ordered Christmas greenery from the local florist and draped it along tabletops and mantles. The scent of pine, the familiar lyrics of "Silent Night" wafting from the RCA phonograph, and the sight of snowflakes drifting past her window lifted her spirits. Satisfied with the festive touches around the apartment, she made herself cocoa and went to the phone, placing a long-distance call to Lena in New Jersey.

There was trepidation in Lena's voice when she answered. "Emily, is anything wrong?"

Emily laughed. "Of course not! I'm just calling to say I'm in the city."

"You are? I'm glad everything is all right. A long-distance call always alarms me."

"I'd like to invite the entire family to New York for Christmas. What do you think?" Emily imagined her sister's concern being replaced with delight, and she waited for Lena's enthusiastic squeal. It did not come. Instead, there was a pause. "Lena?"

"Well, Emily, what a lovely gesture." Lena hesitated. "I—I—don't know what to say."

"Say yes, silly! I'll make arrangements for all of you to stay at the Waldorf, and we can have dinner catered here. All of us Haag girls together. And the children and husbands, of course. It will be lovely." Again, her enthusiasm was met with silence, and she tightened her grip on the phone.

"Emily, I'm not sure. You know, Olga and Louise are already busy preparing. We usually spend Christmas Eve at Olga's, then Christmas Day at Louise's. Um… um… you've been so busy these past few years, so we just assumed…" Lena let her sentence drift off.

Emily's shoulders drooped and she pressed a fist to her lips. "I see." Emily kept her voice light. "I don't mean to interfere."

"You're not interfering, Emily. My goodness, you're our sister! But we've already got plans set and you know how Olga and Louise are. They're probably already baking fruit cakes and stringing popcorn." Lena chuckled weakly.

"Silly me. I didn't think." Emily swallowed a lump in her throat.

"I have an idea. Why don't you and John come to East Orange for Christmas?"

"Hmmm." The thought hadn't occurred to Emily, and she weighed the possibility. She imagined herself in her sisters' homes, gathering around their fireplaces, sipping hot *gluhwein*, eating gingersnaps. But would she be intruding on their festivities whose patterns were so tightly knitted together? She ached to say yes, but wavered. "Do you think Olga and Louise would like me to come?"

"They'd be delighted. We miss you, Emily. And you've shown us all so much kindness. I'll speak to them and let them know you'd like to join us. Please come!"

Her sisters loved her, she knew. She, not they, had drifted away from their bond. After a moment, she said, "You know, Lena, I've been longing to be with all of you. I think, I think I'll come."

"Wonderful! I'm so pleased, Emily. I'll speak to Olga and Louse and write to you with the details. All of us together! What a Christmas it will be!"

"Thank you, Lena. I'll be waiting to hear from you."

They said their goodbyes and hung up. Emily sank back into the chair. East Orange for Christmas!

WITHIN A FEW days, Emily received letters oozing warmth from all three of her sisters. Olga wrote, "Emily, we would be thrilled to offer accommodations to you and John for as long as you'd like to stay." And Louise urged, "Please consider staying in our home. Our guest room is ready!" Lena wrote, "The entire family is eager to see you. My home is too small to offer you a guest room, but both Olga and Louise have lovely homes waiting for you."

How could she choose one sister over the other? She was touched by their welcoming affection. Ove the years, she'd treated her sisters to visits to the city, never considering that each of them would desire the opportunity to reciprocate. Immediately she responded. On three sheets of her monogrammed ivory vellum, she penned, "My dears, I'm gladdened by your generous hospitality and cannot choose between either of my sweet sisters. Perhaps John and I can spend Christmas Eve at Olga's, then Christmas Day at Louise's? We will make arrangements to arrive by train on the morning of December twenty-fourth."

As she tucked the letters into their envelopes, she imagined the bustle of activity these letters would create across the Hudson in East Orange. Would Olga make the *pfeffernusse,* following Mama's old recipe? Would Louise be rolling out the dough for stollen? She imagined their Christmas trees aglow with candlelight and delicate glass ornaments. How could she have put aside these family traditions for so many years?

Her next letter read: "Dear John, I've made arrangements for us to visit all of my sisters in East Orange. On Christmas Eve morning, we will take the train and stay with Olga and her family, and then we will spend Christmas day with Louise. I hope your work is going well. Love, Emily."

She dropped all four letters into the lobby post box on her way out the door. She planned to arrive in East Orange laden with gifts, and she had quite a bit of shopping to do.

EMILY REGRETTED WEARING her mink. Disembarking from the taxi, she had to walk past a line of out-of-work men, some selling apples or pencils, and she feared that her fur made her an easy target for their pleas. Of course, it was not their fault that they were out of work, but their desperation made her uncomfortable. She rummaged through her handbag for some coins to hand out, then escaped into Barney's. Inside, shoppers crowded the aisles and soon she was much too warm. Draping the fur over her arm, she considered checking it into the cloak room, but decided against it.

Every counter in the store was laden with luxurious gifts that belied the financial crisis outside its doors. Emily wandered the aisles, taking in the elegant Christmas décor. Silver bells and trumpeting angels hung from the ceilings, and swaths of gold and silver garland encircled the pillars. Salesmen in dark suits, saleswomen in crisp white blouses stood at the ready to guide shoppers' purchases. What to buy? Choosing clothing for her sisters would be difficult, so she searched for inspiration. Eying a display of leather handbags, Emily decided that this would be a welcome gift. She considered what style might suit each of her sisters. Both Louise and Olga dressed conservatively, so she chose two bags with classic lines, one black, one deep brown. For Lena, she selected a crocodile clutch in a rich maroon.

"Please charge my account and have them sent," Emily instructed the saleswoman, then gave her name and address.

"Certainly, Mrs. Ringling. We also have some very fine men's leather goods you might like." She tipped her head toward another nearby display.

"Thank you. That might be just the thing for my brothers-in-law."

Behind the counter filled with men's accessories, a thin-nosed salesman wearing a pince-nez, his hands folded in front of his chest, greeted her. "May I offer some assistance to Madam?"

Before she could answer, a voice whispered into her ear. "Yes, Madam, what assistance do you need?"

She spun around to see a tall man in a cashmere overcoat grinning at her. "Edward Appleton! You startled me!"

Edward's green eyes sparkled with mischief, and he leaned forward to kiss her cheek. "You're not in Florida, I see. Here for Christmas?"

"Yes, as a matter of fact, I am. My, it's lovely to see you. It's been a long time."

"Yes, I don't think I've seen you since Mary died." He grimaced and a ghost of sadness crossed his face.

Emily closed her eyes for a moment and shook her head. "I miss her so, Edward. She was such a dear friend to me."

"As do I." He shrugged. "But now you're Mrs. John Ringling!"

Before she could answer, the clerk behind them cleared his throat. "May I say, Madam," he began.

She glanced his way. "I'm sorry. Please go ahead and help another customer. I'm chatting with an old friend."

The clerk sniffed. "As you wish, Madam." He strode away, his hands still clasped in front of him.

Emily turned back to Edward who wiggled his eyebrows. A wave of affection for this man stirred through her. Hadn't he always mined the humor in any situation? She burst into laughter.

"What a stiff!" He reached out to grasp her hands. "Say, if you have time, let's get out of this crowd and go for coffee somewhere where we can catch up. What do you say?"

Immediately, Emily's thoughts of more Christmas shopping receded. There was no need to get it all done today. Dear, dear Edward! It was serendipity that brought them both into Barney's on this day. "I'd love to!"

He took her mink from her and held it up so that she

could slip her arms into the sleeves. "We'll grab a cab out front. Let's go."

They settled on the Russian Tea Room and were soon relaxing in high-backed chairs of red velvet, a silver coffee service and a plate of pastries on a table before them.

"How long has it been, Emily?" Edward asked, but of course they both knew the last time they'd seen one another. Mary, her dearest childhood friend, had been the first one she'd turned to when Charles left her. Mary had comforted Emily as she wept, and it was Edward, Mary's husband, who was able to make her laugh by threatening to go out and "Vanquish that cad." It was only two months later when Emily was consoling Edward after Mary contracted pneumonia and died. Numbed by her own grief, Emily was barely able to speak to the bereft Edward who stood at Mary's casket, gripping the hand of their little girl Janey. Later, Emily arranged through lawyers for Edward to purchase her share of Charles' import business, and their lives, once so intertwined by the friendship between Emily and Mary, went in different directions.

Instead of answering his question, Emily asked, "How is Janey?"

Edward brightened. "She's wonderful, of course! Off to boarding school but thriving. She's eleven, can you imagine?" He pulled out his billfold. "Here's a photograph."

Emily examined the photo, then returned it. "She's lovely! Looks like her mother!"

Tucking the wallet back into his pocket, Edward sighed. "Yes, she does. And has her spunk, I might add." He lifted his cup and blew gently into it, cooling it off. "Say, Emily, we certainly have known each other for a long time."

"Edward, I can still recall you as a young college man, sweeping my friend Mary off her feet. I'll never forget her telling me about the night you came and sang "Let Me Call you Sweetheart" outside her window."

He chuckled. "I can still hear her father saying, 'Young man, it is time for you to leave the premises!'" His voice boomed and he threw back his shoulders to demonstrate exaggerated indignation. Their tearoom waitress, appearing alarmed, scurried toward them, but Edward, smiling broadly, held up his hand to wave her off.

Emily set down her cup and giggled. "How could I forget that tale? It must have taken a lot of convincing on your part for Mary's father to allow you to marry his daughter."

"Well, he knew I loved her." Edward lowered his eyes, then looked up at Emily once again. "We were blessed to have Mary in our lives, weren't we?"

Drinking their coffee, first one cup, then another,

Edward and Emily rehashed old stories. But instead of shrouding themselves in grief, Edward's light-heartedness steered them away from heartache and into swells of laughter.

When her second cup was finished, Emily glanced at her watch. "Look at the time! Surely you must have somewhere you need to be, Edward. But this had been a delight. I don't know when I've last laughed this much." Her face flushed as her eyes held his. She had forgotten how boyishly good-looking Edward was.

Edward waved his hand. "I've nothing pressing for today. I'd only stopped into Barney's to look at neckties. Plus, I hate to admit this—I'm a fool for Christmas decorations, and I had to take a look." He summoned the waitress for the check. "I hate to see the afternoon come to an end. It has been wonderful to see you again, Emily. You're as lovely as ever. Let me get a cab. Still at the Barclay?"

"Oh, no. at the Park Avenue Apartments. John and I—" She stopped herself. It was the first time her husband's name had come up in the conversation. She lowered her eyes for a moment. Of course, Edward knew she'd remarried. Everybody did. But the mention of John seemed to throw ice water onto the warmth of the afternoon.

"Ah, of course. The Park Avenue." Edward paid the bill and reached for Emily's hand to guide her out of her chair. As he helped her into her coat, he kissed the top of her head lightly. "Your chariot awaits, my dear." He offered her his arm, and as they made their way to the door, he said, "So, what is your Mr. Ringling up to today?"

Although Edward's tone was nonchalant, Emily heard a sliver of forced casualness. She adopted the same tone. "John? He won't be here for a few weeks. Busy in Florida."

"So, you're rattling around all alone in that big apartment? We can't have that! How about allowing an old friend to take you to dinner tomorrow night?"

Emily eyed the man leading her out the restaurant door. What fun it had been to rekindle an old friendship, to reminisce about good times. His liveliness and humor were good antidotes for the gloom she'd been feeling. "Tomorrow night? I'd love to!"

Chapter Twenty-Three

LIGHTING HER THIRD cigarette and inhaling deeply, Emily paced from the window overlooking Park Avenue and then back to the sofa. Why on earth was she so nervous? Silly, it was only Edward, after all, a man she'd known for years. She caught her reflection in the window and traced her hand along her perfectly coifed curls. Had she chosen the right thing to wear? She once again assured herself that her royal blue shantung dress, cinched at the waist with a black velvet belt, was a good choice—becoming and chic.

She jumped as the buzzer sounded, announcing a visitor. She pressed the button that allowed Edward access to the elevator and opened the apartment door. Taking one last drag on her cigarette, she extinguished it in an ashtray on the foyer table. When was the last time she'd dined with Edward? Wasn't it a dinner that Mary had prepared? How strange to think how things had changed since then.

Emily heard the elevator grind to a halt, and she stepped into the hall to greet Edward. He emerged carrying an enormous package wrapped in florist paper and peered around it, grinning sheepishly, as he approached.

"Thought I'd bring a little holiday cheer, but I may have gotten carried away."

"My, what on earth have you brought?" Emily held the door open. "Come in. That looks heavy."

"Not heavy, just awkward. May I put it here?" he asked, nodding toward the foyer table.

"Of course!" Emily moved the ash tray and slid the lamp toward the edge of the table to make room. "I can't wait to see what's inside."

Edward began tearing away the florist paper and red poinsettia blossoms the size of dinner plates sprang from their confines. "It didn't seem this large in the shop, but when I struggled to get it into the taxi…" He fussed with the blooms a bit and then turned to Emily. "Merry Christmas, just a bit early."

"It's fabulous!" Emily shook her head and chuckled. "And enormous! You must have been quite a sight, getting it into a cab." She grasped Edward's hand. "Thank you, Edward. It's quite cheery and so very thoughtful of you."

"Thank goodness!" Edward buckled his knees and wobbled comically. "I was afraid you'd throw me and this monstrosity right out the door. And then I'd have to hail another taxi and convince a cabbie to let me in."

Emily rolled her eyes. "This poinsettia is perfect!" She giggled and added, "I just hope it doesn't grow anymore while we're out to dinner."

He shuddered in mock horror. "I hope not. So, shall we go? I've arranged a table for us at the Park Central. Tom Truesdale and the Musical Aviators are playing. Of course, I haven't been one for night clubs for a while now but a colleague of mine raves about them."

"Musical aviators? That sounds interesting." Emily lifted her black Persian lamb cape from a nearby chair and Edward took it from her and draped it over her shoulders. Inside the elevator, Emily glanced at Edward, who was staring at the blinking numbers above the door. Why on earth had she been so jittery earlier? This man was so easy to be with, so refreshingly unfettered by the need to impress. Anticipation fluttered through her, and she bit her lip to stifle a grin.

AT THE PARK Central the maître d' led them to a round table for two near the dance floor. "We'll be able to keep our eyes on all of the fox-trotters," Edward commented as he slid in Emily's chair. Emily removed her gloves and scanned the room. Crystal chandeliers sparkled above the marble floors and the windows were swathed in velvety drapes of ruby red. Nearly every table, covered in creamy silks, was occupied—women in well-designed ensembles and men in smart dinner jackets like the one Edward wore. Even though Prohibition had draped a pall over every social gathering, am air of merriment permeated the vast room under a cacophony of chatter and laughter.

"What a lively place!" Emily nodded approvingly.

"I'll say! Shall we order drinks, such as they are?" Edward shrugged. "We won't be getting any martinis here, I'm afraid, but we can pretend." He caught the eye of a nearby waiter who took their order.

Once their tonics were served, they perused the menu, settling on the chateaubriand to share. Their conversation was easy but trivial as they dined—light observations about the ballroom, remarks about the excellent meal.

Once the band began, it was nearly impossible to carry on a conversation, but Edward entertained Emily by cupping his hand over his mouth and speaking into her ear, making wry comments about some of the dancers gliding past their table.

"Don't look now," he hissed as sour-looking gentleman waltzed by with a buxom dowager in his grasp. "I'm sure that couple is planning to run off to Argentina to escape the Feds."

He tipped his head at a giggly ingénue in the arms of her moony-eyed admirer. "It's all an act. He's planning to swindle her out of her inheritance."

"Edward, stop!" Emily brushed tears of mirth from her eyes. She grabbed his hand. "Take me to the dance floor before I die laughing right here."

The Aviators played until one am, and Edward and Emily stayed until the band ended the evening with "Goodnight, Sweetheart." Sinking in the back seat of the taxi, Emily closed her eyes and hummed the melody.

Edward reached for her hand. "I can see that your gloves aren't nearly warm enough for a night like this. Your fingers must be icy. Here, let me warm them for you." He put both her hands between his and rubbed them. "Winter has certainly arrived in New York."

The warmth of Edward's hands around hers enkindled a tenderness within her. "Oh, I love winter, don't you? All of the crisp cold air, the snow." Emily smiled at him. "I don't mind the cold, really, but my hands were freezing, I admit."

They rode along in companionable silence to the Park Avenue Apartments, and as they pulled up to the curb, Emily asked, "Would you like a warm toddy before you head home?" As soon as she suggested it, a ping of conscience poked at the back of her mind. *Don't be silly. We're both in need of a warm drink.*

"Love one." Edward paid the driver and soon they were in the apartment.

"The poinsettia is still the same size, it appears." Edward shrugged off his coat and removed his fedora.

"And so festive! Thank you again, Edward." Emily tossed her cape on a chair, and Edward put his coat and hat on top of hers. "Have a seat in the parlor, and I'll fix us drinks."

In the kitchen, Emily prepared the toddy. Slicing a lemon for garnish, she relived the evening. When was the last time she'd had so such fun? No pretense, no reticence, no weighing every word before it was spoken. When had she last felt this free to be herself? What a happy coincidence that they'd both gone into Barney's.

When she entered the parlor, she found Edward, his hands clasped behind his back, looking out at the streets below. He turned and took the tray from her. "Quite a beautiful place you have here, Emily."

"Yes, isn't it." She avoided pointing out that she had not chosen it or its furnishings. No need to veer off into a conversation about John and Mable. "Hope you like the toddy. My father used to make these for my mother on cold winter nights." Emily kicked off her high heels and curled up in the corner of a sofa.

Setting the tray on a cocktail table, Edward handed her a steaming cup and took the other corner of the sofa. "Smells delicious."

"My mother used to make hot apple cider for us when we came in from ice-skating," Edward recalled. They shared their reminiscences about their childhood winters—warm gingerbread cookies, the chicken and dumpling soup.

"Another thing I recall—the smell of wet woolen

socks drying on the radiators after sledding," Edward made a face and pinched his nose.

"Oh, so do I!" Emily wrinkled her nose and they both laughed softly.

Minutes passed in meandering conversation—a favorite Christmas memory or two, a fond recollection of concerts attended. Edward, his face softened by a lingering smile, sighed contentedly. "Emily, thank you for a lovely evening. I can't remember when I've had such an enjoyable time."

"I was just thinking the same thing, Edward. My, those Aviators were great, weren't they?" She returned his smile and his gaze held hers.

His voice was husky. "Really, Emily, tonight has been special. I—" He stopped his sentence, then turned his eyes away from her and lowered his head to search depths of his now-empty cup.

His unspoken words seemed to hang over them and Emily felt her face redden. Was it the toddy? Why had he stopped himself in mid-sentence?

After several moments, he stood and set his cup on the table. "I… I really should go. Emily. It's late." He reached out and took the cup from her hands and set it on the tray with his. Then he held out his hands to draw her up from the sofa. "Will Madam escort me to the door?" he said in the voice of the Barney's salesman in the pince-nez.

"Of course, Monsieur," Emily answered.

In the foyer, he donned his coat and turned to the poinsettia. Shaking his finger, he scolded, "Now don't do any more growing overnight."

"I'll keep a watch on this beauty." Emily handed him his hat. He brushed her cheek lightly with a kiss as he went out the door.

As the elevator arrived and its door opened and closed, Emily leaned on the foyer table and stroked a poinsettia blossom between her thumb and forefinger.

ONE DAY PASSED, then another and another without a phone call. Had she seen the last of Edward? Was their friendship over? And was it simply a friendship? Images from the evening at the Park Central laced through her thoughts—Edward's green eyes crinkled with laughter, his firm hand on her back as he guided her onto the dance floor, his scent—peppermint and bay—as he leaned forward to whisper a funny remark into her ear. She longed to see him again; didn't he feel the same? Of course, she hadn't been at home the entire time, so perhaps he had called when she was out and about.

With Christmas in the offing, she'd been busy, gathering more gifts for her family. Leather goods for her brothers-in law, driving gloves and a stylish pair of suspenders for Nicholas. In FAO Schwartz, she chose a doll in a frilly dress for Olga's little girl, and enormous teddy bears for her two little boys. As for Louise's baby son, she was stumped until she settled on a velveteen romper in a cheery green. And John, what would she get a man who had everything he could possibly want? She wove her way through the crowds of shoppers in Bergdorf Goodman's and Lord and Taylor, hoping for inspiration. When none struck her, she settled on an engraved silver cigar humidor for his desk.

She lunched with Sophie and a few other friends, a cheery get-together at Delmonico's. Over bubbling ramekins of lobster thermidor, the ladies exchanged newsy tidbits. Sophie, it seemed, had a new beau, an advertising executive, newly transplanted from Chicago to Madison Avenue. "Who would have imagined," Sophie gushed, "that there was so much money to be made selling radio spots for Oxydol?" Emily took note of the light in her friend's eyes, her easy laughter.

"Will there be wedding bells in your future?" Emily quietly asked her friend.

Sophie smiled coquettishly. "Maybe. He seems to really care for me, Emily." She squeezed Emily's hand, and Emily squeezed back. Sophie's joy made her almost luminescent, and her bliss brought a lump to Emily's throat.

"I'm so thrilled for you, my friend. I hope he deserves you." She lifted her water goblet and clinked it against Sophie's. "To you and your new love."

Had she felt as Sophie did just one year ago? She had been swept up in John's persistent pursuit, the flurry of arrangements made, the packing up of her home at the Barclay so their lives could be joined together. Funny, she could barely recall her emotions from last December. Certainly, she'd been happy, hadn't she?

Mildred interrupted her reverie, tipping her cigarette in Emily's direction. "So, Emily, do tell us all about Florida. I can't imagine why you left the sunny climate for New York."

"Yes, we hear you're in the lap of luxury there. Seaside vistas, palm trees, and all that," added Faye, whose mouth twisted sardonically.

Emily sipped from her water goblet. She had never been close to Mildred and Faye, who trafficked in tales of the misfortunes of others Here they were offering best wishes to Sophie, but when Emily had seen them on her last trip to the city, each had cornered her to express concern for her friend, with thinly veiled insinuations about Sophie's financial circumstances. Now, they had their sights set on her, burrowing for fodder to add to their repertoire of innuendo.

"Ca d'Zan is lovely! A living museum actually." Emily lay a hand over her heart. "It's beyond words. But who can forego family at Christmas?"

"But where is your husband? I heard he was still in Florida." Mildred's teeth flashed a feral smile.

"My, Mildred. You seem to know quite a bit." Emily chuckled. "No need to worry about John's whereabouts." She turned her gaze to the far end of the table. "Dolores, did I hear that your daughter is getting married? Do tell."

✧ ✧ ✧

LATER THAT EVENING, when she was back in the apartment, she poured herself a brandy and sat on the chaise longue in her bedroom. Twirling the tassel on a pillow embroidered with roses, Emily inventoried her feelings. These days on her own in New York had been a welcome respite. For months, John's moods were ever-shifting, his affection for her perfunctory. *I don't miss him. I'm happy to be alone.* When had this indifference crept into her being? Once she had ached for the loss of passion in their marriage; now, she felt unmoved. *Perhaps Christmas*—the phone rang.

Edward? She sprang to answer it.

"Emily? John here." His tone was curt. "I've tried to phone several times today and it seems you've been out."

"Hello, John." She would not answer his gruffness in kind. "How nice to hear your voice. I've been—"

"Emily, I'll keep this brief. I received your letter, and I do not think it's wise to plan on Christmas with your family. I may not even be able to complete my business in order to arrive on time. And I certainly don't want to be surrounded by all of your relatives."

"But John! I've promised them! And it's what I want to do. I haven't been with my sisters all together for the holidays in ages." She twisted the phone cord and bit her lip. How could he be so intractable?

"I know this is what you would like, Emily, but I've been working hard while you flit around New York City and—"

She interrupted. "John, please." *Flit around? As if she were shirking some duty down in Florida?* She kept her voice steady as anger pulsed through her. "It's difficult to have a conversation regarding this over the telephone. I will write you. I sincerely hope that you are able to spend Christmas with me as well as with my family."

Silence. Then John said, "I was afraid you'd be stubborn about this." He sighed and cleared his throat. "And I don't want to argue over the telephone. I hope you're having a nice time in the city."

"I am. No need for you to take up any more of your time. Have a good evening." Without waiting for his parting words, Emily placed the phone on the receiver. With clenched fists, she paced from room to room of the apartment while she mocked John with snarling mimicry.

"How I miss you, too, my beloved!"

"I would love to be with your loved ones for Christmas, just to make you happy, my dear!"

"I'm so lonely here without you, my darling Emily."

Soon her anger sank into sadness, and she returned to the chaise. Her marriage was a hollow sham. But what could she do? Asking for divorce was out of the question. Women who sought a divorce often became pariahs in polite society. It was shameful, scandalous.! *Vas ist, ist.* She would have to work to right the course of her marriage, but she wondered if her heart was up to it.

Then the phone rang again.

Chapter Twenty-Four

"HELLO! MAY I speak to the woman who is the hot toddy expert?"

Emily's heart leaped and a smile blossomed on her face. "Speaking! Hello, Edward!"

"Say," he began, his voice hesitant, "I was just wondering if, ... unless, of course if your husband has arrived..."

"No, He's still away. Will be for a while." She smoothed her collar, waiting for his next words.

"Oh, good. Well, probably not good for you." His words tumbled out like those of a nervous schoolboy and Emily imagined him running jittery fingers through his wavy hair. "Anyway, Emily, if you're not busy, would you like to join me for dinner tonight? Someplace very different from the Park Central... quieter."

"Edward, I'd love to. I was going to fix myself an egg and toast for dinner. I'd love to go." She placed her hand on her cheek, suddenly warm.

His voice regained its self-assuredness. "Wonderful. Now, it won't be as swanky a place as the Park Central, but I have a hunch you'll enjoy it."

The melancholy that had been hovering around her had evaporated. "Where are we going?"

"You'll see. I'm going to keep you in suspense."

Through the phone lines, Emily could imagine his soft smile, his twinkling green eyes. "Oh, you! I'll be waiting with bated breath," she teased.

They agreed on a time and said their goodbyes. Hanging up the telephone, Emily hugged herself in anticipation, then dashed into the bedroom to choose something to wear, selecting a simple red wool dress and a strand of pearls. Humming a Tommy Truesdale tune, she ran a bath. No toast and eggs for her tonight!

✧ ✧ ✧

EDWARD GAVE THE cabbie an address and turned to Emily. "Well, now you've heard our destination. Surprised?"

"Surprised? No, just intrigued. Little Italy, right? But I know I'm in good hands." She playfully tapped his leg with her gloved palm, then turned to look out the window. The storefronts became less posh as they traveled along. The sparkling lights of Christmas were nowhere to be found as they neared their destination. Tattered awnings hung over tailors, pharmacies, and hardware stores. Was this safe? Weren't some of the Mafiosi known to be a part of this neighborhood? But

Edward appeared relaxed and confident, so Emily erased apprehensions from her mind. "This is an adventure," she commented as the cab pulled up in front of a small, unassuming restaurant with a neon sign flashing "Tony's".

Edward guided Emily out of the car and gave her a sidelong glance. "What do you think?"

"Well, I won't know until we go in, will I?" She slid her arm through his. "Lead the way, MacDuff!"

Inside, the tantalizing aroma of herbs, garlic, and tomatoes made Emily's mouth water. *No eggs and toast here.* Had she bothered to eat today? Suddenly she was ravenous.

"Welcome to Tony's!" A mustachioed man with deep brown eyes shining under a tuft of thick black eyebrows stood just inside the door. He reached out to relieve Emily and Edward of their coats. "You have a reservation, no?"

"We do," replied Edward. "You must be Tony. My friend Jack recommended you." Emily noticed that Edward slipped a folded bill from his hand into Tony's as he gave him his coat.

Tony raised his considerable eyebrows. "Ah, yes, my friend Jack. We take care of Jack; we gonna take care of you." He jerked his head toward a waiter in the dining room. "Hey, Matteo, show these *brava gente* to Jack's table."

To Emily, this simple exchange appeared to indicate some mystifying code, but Edward seemed nonplussed as he guided her to follow Matteo who led them to a secluded booth in the back of the dimly lit restaurant. There was a smattering of patrons quietly conversing at small tables in the center of the room. The leather banquette crackled and sighed as they slid in behind a table covered in a red checkered cloth. A straw-wrapped Chianti bottle held a lit candle that dripped its waxy strings down the bottle's neck.

As Matteo stepped away, Edward turned to Emily. "So?" He opened his red napkin and arranged it on his lap, then propped his chin on his fist to await her response.

Emily plucked the gloves from her fingers and grinned. "It's marvelous, Edward. Everything smells heavenly!" She scanned the wall that separated their booth from another. "And look at these photos. The Ponte Vecchio, the hills of Orvieto. We've been transported to Italy."

"And so we have. I'm glad you're pleased."

Matteo returned to the table carrying a basket of crusty bread, two goblets and a ceramic pitcher swirled in a yellow and green design. "Shall I pour, Signore?"

"By all means." Edward placed his hand on Emily's arm. "Now for the *ultimo!*"

Emily's eyes widened as she watched a deep red liquid fill each goblet. A rich, fruity scent teased her nostrils. "Wine?"

Matteo finished his task, nodded, and left their table. Edward lifted his goblet towards Emily. "As you see, I have a few tricks up my sleeve. I hear its some of the best Chianti this side of Florence. Cheers to you, Emily." Their fingers brushed as they raised their glasses. She closed her eyes briefly as she savored the rich flavors that trickled along her tongue.

"Edward, this is so lovely—this charming restaurant, the Chianti—thank you." The warmth of his touch lingered on her fingers as she toyed with her pearls. She cocked her head sideways. "Now why did I need this reminder of how much I loved Chianti?"

"I'm happy I could be that reminder. How lucky for me that I popped into Barney's that afternoon." He held her gaze, his eyes soft. Then he chuckled. "Maybe Saint Nicholas was looking out for me."

"But how did you manage the wine?" Emily placed her goblet on the table and propped her chin on her entwined fingers. "Surely this isn't one of those speakeasies I've heard about."

"No, no speakeasy. But Tony has a large cellar here, and when one mentions his friend Jack, well, Tony knows what to do." He swirled his goblet. "Nectar of the gods, isn't it?"

"Yes, it is. And all the better because it's forbidden

fruit." Emily took a small sip. *Forbidden fruit.* She felt her cheeks flush at the unintended innuendo of her remark. Perhaps she should steer the conversation on safer ground.

"You know, I've been thinking about Janey, remembering her as a little girl. Tell me about her," Emily prompted.

Edward's eyes glowed as he spoke. "Ah, she is such a joy. Of course, I may be a bit biased, but she's smart as a whip. Doing well in all her studies, especially French. She runs rings around me in that department. I'm so proud of her. And she's got spunk, too." He paused and lowered his eyes. "You don't want to hear all of my fatherly bragging."

"No, please." Emily touched his arm. "I recall what a sweet child she was, and it's lovely to see your devotion. She sounds like a treasure."

His eyebrows knitted together. "It's been tough on her, losing her mother. So, I'm grateful she's turning out all right."

"Better than all right, I'd say. She sounds like a lovely young girl." She patted his arm.

He took Emily's hand and pressed it to his lips. "You're a kind and caring woman, Emily." Their eyes locked and Emily squelched her desire to stroke his face.

"*MI scusi, signora, signore.*" Matteo appeared tableside, a broad smile twitching beneath his thick mustache.

"Shall you like to order your dinner?'

Both Edward and Emily turned their eyes to Matteo. Heat rose from Emily's chest to her ears, and she slid her hands—fingertips still imprinted with the softness of Edward's lips—below the tabletop.

But Edward assumed an attitude of nonchalance, laying his arm across the back of the banquette. "We haven't looked through the menus yet, Matteo. But may we simply ask Tony to prepare selections he thinks we will enjoy?"

"I highly recommend, signore. Bellissimo!" He loudly smacked his fingertips and headed to the kitchen.

"Bellissimo! I think we're in for a *delicioso* dinner!" Edward gestured toward the wine pitcher."+May I refill your glass, *signora*?"

She nodded and watched as he lifted the pitcher and goblet. In her lap, she clenched her fists, tamping down her desire to trace his hands with her fingertips.

"I hope you can't hear my stomach rumbling in anticipation, Emily." Edward licked his lips. "I haven't had an authentic Italian dinner in quite some time. Have you?"

"No, sure haven't. What fun!" She relaxed into the curve of the banquette. "Such a pleasant change of pace from tuxedoed waiters and heavy crystal."

When Matteo returned, he presented them with plates of steaming pasta covered in clam sauce. "*Primo piatto! Buon appetito!"*

"Grazie!" Edward rubbed his palms together.

Emily lifted her fork, then hesitated. "I'm not even sure how to approach this."

"Let me show you." Edward lifted his fork and spoon, then expertly twirled his pasta into a manageable bite. "A friend from Florence taught me this technique."

Emily did as he'd shown her. "I'm afraid the finer points of my table etiquette have flown out the window," she remarked before she brought a large swirl of spaghetti and clams to her mouth.

Edward's eyes shifted left to right. In an exaggerated whisper, he hissed, "I won't tell a soul." Then he daubed her chin with his napkin. "There. I've eliminated the evidence."

"Oh, goodness. Thank you for taking care of that!"

Matteo eventually returned, removing the first plates and presenting small platters of a variety of dishes with a flourish. "Eggplant parmigiana, veal scaloppini, chicken cacciatore. Prego!"

Emily's eyes widened and Edward chuckled. "Shall I serve?"

"By all means, but just a small amount of each, please."

He scooped some of each onto their plates. "One thing my friend warmed me about Tony's, no one goes home hungry."

They ate with gusto, their conversation focused on the meal before them, speculating about which spices and herbs had been used in the preparation. After a while, Emily set down her fork. "I surrender! I don't think I could eat another bite, but everything was scrumptious."

"But what about dessert? Tiramisu? Profiteroles? We can't insult the chef, you know."

"I'm waving the white flag. But a cappuccino would be nice." She breathed a contented sigh.

When Matteo arrived to clear the plates, Edward ordered cappuccino, and soon delicate cups of the aromatic coffee appeared in front of them.

Edward stirred his coffee absently. "Emily, I'm curious. How do you like living in Florida?" He sipped his drink, then propped his chin on his fist, studying her.

How many times had she been asked this question? In Sarasota, it was all anyone wanted to know. But it always had seemed like the questioners were assessing her by her response. Edith, Mrs. Cumnor, Sam Gumpertz. Even her New York friends asked, and she knew what her answer had to be. To say she loved it; it was beautiful; it was a paradise.

Bu Edward's gaze told her that she didn't have to couch her response in expected platitudes. And perhaps because finally she did not have to pretend, tears suddenly welled up in her eyes, and she looked down into her cup. "I... I..." She looked back at him. "Edward, I so miss New York." Her face crumpled and she blinked away a tear threatening to escape down her cheek. "Silly. I don't know why I'm suddenly teary-eyed."

Edward gently squeezed her shoulder. "I'm sorry my question upset you."

She shook her head. "No, it wasn't your question. It was that with you, I didn't feel like I had to say the right thing. I can be honest." She blotted the corners of her eyes with her napkin. "I apologize for becoming emotional."

"Of course, you can be honest with me." He stroked her cheek to wipe away a tear. "Tell me." Again, he propped his chin on his palm. "I'm listening."

I'm listening. Just those two words flooded Emily with an ease, a contentment she'd not even realized she'd been lacking. She began hesitantly. "I feel isolated there. It's lovely of course, but it's so lonely. My friends, my home, they're in New York."

He nodded, his gaze intense. Should she continue? She inhaled deeply and her voice trembled. "And John and I." She paused, biting her lip. "We don't seem to be right for each other." She turned her gaze toward the wall. *There. I've said it. The terrible, disloyal words I've been carrying around. Have I shocked Edward with her bluntness?*

Edward tenderly turned her chin so that she was facing him once again. "I'm so sorry, Emily. It must be so difficult to carry that sadness." She covered his hand with hers, then brushed his fingertips with her lips.

"Edward, I—"

But he interrupted, taking her face into both of his palms, kissing her forehead, then her lips. His mouth was gentle, then hungrier, more probing, and Emily reached for the back of his head, drawing him closer.

After a moment, he drew back. "Emily. Forgive me. I should not—"

"No, Edward. Don't say that." She wanted only for him to embrace her again, for his kisses to continue. And she saw in the depth of his eyes that he felt the same.

"Let me take you home." Edward slid away from her slightly, scanning the room for Matteo. He signaled for the check, using his finger to scribble on an imaginary pad in his palm. In a moment, Tony appeared at the table.

"Did you enjoy?" he beamed at them, arms akimbo. "What was your favorite, Signora?"

Emily willed her heart rate to steady as she smiled at their host. "Tony, all was superb. But the eggplant, out of this world."

"Ah, so many signora like my eggplant. And you, signore?'

"Hmmmm, let me think." He tapped a finger on his

chin as if in deep thought. "I'd have to say that the clam sauce was my favorite."

"Grazi, grazi. Now you and the missus come back soon, you hear?"

"You bet." Edward replied, returning Tony's vigorous handshake.

The missus. He assumed they were married. And Edward didn't correct him.

Edward settled the bill, arranged for a taxi, and in a few moments, they were on their way back to Park Avenue. The ride was subdued. Edward put his arm around Emily's shoulder, but he seemed deep in thought, staring straight ahead. She eyed his profile, taking in the strong curve of his jaw. What was he thinking? Feeling? And what was she feeling? She was a jumble of longing and of a newfound calmness.

As the cab pulled up to her building, Emily asked, "Nightcap?"

"By all means." Edward paid the cabbie and guided Emily into the building and the elevator.

In the apartment, they tossed their coats on the chair as they had done the night they'd gone to the Park Central. The air seemed charged with electricity. No banter about the poinsettia, no teasing remarks.

"There's sherry in the sideboard. Would you like some?" she said brightly.

"Please." Edward followed her into the parlor. She

poured the amber liquid into crystal cordial glasses, sensing his presence behind her. He seemed to be studying a framed etching on the wall. Was he really interested in it?

She willed her hands to hold steady, then turned and offered him a glass. "Thank you for a lovely dinner, Edward." She lifted her drink in a small toast and managed a weak smile. "I'm sorry I became so weepy. It was uncalled for."

"Please don't apologize, Emily. I should be apologizing to you." He shook his head, then took a sip of his sherry, running a hand through his hair. "I'm sorry you're unhappy. I wish—" He pressed his lips together and glanced downward.

She set her glass on the sideboard and stepped forward. "Edward, please. If only you knew the comfort I've felt, being able to talk to you openly." Her voice was breathy and she laid her hand on his arm.

"Emily." He placed his glass next her hers on the sideboard. In a moment, they were in each other's arms, kissing deeply, passionately.

Edward led her to the sofa, where they sank into the soft cushions, their lips never parting, their bodies pressing toward one another. Emily's breath quickened. She tipped her head back to savor the trail of Edwards's mouth along her throat and murmured his name as waves of pleasure enveloped her.

"Emily," he whispered, then drew back to look deep into her eyes. "My god, Emily, how I want you." He caressed her breasts, her thighs, but then abruptly pulled away from her. "But no. You're too dear to me." He took her face into his palms, kissed her deeply once again, then drew away once more. Reluctantly, he eased her into a sitting position, holding her to his chest, kissing the top of her hair. Emily's pounding heart matched the beat of his, and once again a tear trickled from her eye.

Of course, he was right. This could not happen this way. "I want you too, Edward," she murmured. They sat silently for a moment, arms entwined, allowing the passion to cool.

"I'd better go," Edward said at last.

Emily didn't trust herself to walk him to the door. "I know." She stayed on the sofa, her fist clenched in front of her mouth to keep her sobs at bay, until she heard the click of the door closing behind him.

Chapter Twenty-Five

BRIGHT SUNSHINE STREAMED into Emily's window, nudging her awake. Had she actually fallen asleep? It seemed that she had spent hours, twisting in her bedsheets, pounding her pillow into submission, reliving every moment spent with Edward—every word, every embrace, every kiss. She curled her body around her pillow, as daylight brought back the wretchedness that engulfed her. Her arms and her stomach felt leaden. What could she do? How could her feelings for Edward, a man she'd known only casually for years, have intensified in a few days? Was their encounter at Barney's destiny? Or did it spell only misery? Was a future with this man a possibility or a pipe dream for a lonely, desperate woman?

She rose, steeling herself for the reality of the new day. Once bathed and dressed, she nursed a cup of coffee and lit a cigarette. Would Edward call? Or would he simply vanish from her life?

The buzzer from the building lobby sounded and Emily fingers trembled as she answered. *Was Edward here?*

The voice of the doorman crackled. "You have a telegram, Mrs. Ringling. May I bring it up?"

"Yes please. Thank you," She leaned on the wall. It would be from John. Was he on his way?

Yes. *Arriving in three days.* She crumpled the thin slip of paper that foretold her future and tossed it in a wastebasket. Would John come through the door as morose and preoccupied as he'd been weeks ago, when she'd left him in Florida? She still carried the weight of his dismissive remarks, his disdain for her feelings. With Christmas now only one week away, she wondered if he would he stick to his refusal to join her at her sisters' homes. And did she care enough to be hurt by such a rebuff?

And Edward. With John in New York, she would have no opportunity to see him. She ached to talk to him, to seek comfort in his arms, even for one last time. Should she telephone him? She curled up in her chaise longue, twisting a handkerchief in her hands, she contemplated what to do.

I'll call him. Her heart pounded as she dialed the phone, and was disappointed, then relieved when a housekeeper answered.

"Could you please let Mr. Appleton know that Mrs. Ringing phoned," she asked.

"Certainly, Ma'am."

Now, she would wait. She made one more call—"Sophie, I have a terrible headache, so I'm afraid I must beg off our luncheon today."—and resigned herself to pacing the floor, drowning in the promise of grim scenarios.

By noon, she wondered if he would return her call at all. Of course, he had business to attend to. He couldn't be rushing to the phone just because she wished he would. By one o'clock, she told herself that his silence was all she needed to know. Edward was out of her life.

She slumped into a chair, chastising herself. What did she expect? That a knight in shining armor would descend and carry her off to happily ever after? She was married, after all, and lived a life most women could only dream about. How could she entertain outlandish fantasies after only a few evenings with Edward? She needed to get a grip on her senses, to quash these histrionics. Now might be a good time to wrap Christmas gifts. She stood and headed to the closet where she'd stored them.

The phone rang, exploding her resolve. *Please, let it be Edward.*

It was.

He began by apologizing. "Sorry I didn't call earlier. I've haven't stopped thinking of you but there was an infernal board meeting…"

"Edward, you owe me no explanation. You have a

business to run." She closed her eyes and swallowed.

They both began to speak at once.

"Edward—'

"Emily—"

They stopped, then Emily's breath caught as Edward continued. "Could I come over this afternoon? I'd like to see you, to talk to you." His tone was earnest, his usual cheeriness absent.

Was he running his fingers through his hair, that endearing gesture which had now become familiar to her? "Of course. Come when you can." She kept her voice light, lacquering over her angst.

WHILE SHE WAITED, Emily sat at her desk, determined to busy herself with small tasks. She shuffled through a handful of Invitations to holiday gatherings that lay unanswered. John would have his preferences—a gala hosted by the Ziegfelds, a dinner at Lulu Bohner's—but she imagined he would grumble about attending those given by her friends. Right now, she had no stomach for resuming her duties as Mrs. John Ringling. She set the correspondence aside. Retrieving her cigarette holder from her bedroom, she stood at the window overlooking the street and smoked one cigarette, then another.

You know this can't continue with Edward. It's impossible. But even as she insisted to herself that this was true, her mind created wildly romantic scenarios—life with

Edward on a beach in Bermuda or in a Tuscan villa, far away from everyone they knew. She even included Janey in her musings. She could be taught by a governess, and she'd adore Emily, her charming stepmother. *Stop it, Emily. Come to terms with reality.*

Edward arrived within the hour. He greeted her with a chaste kiss on the cheek, then asked, "May we sit down?" His face was drawn, his mouth a straight line of determination.

"Would you like a drink? Coffee?" Emily asked.

"No thank you." He spoke formally, employing a distant courtesy.

They sat on the sofa facing one another. Emily pinned her arms stiffly against her stomach, as if awaiting a blow, as she took in his anguished expression.

He cleared his throat. "Emily, I am so terribly sorry for the way that I have behaved, for the way I have treated you." He stared down at the carpet, then brought his gaze back to connect with hers.

She shook her head and began to speak, but he interrupted. "Please, allow me to finish. These times I've spent with you, they've brought me so much joy, a joy that has been missing from my life. But I've behaved shamelessly, putting you in a compromising position. I've been selfish and dishonorable. I apologize."

How she ached to move closer to him, to wrap her arms around him. "Edward, no. Please don't apologize.

You have done nothing but show me kindness and affection and have brought happiness into my life, however fleeting."

He winced and rubbed his hand across his mouth. "I've been daring to imagine a life with you. If only—" he began, then stopped and stared at the wall.

"Yes. If only," she whispered. "Edward, I confess I've been thinking along those lines as well. You are so, so dear. I know we can't pretend that circumstances are different." Her voice cracked and her chin quivered. "But your honor, your goodness only make me care for you more. I will never regret the time I've spent with you."

He took her hands in his, enveloping them in his warm grasp. "I never thought I'd feel this way about another woman. But you, Emily, you've awakened a feeling that has long been dormant in me." He brought her hands to his lips and kissed them. "I regret deeply that I've hurt you. And to keep myself from hurting you more, I'm here to say goodbye. It's the right thing to do."

"Yes, I know." Her shoulders slumped and she stared at their entwined fingers resting in his lap. "I agree. But how I wish things were different." They sat in silence for a moment. A door that had opened into her heart slammed shut. "I regret…" she began, but then pursed her lips to keep her regrets to herself. It was not fair to burden Edward with her unhappiness. Her life would march forward, with John, a man she no longer believed she loved. Edward was untethered to another. He could find love again.

What more was there to be said? He was a man of integrity, not a man who would run off with a married woman, disgracing himself, ruining her reputation, causing his daughter irreparable harm. And sneaking around as illicit lovers? The tawdriness, the impropriety went against all of her principles and his. She couldn't divorce John, even for Edward. The scandal would be insurmountable, and they'd be shunned by everyone in decent society. There would be no happiness for either one of them. Even imagining such a situation after their brief encounter was foolish and reckless. She knew that. As did he.

She swallowed the lump in her throat and offered a quivering smile while sliding her fingers away from his. "Thank you for your honesty, for everything, Edward. I wish that you'll find happiness." Standing, she added, "I'll see you out."

He stood, then encircled her in his arms briefly before he stepped back, his arms hanging slack at his sides. In the foyer, he tossed out platitudes while he slipped into his overcoat. "Emily, I hope you have a very merry Christmas. And have a happy new year."

"You, as well. And I'll have the poinsettia to keep me

full of holiday cheer." She plucked a wilting petal off a flower, then snapped off a vibrant red bloom and held it out for him. "A Christmas keepsake."

He twirled it in his fingers. "She's a beauty." He bowed his head as if studying the blossom, then sighed deeply. "Well, I'd better go." He brushed her cheek with dry lips and was out the door.

Emily stared at the closed door for a moment and then turned away, walking with leaden steps back into the parlor, rubbing her chest as if to soothe her aching heart. *Was ist, ist.* Those words her mother had spoken so often resurfaced as she contemplated what was to come. She sat at her desk, absently flipped through her engagement book as she relived her conversation with Edward. It had all been for the best, she knew. But, oh, the chasm he'd left in her.

All at once her eyes lit upon the date printed on the page before her. Today was December 19, the anniversary of her marriage to John, one year ago. Until now, she had not given it a thought. And apparently, neither had he.

EMILY WAS LUNCHING with Sophie when John arrived, but when she returned to the apartment and found him napping in a parlor chair, she was stunned by his appearance. His face was sallow and drawn and dark lines encircled his eyes. He startled when she entered the room, and she leaned over to kiss him. "Welcome home, dear." She smoothed a hand across his wrinkled shirt, noticing his cheeks darkened by stubble. "John, you look exhausted. A tough trip?"

He grunted as he rose. "A bit. Can't seem to shake this malaise. Aching back, legs."

"Well, no sense in your sleeping here in a chair. Why not get comfortable in your bedroom? I've called the cook back in and she's prepared your favorites. I'll just pop dinner into the oven when you're ready. I wasn't sure when exactly what time you'd arrive, with odd train delays and all."

She expected him to object, to tell her that he'd been restored by his nap in the chair. But instead, he plodded towards his room.

"Shall I help you unpack?"

"Not now." He waved her off. "I'll be right as rain after forty winks, I promise. It's good to see you, Emily." He closed the bedroom door, leaving her in the hallway.

Was he really ill or simply tired and overworked, in need of a respite from his business? She told herself to look away from the visions of Edward that came to mind, but she could not. She was struck by the contrast of Edward's face—handsome, lean, youthful—and John's—worn, wan, lined with creases. In the weeks that she and John had been apart she had lost sight of how old John was. Even though he was many years her senior,

John had always seemed robust and bigger than life. But today, he appeared diminished. Edward's energy and virility juxtaposed with John's weariness tore at her heart. But Edward was gone from her life. She would make the best of things, would be solicitous of John's maladies and concerns, but it would take constant resolve.

HER RESOLVE FIZZLED by evening. John emerged from his nap, freshly showered and looking restored, and joined her in the parlor where she was drinking tea and reading the latest *Vogue*.

"So, Emily, what have you been up to?" He poured himself a whiskey and sat across from her. Lighting a cigar, he tipped his head back and inhaled deeply, then puffed out a cloud of acrid smoke.

What had she been up to? A kaleidoscope of images flashed across her mind ... dancing at the Park Central, dinner at Tony's, Edward's arms around her, his eyes locked on hers. She blinked them away. "Mostly seeing old friends, Christmas shopping for the family in New Jersey. We leave in two days, you recall."

He sat his glass on a table with a bang, sloshing the whiskey. "I told you I would not be going to New Jersey, Emily. I have just returned to our home here and I'm exhausted. I have no intention of gallivanting off to New Jersey. We will have Christmas right here."

Emily's eyes turned into slits. A spark of relief was

doused by her irritation. It might be more pleasant if he stayed home, but why should she be the one to acquiesce? She would hold her ground, go without him. "*We*? No John, *we* won't. I will be with my sisters." She tossed here magazine aside. "You've left me alone for weeks while you holed yourself up in your Florida office. And I've made plans for us to join my family, to have a traditional Christmas with my loved ones. I'd think that my husband would want to be with me, to please me."

"And I'd think that my wife would wish to please me!" He crossed his arms across his chest and straightened up in his chair. "You have no consideration for the work I do, Emily."

"No, I suppose I do not. After all, you refuse to discuss any of it with me." Emily's tone was biting. So, they were back to the same conversation, within hours of John's arrival. She stood. "I'll get dinner on the table."

"Fine. And at dinner, we can discuss our plans for after your return from New Jersey."

So, he was truly not going to accompany her to her sisters'. And then, he'd expect her at his side while they gad about New York at parties given by his friends? Would he bother to take into consideration what she might want to do? Emily felt as if a hard crust was forming around her heart as she contemplated the shape of their marriage going forward—two individuals bound by law, not by love.

Her memories of that Christmas were bittersweet. Time spent with Edward, then his departure still had the power to sink her into despondency. But then, she'd spent Christmas with her sisters. After John's refusal to join her, she'd tossed off his absence with a casual, "Oh, he's a bit under the weather," and Lena, Olga and Louise offered sincere expressions of "Hope he feels well soon." But with the flurry of gifts being opened, the bustling about in the kitchen, and the excitement of the children, John was all but forgotten. Emily immersed herself into the family holiday traditions—the spicy warmth of the *gluwein*, the crinkle of Christmas paper being torn from gifts, the glow of embers in the fireplace as all gathered around Olga's piano and sang "*Stille Nacht.*"

Emily had felt at home. On Christmas night, after two days in New Jersey, she curled under a thick quilt in Louise's guest room and wept. She felt more herself in the little room furnished with Mama's old dressing table and pillowcases embroidered by her sister's careful hand than she did in either of her Ringling bedrooms where she was surrounded by Mable's opulent selections.

But the next morning, she'd headed back to Park Avenue, to stay dutifully at the side of her husband. They didn't argue. Neither of them seemed to have the energy for more disharmony. As if no more than a pretty accessory, she was on display on John's arm at one holiday party after another. John basked in the glow of celebrity—the showman Ziegfeld, the colorful Fiorello LaGuardia—and while John held forth on the Tammany scandal and Mayor Jimmy Walker, or on his art acquisitions, or his new acrobatic act, Emily was left to make small talk with the other wives, women she had no interest in getting to know.

And her own friends? Even Sophie, caught up in her new romance, had failed to return her phone calls. Invitations from those in her circle had to be declined to keep their calendar free. John claimed that certain soirees must take precedence, all in the name of business. And besides, he was not well, or so he claimed. It was almost a relief to return to Ca d'Zan in January, where at least she was not confronted daily with a New York life where she no longer belonged.

Chapter Twenty-Six

1932

"Emily, just wait until you see the pirates! And the parade! You'll be amazed!" John turned to Hester and Charles, who had come to Ca d'Zan for cocktails on the terrace to welcome Emily back to Sarasota. "Aren't I right, Hester?" He tipped his cigar in Hester's direction and raised his eyebrows.

"It is quite something, I agree. Emily, please humor us Florida folks. We do have some strange customs." Hester smiled. "But I think you'll enjoy the spectacle. And the Coronation Ball is a lovely event."

Emily returned her smile but was skeptical. The whole thing sounded ludicrous. Notables of Tampa, including business VIPs, dressed as pirates "invading" by boat and demanding the keys to the city from the mayor? Then parades of floats commandeered by said pirates? How childish! And everyone was expected to line the streets and cheer them on. She supposed the Coronation Ball at least gave one the opportunity to dress up, but being proclaimed Queen of Gasparilla was no honor she would covet.

"I always enjoy new experiences," Emily remarked. "I won't have to dress in costume like last year's Depression Dance at the Whitfield Club, will I?"

Hester chuckled. "Oh, no. My, that was a fun evening, wasn't it?"

Both John and Charles nodded in agreement.

"Ralph Caples leading the bread line was sidesplitting!" John's eyes crinkled with mirth as he recalled the event. He slapped his thigh. "And Hester and Emily, your costumes were priceless."

Emily cringed. Hester had helped her fashion her costume, a dress made from gunny sacks and a necklace of small potatoes strung together. Poking fun at the Depression had seemed amusing, but later Emily witnessed down-on-their-luck men and women begging in the streets of New York. Making light of the terrible circumstances of others now struck her as cruel. But she would not lecture her husband or Hester and Charles. She changed the subject. "Tell me what you'll be wearing to the ball, Hester."

THE PIRATE HULLABALLOO of Gasparilla Week was just as absurd as Emily had imagined, and she was chagrined by John's delight in such nonsense. Although his aching legs and the shortness of breath plagued him, he stood in the VIP reviewing stand for hours, cheering as bands of pirates rode by while Emily huddled under an umbrella to ward off the light mist that fell throughout the day.

That evening as they dressed for the Coronation Ball, Emily, noticing John's raspy cough, chastised him for his intemperance, but he waved off her words.

"Emily, don't be such a spoil sport. Can't you allow me even a modicum of fun? Besides, it is important for me to be seen as a man of influence, as a leader of the region. Now hurry along. The car is waiting." He lit a cigar and paced the carpet in their hotel suite.

Emily put the finishing touches on her lipstick and handed John her cape. She had put extra care into choosing just the right gown, an ethereal pink satin that complemented her fair complexion and blue eyes, but John took no notice. Was it only one year ago that he was admiring her beauty, lavishing her with compliments as they headed for the party at Edith's? Now he barely glanced at her as he lay the cape over her shoulders and led her out the door.

The Ball was a crush of people, and Emily was relieved to see that the Tampa elite had shed their pirate costumes for more traditional garb—women in filmy and fashionable pastels and sparkling jewels, men in white dinner jackets. She sat next to Hester at the dinner table and while John held court with their other tablemates, Hester filled her in on who was whom among the throng. It was when the orchestra began playing that the evening took a turn.

John ushered her to the dance floor and swept her along, gliding around the other couples. Even with his health complaints, Emily was reminded of how surprisingly light on his feet John was. As the tallest man in the room, he struck a dashing figure in his white dinner jacket as they fox-trotted around the floor. She took herself back to the ballrooms of Amsterdam where he had first wooed her. As the vocalist crooned, "All of me, why not take all of me," Emily reminisced aloud. "I adore dancing with you. Remember the night we heard Cab Calloway in Amsterdam, John?"

But he was not listening; instead, he was scanning the room. "There's the President of Tampa National Bank, Northam. I must be sure to speak to him." The song ended and the orchestra began "It Don't Mean a Thing." John deftly altered his dance steps, and she followed his lead to the swing beat. But without warning, John stopped dancing and howled in pain. He hopped on one foot, clutching the other. Oher dancers, oblivious to his plight, swirled gaily past them.

Was he having a heart attack? Emily clutched his arms. "John, what is it?"

"That damn woman just trampled across my foot. The pain is excruciating."

Emily's eyes darted round them, seeking the culprit, but only saw a blur of revelers.

"She's gone now. How could she not know that she stomped on my foot?" He managed to stand erect, but his face was ashen. "Let's sit down."

Emily led him to their table, where John endeavored to ignore his injury. But within a short time, he announced that they were leaving, and unable to mask a limp, he steered her out of the ballroom.

In their hotel suite, Emily blanched as John removed his shoe and sock and revealed the bloody gash on his foot. "John! Let me call a doctor!"

"Don't be so dramatic. I'll just wash it off and it will be fine." He hobbled into his bedroom as a trickle of blood stained his path along the carpet.

A WEEK LATER, back in New York City, John's foot was so painfully inflamed that he finally allowed Emily to contact a physician. Dr. Harlow Brooks, an old friend of Emily's, diagnosed John with a blood infection, and prescribed medications and bedrest.

"Bedrest! I have a business to run, good doctor. You don't seem to understand that I cannot wile away my days in a bed." John attempted to stand but sank back into his chair. The angry contour of his mouth was etched with lines of pain.

"Heed my words, Mr. Ringling. I'll be frank. For a man in his sixties, this can be deadly." Dr. Brooks gestured toward Emily, standing behind John. "Your wife will keep me informed of your progress."

"I won't be scolded like a child," John snarled.

"Then don't act like a child," Emily wanted to say, but she held her tongue. She endeavored to be sympathetic and soothing. He was suffering, after all, but his recalcitrance and ill humor pecked away at her kindhearted instincts. "Thank you, Dr. Brooks. I'll keep an eye on him."

But Brooks' comment confused her. Why had he referred to John as a man in his sixties? Escorting the doctor to the door, she waited until he donned his coat. "Just a question, Dr. Brooks. Why did you say 'for a man in his sixties'? John's not."

He tucked a muffler into the lapels of his coat and stared at her blankly. "What do you mean? John is sixty-five. In fact, he just told me that before you came into the room."

Emily froze. Suddenly, as if all the tumblers of a locked safe clicked into place, Emily realized this truth. Recovering, she shrugged at the doctor. "Silly me. I guess I'm so used to thinking of him as a younger man, so full of life as he is. I forget that he's sixty-five." She waved a hand, tossing her question aside. "I'm a little scatterbrained this morning, worrying about John."

Dr. Brooks nodded, then looked at his wristwatch. "Well, I must be on my way. Let me know if you need anything, Mrs. Ringling." He left, and Emily slumped into a chair to absorb the new information. Of course, he was sixty-five! It made perfect sense! Yet, he had told her when they'd met that he was fifty-two, had even written that as his age on their marriage license. And she had never questioned him, never saw what was right in front of her face. How stupidly gullible she had been, swallowing his deception that now seemed so obvious. She could have detected the falsehood when he freely told one and all about all his years in the circus business or wondered about the age difference between him and his older brother Charles, or considered numerous other snippets of chronology he spoke of. Yet she hadn't. *What a fool I am! And what else has he been lying about?* She wanted to barge into his room and confront him but held back. *He's a sick man today, but when he is well, I will confront him. Fifty-two? Ha!*

The infection was one more setback for John but another for her as well. Every day she was confronted with doing what was best for her ailing husband, sitting with him when he fussed, tuning the radio to his favorite programs. No opportunity felt right for confronting John about his lie about his age, so she kept it simmering in the back of her mind. Other issues were more pressing. When Emily came upon past due notices from Bloomingdale's in the mail, her patience evaporated, and she demanded that John disclose his financial troubles to her. After all, their pre-nuptial agreement stipulated that he would pay their living expenses and clearly that was not happening.

Once again, he'd brushed her inquiries aside. "I won't get into my personal finances with you, Emily. Stop haranguing me. Have you no consideration for a sick man?"

"You use your illness as a cloak to hide behind but only when it is convenient for you. Haranguing you? I'm bailing you out, John. You agreed that you would pay our household expenses, yet the servants have informed me that grocery accounts have been unpaid. I've used my funds to set them right, but this was not our agreement. You could make these issues disappear if you simply sold some of the artwork you've acquired," she reminded him. She had never understood his obstinate refusal to part with some of his pieces. Once, he'd bragged that the collection was worth twenty million dollars. Why was it hanging on the walls of a museum no one saw while creditors hounded them?

"I shall never. The collection will eventually belong to the state of Florida. It's my legacy and will remain untouched."

John never wavered and as time passed, arguments increased until Emily had lost track of the times they'd bickered. It was as if they were performing in a radio drama where the characters' travails repeated themselves daily. She was worn out from arguing, worn out from worrying.

Since the doctor had advised against travel, they were required to remain in New York. John grumbled, but Emily was pleased. She invited Lena to stay in the apartment and frequently called old friends in for games of bridge and cocktails. The guests served as a buffer between her and John and although his health was troubling him, he continued to wear the façade of the genial, magnanimous host. Ever the Circus King, he hobbled into the parlor attired in a brocade smoking jacket, puffing on his cigar as he regaled their company with circus stories that Emily had heard over and over.

"He's such a jolly man, Emily," her old friend Olive commented after an evening at the Ringling apartment. "He must keep you in stitches."

"He is one of a kind. So glad you could join us, Olive." When was the last time had John made her laugh? She couldn't recall. Closing the door behind Olive, she drew her finger along the foyer table where Edward's poinsettia had once sat. That was when she had last laughed, but it hadn't been with John at all. It had been with Edward. A lump clogged her throat. Would she ever be so joy-filled again?

BUT JOHN DID not recover, and Dr. Brooks insisted that John be confined to a hospital. His foot infection and his persistent shortness of breath converged to leave him wracked with weakness and pain. Against his protests, John was whisked off to the Coney Island Hospital for specialized treatment. Emily booked a room for herself nearby at the Half-Moon Hotel on the Boardwalk, away from Manhattan and her friends.

"It's dreadful out here," complained Emily to Lena in a phone call. "No one comes to Coney Island in March, and the sea breeze is chilling me to the bone. And this hotel, my goodness. It's completely lacking in good taste. There are plaster busts of Henry Hudson and garish murals of old Spain at every turn."

Lena chuckled. "Not quite the Hotel Astor, I imagine. But aren't you a good wife to tend to your husband while he's recuperating?"

Emily scoffed. "As if he appreciates all that I do. I'm at his beck and call at that wretched hospital. I'm urging Dr. Brooks to send him home soon. Lord knows, John is miserable here. For once, John and I are in agreement about something. We can hire a nurse, and I can supervise his care while being granted a little independence. I feel as if my wings have been clipped completely."

Days ticked by, and John was found fit enough to leave the hospital. Back on Park Avenue, Emily hosted a cocktail party or two, and John, even while recuperating, resumed his attention to business. Meanwhile their arguments continued.

Emily had lost count of the causes of their disagreements, but at the core, their problems centered on money and property, and whose was whose. John continued to insist that his finances were in good order, so Emily, frustrated by John's opaqueness, diverted her attention to redecorating. As at Ca d'Zan, she felt like an interloper in the Park Avenue apartment where Mable's choices in décor surrounded her. Another conflict rose to the surface.

She gave a rug and portieres to the cook; John was indignant. She gave some tapestries to her sister; John was outraged. When she asked Frank Tomlinson, now in New York as John's chauffeur and house manager, to hang some new draperies and he refused, John sided with him and would not fire him. Lingering clouds from their bitter quarrels hung over the apartment.

Emily's discontent smoldered as she found her privacy seeping away. Each day, a nurse—sometimes a Miss Johnson, sometimes a Miss Collins, and sometimes one whose name Emily could not recall—arrived to tend to John's health needs. Their admonishments that "Mr. Ringling needs to rest now" whenever Emily sought to speak to John about some pressing matter like an overdue account filled her with frustration.

ONCE JOHN'S HEALTH improved, he itched to get back to Sarasota. One afternoon in March, Emily was reading in the parlor when she heard John escort the nurse to the front door. Was it Collins? Or Johnson? She hardly cared. She found both women cloyingly loyal to their charge. Emily heard a syrupy voice say, "Mr. Ringling, are you sure? I don't think this is wise."

Whatever were they talking about? Emily set down her book to listen more closely.

"I'm certain," she heard John say. "Thank you for your service. Good day."

Had John dismissed the nurse? If so, Emily was not sorry. The nurses grated on Emily. But how could she complain about those so-called angels of mercy who rendered medical care to her husband? She heard the door close and waited for John to come into the parlor.

He shuffled in, smiling broadly. "I've just told the nurse that I will no longer be needing her. I've got to get back to Sarasota and to the circus, Emily. The season begins in a matter of weeks. Even Dr. Brooks says that this cold weather is detrimental to my circulation issues."

"Well, this seems like a hasty decision. Did it occur to you that you might want to speak to me before you dismissed her?" She modulated her tone, avoiding a sharpness that so often edged her words. Why hadn't Dr. Brooks spoken to her about this? Did he feel that dismissing the nurses was ill-advised? If so, he should have alerted her to John's decision.

He scowled. "I know how I feel, Emily. I'm able to gauge my own health needs."

"I see." Emily considered a return to Florida. She supposed she could stay in New York without him, but the sunless days, the frigid temperatures were wearing on her as well. She'd invited friends in for cocktails but refrained from nights on the town. She imagined the buzzing of gossip that would circle Manhattan air if she were seen at a nightclub while her sick husband remained at home. Possibly a change of scenery would tamp down their growing rancor. At any rate, John was not seeking her opinion about the matter, and refusing to go would speak volumes regarding the future of their marriage.

"Sarasota will be a nice this time of year," she conceded. "But since you'll be so preoccupied with the circus work, I'll ask Lena to join us. She's good company for me while you're tied up with business." She watched John's face, challenging him to object. He didn't.

BACK AT CA d'Zan, Emily was struck by an air of neglect. What had the staff, led by Martha, been doing while they were away? Even Lena commented on the dust balls in out-of-the—way corners, and the windows coated with salty sea spray. When Emily pointed them out to John, he dismissively waved his cigar in the air. "You're the lady of the house, Emily. Take care of it. I'm much too busy to deal with servants."

Determined to keep peace, Emily prepared a list and approached Martha. "I'd like to speak to you in the breakfast room." Martha eyed her sullenly but followed Emily to the table where they both sat down.

Emily slid the paper toward Martha. "The following areas of Ca d'Zan are in need of cleaning and attention. I'd like you to see that these are completed immediately."

Martha's eyes scanned the list. Then she looked up at Emily. "I'm afraid this is impossible right now," she said dully.

"Impossible? I don't think—"

But Martha shook her head. "Listen, Mrs. Ringling, I'm just trying to be honest with you." Her toneless response, the droop of her shoulders caught Emily off guard. She had expected defensiveness and possibly insolence, but Martha displayed neither of these attitudes. Instead, her vacant eyes showed defeat.

Emily placed her palms on the table and leaned forward. "Go on. Explain."

And Martha did. Haltingly, she painted a picture of financial neglect. Mr. Ringling, she said, had left bills unpaid. The grocer threatened to stop deliveries, but Martha had convinced him to wait just awhile more to be compensated. The cook had also threatened to quit when her pay was in arrears, but Martha had cajoled her into staying as well. She had not been able to convince the maids, though. They had left when Mrs. Caples offered them positions with higher pay that would come on time. "I hate to bother Mr. Ringling, as I know he's

THE SECOND MRS. RINGLING

been ill, but I'm at a loss." She dropped her chin to her chest, then looked beseechingly at Emily.

The impatience that Emily had felt toward Martha dissipated. Now, she felt a new respect for this woman who had been struggling to keep things running while facing financial obstacles. No wonder John had insisted that she confront Martha. He was off buried in his circus work, while his beloved Ca d'Zan was in danger of crumbling around them. His avoidance of reality was stupefying. The reality of overdue accounts and unpaid staff had followed them to Florida problems as well.

But she could not allow Martha to see the fissures in John's finances. If the façade of John's abundant wealth showed signs of weakness, it could spell trouble. No doubt Martha already had sniffed out these troubles and might even be spreading what she knew from one estate kitchen to another. Emily forced a smile that oozed a salve of commiseration. "My goodness, Martha. I can see you've been up against some tough problems. Of course, Mr. Ringling has been ill, as you mentioned, so I suspect he inadvertently allowed things to slide. If you'll present me with the accounts and the salaries due, I'll take care of this immediately. And let's hire two more maids. Maybe some girls from Newtown."

Martha let out a long breath. "Yes, Mrs. Ringling. But about the Newtown girls—" She fidgeted with the bib of her apron.

"What's the problem? Don't the colored girls from Newtown work more cheaply? It would be less costly."

Martha nodded. "But Mr. John, he refuses to have them here. He says no ni—." She paused, her face flushed, and began again. "No colored girls."

"Really!" Emily opened her mouth, then snapped it shut. *How bullheaded, how stupidly small-minded!* She thought of Bessie, the gentle and capable maid she'd employed in New York until John dismissed her. It was because Bessie was colored, she now realized. How ignorant. "So, Martha, I was unaware of Mr. Ringling's directives here. I'll handle this. Thank you."

As Martha scuttled off into the kitchen to gather the paperwork, Emily was struck by the change in her. Martha, once haughty and insubordinate, had spoken openly, unburdening herself of the travails she faced managing this household. She had accepted without skepticism the excuse of John's illness. Was Martha now an ally? She hoped so. It was important to keep Martha on board. Emily would pay the bills with her own funds and confront John about this lapse. And about his biases. If he wanted to continue to be known as the fabulously wealthy tycoon of Sarasota, then he was going to have to change his ways. As she had suggested several times before, selling off artwork would be a good place to start.

Later, Emily, armed with a list of bills she had paid, strode into John's office and slapped the pile on his desk.

"For the moment, I've kept you from the humiliation of having the city of Sarasota buzzing about your financial demise. But I want to be reimbursed, John."

He glanced up the ledgers he was studying. "What are you talking about?"

"Don't pretend you don't know. I've paid the grocer, the cook, your driver, and Martha, all loyal employees whom you've taken advantage of. Two housemaids already departed for the greener pastures at the Caples. Our agreement has been that you would pay household expenses, not I." She tapped the stack of bills. "These as well as the fifty thousand you borrowed need to be repaid."

"Don't be shrill, Emily. My fortune is intact but liquidating funds to pay small amounts like these, well, it's not easily done. You will get repaid and before you nag me about it again, no, I won't be selling off any of my art treasures. That's ridiculous." He waved a hand at her. "Leave these for now and I'll get to them. But right now, I'm finalizing the plans for the circus departure in a matter of days, so I'm a bit busy at the moment. I'd expect that as my wife you could see to these things. Mable—" He stopped himself, but Emily heard the implication, the comparison of her to Mable.

Emily seethed. "Did your Mable pay the bills out of her own funds as well? I doubt that. In fact, I doubt that she had any funds of her own in the first place. In the meantime, I am keeping track of my costs for the maintenance of your Ca d'Zan. Don't think for a moment that I will not expect reimbursement. And another thing. Martha has informed me that you will not hire any colored help. I will not abide by bigotry either." She turned and left the room, resisting the urge to slam the door.

Bigotry. Suddenly she recalled a night in New York City months ago, with the Ziegfelds.

ONE EVENING, JOHN'S friend and Broadway showman Flo Ziegfeld invited them to join him and his wife in his private box at his *Follies* on Broadway.

"You're going to love this new gal I've got, Dorothy Dell. What a voice! And wait until you see these Negro tap dancers I've booked, Buck and Bubbles." Flo offered John a cigar and then extended a lighter towards him.

"Negroes? I'd never hire that kind. Can't trust 'em." John examined his cigar. "Say, this is nice. La Corona from Cuba, right?"

Flo lit his cigar and took a deep drag on it, then exhaled. "Nothing like a smooth La Corona." John's comment about the Negro entertainers seemed to drift away like the smoke rings that Flo puffed out toward the ceiling.

But Emily was taken aback. She glanced at Billie, the actress that Flo had turned into a star and then his wife, to see her reaction, but Billie was engrossed in scanning the other theater boxes through a small pair of opera glasses. Had John meant what he said about hiring Negroes? She'd never heard him voice an aversion to Negroes before, but his tone was so nonchalant, so off-the-cuff, that she did not doubt that he meant it.

She recalled that she had once mentioned Hester's housekeeper Gloria, suggesting that she might know of other women who they could add to their staff. John had simply scowled and closed down the conversation.

She was acquainted with very few Negroes herself—the doorman at the Waldorf, the elevator operator at Bendel's, and several housekeepers, and each of them was polite and reliable. She admired the talents of Josephine Baker and Cab Calloway and had read poetry by Langston Hughes. How could John express such a narrow view? Didn't he know that making such comments might be construed as provincialism? Although John had been born in a little town in Wisconsin, he had overcome his humble beginnings to become a sophisticated man of the world. She studied her husband, gesturing with his cigar and recounting a story about when the circus performed in Madison Square Garden.

Billie tapped her on the arm. "Looks like Mayor Jimmy Walker is with us tonight." She tipped her head toward another box nearby. "Didn't John tell us that he was on his boat when it sank?" She tittered, putting her hand over her mouth.

Emily cringed at the childlike timbre to Billie's voice. She shrugged and before she could answer, Flo pointed to the stage. "Curtain's about to go up."

Emily settled back into her seat. As the showgirls, sparkling in silvery sequined costumes, pranced across the stage, she mulled over John's comment. He was misguided. She should set him straight as soon as an opportunity presented itself.

✧ ✧ ✧

BY THE NEXT day, Emily had decided not to confront John about his comments about Negroes. At the time, she had no desire to stir the pot. Now she regretted that decision.

LATER THAT EVENING, John joined Emily and Lena on the terrace, swooping in on their tete-a-tete while pushing a small bar cart. "Drinks, ladies?" As if their harsh words earlier had never occurred, he flourished a champagne flute and grinned. "Since this is one of our last sunsets for a while, I thought we'd take advantage of the beautiful evening air and enjoy some champagne."

Lena tittered at John's showy ceremony of cork-popping, but Emily remained impassive. He handed her a flute, and Emily asked, "What do you mean, one of our last sunsets for a while?"

"Well, you and I leave on the circus train on Saturday so presumably Lena will be heading back to New Jersey." Avoiding Emily's gaze, he held up his glass and squinted at the sunlight shimmering through the crystal.

Lena's eyes darted from Emily to John then back to Emily. She bit her lip and raised her eyebrows as if to ask her sister *"Are you going?"*

"John." Emily took a long swallow from her glass and then shook her head. She had no intention of ever getting into John's circus train car again. The previous spring, she joined him briefly after he promised her the time of her life, and she'd hated every minute. Even though the private car was lavishly appointed, she had felt claustrophobic, living day after day crammed into the small space and only embarking onto a chaotic circus lot, surrounded by terrible smells and nonstop commotion. "You'll recall that you and I discussed my accompanying you on the circus train months ago. I told you then I would not be going along."

"Oh, come now, Emily. You surely don't mean that. We had a wonderful time, seeing the circus all across the Eastern seaboard." John turned to Lena as if to cajole her into siding with him on the matter. "It was a delightful l trip, as it is every year."

Lena remained quiet, but Emily responded. "For you, perhaps, John, but not for me. I will stay back. Now that your health has been restored, you'll enjoy yourself more if you don't have to take my comforts into account." She kept her voice light, tinging it with regret. "I'm afraid I'm just not cut out for circus life."

"But," John began, then stopped himself and looked out to the water for a moment before continuing. "You'll be missed, my dear."

"I'll miss you as well. Here's to a good circus season." *There.* They had both said the right thing. Emily lifted her glass in a salute. "I'm getting chilled out here. I believe I'll go in and see about dinner. Lena, are you chilly as well?"

Lena stood. "Yes, a bit."

The two women headed toward the house, leaving John to admire his sunset.

SO, JOHN LEFT with the circus, boarding his train car alone. Emily settled into a relaxed routine at Ca d'Zan, lounging by the pool with her sister, taking long drives along the shore in the Pierce Arrow. In the months that followed, Emily would look back on those days and long for the tranquility that she enjoyed.

There were rumblings about the circus. Emily was disconcerted to see John's name mentioned in the financial pages of the *New York Times*, speculating on the effects of the Depression on the circus profits, hinting at possible mismanagement. Unproven gossip, surely, or was it? It wasn't long before the *Sarasota Herald* was parroting the *Times* article.

John was so secretive and tight-lipped about his dealings. If only she could gain access into his office while he was away. Emily then recalled the key-filled cabinet in the kitchen. Like a sleuth in an Agatha Christie novel, she investigated, only to discover that the cabinet itself was locked. Could she finagle the key from Martha, or was there a better way? When Martha had retired for the evening, Emily stole into John's bedroom through the door that connected to her boudoir. Her heart pounded as she opened dresser drawers and rummaged through his closet, searching for keys. Had she truly stooped so low that she was skulking around, intruding upon her husband's privacy? What would she say if she was discovered? Of course, it was her right to enter her husband's room. If John had been forthcoming, she wouldn't have to resort to this. She was about to give up when she opened a drawer in a nightstand. There under a pile of monogramed handkerchief lay two keys, one large and one small. These had to be what she was looking for.

She pocketed them and stepped through the door into her own room. So that she would not involve Lena in her skullduggery, she waited until she was sure her sister was asleep, then crept up the short flight of stairs that led to John's office. Holding her breath, she inserted the large key into the lock, gasping when it opened the door. Inside, she turned on a small desk lamp and looked around. John had tidied the office before leaving with the circus and no ledgers or files were on the desk. But when she inserted the smaller key into the desk file drawer lock, she was able to glide the drawer open.

For the next hour, Emily sifted through ledgers along with folders of correspondence. While much of the information was mystifying to her, the letters were not. There were numerous politely worded dunning notices for circus essentials—animal feed, supplies for the circus employees, advertising in newspapers. "Your account is in arrears." "Please remit payments immediately." As she read one letter after another and scanned the ledgers, a knot formed in her stomach. She pinched the bridge of her nose as she absorbed the figures that illustrated a picture of serious trouble for the Greatest Show on Earth. Gate receipts had not kept up with expenses. It appeared that with each new town's performances, the circus was falling further and further into debt.

Emily carefully replaced the files into the drawers and relocked them. And this was only the circus! What about John's other business pursuits? The oil fields? The railroad? John continued to assure her that all was well with those enterprises, but hadn't he said that about the circus as well? She knew that the local real estate development had stalled—empty lots on St. Armand

Key, the construction of a hotel left uncompleted. She caught sight of the framed *Time Magazine* cover from 1924, featuring John Ringling as one of the wealthiest men in America. So, in spite of his braggadocio and optimism, John's fortune just might be in jeopardy. Now, what might she do with this information?

Chapter Twenty-Seven

SEVERAL DAYS AFTER John's departure, Emily and Lena were lounging by the pool when they heard the cheerful ding-ding of a bicycle bell. A Western Union courier hopped off his bike near the front door of the house. The women watched as Martha accepted the telegram, dismissed the courier, and then carried the telegram over to the pool.

Emily shaded her eyes as Martha approached. "Must be John, telling me what town he's in tonight."

"Mrs. Kelly, for you." Martha held the telegram out to Lena who scrambled into a sitting position.

"Thank you, Martha." Emily dismissed the housekeeper as her sister opened the telegram and scanned its contents. Lena's brow furrowed and she bit her lower lip.

"Nicholas seems to be in some trouble. He wants me back in New Jersey." With trembling fingers, Lena, expelling an exasperated sigh, handed the telegram to Emily. "That young man will be the death of me. I've got to leave right away."

Before Emily could absorb the message, Lena was on

her feet, headed for the house. What had Nicholas done this time? He was always full of big ideas but at times landed himself in some shady circumstances. Lena had boasted that he was now a driver for a wealthy New Jersey businessman. But his terse words marching across the flimsy paper: "Lost my job. Boss in trouble. Need to move in with you. Come home" set Emily's teeth on edge as she conjured up potential unsavory situations. Just who was Nicholas's boss? The newspapers were filled with stories of the Feds tracking down bootleggers and she feared Nicholas's boss could be one of them. She told herself not to be overdramatic. Nicholas was a bit of a rascal, but he meant well. No matter what the reason, Lena needed to get on the evening train.

✧ ✧ ✧

WITH LENA GONE and John on the road with the circus, Emily drifted along with little to occupy her time. Her discoveries about the precarious financial state of the circus weighed on her. When a letter arrived from the newly married Sophie, settling in at her new winter home in Coral Gables, Emily eagerly accepted her invitation to visit. The journey by train was a complicated one—first from Tampa to Jacksonville, then another connection to Miami, but Emily welcomed a change of scenery and time spent with an old friend.

Sophie met Emily on the train platform, squealing in

delight as she hugged her old friend. She directed a porter to carry Emily's luggage to a gleaming silver Mercedes parked nearby, and as the chauffeur and porter arranged the suitcases in the trunk, the women settled into the back seat.

Emily squeezed Sophie's hand. "My goodness! Look at you! You're glowing with happiness."

Sophie tossed a hand dismissively as the sun danced off the facets of her new diamond. "Well, what can I say, Emily? I'm over the moon. Remember when I told you that you had caught the brass ring when you married John? It seems I've done the same. My James is a dream come true. I've never been so happy." Sophie blushed. "Who would have thought that we two girls, not quite the young debutantes we once were, would have found the loves of our lives? We are so blessed, aren't we, Emily?"

"We are." Emily swallowed a pebble of jealousy. Certainly she was happy for her friend who continued to gush superlatives at they rode along. But Sophie's bliss was in stark contrast to feelings about her own marriage. Had she ever have been so besotted by John? Had she ever thought of him as the love of her life? *The love of her life.* The phrase conjured up Edward's image, not John's. Yet here she was, Mrs. John Ringling.

Emily turned her attention to the view outside the car. "Sophie, you must love Coral Gables. I was here years ago, but things have flourished even more since then. Such lovely shops under those gorgeous colonnades. And pink trolleys! How utterly charming."

Sophie rolled her eyes. "My dear," she tsked. "Those are not pink trolleys. They are coral."

"And so they are!" Emily chuckled. "I won't make that mistake again, I assure you." She could not avoid comparing the streetscape of Coral Gables with that of Sarasota. Everything here oozed grace and elegance, while downtown Sarasota was chockablock with mundane shops offering little charm—a pharmacist next to a dress shop next to a store that sold shovels and wheelbarrows. When John had described Sarasota to her, this was what she had envisioned, and while Ca d'Zan certainly was remarkable, the environs were almost primitive.

Traveling past the Colonnades and an Italianate sculpture in the center of the street, Sophie filled Emily in on her new home. "James is so pleased to have purchased one of the homes bordering the country club. Of course, he still has a business to run in New York, but we will come here as often as we can. I'm going to learn to golf. Do you play, Emily?" Emily shook her head—no, she did not golf—the car pulled into a driveway flanked by two palm trees.

"Here we are, Emily. I can't wait to show you." Sophie clutched her friend's elbow and led her inside while the chauffeur saw to the luggage.

The home was elegantly designed in the Mediterranean Revival style, and upon entering, Emily was taken in by its serenity and simple beauty. Sleek furniture, uncluttered by gaudy embellishments and unburdened by brick-a-brack on every surface, created an air of sophistication and comfort. "It's so lovely, Sophie!" *How pleasant it must be to live in a home like this, instead of the cheerless museum I'm in.* "Did you choose all the furnishings yourself?"

"Oh, my, no. James and I worked on it together, and I had the help of a designer from New York. You know, we wanted something light and airy and most of all, chic." Her eyes glowed as she led Emily into the living room where sunlight spilled in from French doors that led to a terrace. She paused. "Oh, listen to me. Here you are Emily, living in a veritable showplace, and I'm going on and on about our much more modest home. You must think I'm ridiculous."

Before Emily could respond, a man in tan slacks and a white linen shirt emerged from another room. "And here is the wonderful Emily I've heard so much about." Striding toward her, he reached out to clasp her hands, a warm smile spreading across his face, his blue eyes twinkling. "I'm so happy to finally meet you. I'm James."

"Thrilled to meet you as well. Sophie has told me so much about you." Emily found herself drawn to his relaxed friendliness. She sized him up quickly—an easygoing, unpretentious man, and close in age to Sophie.

"She has, has she? Well, I'm the luckiest man I know to have found my beautiful bride." Casually he placed his arm on Sophie's shoulder, drawing her close to him and kissing her cheek.

"As you can see, Emily, James is as dear as I've told you he was." Sophie tipped her head toward her husband's shoulder. "Let's have Emily get settled first. Then maybe drinks on the terrace?"

SOPHIE LED EMILY to a guest room, decorated in soft shades of blue and white. "I hope you'll be comfortable here."

Emily tossed her handbag onto a tufted chair covered in ivory silk and hugged her friend. "Sophie, it's all lovely, just perfect. And seeing you so in love, I'm delighted for you. You deserve happiness, and I see you've found it in James."

Sophie stepped away from the hug to face Emily. Her eyes glistened. "I never thought I'd be so much in love, Emily. I had become so jaded. But this man—he is good and kind and caring—a dream come true." She waved her hands dismissively. "Silly me. I'll let you get settled and see you in a bit."

Emily hugged Sophie once more, struck by the transformation in Sophie, whose sometimes brittle edges had been smoothed by love. When Sophie left the room, Emily sank onto the edge of the bed. She could not have imagined when she and Sophie embarked on their trip to Europe less than two years ago, that their lives would diverge down such different paths. She glanced round the room, admiring its fresh stylishness and warmth, in contrast to her Ca d'Zan boudoir, swathed in heavy lace and gilded Rococo. The décor of the two places seemed to her to be a metaphor for her life and Sophie's, one bright and forward-looking, the other burdened by pretense. She had come to Coral Gables to temporarily escape the strictures of being Mrs. John Ringling, but she now found herself confronting her unhappiness head-on.

EMILY FOUND SOPHIE and James to be marvelous hosts, balancing time spent entertaining her with outings—dinner on the terrace of the Coral Gables Country Club, scenic drives in Miami—and allowing her to relax alone in her room. Light-hearted banter peppered every conversation and Sophie and James's devotion to one another played out with impulsive pecks on the cheek or a hand affectionately squeezing a shoulder. Emily was particularly struck by the word *we*, a hallmark of their sentences:

"We plan to add some more plantings to the garden."

"We love the Philharmonic concerts when we're in

New York."

"We considered a trip to Italy but decided to put it off until next year."

With every *we*, Emily saw a couple who respected one another, who looked towards their future as partners. She and John never spoke in *We's,* only in *I's. Could something as simple as a pronoun choice indicate what was at the core of a marriage?*

James sometimes had business to attend to. Once, after he ended a phone call with a client, he joined Sophie and Emily on the terrace. "I'm not sure what to do about this. What do you think, Sophie? And Emily, I'd like your opinion as well." He proceeded to tell them about a new advertising campaign. What did they think of the slogan he was considering? Would it appeal to the intended market? Sophie tossed out her opinions eagerly while James, his chin propped up on his fist, nodded at her. "I hadn't considered that, darling. I think you're spot on." He turned to Emily. "What do you think?"

Emily, tongue-tied, struggled to comment. "I—I couldn't really say."

But James persisted. "Sophie always offers a valuable woman's point of view." He patted his wife's knee. "She's been a godsend at times. I'd love to hear your thoughts too, Emily."

"Well, I know Sophie is quite perceptive. I'd take her words into serious consideration." *Take her words into serious consideration. Imagine being married to a man who did that.*

James chuckled, glancing at Sophie. "You know, I always do. She's got a good head on those pretty shoulders of hers." He stood. "I'll get back to work. Thanks, ladies, for listening to me. I'll leave you to your conversation." He kissed the top of Sophie's head before he went back into the house.

"Now where were we, Emily? I think you were telling me about your sister Lena." Sophie retied the headscarf that held her hair in place.

But Emily had forgotten what she was telling Sophie about Lena. "Is James always like that?" she asked.

"Like what?" Sophie removed her sunglasses and tilted her head toward Emily.

"Like seeking your opinion. Telling you about his business. Actually considering what you have to say in order to make a decision for his company." She pictured her encounters with John about business—his curt dismissals of her inquiries, his stubborn refusals to reveal any information. What must it be like to have one's views or insights valued?

Sophie laughed. "Oh, that. Why, yes, he does. I've kept him from at least one disastrous decision, when he tried to sell detergent by making laundry look like a glamorous undertaking. I told him no housewife would be swayed by that!" She tossed her head back. "Imagine!"

Then Sophie's smile disappeared. "Em, what is it? You look so downhearted."

"Oh, Sophie, where to begin?" Emily twisted her mouth as she contemplated continuing. Why should she burden her friend with her troubles? Sophie had suffered her own misfortunes. Ralph had been so terrible to her. She had earned the right to live joyfully.

But Sophie pressed on. "Em, what is it? You can tell me." Her brows drew together and she touched Emily's arm. "If you want...."

Emily stared at her hands clasped on her lap and took a deep breath. "John and I—things are strained. I see you and James—your genuine love and devotion to one another, and it takes my breath away." She locked eyes with Sophie, swallowing the catch in her throat.

"But, Emily, I thought you and John—," Sophie began. "Aren't you—I mean, I assumed you and John were happy. Dear, Emily, what's wrong?" Sophie grasped Emily's hands knotted on her lap.

Emily brought her eyes upward to connect with Sophie's. "I suppose I was so flattered at first. In Amsterdam, John showered me with attention. And back in New York, he seemed smitten. He was charming and his life was exciting. Imagine, King of the Circus!" She paused. "I see now that I should have been more cautious. I suppose neither of us was." She studied her fingernails. "We didn't really know one another, and the next thing we knew, we were husband and wife."

"Has he been cruel to you?" Sophie pressed on. "I've suffered that with Ralph and you helped me see then that I was deserving of better."

Emily shook her head slowly. "Cruel? No, not cruel." Her eyes welled with tears, and she brushed away the path of dampness that now trickled down her cheek. "But we, well, we are like two ships passing in the night. He has his life; I have mine." She had not intended to burden Sophie with her unhappiness, but she found herself continuing. "And then there's Mable."

"Mable? Do you mean his first wife? She was dead before you met John!" Sophie searched her pocket for a handkerchief and handed it to Emily. "Here, wipe your eyes. I can see that you've been bottling up your unhappiness for some time, haven't you?"

Emily shrugged. "Mable may be deceased, but I feel her presence everywhere. Her Ca d'Zan, her museum, her apartment in New York, from the desk I sit at while corresponding with friends to the linens on my bed. And John is passionate about enshrining her memory into an art museum that is costing—" She hesitated. How much could she reveal to even Sophie, her dearest friend? Disclosing John's shaky financial standing would not be wise. "Oh, Sophie, why am I troubling you with my tale of woe? I'm not a child. I apologize." She pulled her hands away from Sophie's and reached for her cigarette case and silver lighter on the table. She busied herself for a moment inserting a cigarette into a holder and bringing it to her lips, drawing on it deeply. "Suffice it to say that John and I have a marriage wrapped in persistent tension. Harmony is rare."

Sophie too reached for a cigarette and the two friends smoked in silence for a moment until Sophie set her cigarette holder onto the ashtray. "What will you do, Emily?"

"Do? What can I do?" Emily sniffed and stared at the bougainvillea bushes lining the lawn. Hadn't she been asking herself this question over and over? And she still had no viable answers. She turned towards her friend. "Sophie, I shouldn't be short with you. It's just that there seems to be nothing I can do. A divorce? We both know that is a terrible option."

Sophie winced and brought her cigarette to her mouth once again. She tapped an ash into the ashtray. "So many people treated divorcees like a pariah. Even those who knew Ralph had deserted me acted like I was in the wrong. 'She must have driven him away' was the constant refrain, wasn't it? I was snubbed by some, humiliated and scorned by others." She shuddered. "And the precarious financial situation added to my anguish."

Sophie was right. "Just my point, Sophie. And you were the injured party; no one disputed that. Imagine if I left the great showman John Ringling. I'd be seen as a gold digger, an opportunistic enchantress who duped a grieving widower for her own gains. Never mind that I have my own money." Emily snorted and waved a hand in front of her. "Headlines: 'Temptress leaves impresario John Ringling with a broken heart.' You see, Sophie? I have no recourse but to make the best of a bad situation."

Sophie's eyebrows knit together as she considered Emily's words. "I see what you mean, Emily. Divorce is not kind to women, no matter what the circumstances. For men, it's a different matter. But you could—"she faltered then shook her head. "For you, it's compounded by the fact that you're married to a famous man everyone claims to know. The publicity would be crushing. I just wish there was something I could do for you."

Emily managed a smile. No solutions had been found to ease her unhappiness, but Sophie's empathy had soothed her. "Well, you've done enough just by listening to my sob story. But there is something you could do for me."

"Just say the word, Emily. I'll do it."

Emily chuckled. "I'm parched. Could you arrange for a tall cool gin and tonic?" Her expression turned serious. "And please, my friend, continue to be so much in love with James. Seeing you two together, why, it brings me joy, knowing that there can be a happily ever after."

After revealing her unhappiness to Sophie, sleep

eluded Emily that night. Sophie's kindness had been welcome but had offered no remedy. She could not leave John; that was clear. But neither could she continue to live under a perpetual cloud of misery. Twisting around in the tangled bedsheets, she told herself she must find a way for them to reconcile. John was stubborn, insensitive, and secretive about his business, but he was not unkind. When they first met, he had been besotted by her and wooed her with attention and compliments. She supposed even lie about his age was motivated by his desire to win her over. Could she captivate him once again?

Look in the mirror, Emily. Yes, John could be insufferable, but she was far from blameless. Had she been demanding? Unwilling to compromise? Unsympathetic? As for the circus, she had exhibited little interest in his life's work, his passion. She recoiled as she recalled a few snide, cutting barbs she had hurled at John. She could do better; she *would* do better.

So where was John now? Somewhere in her handbag she had an itinerary, but she'd barely looked at it. It hadn't really mattered where John was on the circus route; a little town in Pennsylvania was no different from one in Virginia as far as she was concerned. But to John, it did matter. She would write to him and let him know she missed him. Composing a letter to John in her mind, she eventually drifted off to sleep.

Emily woke with new resolve and found Sophie in the kitchen, squeezing halves of fresh oranges over the dome of a cut glass juicer.

"Where is James this morning?" She kept her tone cheerful. "And are you making fresh juice? How delightful!"

"Just one of the benefits of life in Florida." Sophie turned and scanned Emily's face. "James is off golfing. But how are you doing?"

"Sophie, I must apologize for my weepiness yesterday." Emily put out her hand to ward off Sophie's objections. "I've done some soul-searching and I feel a newfound determination to set things right with John. My dear friend, you have helped me see things in a new light."

Sophie dried her hands on a towel and embraced Emily. "I'm pleased you're feeling more positive."

"So," Emily stepped back and continued, "I think I need to do my part to rekindle what John and I once had. Maybe we were too hasty when we entered into a marriage, but regardless, here we are. I'm going to write to him and will do my very best to reconcile. It's the only way."

Sophie smiled. "You've been giving this a lot of thought all night long, I see." She pointed to a chair. "Sit down and let me set out breakfast. Then you can tell me more."

Emily sat, and Sophie bustled around her, pouring coffee and juice, placing a basket of muffins on the table.

"I confess I hardly slept a wink." Emily chuckled ruefully. "Sophie, do sit. You're spoiling me."

Sophie sat. "Now, tell me." She helped herself to a muffin, broke off a piece and nibbled on it as Emily laid out her plans.

She would meet John on the circus route or connect with him in New York. Yes, he had his faults; so did she. But she would focus on the positive. "Who knows? In a few months' time we might be seen as the most romantic couple in all of Florida—except for you and James, of course." Emily eyed her friend, wondering if Sophie viewed her as a Pollyanna or as a realistic and practical woman.

Sophie sipped her juice as she listened, then spoke. "I think you're being wise, Emily. And I wish you the best."

After breakfast, Emily took action. She found John's itinerary and composed a letter, copying it and addressing it to three different locations in care of the post offices in the New England towns where the circus would be performing. One of these letters, she hoped, would be delivered to the John on the circus grounds. She planned for New York to serve as her hub, and when days later, John responded that he would join her at the Park Avenue apartment, Emily bid farewell to Sophie and James and boarded a train for New York.

Chapter Twenty-Eight

ON THE DAY of his arrival, however, Emily was stunned when John walked through the door. How he had aged over the weeks that had passed since he had boarded his circus train. His face, once full and robust, was gaunt and sallow and his deep brown eyes were lined with creases. His shoulders slumped inside his ill-fitting suit coat, once impeccably tailored to fit his now diminished burly frame. While on their wedding day he written fifty-two as his age on their marriage license++++++++++++, that deception was now preposterous.

"Are you well, John?" The words tumbled out of her mouth before she could rein them in. She hugged him, anticipating that he would downplay any malady.

But he surprised her. "I've been a bit under the weather, Emily. Being on the road seems to be taking the stuffing out of me." He stroked her hair and kissed her. "But you are a sight for sore eyes. Your letters were the pick-me-up I needed, and I'm so pleased we can put our silly misunderstandings behind us."

Wrapped in his embrace, Emily murmured agreement, squelching the alarm she felt at his haggard appearance. "It's good to be with you at last, my dear."

John shuffled into the parlor, and although Emily had planned for an evening celebrating their reunion, John struggled to hide his exhaustion. He barely sipped at the drink she poured for him and declined when Emily offered to serve the dinner that the cook had prepared earlier. "Let me get some rest and then we shall spend some lovely days together, Emily. I'm sorry to be such a wet blanket."

Emily stood and held out her hands to guide him to his feet. "You poor dear. You've been working so hard. Time for you to get all of the rest you need." As she linked arms with him and walked toward his bedroom, Emily wondered if John's fatigue could be chalked up to a rigorous schedule or was it something more. No need to panic, Emily told herself. He's simply overtired. "You'll feel like your old self in a day or two," she assured him.

But June turned into July, and John did not improve or return to the circus. The man who always had a sparkle in his eye and a story to tell was now listless and lethargic. Like the foot injury he suffered on the dance floor at the Gasparilla Ball, a small cut he suffered when banging his shin on the steps of his circus train festered.

The summer Emily had planned—dinners with

friends at her favorite New York restaurants, cocktail parties in their apartment, get-togethers with her family—fell by the wayside. During the day, John struggled to attend to circus business while off the circuit and ignored Emily's appeals to consult a doctor. In his office, he telephoned Western Union several times a day and barked out the contents of his missives to his assistants on the road. Couriers arrived with thick brown envelopes stuffed with documents that he attended to. By evening, any good humor that John had possessed dissolved into crankiness and impatience under the weight of his exhaustion and ill health.

Emily's determination to strengthen their marriage was tested. *He's not himself. He's a sick man. Be kind.* Friends phoned to invite her to lunch or to ask her and John to dinner and oozed sympathetic platitudes when she was forced to decline. She felt like a prisoner, bound to the apartment by John's infirmities. In conversation, she remained breezy—"He'll be back to his old self in no time"—but she wondered if that day would ever come.

One morning, when Sam Gumpertz arrived at the apartment carrying a bulging attaché case, Emily met him at the door. "Sam, please don't be too long. John needs rest."

"I've spoken to him over the phone, and he sounds fit to me. I'll try not to overtax him. Aren't you a good wife to be so solicitous?" Sam patted Emily on her arm.

THE SECOND MRS. RINGLING

"But this business cannot wait."

"Sam..." Emily continued but was interrupted by John's booming voice coming from his office.

"Gumpertz, is that you I hear? Come on in!"

Sam eyed Emily and shrugged, then called out, "Will do, John!" He entered the office, reclosing the door behind him.

Emily quelled her impulse to open the door and scold both John and Sam. Couldn't they see that John was unwell? But John would simply accuse her of hovering and wave her away. What good would come of her objections?

When Sam emerged hours later, John was unable to escort him to the door and he beckoned Emily to show out their guest. This time Sam did speak to Emily. "The old man seems to be in some discomfort, eh?"

"Yes, he is. And handling all of this business seems to be taking its toll." She scowled at Sam, crossing her arms over her chest. "Couldn't you—"she began, then stifled her remark. She knew the answer to her question. This was not Sam's doing. John would never agree to relinquish any duties to Sam, insisting that he was the sole decision-maker. She bid Sam goodbye.

When Emily went back into John's office, he was standing, but his palms were pressed on the desktop to keep him upright. His face was red with exertion. "Can you help me into my bedroom, dear? I'm not sure I can walk without assistance. My leg—." He sucked air through his teeth as he attempted to stand erect.

She hurried to his side, slipping her arm around his waist and guiding him toward the office door, then into his room. "John, I insist. Your leg is clearly not getting better on its own. I'm phoning the doctor." This time, he did not argue with her.

AFTER THE EXAMINATION, Doctor summoned Emily into John's room. "Mrs. Ringling, you need to hear this was well. John, your leg is terribly inflamed. I've treated it for now, but it needs to be monitored closely. Wounds that don't heal indicate, John, that you are a diabetic."

John scoffed. "I'm not. It's just a damn cut. Nothing to get worked up over."

The doctor's stern warnings validated Emily's concerns, but she knew that John would continue to ignore the advice he was given. So, when John said, "I have a circus to keep going," and saw the doctor's frustration, she remained silent. If the doctor's words fell on deaf ears, where would hers land?

But the next day, the condition of John's wound worsened, and he was wracked with pain. Emily phoned the doctor once again.

"John, I'm transferring you to Seagate, out on Coney Island where you were last winter," the doctor pronounced. Emily expected John to refuse, to insist that he was fine, to grumble about the bad food he'd had there. But when he offered no rebuttal, Emily's heart clenched in fear. If he was too weak to battle with the doctor over his prognosis and the need for a hospital, then it was clear to Emily that John was seriously ill. The doctor asked to be directed to the telephone to alert the hospital of John's arrival, and Emily ushered him into the parlor to make the call. After he left, Emily made arrangements for their driver and reserved a room for herself at the Half Moon Hotel near the hospital.

In John's room, Emily packed a small valise for him, while John, his face carved with lines of pain, scribbled notes onto a legal pad. "Damn inconvenient. I'm making a list of the work I'll have to accomplish from my hospital bed. Emily, you must not allow anyone to know I'm being hospitalized. I'll telephone Sam, of course, but this remains a private matter. I have a business to run, and it won't serve us well if rumors of an illness start up." His voice was raspy but resolute. "I can't have the press getting wind of this."

Emily nodded and murmured agreement but wondered. The press? Would they really be interested in the health of Mr. John Ringling? She stroked the back of his hand. "I understand, John and I'll see to it. I've already phoned Lena, but she won't be spreading gossip. I had to let her know where I'll be, and she's planning to join me at the Half Moon Hotel. In fact, Nicholas will be driving her out there. He's got himself a new job as a driver, and he's able to use the car, so she says."

John snorted. "Nicholas has another job, huh? I can't imagine hiring that ne'er-do-well, but not my concern. Now help me up so I can get my briefcase packed." He struggled to stand.

"A briefcase of work? John, you're ill." But she knew he would insist, so she acquiesced. *Don't upset him*, she reminded herself. Now was the time to be a loving, devoted helpmeet. He'd be in a hospital room in just a couple of hours, and she would not have to contend with his demands once he was safely installed there. That responsibility would fall to the staff, and she would have some respite.

ONCE JOHN WAS settled into his hospital room, Emily, relishing the prospect of a peaceful evening, bid him a good night and headed to the Half Moon Hotel. Last winter, the place had been eerily quiet, but now it was bustling with Coney Island tourists. Children in bathing togs swatted beach balls at one another in the lobby while harried parents, weighed down with picnic baskets and beach paraphernalia, struggled to rein in their youngsters. Young honeymooners, blissfully unaware of the commotion around them, sauntered along, blocking Emily's path to the elevator. Exhausted from the day's events, she simply wanted to settle into her room, order a pot of tea, and sink into bed.

The next morning, she checked in on John. He'd had a restless night. Fussing with the bedcovers, he issued a litany of complaints. "Why am I even here? Where is the doctor? Isn't he coming to see me? And these nurses—they're impossible. Do you know they won't even let me light up a cigar?"

Emily made soothing sounds as she adjusted his blankets, poured him a cup of cold water—"This stuff tastes like soap!"—and tried to distract him with a description of the boardwalk. "When you're feeling better, maybe we can get a push chair and I can take you for a stroll."

"A push chair? Out in public? Absolutely not! Imagine what a stir that would make—'Invalid John Ringling requires a wheeled chair to get around.' I won't have it." He leaned back onto his pillow and closed his eyes. Underneath all his feisty pronouncements, Emily saw a man withered by pain and illness. Just how long would he be hospitalized before he regained his health? She wanted him well, for his sake as well as for hers.

When the doctor arrived to inspect John's wound, John insisted that she leave. "No need to have you hovering around me all day. Maybe I can get some work done if you're not here." He waved the back of his hand toward her.

"So, you're giving me my notice?" Emily's tone was

light, masquerading the annoyance she felt. Hadn't she demonstrated what a loving, attentive wife should do? And yet, she was being dismissed like she was a chambermaid who'd not attended to the dust under a bed.

John looked abashed. "I'm sorry, dear. I'm not myself, am I?" He turned to the doctor. "Emily has been stalwart in giving me the necessary attention." Then he turned back to Emily. "Come and see me later this evening. I promise I will be less irritable."

She kissed the top of his head, smoothing down stray wisps of hair with her fingers. "I'll be back later. Now get some rest."

Outside, the sun was shining, and a crisp sea breeze stirred through her hair and rustled her skirt. When Lena arrived, she decided, they'd take a stroll, and she could fill in her sister on John's condition. She arrived back at the hotel in time to see Lena emerging from a shiny black Cadillac at the main entrance. And was that Nicholas? She hardly recognized him, dressed in a chauffeur's black suit and cap. She hurried to greet them.

After hugging her sister, Emily turned to her nephew. "My, don't you look official? I hope you can still offer your aunt a hug." Without waiting for an answer, she embraced him and planted a quick kiss on his cheek.

"Aw, Auntie Emily, it's nice to see you." He rubbed his cheek with his palm. "Isn't this a swell car? My new boss said I could use it whenever he wasn't needing me, so I thought I'd help out Mama today and give her a ride. I need to pick up the boss in Manhattan later, but I might check out some of the sights while I'm here, too." He shoved his hands in his pockets and scanned his surroundings, nodding his head in approval.

Lena directed Nicholas to gather the luggage and together they followed Emily to the elevator.

Emily showed them into the small room, simply appointed but with a window facing the sea. "I was lucky to get us connecting accommodations, Lena. Sometimes it helps to mention the Ringling name."

"This is charming. Such a pretty counterpane." She patted the chintz bed covering. While Nicholas stood by the window, peeling back the curtains to study the view, Lena opened her suitcase and piled its contents on the bed. "So just how is John? You've told me so little."

Emily glanced at Nicholas, but he appeared to be oblivious to their conversation, his forehead pressed to the windowpane so that he could view the boardwalk below. "Well, I wish I could be optimistic, but it's pretty serious. His leg is severely inflamed, and the doctor says he has diabetes, so it's not healing well." She lowered her voice to a whisper. "The doctor went so far as to threaten an amputation, but that's unlikely now that he is being treated in the hospital. Lena, John is adamant that all this be kept quiet, so please don't repeat what I'm telling you."

Lena looked in the mirror, removed her hat—a frothy concoction of pink straw and yellow daisies—then fluffed her hair. "Now who would I tell? It will stay between us. I'm just so happy that I could keep you company while you're tending to him away from the city."

Emily smiled at her sister. "I feel better now that you're here. John has sent me away for the afternoon, so how about we find a nice café and have some lunch." She turned to Nicholas whose back was to her. "Nick, want to join us?"

He swung around to face her. "Nah, thanks anyway. I might just wander around by myself for a while. Peruse the scenery, you know." He smirked. "Then I better get back in the Caddie."

Lena reached out to hug her son. "You drive carefully now, dear." He gave his mother, then Emily, a peck on the cheek and was out the door.

"You know, Emily, I believe that young man has come around. Didn't he look handsome in his chauffeur uniform? And he's not asking me for money lately either." She sighed and clutched her hands as if in prayer. "I thank God every day."

LENA ACCOMPANIED EMILY to the hospital on the second day of her visit, and John seemed buoyed by her presence. He had often complained to Emily that Lena was a chatterbox, but Lena proved to be a willing listener to John's tales of life in the circus. He agreed to sit in the solarium and entertained the women with descriptions of the new feats performed by the aerialist Karl Wallenda.

Lena peppered his description with an abundance of *Oh, my*'s and *I can't imagine!* 's that kept John from focusing on his pain. Then Sam Gumpertz arrived, carrying his now-familiar battered attaché case.

"Ladies, time for Sam and me to conduct some business. The circus doesn't stop just because I'm holed up in a hospital. Why don't you run along and take in some of that sea air?"

On the boardwalk, Emily linked arms with Lena. "You're good medicine, Lena. John loves sharing his circus tales with you. I'm afraid I'm a poor audience for his stories. I can't imagine why anyone would want to do what that Wallenda character does."

"Nor can I," Lena said. "But we did distract him from his illness for a bit, didn't we? It's the least I can do since you've treated me to a getaway on the shore."

EMILY ARRIVED IN the Half Moon dining room before Lena the next morning, settling herself in at her usual table. The waiter brought her coffee and offered her a newspaper. "I'm afraid no more copies of the *Times* are available at the moment. Will this suit?" He handed her the *World Telegram*.

"That's fine." Emily scanned the front page as she added sugar to her coffee, but she dropped her spoon when she took in the headline splayed across the page. "John Ringling Near Death! Both legs amputated!"

What on earth! Where had this outlandish story come from? The article had some facts—John's hospitalization at the Seagate, his diabetes diagnosis—but a double amputation? Ludicrous! Emily grabbed her handbag and rushed from the dining room. These lies must be recanted. But how? Her head swam. What would John think if he saw this? Or when he saw it? Surely it would get back to him. How could this have been published in a newspaper? Could Sam put a stop to this? How far had such rumors spread?

She dashed to the concierge desk. "I must be connected to Mr. Gumpertz's room at once," she sputtered to the man behind the desk. "Or send a message up to him immediately."

Over the eyeglasses perched on his nose, he eyed her coolly. "Yes, madam. And you are…?"

"I'm Mrs. John Ringling, a guest in this hotel. Please do as I ask." She spat out her words, then took a deep breath to quell her roiling panic. "Please ask him to meet me here in the lobby as soon as he can. It's imperative."

"Of course, Mrs. Ringling." The concierge motioned toward a chair. "Do sit down and I'll contact him immediately."

THE SECOND MRS. RINGLING

But Emily could not sit. Instead, she paced the lobby, waiting for Gumpertz to appear. When he arrived moments later, disheveled and without his briefcase, Emily thrust the newspaper into his hands. "Have you seen this?"

He quickly skimmed the paper, his complexion paling as he read. "My heavens! What nonsense! Where would they get such ridiculous information?" he searched Emily's face for an answer.

Emily noted that curious passersby in the lobby were watching them. "Let's sit down, Sam. We're drawing attention." Her head was pounding. John would be livid. Her mind conjured up his image, his face purple with rage, his blood pressure rocketing upward.

They found two wing chairs far from the main desk and huddled in quiet conversation. Sam began. "This has to be stopped in its tracks. I'll contact this rag," he said, waving the paper in her direction. "Then I'll call reputable papers and emphasize that John is well, fit, fully recovered." He sank back into the tufted upholstery. "This is terrible for business. It will make the circus look like it's in disarray. This has to be quashed firmly."

"I'm thinking of John, not the damn circus, Sam." Her panic had turned into outrage. "How are we going to break it to him? Or will he already have seen this by the time one of us arrives at the hospital? You know he begins every day by reading any paper he can get his hands on. This false story could affect his health dramatically." She grabbed the arm of Sam's chair. "I will go to the hospital immediately and tell John what has happened. But I expect that you will arrive shortly and will explain to him what you are doing to dispel this gross fabrication."

"See here, Emily," Sam began. But she was already on her feet.

"I will see you later, Sam." She strode across the lobby toward the main entrance.

When she neared the elevator, its door opened and Lena emerged, dressed in a gossamer summer dress the color of cotton candy. "Emily! I'm sorry I'm late to breakfast. Are we going to visit John soon?"

"I'm going alone this morning. Something has come up." Emily tried to skirt around her sister, but Lena grabbed her arm.

"What is it? Has John taken a turn? My, you look as if—"

"I believe he's fine, and I cannot discuss it now. I must go. I'll catch you up on everything later." Emily pulled herself away and hurried forward. Outside, she waved off the doorman's offer of a taxi and hurried down the sidewalk. She only hoped that John had not already been informed of the report she'd found smeared across the front page.

Once in John's hospital room, she found him sitting

in a chair, his leg propped up on a stool. His expression was placid as he focused on a newspaper and his complexion looked rosier than it had in days.

Swallowing hard, Emily leaned over and stroked his shoulder. "You look in a fine fettle this morning, John." *And I'm about to change all that.* "What are you reading?"

"*Variety* from a few days ago. Sam brought it to me yesterday. From the city. No one in this godforsaken hospital could get a copy for me. Doubt if most of them ever heard of it." He held it up and pointed to a story. "Nice piece in here on that Wallenda fellow of ours. He's going to make me millions, Emily. And he's got a whole passel of kids he's training as well. If I do say so myself, showcasing him was brilliant on my part."

"Sounds like good publicity for the circus. Thanks to you, dear, Mr. Wallenda is a star." She sat on the edge of a chair across from him, twisting her fingers through the straps of her handbag. "Has the doctor been in yet today to see you?"

"No, not yet, but I feel like I'm much improved. The leg is not as painful as it was. Maybe I can get out of here." John scanned Emily's face. "Say, Emily, you look peaked. Is staying in that Half Moon getting to you? No Hotel Ringling, right?" He reached out and patted her hand.

"Oh, the hotel is fine. But something has come up." She dropped her eyes to her lap. "I hate to upset you, but

I must tell you." She squeezed her eyes shut, then opened them and continued, describing the *World Telegram* story in detail.

At first, John was speechless. Then he erupted, shouting and waving his fists. "How did this happen? Did you go blabbing to someone? Emily, I told you to keep this under wraps. It's outrageous!" He tried to stand, but when his leg would not allow it, he sank back into his chair. "Damnation, Emily!"

"Me? You accuse me? Why is this my fault?" She breathed deeply, holding in a torrent of angry retorts. *He's upset. Don't make this worse by arguing.* Still, she felt heat rising in her chest. She'd been solicitous, the epitome of the concerned wife, stuck on Coney Island and now he was throwing accusations her way?

"You must have let it slip somehow." Scowling, he pointed at her and then crossed his arms over his chest.

"John, get a hold of yourself. You'll make yourself more ill." She poured a cup of water from a pitcher and handed it to him, but he waved it away.

"I don't need any water, damn it. I cannot believe this! Someone must have told the press. This is terrible! Outrageous!" he continued to sputter while Emily forced herself to remain quiet. Why on earth would he choose to blame her? Who had she told? Only Lena, and Lena had no one to tell. Who could it have been? Some hospital worker? Tuning out John's rant, she ticked off possibilities.

When John barked, "Get Sam in here immediately," Emily brought her attention back to her husband. Compared to when she first arrived, his appearance now alarmed her. He began coughing, his angry words caught in his throat.

Emily offered to fetch a nurse, but John shook his head wildly. She rubbed his back, and eventually he was able to suppress his cough. "Sam is already on his way," she assured him. "This will all be handled." She hoped that Sam would be there soon, filled with assertions that this was going to blow over without a ripple. But would John see it that way? His vanity had been scarred by his afflictions and he detested any loss of his privacy. This would wear on him like no physical ailment could.

When Sam walked in, his eyes darted from Emily to John.

"I see Emily has told you about the *World Telegram* bit. With the trouble the business is in, this is a mighty blow. This is what I'm doing to quell this ridiculous story." He set his briefcase down on the floor and rummaged for a yellow legal pad, already covered with scrawled notes. "I've already sent a strongly worded telegram demanding a retraction."

John gripped the arms of his chair, still struggling to calm himself. "Good start." He pointed at the legal pad. "Read it to me."

Emily interrupted. "Is there anything you'd like me to do, John? Sam?"

John scowled at her. "Well, if you know anyone who would believe this foolishness, you need to set them straight immediately."

Responding to his accusatory tone, Emily spoke through clenched teeth. "Dear, I realize you're upset. Why don't I leave you and Sam to work this out?"

John grunted. "You're right. This is business now, and Sam and I will handle it. Go ahead and be on your way, Emily."

"I will." She forced herself to kiss his cheek before she left the room. Where had her coddling of this man gotten her? Laying blame at her feet? It struck her that he was more than angry, more than a victim of wounded pride. He seemed frightened, she realized. His words, "the trouble the business is in," resurfaced in her mind. So, the business was in serious trouble, as she suspected. Physical vulnerability now coupled with a threat to his reputation and standing in the world of commerce seemed to have worked together to instill fear in him. She headed back to the Half Moon, to find Lena and to decide what to do next.

OVER THE NEXT few days, John rallied every bit of strength he could muster to confront the rumors. To John's dismay, Sam reported that the United Press new service had also gotten hold of the story, and Sam fired off telegrams and made phone calls to demand a recant. The double amputation was simple enough to disavow. After all, John was in possession of both legs. But to prove to skeptics that he was not at death's door, John insisted on leaving the hospital and joining Emily at the Half Moon Hotel.

Emily sent Lena back to New Jersey, promising her sister that she would contact her soon. With Lena out of the way, she discreetly oversaw the arrangements of turning the hotel room into a hospital room for John. This way, he could claim he was no longer hospitalized, when in reality, the medical care was coming to him at the Half Moon. Then Emily wrote breezy letters infused with a light-heartedness she did not feel, informing friends who might have heard the rumors that all was well.

One reporter asked the manager of the Half Moon to weigh in and in a follow-up article, Mr. Goldberg was quoted claiming that Mr. Ringling was only "slightly indisposed." Dressing in his usual business suit, John was interviewed by another sympathetic reporter who verified John's good health in a *Variety* story. Meanwhile Sam contacted the editor of the *Sarasota Herald* and the paper ran a long article on its front page debunking the original report.

"Listen to this, Emily," John crowed, holding up the

Sarasota Herald he'd received by mail. Propped up in bed with several pillows, he was eating his breakfast from a tray that room service had delivered. "George Lindsay has set this to rights. Here's what he wrote for the front page. 'Mr. Ringling is known as a hale and hearty man. He eats sparingly, especially of meats, and smokes de-nicotinized cigars and takes exercise daily. He can do what a younger man cannot—touch his fingers to the floor without bending his knees.'" He handed her the paper. "So, this is all behind me."

Was it? Emily knew George Lindsay, the paper's editor and a friend of John's. A former preacher, he embraced effusive language, both in print and in person. It did not surprise her that he had published this glowing account of John, but she had doubts that Sarasotans would take it at face value. She was astonished at the flurry of speculation this story had sparked in New York. In Sarasota, where everyone knew John and would feel compelled to voice an opinion, she envisioned a stew of wild conjecture, with each acquaintance of John's tossing their own tidbits into the pot.

She skimmed the full story. "John, it says you're rejoining the circus in Cleveland?" She looked up and tipped her head quizzically. "You are not well enough for that." John had left the hospital without the doctor's approval, and he still required daily care.

"Ah, Emily, I'll be fine. And I'm not headed there

right away. Don't fret." Yet he grimaced as he slid the tray away and attempted to stand. Cautiously and with some effort, he managed to place both feet on the floor and to shuffle into the bathroom.

But fret she did. Like Karl Wallenda, John seemed to be teetering on a high wire while his beloved circus, his art and his Ca d'Zan balanced precipitously on his shoulders, and she was struggling to hold the safety net below.

Chapter Twenty-Nine

JOHN WAS DETERMINED to rejoin the circus in Cleveland, but his persistent infirmities prevented him from doing so. "I've got to get out of this cracker box of a hotel room, the doctor be damned. He's not the one crammed in here. The closet in my rail car is bigger and certainly more well-appointed."

"Your health has to come first, John," Emily said, but she too was eager to leave the hotel. Its close quarters were stifling, the food lackluster. She escaped John's bedside by taking her daily walks along the seaside, but it was anything but soothing. She was repulsed by the boardwalk crammed with unkempt frolickers of every stripe—Irish, Italian, Polish—and their unruly, sticky children, where the cloying sweetness of spun sugar mixed with the acrid smokiness of hot dogs under a cacophony of honky-tonk music and skeeball barkers' shouts.

So back to Manhattan they went. John seemed to perk up in his familiar surroundings, and Emily sought out friends to join them for cocktails on occasion. John made sure to settle himself into a large wing chair before guests arrived so that his unsteadiness would go unnoticed, and from there he regaled his visitors with circus tales, old and new, while puffing on his ever-present cigars. A nurse checked in on occasion, allowing Emily to get out of the apartment, to meet old acquaintances for lunch and to frequent her favorite dress shops, where she scrupulously charged her purchases to her own account and not to John's.

Emily had little inclination to dwell on the state of her marriage. For the present, she swallowed little aggravations—John's braggadocio, his insistence that she not be a part of any financial conversations that he held behind his closed office door. She checked herself when she was tempted to toss out a snide remark. At times she felt like an actress on a stage, playing the role of the doting wife. She wondered if her performances might eventually become second nature, a sincere representation of her true self.

Then in August, another bombshell exploded on the front page of the newspapers. This time, the reporting was accurate. While John had been recovering from his illness, Edith Ringling and Sam Gumpertz had united against him, restructuring the Ringling organization. Edith was now the head of the Ringling Brothers Circus and Sam, John's once loyal friend, would manage the daily operations. While the Ringling name was still emblazoned on circus train cars and on the handbills that papered towns across the county, John was no longer the Circus King.

The business editors of the newspapers were unable to resist the story of John's ouster. After *The Chicago Daily News* announced that Edith Ringling had taken over the management of the circus, the New York papers reprinted the story, then opined on the financial health of both the circus and of John himself.

When Emily, skimming the *New York Times* while drinking her morning coffee, read the story, her heart lurched. *Was this true?* Struggling to regain good health so he could return to the circuit, John would be destroyed. Although there was little doubt he relished in basking in his own celebrity, Emily knew how much her husband loved the performers, the animals, and every crew member who pounded a spike into the ground. This could not happen to him, not now.

She glanced over the top of the newspaper at John. Had he seen the story? She assumed he had, since paper was in disarray when she joined him at the table, but he appeared unperturbed, intent on stirring cream into his coffee. Keeping her voice gentle, she said, "Has The *Times* embellished this story of the circus management?"

Her question wiped the calmness from his face. "Don't hector me about it. Months ago, we began to restructure the organization. This is just routine business."

She should have recognized that he would explain no further, but she pressed on. "But John, the paper is reporting that Edith is now—"

"Enough! Enough! I won't hear another word from you." Hampered by his limp, He stormed off as best he could, and slammed his bedroom door behind him.

At first Emily chose to ignore this outburst, recognizing his distress and embarrassment. But no paper would concoct something out of nothing, would they? There had to be something he could do—they could do.

And why must I be the target of his wrath when it's Edith and Sam who have betrayed him? Emily followed him to his bedroom and swung open the door. "I'm sad to see that your world is in a shambles right now. But your world is my world as well, John. Without a full explanation from you, I have no choice but to piece together the true story by reading the papers." She did not wait for a response but returned to her coffee and newspaper once again.

Staring at the article without really seeing it, she recalled earlier meetings at Ca d'Zan when John, Edith, and Sam had met behind the closed doors of his office. One day stood out in her mind, the day that Hester and she had first gone out for a drive. When she returned, she had been shocked to hear John bellowing from behind his office doors. "I'll sue you both," he'd shouted at

Edith and Sam. And what of Edith's rant about his ill-advised investments? "You're running us into the ground, John!" *Were they truly ruined? Had Edith been right or just angry?* Emily replayed the scenes from that day—how only moments later, Edith and Sam bustled down the stairs and shook hands in the driveway before they departed in their own automobiles. Neither had even noticed Emily, out of sight in the solarium as they left.

Then, as always, John had refused to speak to her about it. That evening, they had bitter words about her "interference" in his business dealings. Months had passed, time for the groundwork to be laid for a restructuring, one that she doubted had been favored by John. The *Times* was now reporting that the accounting office had been moved to New York, and John's office would remain in Sarasota. But what would he actually do there, if he was no longer in charge?

LATER THAT EVENING, John shuffled into the parlor and offered a mild apology. "Emily, I should not have spoken so harshly. Edith and Sam want a takeover, but I am still in command of the circus. Take my word for it." He attempted a faint smile but could only manage to draw his lips into a thin line. "When the *Sarasota Herald* arrives in the mail, you will see a completely different version of the story—my version."

Clearly, he was working to put a positive face on things. She wanted to stroke the worry lines from his brow but sensed that he would rebuff any sympathy from her. But she couldn't help but wonder what her role in the ruse would be. He continued to leave her in the dark, all the while expecting her to carry on as if all was well. How could he not understand that she was already worn down from keeping his illness away from prying eyes. Now, she dreaded the hovering around of more rumor mongers. She felt her temper rising.

"So, rather than being informed by you in detail, I must rely on the *Herald*. I see. Precisely what shall I tell those who inquire after seeing the story in all the New York papers? We are here in New York, John. You do realize that people—including our friends and associates—will come to me for information, don't you?" She strode across the room to her desk and held up a stack of telephone messages that the housekeeper had placed there. "I've avoided answering my calls, but I can't do that indefinitely."

"Say nothing. Can you manage to do that? I don't need any more rumors swirling." His eyes narrowed at her.

Could she simply say nothing? Pretend all was well? Keep the gossips at bay by portraying herself as the happy wife of a successful businessman? She sighed. "I'll do my best. Shall I adopt the persona of Helen Twelvetrees?

After all, even when her husband jumped out of that hotel window, she displayed a calm face to the world."

John scowled. "Must you always employ sarcasm?"

"Just trying to inject some light-heartedness in this untenable situation, John." Once he had found her witty, delighting in her clever quips; now she realized that he only found her sarcastic.

"I see no cause for levity here. Really, Emily, do not overdramatize." He hobbled back to his office., leaving her with a half-hearted apology and yet another reprimand.

WHAT FOLLOWED WERE days spent in a turmoil, with John barely speaking to Emily except to demand that all New York City newspapers be brought to him immediately. Emily dutifully returned the phone calls she received, employing her skills as a dramatist by tossing out a practiced tinkling laugh and an "Oh, my! You don't believe everything you read in the papers, do you?" All the while, she wondered if John were fielding similar calls, responding with bravado and hearty laughter at any implication that he had been pushed aside. How painful that must be for him, pretending that all was well while churning with anguish inside. If only he would take her into his confidence. Together, they could defeat Edith and Sam, she was sure of it.

She found herself hovering outside John's closed

door, chagrined that she was now employing a tactic that she had once chastised Martha for using. Eavesdropping on his blistering phone calls to Sam Gumpertz, she heard John accusing his once-trusted friend of backstabbing and treachery. Emily was tempted to confront Sam herself if she had the opportunity. How could Sam have been party to this? Hadn't he been solicitous when John was so ill? And when the rumors of the amputation appeared, Sam had been forceful in discrediting them all.

Perhaps his work to show John as strong and in command had simply been an attempt to ensure financial health of the circus rather than his desire to defend his long-time friend and associate. Emily now saw Sam Gumpertz in a new light. Under his affable exterior, he was a cunning businessman, willing to shove John aside if it meant financial gain.

And what about Edith, the widow of John's brother Charles? From their first meeting, Edith had impressed her as a shrewd woman, not a foolish, flighty one with no head for business. But how could she be so callous as to humiliate John this way? After Edith's initial coldness when Emily first arrived at Ca d'Zan, she became less aloof, even congenial at Hester's Thanksgiving dinner. Emily had cherished the warmth of that day, summoning up the memory of the family gathered at the table as if it were a candle whose glow she could rekindle. The cold breath of betrayal now snuffed out any flicker of good will.

Emily created scenarios in her mind when she might confront either Sam or Edith but told herself that this would be unwise. When the *Sarasota Herald* arrived in the mail, she scrutinized the story that was front and center on page one. The Ringling auditor, J. F. Wadworth denied what he termed as rumor. He explained that the legal operations would be under one roof in New York City, and that John would maintain his office in Sarasota in the Ringling Bank building. The paper quoted a telegram from John: "I still remain as head of all circuses. There has been no change." Again the editor had taken John's words at face value. The piece answered few of the questions that the New York articles had roused, but Emily tried to convince herself that it was enough to satisfy the Sarasotans who saw John as a local hero and luminary.

She knew better. This was not business as usual, no matter what the *Sarasota Herald* said. If things hadn't changed, why was John at odds with Sam? And Edith? One day, Emily intercepted a phone call from her sister-in-law meant for John. Edith offered no pleasantries, asking briskly to speak to John, as if Emily were merely his private secretary and not his wife or a member of the Ringling family. Emily stifled her inclination to ask probing questions. But why bother? Edith would refuse and might even report her inquiries to John. She had no appetite for more of his angry outbursts. "He is tied up at the moment. I will tell him you called." Her hand trembling, she hung up without saying goodbye or awaiting further instructions.

AFTER A FEW weeks in New York, John had recovered enough to return to the circus, now making its circuit in Illinois and Iowa before it headed to Southern states as autumn loomed. This time, he made no pretense of asking her to accompany him. "I believe I'll travel alone, Emily. So much for me to catch up on after my absence."

Emily heard a forced nonchalance in his tone and responded in kind. "I think that's best, darling. Won't it be nice for you to be among your people once again? You always come alive when you're with them. When you return to Sarasota, I'll join you there," she promised.

He gave her shoulder a light squeeze. "That would be best. I'll be so busy."

He could barely contain his delight at leaving the confines of the apartment. Emily had no wish to traipse around the country with him in his train car, but it stung that he expressed no regrets at leaving her behind. When had his desire for her been snuffed out? When the day came for his departure, he hugged her and said, "I'll see you in Florida in a few weeks."

"I'll miss you, darling." Now that his departure was imminent, Emily thought she understood his relief, but it stung. Maybe he was doing the best thing for them for once. Maybe being apart would spark some tenderness between them. Throughout the summer, they had maintained a semblance of peace and harmony but there were many cracks. John was snappish; Emily tried not to respond in kind but was not always successful. Illness, business reversals, rumors had taken their toll. Yes, this time weeks apart would benefit them both.

Once John left, Emily invited Sophie, back in the city with her husband James, to join her for lunch in the apartment. Emily had had her fill of luncheons in Delmonico's and other posh dining rooms where she felt that her every word, every gesture was put under a microscope. She was weary of warding off questions, some well-meaning, some prying.

A so-called friend had placed a soothing hand on Emily's arm and had arranged her face into an expression of concern that Emily found as authentic as her blazing red hair. "How is John's health, Emily? You poor dear, working so hard to keep him well."

Emily had resisted the impulse to slap her hand away. Did this woman, smiling through lips caked in crimson lipstick, really care, or was she implying that John was an invalid, and Emily was chained to his bedside, ministering to him? Emily channeled her inner actress to serve up a gushing, "How kind of you to be concerned!" offering a bright smile of her own. "Why, he is hale and hearty!"

Or, when another woman she knew from her Junior League days, mentioned, "Goodness, I keep seeing John's picture in the *Times*. Of course, I don't pretend to understand the financial news of the day, but—" Emily nonchalantly speared an artichoke with her fork and tossed out, "Oh my dear, don't even think of it. I'm sure you're accustomed to seeing your Lawrence's name in the paper is well, so you know that hints of financial distress are overblown. Gracious, your suit is lovely. Some styles just seem to be timeless, don't they?"

When Sophie arrived, Emily was once again warmed by the radiance of her friend, who wore a summer frock dappled with yellow pansies. Emily saw her own uninspired brown tweed skirt and simple beige blouse in stark contrast to her friend's apparel. When had she become so drab? "Sophie, you look like sunshine itself. Are you and James as madly in love as when I was with you in Coral Gables?"

"I'm pleased to report that we are. Sometimes I wake up and want to pinch myself." She plucked off her white cotton gloves and followed Emily into the parlor. "I'd forgotten how exquisite this apartment is, Emily. Do you love it?"

"You're kind, Sophie. I've tried to add my touches, and subtract some of Mable's, but—." She hesitated. "Let me get us a gin and tonic, and then we'll talk. I gave the housekeeper the afternoon off after she arranged lunch for us, so we won't be interrupted."

Once they had settled in with their drinks, Sophie studied her friend. "So, dear, just how are you?"

Emily slumped into the cushions. "Well, it's been an eventful few months, as you know from my letters. Where to begin?" With Sophie, she could lower her guard and speak freely. Taking a deep breath, her words tumbled out—her determination to reconcile with John, the illness that had led to his hospital stay and the rumors of amputations and his near death.

Sophie interjected. "Your letters only hinted at what a mess this all was. That must have been a terrible time for both of you." She rubbed Emily's shoulder. "But I can see that you've been a stalwart wife. John must be so appreciative."

Emily stared into her glass, swirling the ice cubes. "I don't know if that is true." Then she brightened. "Let me freshen our drinks and set out our lunch. I honestly didn't mean to burden you, Soph." She stood.

"Don't be silly, my friend. Haven't we been through thick and thin with one another? We vowed with a pinky swear to be friends forever, right?" She wiggled her little finger at Emily.

"Right." Emily locked her little finger with Sophie's. "We do go a long way back, don't we? Come, all that 'Woe is me' has made me hungry." At lunch, Emily steered the conversation down other paths. John's tenuous position with the circus was too much to explore with her friend, and how could she put her own feelings of impending doom into words? Sophie had lifted her spirits a bit by listening. She wouldn't inundate her with more.

Chapter Thirty

SUMMER GAVE WAY to autumn and as the weather cooled, the entire city of New York seemed to be under a pall. Thankfully, the details of the Ringling reorganization faded from the pages of the newspapers. Instead, grim stories of tent cities called Hoovervilles, populated by the homeless, sprouting up throughout the city along with the campaign promises of Franklin Roosevelt and the incumbent Herbert Hoover became front page news. Although Hoover proclaimed, "We are turning the corner!" Emily was skeptical. Daily, even in her tony neighborhood, she passed unemployed men huddled on street corners, desperate and homeless. Did they have families somewhere? Who was caring for them? She wanted to believe what Franklin Roosevelt was saying, that "Happy days are here again!"

Emily had little interest in politics in prior elections. Pleased that women had gained the right to vote twelve years earlier, she had not found it necessary to go to the polls herself. This year was different. As a daughter of wealthy German immigrants, she had taken for granted her well-appointed home and wardrobes filled with beautiful clothes and had always stood on a high rung of the social ladder. As the Depression worsened, her eyes opened to the plight of others, even some of her set who had fallen onto hard times. No one was immune, she realized. Even her husband, considered one of the country's wealthiest men, teetered on this ladder of prosperity. She devoured the articles about the election, studying the platforms each candidate was proposing. Both she and Sophie set aside the topics of the latest fashions and pondered the issues in lively conversations. They both agreed that they would cast their first vote for Roosevelt.

What would John think of her decision? There was a time when they had sparred good-naturedly about a range of topics. Were talkies better than silent films? Was the Empire State Building a positive addition to the city's architecture? Should Prohibition be dissolved? He had relished their intellectual give and take, but in recent months he had shown little interest in her point of view. He had once been a staunch Republican, even luring Warren Harding to Sarasota before his death. That was before the Crash, however. Maybe his personal losses had swayed him to consider switching parties, but Emily had no intention of prodding him on that point, especially from afar.

John continued on the circus route and his only

communication with Emily came in the form of brief telegrams. "Sold out show in Appleton," "Fine weather in Springfield draws big crowds," followed by "Fondly, John." *Fondly? Hardly the word that a husband desperately missing his wife would choose.* Reading yet another missive on the flimsy Western Union paper, she crumpled them up and tossed it aside. *He's been unwell, under tremendous stress.*

"Absence makes the heart grow fonder," she told herself and wrote long letters brimming with good cheer and endearments, carefully maneuvering around any gloominess, omitting any reference to Hoovervilles and her political opinions. Peppering her letters with declarations of her devotion and reminders of happier days they'd spent together, she clung to the notion that she and John would once again find harmony.

IN NOVEMBER THEY reunited in Sarasota. Emily welcomed the balmy Florida warmth after the blustery chill of New York, but she and John had made little headway in knitting together their frayed marriage. Days began and ended with a perfunctory kiss on the cheek, but John swaddled himself in a work, leaving early each day for his office in the Ringling Bank building. The unavoidable fact of John's diminished role in the circus stained everything, from whom she might invite in for cocktails to what invitations they might accept.

John was adamant. "I won't be in the same room as Sam or Edith. I'm forced to face them for business purposes, but nowhere else will I be subjected to them." So, the Albees were welcome at Ca d'Zan; the Fields, longtime friends of Edith, were not. One evening, Emily and John found themselves at a dinner party where Edith appeared.

Their hostess, whose deceased husband had known John from the yacht club, was oblivious to the tensions and gushed when she greeted them in her foyer. "So nice that you could be here! The Edwards and the Primes are here, and Edith just arrived." Out of the corner of her eye, Emily saw John's shoulders stiffen and she gave him a gentle nudge with her elbow. How could this woman not know about the rift? Hadn't it been the main course at gossip banquet or months? "So kind of you to invite us. I hope you'll seat us near you so we can catch up. I'm dying to hear all about your little grandchildren."

"Yes, it's been so long since we've seen you." The woman beamed at Emily and beckoned to a maid dressed in a black dress and a frilly white cap and apron. "Milly, please see that Mr. and Mrs. Ringling have a drink. I'll check the place cards just to be sure you and John are right near me." She patted Emily's hand and scurried away.

Drink in hand, John zeroed in on another guest in the living room and steered Emily in his direction. He boomed, "Look who's here! Emily, you know George Prime and his wife Clara." He reached out and shook the man's and vigorously. "Hey, George, you son of a gun! How are you? Clara, you look lovely." They successfully managed to avoid Edith through cocktails and at dinner, Emily feigned interest in the prattling of her hostess about her grandchildren. John, avoiding eye contact with is sister-in-law across from him, steered the subject to his art collection. "It will be opening up after the new year, I can assure you," he promised his listeners.

Would it, Emily wondered. She had not heard this before. In fact, she had all but forgotten about John's dealer, Lulu, and his unctuous fawning over John. At any rate, John had navigated around the subject of the circus throughout the meal, and for this she was grateful.

Once in the car on the way back to Ca d'Zan, Emily twisted her shoulders to loosen knots of tension. "You nicely managed to keep out of Edith's path this evening. My neck is sore from keeping myself from turning in her direction."

John guffawed. "What was that woman thinking, inviting both of us. I nearly walked out."

"Well, I'm glad you didn't." Emily chuckled. "Who would have listened to her go on about those grandchildren?" Then she broached the subject of the art museum. "John, I'm surprised to hear you mention that the museum would be opening. I didn't realize that was in the offing. Have you been working with Lulu recently?"

John scoffed. "Lulu? No! He and I have parted ways. All he's done is hound me for money. I'll handle it all on my own."

"Well, do you owe him money?" She immediately regretted her question. It was as if she stepped on to an ice pond and could hear it crackling underneath her feet.

"Once again, Emily, you've chosen to belittle me." His fingers tightened around the steering wheel.

"No, John, no. I apologize if it sounded that way." She reached out and stroked his hand. "Please let's not quarrel. I'd love to see the museum opened if that is what you want." She sealed her lips together, waiting for his response.

He grunted. "I never want to quarrel, Emily. Let's just drop the whole conversation." He brought the car to a stop in the driveway of Ca d'Zan.

Emily waited for him to open the car door for her until she saw him heading up the steps to the front door. *So, I'll open it myself. Another little nicety seems to have evaporated from our marriage.* Silently, she followed him into the foyer.

He reached into his pocket and drew out a cigar. "I'm going out on the terrace for a smoke. Good night."

He allowed her to kiss his cheek before she headed for the stairs. She heard him call after her, "I need to be back in New York next week for a while. Will you join me?"

"Certainly. Good night, dear." She shivered as she climbed the stairs to the second floor. The ice on the pond hadn't given way completely, but she had come treacherously close to falling into the freezing depths.

Chapter Thirty-One

CHRISTMASTIME IN NEW York had always been magical for Emily, but this year, its enchantment had dimmed. On a shopping trip to Barney's she stopped short when she passed the spot where she had first encountered Edward. The image of his face, exuding warmth and a zest for life, caught Emily's breath.

Was it really one year ago? What might my life have become if Edward—? She shook her head, blinking her eyes to dispel the visage of Edward's smiling face, and headed for the exit. She could not shop here, not at Christmas. The cherubs and trumpets that festooned the ceilings only brought her heartache. The sight of poinsettias that seemed to adorn every storefront reminded her of the one that Edward had brought her.

But Christmas could not be avoided altogether. Once home, she contacted a florist to order garland and greenery for their apartment, stipulating that absolutely no poinsettias be included. Knowing that John would balk at spending Christmas Day with her sisters in New Jersey, she strategized.

The next morning, while pouring John's coffee at breakfast, "John, knowing how busy you've been, I mentioned to my sisters that you will want to stay home on Christmas Day."

"Absolutely. I have no intention of traipsing to New Jersey. I'm not up to the exertion." He smeared a muffin with butter and bit into it.

"But I do love being with family at the holidays." She sighed then sat across from him, propping her chin onto her hands. "What about a little gathering here, maybe a few days before the twenty-fifth? Nothing overblown."

How could he refuse? With no mention about his avoidance of exertion, he'd already informed her of several dinner parties they'd be attending, including Flo Ziegfeld's lavish affair. She saw John, ever the impresario, swanning around with her on his arm while she pretended to be fascinated by his every word. She waited for his response, ready to argue her case.

John sipped his coffee. *Was he searching for a reason to say no?* He set down his cup. "Go ahead. Invite them." Then he smiled. "Ask Olga if she'll bring *pfeffernusse*."

"Will do. She'll be flattered you asked." Altercation avoided; Emily moved ahead with plans for a cozy family dinner.

But a gathering of the Haag family never happened.

On the morning of the Ziegfeld affair, John woke in excruciating pain. "Emily," he shouted. "I can't get out of bed."

Emily found John sitting on his bed's edge, his pajamas rolled back to reveal his right leg, hideously inflamed. She bent to examine it.

John was panting, his face flushed. "Don't! Don't touch it!'

Emily had never seen him in such physical distress, so much worse than his previous episodes. "I'm calling the doctor." When John didn't argue, she knew he shared her alarm.

Christmas went by uncelebrated.

AND SO, 1933 began. Thrombosis, a small stroke, and a weakened heart proved to be fierce adversaries, keeping John in the hospital for weeks. While Dr. Ewald prescribed numerous medications and bedrest, he cautioned Emily that John would require a long convalescence. "He's not the man he once was," he intoned.

No, he is not. Emily could barely conjure up the John Ringling who had wooed her along the canals of Amsterdam, who had pursued her with ardor in New York City. The once robust figure who once exuded so much dynamism and energy was now a sallow-faced man who could barely stand on his own. His illness had sapped his vitality, drained away by constant pain and physical impairments. Rarely did he smile, and when had she last seen him laugh? "You'll feel more like yourself when we get you back to our apartment," she told him, but she had no idea if that were true.

Sitting in a hospital chair, plucking absent-mindedly at the thick gray blanket covering his lap, he murmured, "I hope so."

When Dr. Ewald gave permission for John's hospital release, Emily busied herself with arranging for the paraphernalia that he would require. John's classically appointed bedroom was now cluttered with a metal pieces—a bed tray on wheels, a nurse's stool, a storage rack for medical supplies. A brocade wing chair was replaced by a drab gray one, easier for John to sit in.

John arrived accompanied by his new nurse, Ina Sanders, who had been highly recommended. Listening to Dr. Ewald tout her experience, Emily had pictured a stout, gray-bunned woman in silver-framed spectacles, but Nurse Sanders did not fit this description. Emily guessed she might be thirty years old, possibly younger. She was tall and slender and wore her dark brown hair in a bob not a bun. Even her crisp white uniform did not conceal her shapeliness.

Hospital orderlies wheeled John into his room and lifted him into his bed while Ina bustled around, issuing directives. In a voice as starched as the white cap she wore, she pointed Emily toward the door. "Mrs. Ringling, please step out of the way. I will have Mr.

Ringling settled in just a moment."

As Emily exited the bedroom, Ina's voice changed, oozing sing-song treacle. "There now, Mr. John, isn't this nice. Aren't we happy to be in our own room?"

We? Own room? Emily smirked. *John will never abide with this condescension.* But then she heard John's tremulous response. "My dear, you're heaven sent. Thank you." This was hardly the John she knew, the one who barked orders rather than accepting them, who readily snarled at those who attempted to fawn over him. That John had been replaced by an invalid, meekly submitting to the aid of the nurse at his bedside.

I'm married to an old man.

Ina Sanders peered into the hallway where Emily stood. "You may come in now, Mrs. Ringling. But take care not to overtax Mr. John. We've had a long afternoon."

"Yes, *we* have," Emily said coolly, walking past the nurse and sitting on the edge of John's bed. "Please allow my husband and me some privacy, Miss Sanders. You may close the door behind you."

Ina opened her mouth and tsked but did as Emily directed.

Emily brushed a wisp of hair from John's forehead and kissed his cheek. "I'm happy you're home, John. You'll recover much more quickly here." She cradled his face in her hands. "I'll do whatever it takes to get you well again, my darling."

John lay his hands on hers. "I'm already feeling better, just by being home." He closed his eyes for a moment, breathing deeply. "But the commotion of getting from the hospital to here has worn me to a frazzle. Could you please leave me to rest, Emily? Perhaps you can ask Nurse Ina to come in."

"As you wish, darling. Rest well. Before long you'll be as right as rain." She lightly tucked the sheet around him and left the room.

As right as rain? Was she now reduced to tossing out hollow bromides to soothe her ailing husband? Is this where life had taken her? She nearly collided with Ina, who had been hovering just outside the door. "I see you're only steps away, Nurse. Go on in. And when you are finished tending to my husband, I will need to discuss his care with you."

"Certainly, Mrs. Ringling. We both have his best wishes at heart, don't we?" She beamed a broad smile through ruby red lips, but her eyes remained cold. "Don't you fret."

Emily detected a tone that one might use when addressing someone of advanced years who needed gentle reassurance. *Does she take me for some doddering wife in need of appeasement? I'm a lot closer to her age than his!* "I have no intention of fretting, as you put it. I will be in the parlor when you're available."

When Nurse Sanders appeared in the parlor, Emily began. "Your room will be right down the hall. John will wish to keep working and he will not be swayed to do otherwise. As for John's care, I will expect you to apprise me of any change in his condition."

Ina simpered. "Mrs. Ringling, you do understand that I am in Mr. Ringling's employ and not yours. I will take directives from him."

Emily's glare was steely. "My husband is your patient, and you will keep me, his wife, informed. As his wife, I will determine the best course of action. Of course, I will consider your opinion as his nurse. Now that I've made myself clear, you are free to get settled in your room." She stood, dismissing the nurse. If Ina had more to say, she kept it to herself and left the room.

IN THE WEEKS that followed, John rallied somewhat, but as Dr. Ewald continued to admonish, "He's not out of the woods yet." Emily lamented the toll illness had taken on John, but she also lamented the toll it was taking on her. Yes, his health was of the highest priority, but she was tired of staying home, tired of being cooped up with no social outlet. How could she escape for a day on the town when her husband was struggling so? The weight of guilt would outbalance any enjoyment she might find outside the walls of the Park Avenue apartment.

And then there was Ina, constantly cooing over John,

tidying his lap blankets when he hobbled into the parlor, making herself at home on the sofa. "I hope you don't mind if I stay nearby, Mrs. Ringling. I want to be able to hear Mr. John when he needs something."

Emily did mind. She and John had lost the opportunity for any private conversations. But John always insisted, "Ina, you sit right down and join us." So Ina sat with her shoulder turned away from Emily. On the evening when John was well enough to have his meals at the dining table, Ina joined them there as well. "This way I can insure he's eating right, Mrs. Ringling."

Emily stabbed at the meat on her plate. "You're so thoughtful, Ina. I know John appreciates it."

Each morning, Emily woke with a new determination to be the wife John required in his recovery. She made daily resolutions to be upbeat and attentive. Although Dr. Ewald had cautioned against rich foods, John pouted over a diet of soft-boiled eggs and dry toast. Instead of scolding him, Emily acquiesced, delivering the buttery English muffins topped with thick jam that he loved. She sat next to his bedside where, propped up like a sultan surrounded by pillows, he ate from his tray.

She made a point of finding light-hearted stories in the papers to distract him from the business pages that he pored over with intensity. So many of her sentences began with, "When you're well."

"When you're well, we must see that new movie

called King Kong. It sounds thrilling!"

"When you're well, we'll see the new Follies."

"When you're well, we could go to Chicago for the World's Fair. They're calling it Century of Progress."

At the mention of the Century of Progress, John's face lit up. "Going to be better than the one in 1893, or so they say. Say, I heard that Frank Buck is featuring a jungle show there. That rascal! Did I ever tell you about the elephants I gave him for his San Diego Zoo? Empress and Queenie?"

"No, I don't think so. Do tell." She noted the sparkle in his eye. "I'm all ears." She fluttered her hands at the side of her head to mimic elephant ears and was rewarded with a hearty chuckle from John.

But before he could begin his story, Ina bustled in the room. "Mr. John, you shouldn't be eating this." She whisked the plate with the remains of the muffin from his tray and scowled at Emily. "Mrs. Ringling, we've discussed appropriate dietary needs, haven't we?"

John looked chastened, like a small boy caught with his hand in a cookie jar. His submission to the scolding rankled Emily. *Since when had he become so docile?* "Mr. Ringling requested this, and I am intent on pleasing my husband. I'm certain one muffin and some jam will have no ill effects."

"Now see here, Mrs. Ringling—"

"Nurse, I beg your pardon. I do not take orders from

you; nor does my husband. You are just here to care for his medical needs." Emily glanced at John. His mouth gaped open and shut. "You and I can speak of this later. Right now, I'd like you to leave the room until I let you know that my husband requires your attention."

"As you wish," Ina huffed, turning toward the door. Before exiting, she paused and faced John. Adopting her obsequious tone, she added, "Mr. Ringling, we'll have your bath whenever you're ready."

When she was gone, John found his voice. "Emily you can't speak to her like that. She's such a godsend. I won't have you at odds with her."

"John, she is a nurse, not a dictator. I won't have her ordering us around as if we were children."

"Must you make this unpleasant?" He slapped his bed tray and his coffee cup rattled in its saucer. "Don't drive her away, Emily. I need her."

She flinched. *He needs her? A paid employee takes precedence over his wife?* Emily stood and folded up the newspaper. "I see. I'll leave you to your bath time, John. But then Ina and I will discuss our arrangements." She left the room and retuned to hers, where she paced back and forth, composing retorts she knew she could never speak aloud.

Once again, Emily spoke to Ina. "Nurse Sanders, if my husband wishes to have a muffin or anything else for that matter, he may do so. You provide his medication, administer the therapeutics he requires, and nothing more."

"Mrs. Ringling, your husband's diet is of great concern. He—"

Emily held up her hand. "He will eat what he likes. Do not interfere again."

Ina tossed her head, but before Emily could accuse her of insubordination, she replied, "As you wish," and turned and headed for John's room.

Emily glared at her back. *I'd fire her if I could.* But then what? John clearly needed the care she provided, and Emily had no interest in sitting at his bedside morning, noon, and night. As irritating as Ina was to Emily, John found her an eager audience for his tales, and this spared Emily from listening to them over and over. Ina provided Emily with some element of freedom as well. She could dash out briefly without worrying that John was alone. No, Ina needed to stay.

An uneasy truce was established between Emily and Ina but the sound of the nurse's chirpy laughter from behind John's door rankled Emily. When Emily sat with John, he was often morose, complaining of his confinement, grousing about his discomfort. Yet when Ina entered the room, his face lit up and he puffed out his chest. "My dear Ina," he'd say, "just the dose of sunshine I need!"

"Oh, Mr. Ringling, you flatter me," she'd say, her

cheeks pinking at his attention. "Now let's have our medicine, shall we?"

Emily took this as her cue to leave them. *Our medicine, shall we?* The use of the royal we poked under Emily's skin. How she wanted to point out that it was John, not any "we" who were undergoing treatment.

EACH DAY FADED into the next. Emily felt like one of John's circus ponies, going around and around in a circle, with John, the ringmaster assisted by Ina, leading her on. The apartment walls were closing in on her, but where was she to go? Was this all the future held for her?

She telephoned Lena. "Please come to New York. I'm desperate for company."

Lena hesitated. "What about John? Won't a houseguest disturb him?"

"Not in the least," Emily assured her sister. Would it disturb him? Undoubtedly, but she could not remain confined. Perhaps her sister would provide a buffer between her and John and the ever-present Ina that might ease the tension in the apartment. Lena was a reliable companion, always eager for conversations or jaunts around the city. She tended to jabber but was a willing listener for John's tales.

"In that case, I'll come. It's always lovely to spend time with you."

Emily could imagine her sister on the other end of

the line, already mentally packing her suitcase and wondering what to wear. Lena would be the diversion she needed.

Impulsively, Emily added, "And I'll throw a cocktail party when you're here. It's been so long since we've invited friends in." Yes, a party was just the thing. Nurse Ina would hate that, she supposed. She could just picture her fussing about "overexcitement" and "rapid heart rates."

"I'll be on the train tomorrow." Lena added a goodbye, then hung up.

As Emily set the phone receiver in its cradle, she was already creating a guest list in her mind. Twelve, no fourteen people? She'd arrange for guests to arrive after John had been tucked into bed for the night. It would be her party, not his, and she could toss off Ina's simpering handwringing regarding John.

Then, just to escape the apartment, Emily telephoned her personal assistant at Bendel's and made an appointment. In front of the apartment building, the doorman hailed a cab for her and as she was whisked down the busy streets, she relished the thought of indulging herself with some spring shopping. The store's Christmas decorations were long gone, replaced by baskets of paper daffodils and tulips. In the private salon, a saleswoman in a crisp white blouse and navy skirt greeted her. "Why, Mrs. Ringling! How nice to see you."

She pointed to a display of spring hats arranged on stands of varying heights. "Lovely confections, aren't they? Would you like to try some on?"

"Hello, Anna. Please. They're divine! It's lovely to see some signs of spring." Emily settled herself at a skirted table and gazed into the mirror. She shrugged off her cashmere coat, lifted her black velvet cloche from her head and fluffed up her hair. For the next thirty minutes, the clerk fawned over her, placing one hat after another just so on Emily's blond curls.

"This season, the cloche is featuring a rolled brim. So fetching." Anna nodded approvingly into their reflection in the mirror as Emily tipped her head side to side.

Anna's sprinkling of compliments continued with each new selection.

"The little blue plate hat is so flattering. Brings out the color of your eyes."

"Mrs. Ringling, the turban is *tres chic*. You look lovely."

How delightful to be indulged this way! A new hat is just the thing after enduring a bleak winter. "Anna, how will I choose? I don't think I can resist the emerald green"—she pointed to one perched on its stand—"but I must have the blue as well. I'll take them both."

"Excellent, madam. I'll add them to your account. Would you like them delivered? Or will you carry them?"

"I'll take them in the cab."

"Of course. I'll box them up." Anna carried them into the back room while Emily remained at the mirror. She reapplied her lipstick, then searched through her handbag for a tissue. *Maybe I'll ask Anna to show me some shoes as well.*

Moments later, Anna returned. Clasping her hands in front of her, she opened and closed her mouth before she took a deep breath and delivered her news. "Mrs. Ringling, I'm afraid you won't be able to take the hats with you after all. My manager has requested that you kindly stop in the accounts department, and then Bendel's will be happy to deliver your hats to you." Anna stared at her feet, unable, it seemed, to look Emily in the eye.

Emily felt heat rising up her neck and on to her cheeks. *This is impossible! How dare this store—.* But in her heart, she knew it was not impossible. It was very likely that their account had not been paid, that John had ignored it or shoved it off to the side. The pity she detected in Anna's tone chilled her as if Anna had torn away her clothing, leaving her naked and stripped of her dignity.

Veiling her humiliation, she gave a toss of her hand. "Oh, how dreary. This is most inconvenient." She frowned at her wristwatch. "I'm in a bit of a rush, meeting a friend, So I'll have to tend to this at another time. Most inconvenient. Anna, I don't blame you, of course, but after all my years as a good customer to this establishment, this treatment is appalling. I would expect some respect and gratitude."

Anna twisted her mouth in a show of sympathy. "Of course, Mrs. Ringling."

Emily gathered her hat and her handbag and strode toward the elevator. When the door slid closed behind her, she ignored the greeting of the uniformed operator and huddled into the corner to blink back the angry tears that threatened. *Damn John! Damn him! How could he put me in this position? How stupidly arrogant can John be. And how foolish of me to imagine the accounts were in good stead.* On the first floor, she headed for the door, the heels of her pumps clacking along the marble floors. This was the limit! She would go home, confront him, demand an explanation. But as she exited the store and sought a cab, she changed her mind.

He will only avoid the issue once again and I won't allow this disaster to continue. She needed a new approach—a way around John's constant avoidance. She gave the cabbie the address of the Ringling office downtown. As the cab headed toward the financial district, Emily planned a new strategy. Sam Gumpertz would know the truth of John's financials. She'd convince him to reveal the true picture.

In the Ringling office, Emily was greeted by an unsmiling receptionist. But when she said, "I'm Mrs. John

Ringling, here to see Mr. Gumpertz," the woman straightened to attention and quickly announced her presence.

Sam, his face marked by concern, rushed from his office to greet her. "Is John all right, Emily?"

"Oh, yes, Sam. He's recovering rather well." She allowed him to lead her into his office. He directed her to a leather Chesterfield sofa and perched himself on a matching wing chair. It felt odd to be here. She had not seen Sam since last summer when he had been so helpful about quashing the rumors about John's health, and so much had transpired since then. John was bitter, claiming he'd been deceived by Edith and Sam in the take-over of the circus, but he had never explained to Emily what had occurred. But anger or coolness would not serve her purposes today. Charm was her best tactic.

"Cigarette?" Sam opened a burled cigarette box on the table. She took one and leaned forward toward the lighter that Sam held out for her. "So, what brings you in, Emily?" He steepled his fingers and tilted his head to the side.

"I really don't know where to begin." Emily drew on her cigarette, then exhaled a thin trail of smoke. John would see her presence in Sam's office as a betrayal, if he knew she was here. *So be it.* "Sam, I'm concerned about John's finances. I need to know just how things stand."

Sam grimaced. "Emily, I don't think I can—"

She interrupted. "I realize I'm putting you in a difficult position, Sam. But you've been a friend to John for years, notwithstanding the new organization of the circus. Please hear me out."

Sam ran a finger under his collar and fidgeted with his necktie. "You realize that the Ringling business is confidential."

"I understand. But please listen." Emily drew on her cigarette once more and began her story—all of it. The unpaid bills at Bloomingdale's and now Bendel's, John's insistence that she be kept in the dark about his assets, her taking on of household expenses.

Sam said little and his expression remained impassive. Should she go further? *Discretion is the better part of valor*, she'd always heard. No. *After Bendel's today, I'm plowing ahead.*

"Are you aware, Sam, that John has yet to repay a substantial loan I made to him before our marriage?"

Sam's eyes widened and he sucked a sip of air through his teeth. "Emily, really, I don't see—" His voice trailed off and he cleared his throat.

Her revelation had gotten his attention. She continued. "And, then there's the museum, filled with valuable art works, none that John is willing to liquidate. I'm at my wit's end, Sam. Is he losing his financial empire? Or is this just a temporary setback due to the Depression?" She stubbed out her cigarette in a bronze ashtray. "I need to do something, especially considering his precarious health."

Sam had listened quietly, and now she waited for his response. He spoke in a measured tone. "Emily, my dear, you have reason to be concerned, but no reason to be unduly alarmed. Yes, there have been financial setbacks, as you've observed. But I'm not at liberty..." He stopped mid-sentence as a groan of frustration escaped her. "Emily, let's not become overwrought."

How ridiculous! "I'm decidedly not overwrought," she nearly exclaimed. Instead, she squelched her irritation and applied some of the feminine wiles men like Sam were used to. She pulled a handkerchief from her bag and dabbed at the corner of her eye, then gazed at him imploringly, widening her eyes. "But what can be done? You've got such a head for business, Sam. I'm wondering if it would be helpful to sell some art at this time, to cover expenses while things are in flux?"

"That would be a wise course of action, I believe. But can you convince John of that? I've proposed that myself on occasion." Sam shook his head. "How he loves his art! He and Mable—"

"Yes, he and Mable. I'm well aware. But clinging to dusty old artifacts does not solve some immediate problems." Emily twisted her hands into a knot. "What am I to do, Sam?"

Sam tapped an index finger against his chin. "I do

know a dealer who may be interested in some smaller items of art, if you could convince John."

If I could convince John. How impossible might that be? But could there be another way? Why would John have to know? A solution sprang in her mind. *Of course! I can make this work.*

She brightened and offered a smile as her earlier despair turned into inspiration. "You know, if he had a concrete offer..." Her sentence hung uncompleted as she created a scenario in her mind, one she would not share with Sam. John would not have to know, not if she did this right. "Let me give it a try, Sam. Can you give me the dealer's name?"

"Surely." Sam rose and turned toward a file cabinet. After a moment or two of combing through a drawer, he pulled out a folder. "Ah, here we go. Very discreet as well." He jotted the name and contact information on a card and handed it to Emily.

Emily scanned the card and tucked it into her handbag. Standing, she said, "I won't trouble you anymore, Sam." When he stood as well, she gave him a peck on the cheek while running her hand along his arm. "You've been a dear, so kind to listen to me ramble on. Now, we'll just keep this get-together between the two of us, won't we? Neither of us wants to add more to John's plate now."

Sam chuckled. "Heavens, no. And I'm happy I could

be of some assistance. John and I go way back, and sometimes difficult business decisions can impair a friendship. It's been trying." He laid a hand over his chest and shook his head.

"Oh, I understand completely, Sam. Business is business, that's what I always say. I'll be on my way." She planted another kiss on Sam's cheek and left the office.

On the cab ride home, her earlier humiliation at Bendel's drifted away as she strategized. Why couldn't she approach this dealer with a few small items, ones that John would never realize were missing? This would be some payback for the expenses she'd accrued, the ones that John was supposed to pay. It was only fair that she be reimbursed, and the art wasn't benefiting anyone just hanging on a wall or cluttering shelves. By the time she exited the cab, she already had some pieces in mind. Mable, dead for years, still emanated from every corner of the New York apartment as well as Ca d'Zan. It was long past time to benefit from some of her precious treasures. *I'll start with that ridiculous old-world gewgaw covered with gold filigree on the dresser, some time-telling instrument no more useful than a sundial. it surely has monetary value, and I could easily fit it into my handbag and whisk it out the door, straight to the art dealer.*

Chapter Thirty-Two

WHEN EMILY RETURNED to the apartment, she found John smoking a cigar in the parlor while Ina sat nearby, darning some hosiery. Ted Lewis's rendition of "On the Sunny Side of the Street" floated from the Victrola. The tableau of cozy domesticity jabbed at Emily. First the sainted Mable, now the doe-eyed Ina as Florence Nightingale. Just where was her place in the picture?

"Ah, Emily, here you are. We were wondering when you'd be home." John smiled at her, but Ina added, "He was becoming worried."

"Darling, you look well." Emily planted a kiss on John's forehead. "Let me hang up my coat and then we can chat." Shrugging off coat, she turned to Ina. "Nurse Sanders, you're free to go now. I'd like to speak to my husband."

Ina gathered her sewing then walked to John's chair. "Is there anything you need, Mr. John?"

"I don't believe so." John patted her hand she had placed on the arm rest.

Emily waited, teeth clenched, until Ina had left the room. With Ina out of sight, Emily turned to John, "I don't see how you can bear her cloying."

"Don't be so harsh, Emily. Had it not been for Ina's attention, well, who knows where I'd be."

"Yes. Of course." She would not argue. Tossing her coat on a chair, she sat on the sofa. "Anyway, I have some news. I spoke to Lena earlier and she's coming to visit for a while. She arrives tomorrow. Won't that be grand?" She beamed at him, hoping her enthusiasm would be infectious.

"A houseguest?" He heaved a weary sigh. "I don't think I'm up to it."

"We won't disturb you; I promise. And you know how much you enjoy Lena." She stood and leaned over his chair, her arms encircling his shoulders. "She'll be a diversion we both need."

"I suppose…" he drew on his cigar. "She may come."

Had she needed his permission to have her sister in her own home? Should she thank him for his almighty benevolence? She returned to her place on the sofa. "And on another note. I shopped at Bendel's today."

He scowled but Emily detected an underlying sheepishness, revealing his knowledge that bills had been unpaid. "Can you imagine what I experienced? It was humiliating. Have you simply closed your eyes to your financial obligations?"

John studied the ember at the tip of his cigar. "My illness..." he mumbled.

She did not point out that John had assured her that he could handle things during his recuperation. How tired she was of this discord. But with the art dealer's card tucked into her handbag, she saw a glimmer of a solution. Her eyes fell on a Chinoises figurine on an end table. *What might that ugly little thing sell for?* "I will pay the account, John, this time, as I have done in the past. I'm sure you'll consider this a loan that is to be repaid, just like the loan I made before our marriage. Now let's close the subject. Would you like a cocktail?"

LENA DID NOT arrive by train. Instead, Nicholas delivered her to the apartment in late afternoon. When Emily buzzed them into the apartment, Nicholas led the way, wearing his chauffeur's cap and a pin-striped suit with lapels as wide as dinner napkins.

"Hey, Aunt Emily! Don't you look grand!" He plopped Lena's luggage down in the foyer and embraced Emily. Lena followed and hugged her sister, wrapping her in ribbons of "Oh, my goodness!" and "I'm so happy to see you!" Nicholas, hands tucked into his pleated trouser pockets, sauntered into the parlor. "Uncle John! You're looking spry!" He chuckled and then offered John, seated in his usual chair, a handshake and a clap on the back. "Never thought I'd see you looking this good again." He surveyed his surroundings. "Still quite a snazzy place you've got here, Uncle John. Not quite Ca d'Zan, but nice, really nice."

"Nicholas! Such a thing to say!" Lena scurried behind her son, hands aflutter. "John, you're looking well." She gave his shoulder a squeeze.

John offered a tepid smile. "Good to see you, too, Lena. And you, Nicholas. And this is my nurse, Ina Sanders." He waved a hand toward a nearby chair where Ina sat primly, her hands folded in her lap, the toes of her white shoes perfectly aligned on the carpet.

Nicholas, who had brushed past her to view the streetscape below, turned around. "Why, hello to you!" His eyebrows shot up and he stepped forward to take her hand in his. "I'm Nicholas. Isn't Uncle John lucky to have you taking care of him instead of those old battle axes out on Coney Island?" He chuckled at this joke, and although no one joined in, he continued. "Say, Uncle John, guess Nurse Ina here is just what the doctor ordered."

"Nicholas, really!" Emily scowled at her nephew, but Ina tittered and stood behind John's chair.

"I do my best to give dear Mr. John the best care he deserves." She scrunched her shoulders coquettishly, while John gazed up at her.

"She's my angel of mercy, I always say," said John.

"Oh, I'm sure." Nicholas licked the corner of his lips.

Emily had seen enough. Nicholas was ridiculous, ogling Ina as if she were some cigarette girl in a night club. And Ina, years older than Nicholas, batting her eyelashes and ladling flattery onto John. "I'm sure you need to be rushing off, Nicholas. Your employer surely needs his vehicle, doesn't he?" She grasped his elbow. "John, Lena, say goodbye to Nicholas and I'll escort him to the door."

Nicholas hesitated. "So, Aunt Emily, as it turns out, the boss wants me to stay in the city. So, I can pop in any time." Again, he turned to Ina. "I work for a guy who's rolling in dough, driving him all over. Kinda his right-hand man, so to speak."

Emily did not let go of Nicholas's arm. "Well, your mother and I will be out and about while she is here, and Uncle John requires his rest, so let us know before you plan to come over."

"Yeah, sure! Nice to meet you, Nurse Ina. See you, Mama, Uncle John!" He tipped his cap at everyone and allowed himself to be led to the door.

LENA ARRIVED AT the breakfast table well after John and Ina had finished their meal and had returned to John's room for his therapeutics. Still in her chenille dressing gown, she nibbled at the edges of a piece of toast she'd slathered with marmalade while Emily sipped her second cup of coffee. "You look fresh and ready for the day,

Emily. Do we have plans?"

"As a matter of fact, I do have an outing for us. But it's hush-hush, so don't mention anything to John or Ina." Emily, dressed in a mauve boucle suit, pressed her index finger over her mouth in an exaggeration of secrecy. "Shhh. Top secret."

Lena clapped her hands. "Ooh, sounds intriguing! Do tell."

"Let's get dressed to go out, shall we, and I'll explain. Just put on something simple."

When Lena emerged dressed for the day, Emily, who had added a navy-blue cloche to her ensemble, noted that her admonishment to dress simply had fallen on deaf ears. Nevertheless, she linked arms with her sister as they took the elevator to the lobby and allowed the doorman to secure a cab. Lena's brilliant teal hat adorned with tall peacock feathers nearly snapped off when she climbed into the cab.

"What's in there?" Lena pointed to the leather train case that Emily carried. "Hopping on board the New York Central?"

"I'll tell, but don't breathe a word. They're a few art pieces here that I'm showing an art dealer. But this is confidential, so please keep this under that magnificent hat of yours." She ran her finger along the largest of Lena's feathers, scraping the ceiling of the cab. "I'm planning to liquidate a few of John's assets as a surprise for him. After I meet with him, we'll find somewhere charming to have lunch. Then maybe a movie?"

Emily left Lena in a coffee shop in the building's lobby and headed for the elevator. "Sixth floor, please," she said to the operator, who closed the bronze gate and pushed the button to send them upward. Once out of the elevator, she searched the frosted glass doors until she found the one labeled Smythe and Son. Reassured by the tidy, respectable look of the building, she opened the office door. Inside, a middle-aged secretary peered over her spectacles to welcome her.

"I have an appointment with Mr. Roland Smythe. I'm Mrs. Ringling."

"Certainly, Mrs. Ringling. Mr. Smythe is expecting you. Please come this way." The secretary stood and gestured to the closed office door behind her. She tapped on it and opened it slightly to announce Emily, then stepped back so Emily could enter.

Although Emily had no notion of what Roland Smythe might look like, she was surprised by his appearance. He was a rotund little man with rosy cheeks and a halo of gray curls spiraling from his head. His suit was rumpled, his tie askew and the smudges on his bifocals made Emily wonder how he could see clearly. While his secretary's domain was uncluttered and organized, his office was not. Stacks of art catalogs teetered on the edge of his desktop and papers and folders drifted across his desk. Framed canvases leaned against the wall and a credenza was lined with various *objet d'art*. Spotting an ancient bronze rubbing shoulders with a Renaissance Madonna, Emily wondered if Sam had led her astray with his recommendation.

Her trepidation was immediately disarmed by the warm smile and hearty greeting. "Welcome, welcome! So, Sam sent you, Mrs. Ringling? Ah, he's an old friend. Please have a seat." He removed a pile of folders from a chair and patted the cushion. "Here, here, please, Mrs. Ringling. Excuse my disarray." He took a chair beside hers, then patted the arm rests. "I'm interested in hearing what I can do for you."

"Well, Mr. Smythe, Sam tells me that you may have buyers for some of the items of the Ringling art. My husband—I'm sure you're familiar with him—has a vast collection. I'm here on his behalf." She chuckled. "John loves his art, as you may know, but I suppose one might say he has acquired too much. So, we are considering parting with a few pieces, some that are similar to others in design or significance." She opened the train case at her feet and brought out the pieces inside, each carefully wrapped in cottonwool, and set them on the desk. "Here are a few."

"I see." Smythe's eyes lit up as she revealed each object—the timepiece and two Chinoises figures. "May I?" He raised his eyebrows, seeking permission to touch the pieces.

"Certainly."

Smythe lifted the timepiece gently and scrutinized its every feature—the enameled images encircling its base, the tiny door to the mechanism. After a few moments, he removed his eyeglasses and cleaned them with a handkerchief, then returned them to the bridge of his nose and continued his examination without comment. Finally, he moved on to the Chinoises pieces and conducted the same methodical process.

Emily's mind swam as she waited. She had selected these items randomly; they'd fit easily into her train case, and she doubted that John would notice their absence. Were they inconsequential bric-a-brac that had once caught Mable's eye or valuable treasures? Just how long would it take for Smythe to speak, to give her his assessment? She resisted the urge to tap her toes or to click her fingernails on the arm of the chair and willed herself to remain still and unperturbed. She thought of Lena in the coffee shop and pictured her impatiently checking her watch every minute. Or had she found an affable listener for her friendly chatter?

At long last, Mr. Smythe returned to the chair beside Emily. "Mrs. Ringling, each of these pieces is remarkable in its own way. I'd say that your husband has made a very sound investment in each one."

Without revealing her pleasure at his opinion, Emily

nodded. "As we suspected. My husband has been an astute connoisseur for many years. But do you believe you might be able to successfully broker each of them?"

"Ah, most certainly." Mr. Smythe removed his eyeglasses and rubbed them with his handkerchief in a futile attempt to remove the smudges. "Several of my clients are in a position to invest and are steering clear of the stock market these days. In fact, I have a few people in mind who undoubtedly would be interested." He put on his glasses. "Let me write up an estimate quickly for each piece and you can present them to your husband. If you're willing, I can keep the pieces here in my safe, giving you a receipt of course, so that you don't risk damaging them in transport."

"I'd appreciate that. One can never be too careful."

Smythe returned to his desk chair and painstakingly composed three documents. Without showing them to Emily, he tucked them into a brown envelope and daubed the flap with mucilage from a rubber-tipped bottle. "After your husband has made his consideration, he or you, on his behalf, may inform me of your decision."

She accepted the envelope and rose. "Thank you. And since John has been so busy these days, all the while recovering from some health issues, I'm sure he'll want me to continue to communicate with you. Dear man! I'm pleased to be able to take something off his plate."

"You're an asset to him, for sure." He ushered her to the door, and she made her exit.

The envelope seemed to throb in her hand as she rode the elevator and crossed the lobby to find Lena, sitting in a banquette with an empty cup of coffee in front of her.

"My goodness, Emily! I was beginning to feel deserted."

"Sorry, dear, but my business took longer than expected. You must be starving for lunch by now. Come, let's get a cab. You choose your favorite spot." Emily pulled some coins from her handbag and left them on the table. "Where to, my lady?"

Lena laughed. "I'm always so fond of that darling little tearoom at the Windsor. Remember when you took Olga and me there years ago? They had such divine tea sandwiches and sponge cakes with lemon."

"The Windsor it is. And maybe a movie afterwards."

"Ooh, what about *Tonight is Ours*, with that dashing Fredric March?" Lena clasped her hands together in a swoon.

And although Emily wanted nothing more than to rip open the envelope, she folded it and slipped it into her handbag. Lena, with her talk of tea cakes and stars of the silver screen, seemed to have forgotten what Emily's business entailed. That would probably be best in order to keep her secret.

The lunch and the movie took up the entire afternoon, and back in the apartment, she and Lena joined John and Ina in the parlor.

"What have you ladies been up to today?" John asked as Emily kissed his cheek.

Would Lena remember to keep the morning's business quiet? Emily tried to catch her sister's eye in reminder, and although Lena didn't notice, she was true to her word and avoided revealing the morning's errand.

"John, we saw the most wonderful film. Ina, are you a movie goer? This one featured Claudette Colbert and that handsome devil, Fredric March." Without giving the time to respond, Lena continued, summarizing the entire plot.

Itching to escape the room, Emily held herself in check. When Lena eventually stopped talking, Emily stood. "Come, Lena, let's freshen up. I'm sure I've worn you out and dinner will be ready soon."

Finally! Emily closed her bedroom door and drew the envelope from her bag. Carefully peeling back the flap, she slid the papers out. First, the timepiece. Her eyes jumped to the numbers at the bottom of the page, and a gasp escaped her lips. This was beyond her imagining. That silly piece, once sold, would pay the entirety of the Bendel's bill, with money remaining. Then she turned to the papers detailing the Chinoises pieces. Incredibly, these were even more valuable. And here they were, taking up space on end tables and dressers when they could be put to practical use, relieving their financial pressures. She could have jumped for joy. Instead, she tossed her hair back and jutted out her chin. *"I told you so, John Ringling!"*

There was a tap at the door. She slid the papers into a bureau drawer. Expecting to see Lena, she was surprised to see the housekeeper Catherine standing at the threshold.

"May I speak to you, Mrs. Ringling?" Catherine spoke in a near whisper and her face was pinched into a spiderweb of wrinkles.

"Of course."

Catherine glanced behind her. "Privately, if you please, missus."

This was so unlike Catherine, to knock on Emily's door. For the most part, the diminutive, soft-spoken Irish housekeeper was nearly invisible, managing the cleaning and the cooking seamlessly. Silently, she bustled about, wielding a cloth and feather duster, warring against any speck of grime that dared to show itself. Emily had never had reason to find fault with her efficiency. When they had occasion to speak, it was to confer on some menus or to arrange dinner times.

"Certainly. Come in, Catherine. You look upset. What's troubling you?"

Inside the room, Catherine drew a deep breath and

bit her lip. "I don't know what to make of it, Mrs. Ringling."

"Make of what? Tell me."

"I was doing me cleaning this afternoon while Mr. Ringling was resting and I, I noticed something gone awry." Again, she diverted her eyes, drawing a deep breath as if to find the courage to continue.

"So, Catherine, what is it?"

Catherine forged ahead. "Well, Missus, for one thing, that brass thingamajig on your dresser has disappeared." She nodded her head vigorously, confirming her own statement. "And then that China girl in the parlor, and a vase. Gone."

"I see." Emily froze. She had only considered that John might note the disappearance of his possessions, not that this eagle-eyed woman would as well.

Before Emily could explain, Catherine continued. "Now I don't like to be sayin', but that nurse, could she have taken them? We've never had things walk off until now." She squinted at Emily. "Couldn't help but wonder... and Lord forgive me for casting blame, but might that nurse be up to no good?"

Emily patted Catherine's arm. *How rich!* Catherine was no more enraptured by Nurse Ina than she was. Emily momentarily imagined a scenario where she could cast out John's Florence Nightingale as a conniving thief who'd wormed her way in to John's good graces only to steal from him. Still, that would leave her in charge of John's care, and as annoying as she found Ina, she could not allow her to be a suspect in a crime that didn't exist. "You are observant, Catherine, and I can see why you might suspect that Nurse Sanders had a hand in it. But I must apologize. I never considered how vigilant you are." She tossed a little laugh into the air. "No need to worry, Catherine." She hunched down to face the diminutive maid eye-to eye. "Just between us, I wanted the apartment to be less cluttered with all these pretty things. Too many, I think, don't you?"

Catherine tucked a stray strand of gray hair behind her ear and nodded. "Well, missus, there's an awful lot needs dusting, and I live in fear of dropping some of them, imagining Mr. Ringling so distraught at the sight of a broken vase or figure."

"Exactly, Catherine." She grinned conspiratorially. "Now I've packed some items out of harm's way, hoping that Mr. John might never notice, just for safe-keeping. But let's not mention this to him. No need to upset him over something that hasn't even drawn his attention."

"I see, Missus. I see." Catherine's eyebrows knitted together. "Shame on me for casting doubt on the good nurse. May the good Lord forgive my evil thoughts."

"Catherine, don't think a thing of it. I appreciate your vigilance, and it's understandable that you might suspect this new person in the household. Can't be too careful, can we."

"No, missus."

Emily reached for her handbag and extracted a dollar bill. "Here, Catherine. Thank you for telling me about this. You were right to be concerned. Now I may pack away a few more curios and such, so don't be alarmed. And as a favor to me, please don't say anything to dear Mr. Ringling." She rolled her eyes. "We know how he is about his bits and bobs and pretty things."

"Certainly. Missus. And I won't be botherin' you any further. Good night." Catherine pocketed the dollar bill and backed out of the room.

Emily closed the door behind her. *So, I have another ally.*

Chapter Thirty-Three

EMILY ITCHED TO contact Mr. Smythe immediately and give him the approval to solicit buyers for the pieces she'd shown him. But she restrained herself for a few days. It would not behoove her to look to anxious, and she wanted to continue the charade of John's involvement.

When three days passed by, she secluded herself in John's office and telephoned Mr. Smythe, picturing the man at the other end of the line, his hair disheveled but his mind keen. Although Emily found the proposals to be more than adequate, she knew that a first offer was generally low. An experienced art dealer would expect some dickering and she was up to the task. Aligning some pencils and a letter opener on the desk blotter, she chose a businesslike tone of voice. "Mr. Smythe, my husband asked me to phone you, now that he's looked over the proposals you've sent. He was, frankly, a bit taken aback at the low price of the timepiece and wished me to convey to you that this was more valuable than you've assessed. Can you do better?"

Waiting for Smythe's response, she imagined him rummaging through files on his desk and she wondered if he even recalled his initial offer.

"Ah, here it is. Well…" he hesitated, "I suppose I can increase the offer a bit. But in these tough economic times…" his voice trailed off.

"Mr. Smythe, John is fully aware of the tough economic times you speak of. But that is what makes this rarity such a valuable investment. Of course, I can always take the pieces to another dealer if you're unable—" She paused and allowed a silence to hover over them. *This is fun, setting a businessman back on his heels.* She smirked, grateful that a telephone conversation gave her more pluck. *I'm rather good at this game.*

When Smythe responded, his tone revealed that she'd been the victor. "Your husband drives a hard bargain, Mrs. Ringling, but I believe my client will go higher." He offered a new number, one that far exceeded Emily's expectations.

My husband's hard bargain? Emily nearly chuckled aloud. *My husband has no inkling.* "I'm sure that will be acceptable, Mr. Smythe. As you can imagine, John is quite busy these days, but I can find the time to deliver the papers any time this afternoon. And one more thing, this must be a cash transaction. With the state of banks these days…"

"Certainly, Mrs. Ringling. If you give me a few

hours, I'll have everything in order for you and your husband. Just have him sign the dotted line and we have a deal."

Replicating John's signature would not be difficult. She'd seen his flourish scrawled on many a document. "I should be able to reach your office by three o'clock, Mr. Smythe." By late this afternoon, she would be in possession of a great deal of cash and John would be none the wiser.

She found John and his nurse in his room, where John, dressed in an undershirt and a pair of boxer shorts, was sprawled face down on a massage table while Ina, her breasts straining at the buttons of her white uniform, leaned over him and kneaded his back. The intimacy of the scene made Emily cringe. Yes, this was a prescribed therapy, but Emily felt like an intruder. John barely lifted his head to acknowledge her presence, and Ina continued pressing her fingertips into John's shoulders as Emily spoke.

Emily bent down to John's eye level. "John, I have a glorious idea! We've been cooped up so long, and with Lena here, it would be nice to invite a few friends in, cocktails and such, a small soiree for tomorrow evening."

Before John could respond, Ina spoke. "Mrs. Ringling, I'm afraid I must object. Such excitement could affect Mr. John's heart rate. We can't have that." She shook her head and bit her lip in disapproval, her fingers continuing their manipulations along John's spine.

Emily's lip curled as she glanced at Ina, then focused on her husband's face. "I am speaking to my husband, Nurse Sanders. John, I'm planning on a few friends. Are you interested in joining us in the parlor or would you rather remain with your nurse in your room?"

John grunted. "Who are you thinking of inviting? Your friends, I suppose."

"Well, yes, my friends. And aren't they yours as well? The Sampsons? The Weatheringtons? And a few others. Sophie, James. And Jasper and Margo Lawrence. You know how she adores you." Emily found Margo insipid, and her husband, who fancied himself an expert on British theater, was a crashing bore. But she'd tossed their names in the mix, just to appease John.

"Oh, that Sampson woman is nothing but a flibbertigibbet, but her husband isn't a bad sort. Go ahead. I may not be able to be the host all evening, though," he warned. "Ina, your fingers are like magic." With effort, he pulled himself to a sitting position at the edge of the massage table. "Now, let me get dressed, Emily. Go ahead and plan your little gathering. I'll do my best."

THE GUESTS WERE expected at eight o'clock, and Emily had dressed early, choosing a simple navy crepe de chine, adorning it with a leaf-shaped brooch studded with small emeralds, an heirloom piece that had been her mother's. She entered the parlor to find Catherine adjusting the barware at the sideboard.

"Everything's all set, I see." Emily lifted a cigarette from a Lalique crystal box and slipped it into the jade holder she carried.

"The canapes are all prepared, Mrs. Ringling." Catherine plucked at her sleeves. "But, ma'am, I'm afraid…" She blinked at Emily then fidgeted with her sleeves again.

"What is it, Catherine?"

"It's me mister. He's a conductor on the streetcar, you know. Well, there was an incident last night and he was injured, leg all banged up. O'course, he doesn't like to complain, but he's not fit to work, can barely get around, and no one home to see to him. I hate to ask, what with you having a party, but I was wonderin', if it would be possible, if I could—" She looked beseechingly at Emily, her fingers entwined.

Emily lit her cigarette with the tall silver lighter next to the ice bucket. *So who would serve the canapes? What a nuisance.* Even as the thought crossed her mind, Emily recalled the maid's willingness to stay mum about the missing art pieces. *I'll be magnanimous, this once.* "Catherine, No need for you to serve. You may go home for the evening, and I'll take it from here."

"Well, if you're sure." Catherine straightened a pile

of linen cocktail napkins and then tucked her hands behind her back. "That'd be grand, missus. And I'll be back in the mornin' to do all the washin' up."

"Of course." As Catherine scuttled toward the kitchen to make her exit, Emily brought her cigarette holder to her lips and scanned the room. Managing guests without the maid would be a bother. What conclusions might people leap to with no help available to serve them? She could enlist Lena, but she was so flighty. But Ina? That would work.

She scrutinized the living room, mentally redecorating it with a sleek sofa, perhaps in a deep jade, flanked by unconventionally shaped burled end tables replacing the ornate, fusty pieces she saw before her. After three years of marriage to John, wasn't it past time for her home to reflect her tastes, not those of a woman who had been buried years ago? She promised herself that she would not allow another week to go by without contacting an interior designer. She'd tell John she would pay for it all, and he'd never realize that those silly Chinoises figures were footing the bill.

Lena broke her reverie as she swept into the room. She had chosen a sequined gown in an unfortunate shade of lavender and a feathered fascinator perched atop her curls. Her butterfly sleeves fluttered around her as she gestured to her sister. "Emily, so chic as always. Perhaps I'm overdressed?" She clutched at the strands of crystal beads that dangled from her neck.

Emily smiled. Had Lena ever been underdressed? Even as a little girl, she layered her dolls in frilly ribbons and bows, and she had never vacillated from her love of showy fashions. "Lena, you will be the star of the show."

Lena swayed from side to side, sending her chiffon skirt in motion. "I do love a party. And I know you don't mind, but when I spoke to Nicholas this morning, he mentioned that he might want to stop by." She twirled her beads. "He loves a party as much as his mother."

Nicholas inviting himself? How typical! Emily couldn't imagine him mingling with her party guests.

Then John, in a deep burgundy smoking jacket and gray trousers, entered the parlor, with Ina by his side guiding him to a chair. But it was Ina's appearance that caused a hitch in Emily's breath. Her uniform had been replaced by a sleek ruby-colored silk that accentuated her figure. Her dark brown hair cascaded in soft waves around her face. Sheer silk stockings and gleaming black pumps completed her ensemble, along with a distinctive pearl choker. Emily stifled a gasp. The necklace was undeniably from Mable's jewelry collection that John kept in his room. Had John lent it to her for the evening, or was this a gift? Just what was Ina's place these days?

"My, don't you look handsome, John." Emily turned to Ina. "Nurse Sanders, how nice you look. I didn't expect—"

The buzzer sounded, announcing guests. Soon the apartment was a hubbub of conviviality—the Sampsons and the Weatheringtons, then the Lawrences and Sophie and James arriving all at once.

"So good to see you all. I know you remember my sister Lena." Emily exchanged air kisses with everyone while Lena twittered her greetings. "John is in the parlor."

The guests shrugged off their coats and with Catherine not available to collect them, Emily found herself gathering them in her arms. "I'm afraid I had to give the maid the night off. Such a bother, but you know their kind is always having one calamity after another. So, *nobless oblige*! Please come in!" She led them into the parlor, where John brought himself to a standing position, booming hellos and accepting the cascade of "So good to see you! My, you look well!" that rained upon him.

John laid a hand on Ina's arm as she stood at his side. "This is my dear nurse, Ina Sanders. She's been looking after me." He gazed at her fondly, then rattled off the names of the guests.

Emily took in her friends' reactions to Ina. The men were agog, their eyes scanning her from head to toe, but the women were more quizzical. *What were they thinking?* She could imagine a tete-tete where Margo Lawrence would serve up a description of John Ringling's young and beautiful nurse along with the coffee and croissants. Emily handed Ina with the armload of wraps. "Nurse Sanders, could you please take care of these?"

Ina, her expression bland, accepted the pile. "Certainly, Mrs. Ringling."

There. This would show the group that this woman was simply an employee. She beamed and linked her arm through John's. "Drinks, anyone? James, could you be a dear and help with the cocktails? And Lena, please select some music and get the Victrola going. it's so good to have all of you here, isn't it, darling?" She leaned her head into her husband's shoulder. "Now let me run and get the canapes. With the maid out for the night, what's a hostess to do? Believe it or not, I can manage, everyone!"

Surrounded by the mellow music of Cole Porter that drifted from the Victrola, the party was pleasant and lively. No one, not even the tedious Jasper Lawrence, dragged the conversation down into the depths of the Depression, and Margo, batting her Kewpie doll eyelashes, cajoled John into telling some of his best circus stories. Emily was warmed by the air of geniality and even the sight of Ina's hovering over John failed to annoy her.

She was just about to suggest some dance music when the buzzer sounded and Lena hopped up from her seat and said, "Oh, that must be Nicholas! I'll answer."

Yes, it was Nicholas, but not only him. Leading a gaggle of young people into the parlor, he called out, "Hey, Aunt Emily, Uncle John! Mama said you were having a party, so I brought a few of my pals and a couple of gals. Hey everybody, meet my famous uncle!"

Emily was momentarily speechless as the group swarmed into the room. The young men—there were three of them—swaggered about, shaking hands with John and hugging Emily in a too-familiar way. "Say, quite a swanky place, Aunt Emily!" one said, winking at her, while another exclaimed, "Ritzier than the Ritz, if you ask me!"

Nicholas put his arms around the shoulders of the two girls he'd ushered into the gathering. "Everybody, this little beauty is my gal Dotty"—he squeezed the shoulder of the ingenue on his right—"and this is her pal Gracey." Barely out of their teens, the girls appeared to be carbon copies of one another, their eyes laden with thick mascara under arched brows drawn on to give them a look of perpetual surprise. They both posed, one hand on hip, in low cut gowns more suitable for a Vaudeville stage than a Park Avenue apartment. A rhinestone tiara sparkled on Dotty's gossamer yellow waves, while Gracey's flaming red tresses were held in place by a sequined comb. "Charmed, I'm sure," they responded in unison.

"Say, Uncle John, got any champagne?" Nicholas

eyed the bar and didn't wait for an answer. John watched, his mouth agape as Nicholas searched through the liquor cabinet. "Guess not, but we'll settle on the gin and other stuff that's here. Hey, chaps, what'll you have?"

His friends clustered around as Nicholas filled glasses to the brim.

Lena looked on fondly. "He is so high-spirited, my son."

Emily could not decide between being amused or outraged. *Maybe this party was a little dull, all this polite conversation and decorum.* She scanned the room, noting the bemused expressions on her friends' faces, contrasting Ina's uneasy scowl and John's reddening complexion. Observing John as he fidgeted in his chair, she felt as if she were watching a play, one of those drawing room comedies. She settled in to watch the plot unfold.

Nicholas and his entourage soon took center stage. Cole Porter's melodies were replaced by the thumping beat of Cab Calloway. One of the boys, a fresh-faced fellow named Tommy, asked Emily to dance. She demurred, but only for a moment. "I'll dance but only if you all join us, Sophie, James, everybody."

"Let's, Sophie!" James led his wife in a spirited fox-trot across the carpet.

"Jasper, don't be a stick in the mud! Dance with me!" Margo tugged at her husband's arm until he guffawed and, much to Emily's surprise, sprang to his feet. Claudette Sampson coaxed her husband off his chair, and soon the Weatheringtons joined in. Nicholas pulled Dotty to him and cheek-to-cheek, and they twirled around the other couples.

When had she last danced like this? It was exhilarating! She felt as effervescent as a flute of champagne.

"Say, Nurse, wanna dance?" The fellow named Stanley sidled up to Ina. She frowned and shook her head. He shrugged. "You're missing out. I do a heck of a Lindy."

"C'mon, Mama, let me show you the Harlem Lindy Hop. Stan, put on something jazzy." When "Cotton Club Stomp" erupted from the Victrola, Nicholas grabbed Lena's hand and swung her around the room until one of her butterfly sleeves became entangled with a vase and sent it smashing to the floor.

"Sorry! Sorry!" Lena squeaked as she and Nicholas stopped in mid-step to retrieve the shards scattered about. Emily dared not look at John, imagining his displeasure, and waved her hand dismissively. "Accidents happen. Don't worry."

John signaled to Emily to step towards him and hissed through ragged breaths. "It's a valuable antiquity. Mable cherished it. Do put a stop to this."

She hissed back. "John, it was unintentional. I won't spoil a good time."

"Emily, what on earth has gotten into you? This is foolishness." He spat out his words, his face florid.

"What has gotten into me? It's called fun. Maybe you remember."

Ina stepped in front of Emily and held John's wrist between her fingers. "Mr. John cannot handle this commotion. His heart rate is becoming dangerously high."

Emily spoke through gritted teeth in a voice only Ina could hear. "Then I suggest that he retires to his room for the evening. I won't be turning our guests away." She turned to Nicholas who held the broken pieces of the vase in his hands. "Nicky, toss that in the trash and fix me another cocktail please."

The record ended and Emily clapped her hands to get everyone's attention. "Stanley, before you find a rumba for us, I'm afraid that John's nurse feels he needs to call it a night, so let's all wish him a good evening and then refresh our drinks."

John stubbed out his cigar and offered a limp wave. "It's been a pleasure to see you all." He shuffled out of the room. Ina by his side as the guests called out *good nights*.

Emily was not sorry to see him go. She lit another cigarette and accepted another gin from Nicholas. "Shall we roll up this old rug? Then let's keep dancing!"

And so the party continued. Lubricated by free-flowing cocktails, the guests cavorted across the room, singing "It Don't Mean a Thing If you Ain't Got That Swing" while Duke Ellington's band blared from the Victrola. A canape or two dropped onto a tufted sofa, leaving smears of pate. Whiskey sloshed from crystal tumblers; ice cubes skittered across the floor when a drink was carelessly poured. A record shattered on the parquet when it toppled off the record cabinet. The gentlemen's ties were loosened, the ladies fanned themselves with perfectly manicured fingers. Even the inanities uttered by the doe-eyed Gracey whipped up loud guffaws.

A mantle clock chimed two. "We really must be leaving," Sophie said, leaning heavily on James. "Emily, I can't remember when we've had such a lark."

"Oh, if you must. But we will do this again." Then the rest of Emily's friends departed, and Nicholas rounded up his friends as well. He managed to rouse Dotty, curled up and asleep in a love seat. "Thanks, Aunt Emily! You're a peach." He guided Dotty forward, gently removing the spidery false eyelash that had drifted onto her cheek, as he and his band of merrymakers headed out the door.

Back in the parlor, Emily found Lena ineffectually daubing at a spill with a linen cocktail napkin. "I think everyone had a good time, Emily, but I'm afraid there's a bit of a mess."

Emily scanned the disarray that remained and hugged her sister. "Go to bed, Lena. Catherine will deal with this in the morning."

In her room, Emily stepped out of her dress and peeled off her undergarments, leaving them in a heap on the floor. Too exhausted to remove her make-up or brush her hair, she slipped into a nightgown and crawled into bed. The melody of "It Don't Mean a Thing" drifted in her head, but she was asleep before the first verse ended.

Chapter Thirty-Four

EMILY LINGERED IN her boudoir the next morning, savoring the afterglow of the party. Evenings of dancing and light-hearted banter had once been central to her life, and last night's merriment sparked a carefree joy that had been snuffed out by John's infirmities. Oh, how she missed it. Did John miss it as well? His unabashed self-confidence and vitality were what had drawn her to him, but these traits had diminished, often leaving him cranky and querulous. She wanted her old life back, a life where fun was around every corner, where laughter laced every conversation. It was well after breakfast before she emerged, freshly bathed and coifed, to begin her day.

Maybe she and Lena could take in a matinee. She quietly peered into the guest room, but Lena was still asleep, the curtains drawn against the morning sunlight. *Too many cocktails, I suppose.* In the parlor, Catherine was rubbing furniture polish into a water ring on a table. The room had been set to rights, as Emily knew it would be.

"Good morning, Catherine. I trust your mister is

doing better." Not waiting for Catherine to respond, Emily strode toward the dining room. "Coffee in the urn?"

"Yes, missus." Catherine stood. "Beg pardon, but Mr. John asks you to join him in his office."

How tiresome. She was in no hurry to rehash the evening with John. Was he calling her on the carpet, like some recalcitrant employee? She poured a cup of coffee and headed for his office. He was seated at his desk, a cigar in one hand, flipping through a stack of papers. In a nearby armchair was Ina, holding a notebook in her lap. Ignoring her, Emily approached her husband and hugged his shoulders from behind. "Good morning, John. You're to work bright and early, I see."

"So, you're finally awake, Emily. It's nearly noon. A late night, and a noisy one." He scowled at her and shoved the papers aside.

Emily chose not to mention that it was ten forty-five, not noon, and kept her voice light. "Oh, it was such fun. Too bad you felt that you had to duck out early. You could have shown those young ones a thing or two about dancing." She raised her eyebrows and flashed a teasing smile, waving her palms back and forth in a lively rhythm.

He swatted at the air. "With all my health problems, you certainly couldn't have expected me to dance. It's almost cruel of you to suggest it."

Emily sat in a chair next to the desk. "A pity, truly. You're such a superb dancer. I wonder if you're not as frail as you think you are."

Ina cleared her throat. "Mrs. Ringling, allow me to interrupt. Mr. Ringling should not become agitated, in spite of the improvements he has made in recent weeks. In fact, after his episode of rapid heart rate, I arranged for the doctor to make a house call this morning. He left about an hour ago."

Emily looked from John to Ina. "Really? How efficient of you, Miss Sanders. And you didn't feel it was necessary to inform me?"

"After your late evening, I did not feel I should disturb you." Ina lifted her chin. "I have my notes from Dr. Ewald's visit right here." She held up her notebook.

"I see." She turned to John. "And what did Dr. Ewald have to say? John, perhaps you can speak for yourself without relying on Nurse Sanders' copious notes."

"Well, despite the strain on my blood pressure that arose from the commotion here last evening, I seem to be doing rather well. Doctor Ewald prescribes continued rest and relaxation and he advised that I avoid any incidents that might cause me any nervous tension. Like that rake Nicholas." He sneered. "Inviting your nephew here has done me no favors."

Before Emily could object, he turned to his nurse.

"And Dr. Ewald complimented Ina here, on her thorough care. She seems to be the best elixir I could have found."

"Well, aren't we fortunate to have Nurse Sanders in our midst, keeping track of your every heartbeat?" Emily swallowed to quell her annoyance. Why did Ina grate on her so? After all, she was efficient and competent. Wasn't that what one wanted in a nurse? But her "I know best" demeanor ignited a mean streak in Emily. She fought the urge to lash out first at Ina for her unctuous displays and then at John, who reveled in the daily bath of devotion she provided.

"But here's the best news." John puffed on his cigar and set it on an ashtray. "The doctor has given me permission to return to Ca d'Zan. In fact," he threw his shoulders back and paused, adding weight to his next words. "We can leave immediately! Doctor Ewald feels it would be the best place for me to continue my recuperation. While you were still lollygagging this morning, the arrangements have been made for my *Jomar* to be here in New York in a few days." He tapped on his desk to add a flourish to his announcement.

"Really?" Emily's heart sank at the mention of Ca d'Zan. John's illness had confined them to New York, and her wings had been clipped by the reality of an ill spouse. But at least she was in her home city. Florida offered her no pleasure. Just as John's improving health might hold the promise of more freedom in the city she loved, she was now being pulled back to the mansion of Mable, where she would spend her days under the provincial scrutiny of the Sarasota elite. Her mind swirled to find objections to John's plan, to line up roadblocks that would keep them in New York.

"But, John, what about your nursing care? I don't see how that can be arranged. I won't have you endangering your health." Surely with all the talk of heart rates, that would give him pause. She turned to Ina. "Nurse Sanders, you must see the folly in this plan."

But John continued. "We've already taken that into account. Fortunately, Miss Sanders has agreed to accompany us to Ca d'Zan and continue providing my care. I've managed to convince her that she will come to love Ca d'Zan as we do, haven't I, Ina?"

Ina offered a simpering smile, the kind that Emily so despised. "Mr. John has told me how beautiful it all is in Florida. What a privilege for me to have this opportunity to care for him in such a paradise."

John chuckled. "A paradise for sure. Just you wait and see!"

Emily rubbed a finger across her mouth. "So, it's all decided," was all she could manage as disbelief turned into anger. *How dare he? Does he have no regard for what I might care to do?* "Nurse Sanders, I'd like to speak to my husband in private. Now."

The curtness in her tone brought Ina to her feet. "Certainly, Mrs. Ringling. Mr. John, just let me know when you're ready for your massage." She straightened her white cap and left the room.

When the door closed, John reached for his cigar and wagged it at Emily. "You needn't be so dismissive of her, Emily. She—"

"Stop right there, John Ringling. If anyone has been dismissive, it is you. Without even consulting me, you have arranged for us to travel back to Florida and to bring this woman into our house. Have I no say in anything?" She clenched her fists. "For a hundred reasons, I am furious." Grievances large and small enveloped her—his indifference, his evasiveness, his disregard for her opinions and feelings—but there was no point in rehashing all of it now.

He rolled his eyes. "Here we go again. The poor mistreated Emily. So tiresome."

"Yes, that's it. exactly. And I won't waste my breath going into detail since you clearly do not care about me." She grabbed his shoulder and brought her face within inches of his. "I don't know why—" She stopped herself from finishing her sentence, but the words hung in the air. *Why I did I ever marry you?* Unhanding him, she stepped back.

"Good lord, Emily! There you go stalking off again! But before you go, I need to ask you a question."

"What is it?" Her eyes were narrow slits.

"Do you know what happened to the two Chinoises pieces of Mable's that were in the parlor? They're missing. Did that ne'er-do-well Nicholas or one of his chums break them? Or swipe them?"

Emily's chest tightened. She had been sure that he would never notice, but this morning he must have been in the parlor, considering the party's aftermath. Would he uncover her secret?

She recovered in an instant and sneered at him. "Mable's Chinoises? Mable's? Mable isn't here anymore, John. And I have no idea what might have happened to those ugly things. But here's a thought. I noticed last night that your nurse was wearing Mable's pearls, so maybe she got the idea that she could help herself to those figurines as well. Why don't you ask her? And here is another question you might answer for me. Why did you claim to be fifty-two when we married? You're long, long past fifty-two, you old fool, and I cannot believe I was ever so blind as to believe a word you utter." *Finally, I've said it!*

He began to sputter a reply, but Emily was out the door, slamming it behind her, so his words never hit their mark.

Emily was not surprised when John never returned to the subject of the missing figurines. He was too distracted with preparations for the return to Sarasota, and he would never fathom that Emily had sold them. Maybe he assumed they were broken on the night of the party and blamed Nicholas. Regardless, Emily had the funds she had collected tucked away for her own use and did not regret her decision to sell the pieces.

The trip to Sarasota seemed interminable to Emily, with her, John and Ina sharing the *Jomar*. She avoided the observation room to escape John's grandiose descriptions and Ina's saccharine exclamations of wonder and spent most of the time in her room, the one that had belonged to Mable and still featured all of Mable's overblown décor.

They disembarked in downtown Sarasota on a warm afternoon. *Back at Ca d'Zan.* To Emily, the *Jomar* had seemed claustrophobic, but so did life in Florida. As their driver steered the Rolls Royce through the gates and down the lane, John pointed out the home's every feature to Ina, blinking in amazement and oozing little utterances of awe at the sights before her. Mable's rose garden, the museum off in the distance, the regal palm trees with branches swaying above their heads and the swimming pool were all described in minute detail as they neared the house.

Emily slumped in her seat as the automobile neared the mansion's front door. John's descriptions were the same ones she had heard only a few years ago. When had her admiration devolved into a jaded indifference? As Ina oohed and aahed, Emily caught John's eye. "I believe Miss Sanders is impressed, John." He had not sounded this buoyant, this robust in months. Perhaps the time in some fresh air would erase the pallor of his skin and the lines drawn at the corners of his mouth. Here, his health might be restored, and life could return to normal.

"My goodness, Mrs. Ringling! I'm dazzled!" Ina's voice bubbled with excitement.

"And this is only the exterior, my dear!" John waved his cigar toward the home's exterior. "Wait until you see all the wonders on the inside."

The driver stopped and hurried to open the car doors. As they stepped out, Martha stepped out onto the front steps to greet them. John clutched Ina's arm and barely paused his narration as they entered the foyer.

"Hello, Martha." Emily waited until John introduced Ina to the housekeeper. Then, removing her hat and gloves, she laid her hand on Martha's elbow. "It's been a long journey and I'm dying for a bath, just as soon as you arrange the luggage."

"Certainly, Mrs. Ringling." Martha glanced at Ina and John, now deep into John's explanation of the artistry on the ceiling. "Which room is your preference for the nurse?"

"Hmm, I hadn't considered. What might you suggest? One of the rooms along the north balustrade, I suppose." Emily stepped forward into the vast parlor and pointed upward at the mezzanine. "Any of those should be fine."

"As I thought, Mrs. Ringling. We'll have her things brought up to the blue room."

Without interrupting John's storytelling, Emily ascended the stairs to her suite that extended along the east side of the home. The blue room, now Ina's, was quite a distance from John's, but what was one to do in a house this large? In the city, Ina had been assigned a small guest room across the hall from his. Here, he would need an annunciator from his south corner suite to hers in case he needed assistance during the night. *Will I be hearing her scampering past my door in the middle of the night?*

"NO NEED TO stand on ceremony here, Ina," John said at breakfast on their first morning in Florida. "Now that we are out of the city, I'd much prefer to see you in something pretty that does not harken me back to my hospital days." He pointed a fork tipped with a chunk of cantaloupe toward Emily. "I'll arrange for Ina to have an account at one of the local shops. She can choose some clothing suitable for this warm climate. What shop do you suggest, Emily?"

So, John, whose Bendel's bills had been paid by her, was now underwriting the clothing of his nurse? Emily's coffee cup clanked onto the saucer. *What do I suggest? As if Ina and I would shop at the same places!* Bitter retorts surfaced but she focused on mopping up the coffee droplets that had splattered on the tablecloth.

"How generous of you, Mr. John." Ina nibbled at the edge of her lip and clasped her hands together. "And Mrs. Ringling, you're so kind to help me."

What was the name of that dowdy little place that hung big price tags from the garments in the window? She had never stepped foot in here, but it would be good enough for Ina. Emily spoke through gritted teeth. "Have Frank drive you to the Daisy Shop on Main, whenever you can get away. I'm sure they can help you."

By dinner time, Ina's white uniform was packed away, and she appeared in a flowery shirtwaist cinched at the waist by a patent leather belt.

"Doesn't she look like the breath of spring, Emily?" John said, and Emily had no choice but to agree.

Within a few days, a new pattern of domestic life emerged, one that left Emily feeling increasingly isolated. In the past, it seemed that the ghost of Mable was everywhere. Emily breakfasted under Mable's green Murano chandelier, sipped coffee from Mable's china cups, read the newspaper while her feet rested on Mable's tapestry footstool. But now, in addition to Mable, Emily was confronted constantly by the presence of Ina. Rarely far from John's side, Ina became a constant fixture at every meal, and John insisted she join them at every cocktail hour on the terrace.

Emily considered ways to tried to bring her husband's attention back to her. Determined to engage John in a reminiscence that only the two of them shared, she made a mental list of topics.

One evening, while she and John, with Ina by his side, were having drinks on the terrace, and Emily, wearied by Ina's incessant exclamations about the view, pulled her chair closer to John's and laid her hand on his knee. "John, dear, remember that wonderful evening when we first strolled through Amsterdam? And the moon over the canal, shimmering on the water?" She and hummed a few bars of "Them There Eyes" and gave his knee a light squeeze. "I close my eyes and I'm back there with you."

John drew in on his cigar. "But not as wonderful as this view." He nodded toward the gulf.

Emily forged ahead, training her fingers lightly along his leg. "But the romance, the air was filled with it, wasn't it? I can still see how handsome you looked."

John snorted. "Well, the years have passed." Absentmindedly he patted her hand on his leg, then turned to Ina. "Don't suppose you've been to Amsterdam, have you, Ina?"

"Oh, no. Maybe someday." Ina sipped her seltzer, having refused anything alcoholic while "on duty." "But I'm kind of a homebody, I suppose."

John chuckled. "Well, I've turned into a homebody

too, it appears."

Like a shawl of thick wool, a heaviness descended on Emily. *He has lost all interest in me. And now I'm just a reminder of what he can no longer do—travel the world.* She pulled her hand from John and lifted her glass, draining her Rob Roy. "I think I'll head in. Getting rather chilly out here."

She stood, a lump forming in her throat, and walked toward the house. The sinking sun had painted the stonework with a rich golden glow and the terracotta adornments shimmered in the light. *I hate this place.*

Inside, she passed Mable's unoccupied Delft birdcage, larger than a telephone booth, and stopped to peer in through its bars. *I'm like one of those tropical birds kept in an exquisite home, trapped, my freedom exchanged for a life defined by another.*

Chapter Thirty-Five

JOHN'S INITIAL BURST of vigor upon arrival at Ca d'Zan dwindled within a week or two, and his health see-sawed from surges of a robust spirit to bouts of leg pain and episodes of heart palpitations. Each morning, Emily, determined to present a cheeriness that she did not feel, entered his bedroom to gauge his condition and to jolly him out of any ill humor. Her happiness and freedom rested on John's condition. The sooner he was well, the sooner their marriage might be revitalized.

One sunny morning, she burst in with only a light tap on the door, calling out, "John, the day could not be any lovelier! Why don't we—" She stopped in mid-sentence. Seated at a small table set for breakfast was John, unshaven and still in his bathrobe, and across from him sat Ina wearing a pink satin dressing gown. A pot of tea sat between them. Behind them were John's beds. His room was furnished with two, a gilt-encrusted pair arranged side-by-side, and it was obvious that both had been slept in.

Emily froze. Swept with a wave of dizziness, she

grasped the doorframe to steady herself. Then she stepped forward and pointed a finger toward Ina. "She slept here? She slept here?"

Ina's cheeks pinked and her hands fluttered. "Mrs. Ringling, your husband—" but Emily would not let her finish, thrusting her palm forward.

"Quiet! How dare you!"

John stood. "Emily, I don't like your insinuation here." He scowled and shook his head.

Emily spit out a derisive laugh. "Insinuation? This woman has spent the night in my husband's bedroom." Her voice rose and she jabbed a finger in his face. "This is intolerable! I want her out now."

John turned to his nurse. "I apologize, Ina, for my wife's outburst. Why don't you return to your room now and I'll speak to Emily privately."

As Ina slipped from the room, Emily clenched and unclenched her fists. When the door closed, she stepped closer toward John, her nostrils flaring. "How dare you, you bastard, bringing that trollop in here right under my nose." She slammed her palms into his chest.

He grasped her wrists. "You are jumping to ridiculous conclusions, my dear. Get a hold of yourself."

His quiet tone only incensed her further. "I hate you!" She tried to wrench herself from his grasp, but he held tight.

"I'll ignore that comment for now. But I will tell you

that after you retired for the evening, my heart rate became erratic. Ina and I felt it best that she remain here so she could monitor it, and so that I could call out to her if necessary."

"You can reach her through the annunciator, just like any other servant." Emily yanked her hands away from John's loosened grip. "There is no need for her to sleep here." She smeared tears across her cheeks. "It's outrageous!"

"Emily, I cannot tolerate your theatrics. This is simply a practical matter. Ina's room is on the other side of the house, and if she is to provide care for me, she must be with me, even during the night. She and I agreed that this would be best." He slumped into his chair and mopped his brow with his sleeve. "Really, your behavior is most upsetting. I can feel my blood pressure rising due to your outburst. Please settle yourself down, for my sake."

Emily glared at him. "You demean me constantly, John Ringling." Then she grabbed the teapot and hurled it at the bed where Ina had slept. As the pot crashed onto a golden cherub perched on the headboard, splinters of porcelain and swaths of tea flew in every direction. "That's what I think of you and your nurse."

BACK IN HER room, Emily allowed her tears to flow. John and Ina in their dressing gowns, the tumble of sheets on unmade beds, the cozy domesticity…the images filled her with a bitterness she could taste, a wrenching in her stomach. Once her tears dried, she paced the room, parsing her emotions. She was angry, but what else? Humiliated. Mortified. Contemptuous. Vengeful. The words tumbled around within her, each taking precedence momentarily, only to be bumped aside by another stronger one. Questions presented themselves, but no answers. Should she divorce John? Their marriage was a sham. But to divorce the beloved, the renowned John Ringling? Where would that leave her? She told herself not to be hasty, all the while wondering how she could bear another day. For the moment, she knew that she had to escape, to clear her head.

She slipped down the stairs, hoping she would encounter no one, and headed for the garage. Frank was there, buffing the shine on the Rolls.

"Can I help you, Mrs. Ringling?"

She faked a carefree smile. "No, I'm off on my own today. I'll just take the Pierce."

"Of course. Just getting the Rolls ready for Mr. Ringling, but I can back out the Pierce for you if you like." He wiped is hands on the buffing cloth.

Where was John going? She wanted to ask but stopped herself. She would not succumb to asking the help to inform her of her husband's whereabouts. "Sure. Then I'll be on my way."

Once in the car and out the gates of Ca d'Zan, Emily felt the tension ease from her shoulders. She savored the wind that tousled her hair and the spray of crunchy paving shells that erupted under her tires as she sped along. *Where to?* The question hung over her as she continued down the road. *Where to today, this moment, and where to, in the future?* She mulled over the question and without thinking, found herself heading over the causeway to Lido Key. She parked the car and headed for a quiet spot on the beach.

She wandered far from other beachgoers, removed her shoes and stockings and dug her toes into the sand. Tucking her skirt under her knees, she sat down and sifted grains of sand through her fingers as she stared at the Gulf. *What to do?*

Was John having an affair with Ina? The scene she'd come upon that morning certainly made it appear so. But would Ina be quite so bold? Wouldn't she at least attempt to hide any improprieties from Emily? But what about John? She had chalked off their lack of intimacy to his weakened health. Could it be he had simply lost his desire for her, and was now pursuing his nurse?

Or could what she had seen this morning been just what John said it was—a nurse staying close to her patient? After all, it was hard to imagine that Ina, young and, Emily had to admit, quite pretty, would be attracted to an aging invalid, no matter what riches he might offer.

It was laughable, really.

Should I divorce him? She slid her wedding ring off her finger and held it in front of her, twisting it back and forth so that the diamonds winked in the sunlight. She thought back to her life before John, alone in the world. She had been lonely, but she also had independence. Setting the ring onto the sand, she dug a small hole, set the ring inside, then buried it. Without the ring on her finger, she felt lighter. Maybe a divorce would be for the best.

But wouldn't that be simply playing right into his hands? If she divorced him, he could wash his hands of her, accuse her of abandoning him in his time of need. John's influence was far-reaching, from Florida to New York, and the headlines of gossip columns would scream her name. And if she dragged Ina into it, wouldn't that reflect on her, a wife who couldn't keep her husband happy? She would be a laughingstock and a pariah. Life with John was difficult; life without him would be hellish.

She unburied the ring and returned it to her finger, then scooped up a fist full of sand and flung it forward.

No. She would not make this easy for him. She had given him some of the best years of her life. She and Edward had parted ways, all because of her marriage to John. She had been steadfast through his illness. And he still owed her the money he had borrowed when they married. If she divorced, she could kiss her money goodbye.

He may wish to be rid of her, but she was going nowhere. She was Mrs. John Ringling and she intended to keep it that way. No insipid little nurse was going to get the better of her.

Spring melted into summer and Emily and John settled into an armistice dotted with stilted pleasantries coating an undercurrent of disdain. Emily insisted that if Ina found it necessary to stay in John's room, she would be informed, and Ina, contrite at having been discovered there in her dressing gown, quickly acquiesced.

Occasionally, Hester invited Emily to join a bridge game or a lecture at a woman's club meeting where she cultivated a few friends. Emily surmised that Hester had found the rift between her mother Edith, the Gumpetrzes and John to be awkward, but had decided to forge ahead with good will toward Emily. For that kindness, Emily as grateful, and she and Hester steered clear of any conversations regarding the circus or the bank.

"We won't let family finances get in our way," Hester assured Emily, but at times it was difficult to navigate around the topics that were central to their lives. Emily wished she could be frank with Hester and pry loose some of the details that John concealed from her, but at the same time, she hesitated to admit that her husband willfully kept her in the dark.

When the Ringling Bank was sold after the National Bank Holiday, she found out by reading the Sarasota paper. She brought the article to John, busying himself in his home office. "Must I learn about your business strictly from reading the *Herald*?"

John heaved an exasperated sigh. "We've gone over this before, Emily. I'm not required to fill you in on my business."

"But the bank! Do you not suppose everyone in Sarasota has been talking about this? I imagine I've at sat at bridge tables with women whose funds have been tied up there. No wonder I'm so often met with aloofness."

"All the reason why you don't need to know. I won't have my wife involved in tittle-tattle about my business."

"Well, it appears that Edith has taken the credit for reimbursing the depositors."

John snatched the paper from her, and she knew that her retort had hit its target. But at least no one could accuse John of defrauding his neighbors. It was difficult enough to live in a town where everyone knew her name, and she did not relish the thought of her reputation tainted by any of her husband's failures.

UNDER THE WEIGHT of incessant tropical heat Emily fought to chase away a torpor that settled over her. She was tired of sweltering sunshine followed by sultry nights, of superficial conversations, of the ubiquitous Nurse Sanders hovering over John.

She took long drives alone in the Pierce Arrow, exploring the rural areas that surrounded the city, corresponded with faraway friends, and devoured the commentary and society news in every issue of *The New Yorker* that made its way to Ca d'Zan.

One afternoon, John was restless, so he arranged for Frank to take him, Emily, and the ever-present Ina on a drive to St. Armand Key, and the three of them lined up in the Rolls' back seat with Ina in the middle. Crossing the Causeway, John informed Ina that he had been the mastermind behind building it and then donating it to the city of Sarasota. Once on St. Armand, John pointed out where he'd had his hand in the development. Emily had heard it all before and noted silently several unkempt and uncompleted projects surrounding a few well-appointed homes. The Circle, its lawn a mass of weeds, was especially shabby.

But Ina was agog. "Mr. John, this is incredible. It's as if you've waved a magic wand and there was this beautiful city." Ina's eyes were glossy with admiration, and John preened.

"You know, I have to admit that the city of Sarasota loves me. You should have read the accolades in the paper when I gave the Causeway to the city."

Emily curled her lip in disgust and pointed at the bandshell in the center of the Circle. "This looks more derelict than the last time we were out here. I've had enough, John. This heat is stifling. Let's head back."

John's eyes flicked upwards. "So negative, Emily. If you insist. Frank, Mrs. Ringling is ready to return." He glanced toward Ina whose lips were pressed together in disapproval.

"Certainly." Frank steered the car around the circle and headed back across the Causeway.

On the shell road, Ina leaned forward. "Remember to take it slow, Frank. We don't to jar Mr. Ringling along this bumpy road."

"Ina, for heaven's sake. Must you mollycoddle him?" Emily crossed her arms over her chest. No wonder John was so smitten with his nurse. She hung on his every word, then indulged him like a child, while Emily was cast as the complainer simply because she pointed out the truth. Under her breath, she muttered, "I wish Frank would drive faster and let the son of a bitch feel every bump!"

"What did I hear you say, Emily?" John jerked his head to look at her, his brow puckered. "Damn it, Emily, have you gone mad?"

"Mrs. Ringling, my goodness!" Ina threw her shoulders back in umbrage while Frank stammered his noncompliance.

Had she spoken the words aloud? She had not meant for her comment to be heard, but now that it was out, she felt no regret. She was tired of John's infirmities that seemed at times to wax and wane depending on his mood, and of his insipid nurse, even now wedged between them in the car. She responded with a shrug and an "I was only kidding!" and stared at the Bay, willing her furor to subside.

Once they reached the curved driveway of Ca d'Zan, Frank got out of the car to assist John. As Emily opened the door on her side of the back seat, Ina grabbed her arm. "Mrs. Ringling, I must remind you that Mr. John cannot endure such upheaval. I advise you—"

"I don't need your lectures, Ina." Emily bolted from the car and stalked up the steps, not stopping until she reached her bedroom.

What had gotten into her? Where had this malice come from? She recalled a long-ago trip with Charles, in the early days of their marriage, to Taormina, Sicily. There, well-heeled tourists basked in the warmth of the Ionian Sea, dined on the local seafood, and explored the ancient temples, all the while ignoring the volcanic puffs that rose from nearby Mt. Etna. Wasn't anyone afraid of a full-blown eruption, she wondered. But someone explained. Mt. Etna posed little danger. Those thin streams of smoke were a good thing, allowing the volcano to expel some of the heat without bursting forth with a major explosion. She found herself becoming a Mt. Etna, disgorging small wisps of ugly remarks toward John to keep herself from a catastrophic eruption.

That evening at dinner, she wore her best smile, determined to wheedle her way into John's good graces. But on this night, he had another topic on his mind, his yacht the *Zalophus*.

"You should have seen it, Ina. It was quite a vessel, the showpiece of the yacht club back in its day. Famous all over the west coast of Florida, featured in every boating magazine. One hundred twenty-five feet, if you can imagine. Much longer than the *Jomar*." He smiled and tipped his head. "Sure was a beauty."

Ina murmured a wistful sigh and Emily recalled when she had first heard of the *Zalophus*. She tuned out John's ramblings as she recalled the dinner with the Ziegfelds.

AFTER THAT FOURTH of July gala In Amsterdam, it seemed that John never left her side. During the day, he was busy, acquiring art works for his museum, but in the evenings, they often went dancing or out to dinner. One evening, she and John had been dining at the Schiller Café with the Ziegfelds. At first, Emily had been dazzled by this glamorous couple, but after spending several evenings with them, the glitter had faded. She found Flo tiresome, full of show business stories that always centered on his perceived acumen, and his wife, the film star Billie Burke, spoke in a twittery voice that set Emily's teeth on edge. Yet, she feigned admiration, knowing that John found them amusing.

After a meal of heavy schnitzels and potatoes that Emily only picked at, a waiter with slicked back hair and a precisely curled mustache brought a silver tray of aperitifs to the table. Emily held her delicate crystal up to the candlelight, admiring the amber glow of the cognac. She pondered when she and John could escape these two. Could they never dine alone?

"So, John, what's that I hear about your yacht sinking? Sounds like an amusing story," said Ziegfeld, leaning back into the velvet upholstery of the booth. He tipped his head back, drinking the entire aperitif in one gulp, then signaled to the waiter for more. "Remember it, Billie? We took a spin around the bay with Mable a few summers ago."

Billie nodded, placing her hand on her chest dramatically. "Oh, it was a grand day! We had so much fun with darling Mable. What happened, John?" Her face sank into a theatrical pout, one that Emily had seen playing out on Billie's face with frequency.

It seemed to Emily that Mable was never very far removed from any conversation. Mable... Mable... dead over a year and that was all anyone talked about with John.

She leaned forward, her fingertips touching John's suitcoat. "A sunken ship? Oh, my! Do tell!"

But John was not amused. He puffed on his cigar, then waved it at his listeners. "That damned Sam Gumpertz... he's my circus manager. Trying to be a big shot while I was away on business. Took our *Zalophus* out at three in the morning, then crashed it into rocks near Lido Key. Boom! Her steel hull completely smashed in, and she sunk." He shook his head in disgust, then took a gulp of his cognac.

"Goodness, John. Was anyone killed?" Emily leaned forward, her wide eyes looking intently into John's.

"No, thankfully. Just my beautiful Zalophus, all one hundred twenty-five feet of her. Never to be seen again. Thankfully Mable wasn't around to see it. She would have been bereft." He turned away from Emily, staring toward the bar, and Emily sensed that he was miles, no, years, away.

Ziegfeld dug in. "Wasn't Jimmy Walker on the boat? The Mayor of New York? And that actress, you know, Betty Compton. I heard about some hanky panky. Just imagine them being plucked from the water dripping wet! Har, har. Pretty titillating stuff, John!" he guffawed. "Got you some press."

Emily's brow furrowed at Ziegfeld. Didn't he see John's pain? Then she turned to John and patted his arm. "Well, I think it's terrible. I'm so sorry you lost your lovely boat." Her blue eyes were full of sympathy, and John's frown faded.

"Thank you, dear Emily. There were so many good times on that beautiful vessel." He sighed. "Let's call it a night, shall we?" he reached over and gave her hand a squeeze. "You've already lifted my melancholy."

✧ ✧ ✧

ON THAT LONG-AGO night, she had listened sympathetically to John's loss of his precious yacht. Tonight, she felt only annoyance at his incessant boasting to impress Ina.

"Don't forget to tell her how the boat sunk with the Mayor of New York on board." Emily snorted. "An inglorious end."

John glared at Emily as Ina put her palms to her cheeks in distress.

"Oh, how sad!" she cried.

That's exactly how I reacted when I heard the story. But tonight, she felt hollowed out. She had become nearly invisible to her husband unless it was to be on the receiving end of a rebuke. She could not recall the last time he had complimented her, engaged her in a conversation, or had shown her any affection. Yet here she was, steadfastly by his side, traveling from New York to Florida as he wished, far from the company of family and friends, cut off from her New York way of life. Isolation gnawed at her.

She stood. "I'm going to retire early. I'm feeling headachy."

John muttered, "Feel better," as she left the dining room.

SOON AFTER, SHE wrote to Lena.

"Please come to Ca d'Zan. I'm at loose ends and I cannot bear to attend one more luncheon where all the ladies wish to discuss is whose magnolia trees have the most blossoms. John is often out of sorts, and we rarely entertain. I know it's brutally hot here, but we can dip into the pool and catch a breeze on the terrace. I miss you, dear sister.

Chapter Thirty-Six

July 1933

EMILY FOUND HER sister Lena in the solarium, stretched out on a chaise under the ceiling fan, concentrating on a crossword puzzle in the newspaper folded on her lap.

"Good heavens, it's warm!" Lena dabbed at her cheeks with a hanky. "I'm clammy from this Florida heat."

"I agree, dear. But I just can't leave John alone." She wrinkled her nose. "I need to be here."

"Alone?" Lena scoffed. "John is never alone, Emily, not with Nurse Ina hovering around." She rolled her eyes.

"That's exactly what I mean. He is held in her clutches, but if I were to go to New York, I'd have no idea what was going on. So, I must stay and be vigilant." Emily perched on the edge of a chair. "But let's leave the house for a while. I've checked in on John, and he's planning to go to his downtown office this morning. I thought you and I could drive into town, pop into some

THE SECOND MRS. RINGLING

of the shops, and have lunch on the hotel terrace. There should be a nice breeze from the gulf."

"Oh, let's." Lena set her newspaper and pencil on an end table. "I'll get my hat and be ready in five minutes."

DOWNTOWN SARASOTA WAS no less steamy than Ca d'Zan, but Emily and Lena wandered in and out of the shops where electric fans stirred the air. In La Mode, Emily purchased a linen blouse for Lena, who had admired its crisp light fabric and stylish collar. Then, they headed into Kress's.

"One always needs something from Kress's," Emily remarked as they entered its doors. "Today, it's some hair pins and emery boards." She and Lena headed for the aisle that displayed hair goods.

"I as well. I hope they have the blonde pins, not just the black ones." Lena scrutinized the racks. "Ah, here they are!'"

Neither woman noticed the man in a gray suit and fedora approaching them until he spoke. "Mrs. Ringling?"

Emily turned to face him. Who was this? He did not look familiar, and his expression was dour. Was he soliciting for some charity? So tedious to be hounded while out running errands. In New York she could go about her business unnoticed, but not here in this provincial town. "I am Mrs. Ringling. How can I help you?"

"I'm a process server from the Sarasota courthouse, here to serve you these papers." He tapped the brim of his hat as he handed her a large envelope. "Good day, Mrs. Ringling." Before she could respond, he turned and left the store.

"What on earth!" Could he have meant this for Edith Ringling? Surely there had been some error. She studied the envelope. No, it was addressed to her. Emily Ringling.

Lena looked over her shoulder. "What is it?"

"I can't imagine. Looks official, though." Emily glanced around the store. A woman in the aisle next to hers was studying a selection of headscarves, but her eyes were darting over to Emily and Lena. Two others, their mouths agape, were staring at them. Yes, she'd been recognized. Had they heard the man say he was a process server? Emily imagined the tornado of gossip that would commence. "I can't open this here. Let's pay for our items and leave."

Emily nudged Lena toward the counter where the clerk stood to complete their purchase. "Just these today." Emily handed the clerk the pins and managed to pull some coins from her purse without dropping them. What was in the envelope? And why was it given to her in Kress's, of all places? Once outside, she and Lena headed for her Pierce Arrow parked nearby.

THE SECOND MRS. RINGLING

In the car, Emily opened the envelope and slid out an official-looking document. She blanched as she read. Disbelief, mortification, then anger pulsed through her as she scanned the document page by page. "That bastard! That bastard!"

Lena snatched the document from Emily. "What is it?"

"He is filing for a divorce!" Emily slapped the steering wheel and hot tears clouded her eyes. "How dare he! How dare he!" Overcome by dizziness, she swallowed bile that had risen in her throat. Was she going to vomit? This could not be happening.

Lena shook her head as she studied the papers and then she grasped her sister's arm. "How could he? Did you have any inkling?"

"No, none whatsoever." Emily let out a low moan. She had toyed with the idea of divorcing him for months, but never expected that he would be the one to initiate this. She was the one who'd been suffering in this marriage, not him.

"Emily, take a deep breath, dear. Let's not stay here. Are you able to drive?" Her voice was calm. "Look at me, Em. We need to get you home. We can't sit here on Main Street." She noted a few passersby looking with curiosity at them in the parked car. "People are wondering what we're doing, sitting in this hot car."

Emily brushed the tears from her cheeks. "You're

right. I've got to get out of here." She bit her lip and focused on starting the car and although her legs were trembling, she managed to put it in gear and pull away.

Her heart thudded in her chest. What was she going to do? She must confront him at once. "He's at the downtown office right now. Maybe I should go in and demand an explanation. Have it out right there for all of the staff to see."

Lena shook her head. "No, I don't think so, Emily. Let's consider."

Emily whimpered as she stared at the road ahead. Who else might know? Did that horrible nurse Ina have a hand in this? "I'm so humiliated. That bastard! If anyone should be filing for divorce it should be me."

"I agree. He treats you shabbily." Lena crossed her arms. "I don't know what to say, Emily."

I won't be shamed like this. I won't. Emily willed her tears to cease as she struggled to weigh her options. She would not be tossed aside, disgraced by this man who she'd catered to these past years. She'd spent the miserable summer here in Sarasota, nearly dying of heat and boredom, and what good had come of it. She had to get away, do her thinking and planning outside of this stifling atmosphere.

They rode in silence until they drove through the gates to Ca d'Zan. Emily stopped the car in front of the house and turned toward her sister. She wiped the tears from her face and spoke decisively. "We're leaving, Lena. Clearly, I cannot stay here. Pack your things. We can be on the evening train for New York if we hurry."

Up in her room, Emily tossed clothing into open suitcases she'd had Martha deliver to her room. Folding a blue cocktail dress, she recalled when she had first worn it—Christmastime of '31, the magical night at the Park Central with Edward. She should have left John then. She'd had ample reasons. But no, she had chosen to salvage her marriage. And for what?

When she finished packing, she rang the annunciator. "Please send the driver to collect my bags. And my sister's as well."

When a knock came at her door, she opened it to allow her bags to be carried to the car. But standing there was John. He cleared his throat, began to reach toward her, then pulled back.

"Get away from me, John." Emily began to close the door, but he stepped forward and grasped its frame.

"Let me explain all of this, Emily."

"Explain? You've filed for divorce. A divorce you've never even mentioned to me. And now you wish to explain? You bastard. You damn bastard." Impulsively, she slapped John's face with a resounding smack. Had she really struck him? She was not sorry. He'd provoked her. She pushed the door again but when he did not withdraw his grasp on the frame, she crossed her arms and sneered. "I'll be out of Ca d'Zan in a matter of minutes. Lena and I will be on the evening train for New York."

"Get a hold of yourself, Emily. You're overwrought." He rubbed his cheek. "This is nonsense. No need for you to leave. You can remain in Ca d'Zan." He pursed his lips and inched forward, still grasping the door frame. "Come now. No reason to overreact."

Emily's head swam. Overreact? He could not be serious. She had just been served with a divorce filing and now he was suggesting she remain under the same roof as he? Suppressing the urge to hit him again, she spit out, "You bastard. You bastard." She could summon no other words but stopped herself from slapping him again. Of course, she would leave. Just the sight of him feigning concern enraged her. He had shown her nothing but callous disdain, sending the server into Kress's, publicly shaming her.

"Now, Emily, let's be reasonable. Perhaps we can come to some agreement, some meeting of the minds."

His words may have been meant to mollify her, but they had the opposite effect. She pushed her hands against his chest. "I won't be humiliated this way, John. Why have you been so cruel? Is it that conniving nurse of yours? Or your miserable financial losses?"

"Emily, surely you realize that our marriage has not been a strong one for quite some time. You've shown little regard for—"

"I have shown little regard? You must be joking." Again, she slapped his chest. She thought of the gossip that would bloom, tittle tattle in the society columns, with her name tossed around for the amused speculation of others. If he were the initiator of the divorce, he would be the sympathetic character in the story. Then there was the fifty thousand dollars he had yet to repay her, money she had lent him even before they married. If she left, would she ever see that money again? No, she would not allow John to orchestrate their lives this way. She would write a different scene, one where she would be the righteous one.

She clenched her fists at her side. What choice did she have? Would fleeing to New York be in her best interest or would it be playing right into his hands? She thrust out her jaw and sneered at him. "I'll stay. For now. And you will need to drop this divorce. For your sake as well as for mine. Now get out of my sight."

He let go of the door frame, nodding his head and wiping his brow. "We will discuss this later, Emily. I need to rest. My palpitations."

His face, she noticed, had reddened, but she felt no sympathy for his affliction. "Better go back to your nurse." She slammed the door.

AND SO, SHE had stayed, as had Lena. Emily, usually the

one with advice and counsel for her sisters, now clung to Lena as her sounding board. On the morning after the delivery of the divorce papers, they walked around the withering rose bushes that had once been Mable's prized garden, now neglected after John had stopped paying the gardeners. Out of earshot of the household, the two sisters mulled over Emily's future.

"Maybe a divorce would be to my benefit. I could take up my life in New York once again, without the encumbrance of a sickly husband." Emily plucked a limp blossom from a bush, tearing the petals off one by one.

"But think of the degradation, tossed aside by the wonderful Mr. Ringling. Could you bear it? The rumors swirling around you everywhere you went?" Lena shook her head. "I can hear the comments. 'She couldn't keep him happy. She's a heartless shrew.' I'm being blunt, Emily, only because others will be."

"Do you believe it would be that bad?"

Lena hugged her sister's shoulder. "You know it would be, Emily."

"But maybe, then," Emily paused. Dare she say the name, Edward? While she still nursed improbable fantasies involving the two of them, she would not reveal them now to Lena, who had never known Edward. She continued. "But maybe then I could find a new life, somewhere far away." She knew this sounded improbable even as she spoke the words. Where on earth would she, a woman alone, go to begin anew?

"Emily, really."

"I know, Lena. I know. But I won't make this easy for John. I'm not giving up what is due me. He still owes me a small fortune."

EMILY AVOIDED JOHN as well as Ina, requesting that her lunch be served in her room. Later that afternoon, Martha knocked on her door. "Mr. Ringling would like to see you in his office."

He treats me like a business adversary instead of a spouse. But what choice did she have? Steeling herself to remain calm, she complied. She discovered that she and John would not be alone, for seated on a chair was a man she recognized.

"Emily, you remember Henry Williford." John, seated behind his desk, waved his cigar in the direction of his attorney, a plump, bespectacled man with a nest of unruly gray hair.

Williford stood up and bent at the waist. "Good day, Mrs. Ringling."

Emily looked coolly from Williford to John and perched on a chair. "I didn't expect that we would need a lawyer present, John, to discuss our marriage."

John rested his cigar on an ashtray. "Emily, your increasingly volatile and cruel behavior has led me to file for a divorce. But I'm willing to compromise. Henry, why don't you explain what I am proposing."

Williford peered over his spectacles. "What your husband is proposing is quite straightforward." He reached for a folder on the table next to him and cleared his throat. Lifting a paper from the folder, he began to read in a monotone.

The words, dry and lawyerly, washed over her as she concentrated on absorbing their substance. *So it is a business transaction.* John was demanding that she relinquish her dower rights and any rights to the museum. In addition, she must cease demanding the immediate repayment of the loan she had made to him. If she agreed, he would rescind the divorce filing.

When Williford finished reading, he laid the papers on the table. "Those are the terms, Mrs. Ringling."

Emily shook her head and turned to John. She dug her nails into her palms and struggled to swallow her humiliation and anger, like lumps of gravel clogged her throat. "You're treating me like an unscrupulous business associate. Where is your heart?"

"My heart?" He sniffed. "How ironic that you should inquire about my heart. Your shrillness, your interminable outbursts have affected my heart to its core."

"But you owe me! I'm your wife." She massaged her forehead and sat in silence for a moment. When she began to speak again, her voice was firm. "I can tell my side of the story as well. Your failure to repay me fifty thousand dollars puts you in a bad light, and then there is the matter of close relationship with your nurse."

"Ina?" He chuckled. "You should know that she has kept records of times you've lashed out at me and then recorded its effects on my blood pressure." He inhaled on his cigar and then pointed at her. "Listen, Emily. You must understand you are powerless to fight this. Do you realize that in the state of Florida, I can do no wrong? Isn't that right, Henry?" He looked to his lawyer who nodded in ascent. "Here in Sarasota, public sentiment is strongly in my favor. I have influential friends in every court across the state. And Florida wants the Museum, so they will do anything I request. Abide by my terms, or I can promise you, your name will be dragged through the mud in every state. Neither of us wants that, do we?"

Williford cleared his throat again. "Mrs. Ringling, I advise you to strongly consider your husband's proposal here. And then sign it." He slid the papers in her direction.

She sat without moving, ignoring the expectant gazes from both John and Williford that bore into her. Of all that she had heard, the discovery that Ina had been creating a record, attempting to link her to John's heart condition, was the most shocking. Had Ina been plotting with John all along, while ingratiated herself as his indispensable companion? How dare Ina be so conniving?

In hindsight, she realized that she had made a mistake with Ina. She had seen the nurse as an intrusion into their lives and had voiced her displeasure repeatedly to John. It had gotten her nowhere. Instead, John had not only defended Ina, but had protected her from Emily's ire. Too late, Emily realized that by making Ina an adversary, she had all but handed her over to her husband.

Managing to hold her emotions in check, Emily snatched the papers from the table. "It appears you've made yourself clear." She stood and left the room, resisting the temptation to slam the door behind her.

A PALL OF tension settled over Ca d 'Zan, as if all were actors in a well-directed play who could not appear on stage at one time. Emily and Lena claimed the solarium and the terrace and dined upstairs, while John and Ina kept to John's room except when eating in the breakfast room. Emily's emotions roller-coastered from anger to inertia, from revenge to grief. When the *Sarasota Herald* splashed the news of the divorce filing on the front page, Emily brought it to Lena, weeping. "I'm the laughingstock of Sarasota!"

Lena rubbed Emily's shoulder and murmured soothing noises. "No, dear, no. You're not."

But Emily read the pain in her sister's eyes. Then a telegram arrived from Sophie, offering sympathy and support. Her friend's kind words only fueled her despair as she recognized that word had traveled to New York as well. Still, she had not signed the papers that would reverse John's decision to divorce her.

A few days later, Emily was in the solarium, paging through the social pages of the New York Times, wondering if her name would appear in one of the columns. Instead, she came upon a wedding announcement.

"Mr. and Mrs. Michael Rogers announce the marriage of their daughter Caroline to Mr. Edward Appleton."

Emily's heart sank as she scanned the article and its accompanying photograph of a dreamy-eyed bride clutching a bouquet of calla lilies. The couple, the article said, would be making their home in Connecticut after honeymooning in San Francisco. Emily told herself to be pleased for him. The young bride looked lovely, and wasn't he deserving of happiness? And hadn't it been more than one year since she'd seen him? But her lip quivered, and grief washed over her. *You foolish woman. Was ist, ist.*

AFTER ANOTHER NIGHT contemplating her life as John's divorcee, she approached him in his home office. She could not, would not allow John to divorce her. "I'm begging you to end the divorce proceedings. I know I've been unkind at times, but your illness has burdened me as well as you. I vow to be more sympathetic, more even-tempered." She winced at the sound of her groveling whine but continued. "Please, John."

"Is that so?" His voice was bland, devoid of emotion. "Well, then, I'll rescind the divorce. But as I've told you before, you must first sign away any dower rights, including any claim on the Museum. In addition, I need a four-ear extension on that loan you made to me. Emily, divorce is not a pretty option, but I will follow through if you choose not to acquiesce." He leaned back in his chair, studying her. "You're not the woman I married, Emily. You have a harshness that has become more apparent. And I have witnesses that will testify that you have been cruel to me."

"But—" Emily felt her face redden with indignation but reminded herself not to take the bait. Tears pricked her eyes. "John, I want to remain married. Please, do not go through with this."

"You know my terms. Now dry your eyes, my dear, and do what's best for both of us. My offer stands for just a short time. And my word is my honor." He offered her his starched handkerchief, plucked from his shirt pocket. She crumpled it in her lap.

"Your word is your honor? Please spare me that sanctimonious drivel. You began our marriage by lying about your age on our license." She wanted to continue, to lash out to remind him of all the times he had shown indifference to her, but she checked herself. "I had hoped you would soften your stance, John, but I see that you have not. I won't take up any more of your time."

She left the office, and descending the stairs, she came face-to-face with Ina. How Emily wanted to lash out at her, for her simpering obsequiousness, for her perfectly applied red lipstick and gauzy summer frock that now replaced her nurse's uniform, for carefully plotting against Emily with a log connecting arguments with John to his episodes of hypertension. This woman was a snake in her midst, poisoning her marriage.

"Good morning, Mrs. Ringling." Ina stepped aside on the stairwell so Emily could pass. Emily did not return the greeting. Instead, she raised her chin and kept her eyes focused on the steps. *I will not acknowledge her presence.*

DAYS, THEN WEEKS passed, and Emily flitted from episodes of despair to bouts of righteous indignation. John remained polite but aloof, issuing an occasional reminder regarding the papers he expected her to sign. Sometimes Emily sounded off to Lena about the benefits of a divorce, the freedom to do as she pleased, but in her heart, she knew that the glaring notoriety as the woman cast off by John Ringling would be too grim.

"Should you hire your own attorney?" Lena suggested.

Emily raised her palms to the sky and heaved a sigh. "But who? Certainly, no attorney in Sarasota or even Tampa would side with me, and any I know in in New York are not apt to take on my case so far from their practices in Manhattan. Besides, John's influence reaches there too. Who would be willing to fight my battle against him?"

Restful sleep escaped Emily as her mind twisted from emotional turmoil to shrewd calculations. One night, when no breeze pierced the August heat, Emily left her bed and slipped down the stairs to the kitchen, hoping to find a pitcher of lemonade in the refrigerator. After pouring herself a glass, she sat in the parlor, turning on only one small lamp. She sat on a tufted ottoman and slid the cold drink across her forehead and along the back of her neck. Sipping the lemonade, she scanned the room, illuminated by the moonlight that streamed through the skylights. How she despised this place! The specter of Mable was everywhere—her fussy fabrics on every chair, her old-world bric-a-brac on every surface. Even after almost three years of marriage, Emily found no traces of herself, no sign that she was the mistress of Ca d'Zan. It was as if she had been swallowed up by the Ringling mystique. She stood and faced the portrait of Mable that still hung on the wall. Mable, swathed in ivory, her hands placidly folded on her lap, seemed to stare back at her impassively as Emily scrutinized her face.

"So, Mable, you may be dead, but you've never left, have you? You have never allowed me a moment's happiness in your precious Ca d'Zan." *Why have I tolerated having this portrait on the wall? I should have insisted she be removed, relegated to the attic and out of my sight, out of John's sight.* "Will you be happy if I leave?"

What if she gave in to John's demands? Perhaps it would be the most practical thing to do. How much longer would John live? One year? Two? If she held on to her marriage until his death, surely there would be some assets from his estate that she could claim, unrelated to his Museum. That Steinway no one ever played, those musty tapestries that John loved so much, each would draw a hefty sum. And, as John's widow, she would be garner sympathy; as his divorcee she would only garner scorn. *Have I really sunk this low, imagining the death of my spouse?* While she shrank back from her coldly pragmatic musings, she reminded herself that as a woman under the threat of a divorce, she had to put her best interests to the forefront of her decision-making.

"No, Mable, I won't go that easily." She set the lemonade glass on the piano, knowing that a water mark would result, and returned to bed.

THE NEXT MORNING, Emily awoke with her decision made. She joined Lena, sunbathing by the pool. "I'm giving in."

Lena sat up on the chaise and removed her sunglasses. "Giving in? What do you mean?"

"I'm signing what John wants me to sign." She shrugged. "I'm hollowed out. You and I have been over this and over this. There is no other way."

Lena ran her hand along Emily's shoulder. "You've been so tormented. Perhaps this will set things to rights."

"I hope." She let her eyes wander towards the Museum at the far corner of the property. "That Museum and its contents are what's important to John, not me. I have to accept that."

On August 31, 1933, Emily gave up her dower rights including to the Museum and extended the promissory note on the money that John had borrowed from her. John agreed to dismiss the divorce. Each of them agreed to keep the façade of their marriage in place, despite the spider-webbed threads of grievances and hurt that threatened to ensnare them both.

Chapter Thirty-Seven

AFTER SIGNING THE agreement that John demanded, Emily was relieved when John claimed that he needed to return to the city for business. Autumn in Manhattan was a welcome reprieve from the stifling heat of Florida and Emily found renewed energy as she made her way down the busy sidewalks, anonymous among the throngs of New Yorkers. In Sarasota, she had seldom ventured out after she was confronted with the divorce papers in Kress's, and when she did, she had regretted being in public. Even on a simple outing to the post office, she became the object of thinly veiled stares and smirks. Once she stopped in Liggett's Drugs to purchase aspirin and had encountered two women who had mistakenly assumed that a cupped hand over a mouth kept a whispered remark from reaching her ears.

"Isn't she the one Ringling is divorcing?" one woman in a straw hat bedecked with a cluster of paper cherries hissed to her companion.

Emily had glared at them and barked, "Yes, I am Mrs. Ringling, not that it should be any of your concern," then hurried past them as they huffed, "Well I never" as she made her exit.

But in Manhattan, its air crisp and cool, she could stroll the avenues, stop for tea at the Waldorf, or simply absorb the cacophony of automobile horns honking without her movements being observed and commented on by others. Escaping the apartment, she could avoid thinking about the tensions that existed between her and John, and could pretend, if just for a few hours, that their marriage was on a smoother path. It was exhilarating to be back in the city, and she vowed to stay away from Ca d'Zan as much as possible.

After the rescinding of the divorce filings had been published in the papers, John had simply said, "Let bygones be bygones," while making little attempt to change his habits. Although his health had shown improvement, Ina remained a part of the household, traveling with them back to the Park Avenue apartment. Emily dared not object, fearing the strife that would lead to another demand for a divorce, so she held her tongue. Her marriage was a charade, but she had come precariously close to the abyss, and she did not wish to hover so close to the edge again.

So, she seasoned her speech with "darling" and "dearest", invited John's New York associates in for cocktails, and play-acted the part of the doting wife while he held the floor, opining on the newly installed

President's plans to end the Depression, on the repeal of prohibition, and on his connection to the fan dancer Sally Rand, the star of the Chicago World's Fair. Instead of turning her nose up at Ina's dewy-eyed fawning over John, she found that if she sprinkled on more flattery of her own, John's temperament softened. This was the price she had to pay.

But despite her resolve to tamp down her emotions, eruptions threatened. When Bloomingdale's sent a notice that they were filing a lawsuit against both Emily and John, demanding payment, Emily burst into John's room, waving the notification in his face. "These are your bills to pay, John, and yet my good name is being dragged down by your financial failures."

John took the notice from her and laid it on his desk. "The small matter of Bloomingdale's is not worth my time right now, Emily. Now calm down and leave me be."

His dismissal lit a spark of fury and she lashed out at him. "You're an embarrassment, John, and a colossal failure. You can't even manage to pay simple household expenses. How low you've sunk."

"Enough, Emily! I will not tolerate your harping. Your shrillness is a detriment to my health." He pointed toward the door. "Out."

And so, she left the office, carrying with her dark thoughts about his health.

AND THEN THERE was Ina, who insinuated herself into all aspects of the household management. One afternoon, Emily stepped into the kitchen and observed Catherine preparing chicken for dinner. "I thought I requested lamb chops for this evening, Catherine."

Catherine wiped her hands on a towel and nodded. "Yes, missus, but then Nurse told me to prepare chicken." She stared at the counter and chewed her lip.

"Oh, did she?" Emily's eyes narrowed, but she stopped herself from scolding Catherine. Clearly, the woman was caught in the middle. "I see. I will speak to Nurse regarding menu decisions in the future. I'm sure the chicken will be fine."

Emily refrained from approaching Ina on this matter, but incidents piled up. Could their driver take Emily to visit her sisters in East Orange? No. he was already tied up with chauffeuring Nurse Ina for the day. Ina's directives, once centering on John's care—"The towels in Mr. Ringling's bath need to be changed."—now branched out in all directions.

"This carpet needs vacuuming."

"Dinner must be served no later than seven."

When Emily greeted an elderly neighbor, a Mrs. Willoughby, in the elevator one morning, the usually garrulous old woman barely acknowledged her hello, staring straight ahead at the descending numbers above the door. *Is she snubbing me?* Emily wondered, then brushed the thought aside. But later, when Emily returned from her errands, she found Ina and Mrs. Willoughby at the mailboxes, chuckling together like old friends.

Day after day, Emily observed Catherine, their driver, even the building's concierge, scurrying to do Ina's bidding. Where did that leave Emily, the mistress of the Ringling household? Should she broach this with John? Confident that she could present this as simply a matter of household logistics, Emily stepped into John's room where he and Ina were seated in side-by-side armchairs. "Excuse me, Ina, I need to speak to my husband alone."

John glowered. "Why?"

Ina made no move to leave.

Emily tightened her fingers into fists at her side. "I'd like to speak to you privately, John."

"And I don't see why you feel the need to rudely dismiss Ina from the room."

And without any premeditation, Emily's composure was engulfed under a geyser of steam. Hot angry words burst forth as she ticked off every incident, large and small, that had stuck in her craw for weeks. "You are a fool, John, if you don't see how she is manipulating you! She is calculating and conniving, out to usurp my role as your wife. And you are too besotted to see her for what she is."

Before either John or Ina could reply, Emily stormed

out of the room. Her flareup had left her weak and trembling. She crumpled onto her bed. *What have you done? What have you done?* She imagined John at this moment, calling his attorney to refile for a divorce, Ina at his side cooing assurances that it was the right thing to do. No. this could not happen. She'd have to apologize, beg forgiveness, and wrap herself in humble contrition. If not, her marriage, dismal as it was, would end, leaving her stripped of shred of dignity she possessed. So, she returned to John's office, mouthing words of apology she did not feel. John offered no conciliatory words of his own, as was his way.

ONE AFTERNOON, SOPHIE telephoned. "Emily, it's been months since we saw you in Coral Gables, and here we are just a few blocks from one another in the city. Maintaining two homes has been keeping me hopping, but you know all about that. The painters here have finally finished, and everything has been set to rights. Please come for lunch and see what James and I have done with the place."

Emily felt a flush of affection for her friend. She knew that Sophie was aware of all that had transpired—the divorce filing, its rescindment. How like Sophie to skirt around the unpleasantness and simply offer her friendship. "Sophie, we have so much to catch up on. Yes."

A few days later, Sophie welcomed Emily into her Eighty-ninth Street apartment. "When James and I married, it made sense for us to live in his place. But you know my James. He wanted me to feel that it belonged to me, so he's encouraged me to redecorate." Just as when she visited the couple in Coral Gables, Emily immediately felt at home. The rooms were decorated in an up-to-date style, and the color palette of soft golds and deep greens was warm and welcoming.

"It's lovely, Sophie. You have such an eye." Emily hugged her friend, swallowing her envy. John had never allowed her to redecorate, acting as if it were an affront. Every element in this home reflected Sophie and James. *The homes where I reside display only Mable, not me.*

She recalled the day, perhaps a year ago, when she could no longer countenance the sight of the garish gold columns in the Ca d'Zan foyer. Impulsively, she bought a can of black paint to cover the gilt and without discussing her plan with anyone, set to work. Satisfied with the results, she stopped for a moment to admire the rich, velvety black that added a contemporary drama to the room. Just then the elevator door opened and John appeared.

"Emily! What on earth have you done!" He hobbled toward her, his face menacing.

"Just adding some modern flair, John. The gold paint is so dated and frankly, rather vulgar." She daubed on a few last strokes with the brush and wiped the bristles with a cloth. "Black is all the rage these days."

John erupted. How dare she? Didn't she know these were authentic Venetian columns that he and Mable had obtained on trip to Italy? On and on he fumed as she tidied up.

Finally, she turned to him. "I refuse to debate this with you. This is my home too and I have every right to make a simple change without consulting the long-deceased Mable." Coolly, she strode past him as he continued to sputter. Not for one moment had she regretted her actions. The appearance of the foyer was much improved in her eyes, and more importantly, the black paint reflected her taste, not Mable's.

✧ ✧ ✧

AS SHE SERVED lunch, Sophie skittered around inconsequential topics.

"Have you seen Douglas Fairbanks in *Morning Glory*?"

"We saw Eddie Duchin and his band last week."

"There's an intriguing little mystery in this month's *Vanity Fair*. Have you read it?"

Finally, Emily reached out and grasped Sophie's hand. "It's okay, Soph. We can talk about it."

Sophie squeezed Emily's hand. "I don't need to pry."

"You're not prying, and I could use a sounding

THE SECOND MRS. RINGLING

board." Emily threaded her fingers through her necklace, then fidgeted with her wedding ring. "I'll start from the beginning, if you're willing to listen."

"Of course. My heart has been aching for you, but I didn't know..." Sophie's voice trailed off.

Emily recounted her story—the serving of the divorce papers in Kress's, John's push for her to sign away her dower—and ended with, "I've got to stay with him." She pressed her lips together and closed her eyes. When she opened them, she met Sophie's gaze. "Am I a fool?"

"No, you're far from being a fool. You've endured so much, Emily, and I understand the choice you've made. I can only offer my friendship, and if you ever need anything, you know I'm here."

"A friend is just what I need. And I'm sorry for burdening you." Emily forced a weak smile. "I just need to watch my p's and q's. It's like walking a tightrope around John."

"I know you, Emily. You'll keep your balance on that tightrope." Sophie patted her hand.

Emily chuckled. "Listen to us, talking in circus jargon. Thanks for your loyalty, Sophie."

THE TIME SPENT with Sophie lifted her spirits. October turned into November, Emily urged John to spend Thanksgiving Day with her sisters and their families in East Orange. But John brushed off the invitation, as she suspected he would.

"Of course, when it comes to something that pleases me, you'll have no part in it," Emily observed, her voice tart with disdain.

"And your caustic attitude does nothing to sway me to change my mind," John retorted.

Go to hell. But she held her tongue. When had she become so nasty? She had often been described by others as vivacious. John had once said, "You're like a bubbly glass of champagne!" Now, there was no effervescence left within her.

In truth, she was not sorry that he'd turned her down. The holiday was much more pleasurable without having to weigh her words and gauge his frame of mind, to manage to enjoy her family while keeping John entertained and content. Around Olga's dinner table, she felt the tension dissolve, as savory dishes and familial affection were doled out in equal measure. Maybe as Christmas approached, she might spread some holiday cheer and good will into her marriage.

After the Thanksgiving weekend, Emily broached the subject of Christmas with John, reading a newspaper in the parlor. "Darling, with Christmas right around the corner, I've been thinking. Perhaps we could do some entertaining. Wouldn't that be fun? Say, a dinner party, with the apartment all decked out for Christmas—a lovely tree, holly and ivy on the table."

John looked askance at her, but she perched on the ottoman in front of his chair and laid her hand on his knee, choosing a pose of supplication. "I'll do all the planning. I love decorating for Christmas. As for the guests, that's up to you. But it's been an age since we've seen the Ziegfelds. And you and Flo go way back."

John dropped the newspaper to his lap and scowled. "The Ziegfelds? You can't be serious. What a ludicrous idea."

She flinched. *What had she done now?* "Ludicrous? Why?"

"Surely you are aware that he and I have had a falling out over business. Your suggestion that we invite them in as if everything were rosy is simply ridiculous." He slid her hand from his knee and curled his mouth into a sneer.

Emily sat back. "I had no idea. But then how would I know? You haven't confided in me."

"Well certainly you read the newspapers. I can't be expected to fill you in on what you can easily find in print." He lifted the paper and opened it with a snap. "As for a Christmas party, I'm hardly in the mood. But do as you please. Just don't let Nicholas in again, after the disaster last time."

She stood. "I was only trying to inject some fun into our lives, John. 'Tis the season, you know." She swallowed a lump that had materialized in her throat and left the room. *So much for holiday cheer.*

But why not go ahead with my plans, John's crankiness be damned? What could be the harm of a small Christmas gathering? Maybe John would rise to the occasion once guests arrived at his door, and he would appreciate her efforts once a party unfolded. Pushing aside her feelings of dejection, she forged ahead.

This time, she did not ask John his opinion, but presented her plan as a *fait accompli*. "I've set a date for a small gathering for the twenty-second, John," she announced at breakfast the next morning. "And here is the guest list." She slid a paper toward him, confident there was no one he could object to. Hadn't he mentioned in the past that Sophie's husband James was a fine fellow? Two other couples with no Ringling business connections were on the list. And the Lawrences—that silly Margo always fawned all over John. She'd even included that Willoughby woman from the building. Wouldn't the old dowager be tickled? Turning to Ina, she said, "And of course you'll be part of the merriment, I hope."

He scanned the list. "So, fine. Go ahead."

"You'll see. It will be lovely." She busied herself with sending invitations, arranging boughs of greenery and sprigs of holly, selecting china and festive table linens from Mable's collection, and planning a menu with Catherine, all as if John had never shown any objection.

Keeping things merry and bright, she hoped to soften the friction that dwelled within her and John.

But on the evening of the party, Emily, dressed in an ivory velvet sheath belted with a red satin bow, was making last minute adjustments to the dining table when John came up behind her.

"Emily, I need to speak to you." He leaned heavily on his cane. "Come in the parlor, please."

She turned toward him, puzzled. *Was he ill? But he looks well.* "My, don't you look dashing," she said, following him into the parlor.

John eased himself into a chair. "I want to let you know that I'm returning to Ca d'Zan."

Was that all? "Oh, I assumed you would want to head back to Florida after the holidays. I'm actually looking forward to escaping the cold of January—"

He held up his hand, stopping her. "No, Emily. Not after the holidays. Tomorrow. And I do not wish to have you accompany me there."

"What?" Her voice trembled. "Tomorrow? And without me?"

He crossed his arms across his chest. "Yes, I've made up my mind. We'll have your little soiree this evening, and then I've arranged for the train car for tomorrow." His voice was bland, emotionless.

"And you've chosen to fill me in on this just now?" Emily stroked her throat, then turned her eyes away from

John. She absorbed the holiday glow she had orchestrated—the glimmering candles, the little Christmas tree bedecked with glass baubles and twinkling lights, the punch bowl on the sideboard. Had she done all of this for naught?

"Well, you've been so wrapped up with Christmas. I'll keep in touch, of course. I just need to get back to Sarasota." He rubbed his hands together as if cleansing himself of the matter. "Now, don't get worked up and put a damper on your party."

She trailed her palms along the arms of the chair, swallowing rapidly to keep dizziness at bay. "I see" were the only words she could utter as questions crowded her mind. *Was this as casual, as innocent as he wants me to believe? Why now? Why does he want me to stay in New York? Why hadn't he told me before now? And was Ina accompanying him? But she couldn't lash out now; guests were arriving in a matter of minutes.*

John rose, leaning on his cane. "I think I'll sample the eggnog before your guests arrive." He shuffled to the sideboard.

Emily covered her face with her hands. *Do not cry.* Then she forced herself to stand. "They are our guests, John, not only mine. I'll be right back. I'm going to touch up my lipstick."

In her room, she plopped down at her dressing table and willed herself to take deep breaths to swallow her indignation, her anger. Glaring into the mirror, she hissed, "I hate him," then reached for a comb and snapped it in half. How sinister, how calculating of him to time this announcement so that she could not question him. And why did he insist that she remain in New York?

Before she could mull this over, she heard the annunciator buzz. She blotted her warm cheeks with a tissue, stiffened her spine and went to the foyer to greet her company. Ina had gotten there before her, and was complimenting Mrs. Willoughby on her dress, a dreary maroon shantung that had no doubt been trotted out at Christmastime for at least a decade. Emily joined the chorus. "How nice you look, Mrs. Willoughby. So delighted you could come." She could ooze as much flattery as Ina could. And she could survive this evening with her self-respect intact. *It will be a long evening, but tomorrow that bastard will be out of my sight.*

EMILY SPENT CHRISTMAS alone, not wanting to evoke sympathy by mentioning to her sisters or to Sophie that John had left for Sarasota. She'd given the help the day off and found comfort in her solitude. John had telegrammed a breezy line that he'd arrived in Florida; she'd responded with a "Merry Christmas, dear." Was this how they were going to be, exchanging pleasantries over the wires? She tossed the holiday greenery in the trash chute. Christmas was over.

A few days later, Sophie telephoned. "Emily, your party was lovely. Such a festive table you set. And James is still marveling at the Wellington you served. Splendid!"

Emily winced. She'd have to tell Sophie about John's departure. "So, you didn't feel that anything was off-kilter?"

"Off-kilter? What a strange question! No, unless you mean that garish brooch on the considerable bosom of that neighbor or yours, Mrs. Willoughby." Sophie chuckled. "She was bit of a bore, but the Nurse seemed to get on with her." When Emily did not return a chuckle, Sophie said, "I'm sensing something is off kilter, though, Emily. What is it?"

"Yes, or I could say unsettled." Emily slumped against the wall. "John's in Florida; I'm here. Alone."

"I see." Sophie paused. "Would you like me to stop in this afternoon for a drink?"

"Sophie, I'd like nothing more."

When Sophie arrived, Emily prepared a shaker of Martinis and poured each of them a glass, then added an olive speared onto a swizzle stick.

Sophie accepted the drink, then took a sip. "Excellent! Now, my friend, what is troubling you?" She set her drink down on the cocktail table, then spread her arms across the back of the sofa.

Emily curled up in a nearby chair. "I'm not quite

sure, to tell you the truth. John is at Ca d'Zan, but he asked me to stay here. Still, he's been cordial, sending chipper telegrams as if things were fine between us. I don't know what to think." She plucked the olive from the drink and nibbled on it. "I'm a bundle of nerves and I vacillate from "*Good, he's gone*" to "*I must save my marriage.*" I've toyed with hopping on a train to Florida, but don't think that would be my wisest course."

Sophie sipped her drink. "Where do you see your marriage going, Emily?"

"Oh, we've been through all of this. I cannot survive as the woman who John Ringling tossed aside. It would be social suicide. So, I want to hang on, somehow. Maybe being in two different states is what is needed." She set down her martini, then studied her fingernails, biting at the edge of one.

"Now don't go ruining your manicure over this, Emily. You've got a goal, now let's see how you can best attain it. And it won't be achieved with you acting downtrodden and hiding in your apartment."

Emily smiled. "You always manage to say the right thing. So, what do you think is my best course of action?"

As if plotting for battle, Sophie issued several directives. "Be lively. See your social set. Show New York that you and John are apart only because of business, and you miss him dearly. Keep in contact with John, telegrams, and even better, letters. Cheery ones, filled with your signature sense of humor, your sunny optimism. Shower him with affection in every missive and don't shrink from reminding him of the pleasures he is missing by being apart from you." Sophie's eyes sparkled. "You'll have him begging at your feet before long."

"Do you really think this will repair our rift?" Emily sighed. "We began our marriage with optimism, and everything seemed like a happy new adventure. That's over, but a divorce? No."

"Mark my words, Emily. John will be pursuing in a matter of time." Sophie's eyes twinkled.

"You may have read too many romance novels, my friend. But for the sake of appearances, we cannot end this marriage."

As THE WORLD rang in the new year of 1934, Emily found herself caught up in the optimism spreading across the land. Newspapers touted FDR's New Deal and the lessening of unemployment rates. Social columns were chock full of breathy descriptions of sumptuous gatherings where champagne corks popped unabated, now that the scourge of Prohibition was a thing of the past.

Sophie commandeered Emily's return to the social circuit, explaining that John's improving health allowed Emily more free time. When a curious acquaintance inquired about why John and Emily were not together, Emily tossed it off with a much-rehearsed line. "Oh, my, John is so very busy with his interests in Florida, and he suggested I enjoy the city while he is so tied up." She layered her comment with a bright smile and a "But enough about me. Tell me how you are doing."

At home, Emily wrote long letters to John almost daily, and although he telegrammed occasionally and was warm when she telephoned him, she had not encountered any sign of romantic feelings that Sophie had predicted. So be it.

On a blustery February evening, she penned, "My Dearest One," then blotted her stationery as she searched for inspiration. What was there to say, day after day? Truth be told, she did not miss him. Here in New York, she was free to come and go as she pleased. No tiptoeing around his moods, no fretting about his health. She was busy with a circle of friends and acquaintances, and it wasn't unusual for husbands to be away on business or tied up at their offices, leaving their wives to socialize solo. With a prominent husband, doors were open to her. But those doors had come perilously close to slamming shut when John filed for divorce. Keeping John content as her husband, even from a distance, was essential to her social standing.

She forged ahead, commenting on the winter cold, layering in "I wish I was with you, my darling boy." She could not resist adding, "Here is a good laugh. I saw this article the other day. 'John Ringling loses 120,000,000 in three years.' Oh, boy that surely sounds like money." Had John been aware of this dire headline? Was it true? Would he dismiss it as simply some columnist speculating out of thin air, or would he cringe at a precise accounting of his wealth? How she wished to know the accuracy of this statement!

Tread lightly, my girl. She continued. "Dearest, you can't imagine how lonesome I am for your sweet dear self. I love you until my dying day. God gave me that love for you, something I never knew before…" After three more pages, the letter was complete. She signed off with "Here's a big kiss," then a row of "xxxxx". Surely this constant outpouring of devotion would bring about a tenderness, and a warming of his heart. *He'll be calling me any day now, asking me to join him in at Ca d'Zan.*

As February ended and days passed without word from John, Emily placed a phone call.

He responded to her "Hello, dearest," with a terse "What is it, Emily?"

She forged on, choosing to ignore his abruptness. "Just missing you, John. Thinking of you each day."

"I see. So, nothing important to talk about then."

Emily imagined him at his desk, piled with folders. Was he alone, or was someone—Ina?—in the office with him? Maybe that would explain his reticence to speak of his affection if he even felt any. "No, nothing crucial to discuss. I played bridge the other day. You'll be amazed at how I've improved."

"Well, good for you." After a few seconds of silence, he added, "I will call you in a day or so, but right now I'm quite busy."

"Oh, I see." She ended with a breezy, "Well, darling, I'll let you go back to work," and hung up. Absence was clearly not making his heart grow fonder. She toyed with announcing her arrival in Florida but held off. Maybe by April.

A week later, as Emily sat down with the newspaper, her phone rang.

It was Sophie, her voice tense. "Have you seen Winchell this morning?"

"My, no. I've just poured my coffee and was going to begin on Page One. What's that rapscallion Walter spouting off about today?"

"Emily, dearest, I'll wait while you take a look." Sophie spoke softly.

"Okay, if you insist." Emily set down the phone, then flipped through the paper until she found Winchell's column. The first sentence punched out at her. "John Ringling once again files for divorce against his wife Emily, citing 'mental cruelty and ungovernable temper.'" She dropped the paper to the floor and picked up the telephone receiver, her hand trembling.

"How can he have done this? Why?" She cried into the phone. "I had no inkling! No inkling!"

"I'll be on my way in a few minutes, Emily. But maybe Winchell is wrong. It will be all right," Sophie assured her.

"All right? It won't be all right! That bastard is out to ruin me. And Winchell'd never write anything this scandalous unless he knew for sure." Emily hung up the phone and slumped to the floor clutching her stomach. *He's been plotting all along, too cowardly to face me, leaving me to find out by reading a damn newspaper. And what should I do now?*

Chapter Thirty-Eight

Sarasota 1935

EMILY COULD NOT have imagined the months that would tick by before the divorce hearings took place. Retaining a lawyer, wrangling with John's attorneys over details large and small, filing papers, then more papers, dragged out through spring, summer, and fall. Finally, in November, the hearings began in a Bradenton courtroom, a few miles north of Ca d'Zan.

Emily had not been to Florida since John had filed for the divorce and returning to the place where she had been so unhappy had filled her with dread. When John's attorneys had arranged that she stay in the Ringling Hotel, she phoned her attorney Michael Parker and objected. "I won't say in his hotel! John is purposely taunting me!"

But Michael had explained that John had agreed to pay her expenses there. "It will be only for a few days, Emily. We should not waste our objections on trivial matters when there are bigger issues on which to focus."

Reluctantly, she agreed. But simply crossing the

lobby was an ordeal. She imagined all eyes upon her, from the bellhop to the Sarasota matrons gathering for tea. She remained in her room as she awaited the courtroom appearances. Even the private terrace offered no respite, as from there she could see Ca d'Zan off in the distance, further down along the bay shore. *Whatever possessed me to marry this man? How did I fall under his spell and succumb to his wishes?* The questions tormented her as she paced like a caged lion, waiting for her day in court.

LIKE SHE HAD done each day of the trial, Emily and Michael Parker entered the courtroom and proceeded to their seats at their table while ignoring the whispers of the onlookers in the gallery. Faint glimmers of sunshine filtered through the narrow windows, and brass pendants hanging from the tall ceiling cast pools of dim light upon the room. Surrounded by pecky wood paneling and facing the judge's bench that loomed before her, Emily steeled herself for the events to come. This day was her day.

As Emily had trained herself to do, she kept her eyes straight ahead. Dressed in a navy-blue suit and an unadorned felt cloche, she plucked the dove gray leather gloves from her fingers, tucked them into her handbag, and then folded her hands on the table. She gathered strength from Michael's presence beside her, and she allowed herself to glance in his direction, drawing confidence from his strong-jawed profile. She noted his steady hands and the fountain pen he held poised over a legal pad. Then, staring straight ahead, she donned a practiced placid expression, one that masked the frustration and anger that smoldered within her. Day after day, she had listened to lies, innuendo, vile depictions of her character and demeanor and her lack of integrity. John's lawyers had brought forth an ensemble of individuals who portrayed her as a cold-hearted shrew hell-bent on making one man miserable. After hearing her name smeared with tawdry untruths and exaggerations, it was finally her turn to set things right.

While waiting for the judge to appear and the day's proceedings to commence, Emily replayed the worst of the testimony against her.

Early on, Mr. Choate, one of the phalanx of attorneys that lined John's table of legal representation, had called Miss Ina Sanders to the stand, casting her in the role of a selfless angel of mercy. Ina, dressed in a crisply ironed white uniform, sat primly in the witness chair and, her brow furrowed with concern, apparently ready for her opportunity to malign Emily.

When had she last worn that white uniform, the blue cape, the starched cap? It was as if Ina was in costume for the occasion, when in the Ringling homes Ina only wore frocks chosen to please her employer. Thick white stockings and heavy-soled white brogues now replaced the sheer hosiery and stylish pumps Ina wore while hovering around John each day. *Spare me your sanctimony*, Emily wanted to shout.

Choate, gaunt and sallow-complected, encouraged Ina with sympathetic strokes of his limp jowls and an air of concern as she related incidents that put her patient, Mr. Ringling, in mortal danger. She produced a notebook that she had been maintaining while providing his care. Each time Mr. Ringling's heart rate elevated, she recorded the circumstances surrounding the incident. Had Dr. Ewalt ordered her to keep such a notebook?

"No," she replied. "But I believe it was my duty as a nurse to keep meticulous accounts of Mr. Ringling's condition."

"And isn't Mr. Ringling fortunate to have been under your fastidious care," Choate opined, nodding gravely.

Michael Parker stood so abruptly that Emily flinched. "I strongly object, your honor. Mr. Choate is not questioning his witness; he is proselytizing."

The judge scowled at Choate. "Keep to the questions, Mr. Choate."

Choate held up a hand in apology. "Go on, Miss Sanders."

Ina spoke earnestly, oiling her voice with compassion. "I warned Mrs. Ringling that Mr. Ringling should not become agitated, but she paid no heed." She shook her head and wrung her hands, then dabbed her eyes with a starched linen handkerchief. "It was sad to witness such cruelty."

"Please continue, Miss Sanders." Choate extended his hand toward her. "Your observations are most insightful."

Ina straightened her spine. "I'm afraid there are many incidents that I observed." Courtroom spectators gasped and tabloid reporters scribbled in their notebooks as Ina claimed that Emily often flew into "fits of rage." Once, Ina recalled, Mrs. Ringling harangued John incessantly, hour after hour, demanding that John sell his property, until his heart rate rose to dangerous levels. Another time, Emily became so incensed that she threw bed linens around the room. Then there was the time when Emily prodded the chauffeur to speed down a bumpy road. "I told her that her husband would suffer, but she rudely dismissed me."

The judge rapped his gavel and issued a reprimand when the volume of the courtroom murmuring rose behind her, and Emily ground her jaw and squeezed her hands together so tightly that her knuckles ached. *This woman is diabolical. She plotted against me, turned my husband away from me, and now she presents herself as John's savior.* And what would the newspapers make of it all? She imagined the salacious headlines: *Ringling's bride out to kill him, nurse contends; Emily an evil shrew; JR barely survives.* With the daily rags screaming her name, readers from Florida to New York would be feasting on the demise of her reputation along with their breakfast muffins tomorrow. After these ugly accusations, would anyone be willing to hear her side?

It seemed that others on John's side had been lying in the weeds, waiting to pounce. Even Joe Cooke, a Ca d'Zan driver she'd always found affable, was called to the stand. Choate led Joe to explain how she and her sister insisted he drive them to Tampa constantly, and he often overheard Mrs. Ringling and Lena disparaging Mr. Ringling. "Once I heard Mrs. Ringling say that her husband was just an old skinflint."

Choate added, "So, while Mr. Ringling was recovering from his illness, his wife would be off to Tampa for her shopping and such? And while in Mr. Ringling's own car, she would confide in her sister, ridiculing her husband?" He shook his head in a show of sadness.

Michael Parker rose. "Objection, your honor. Counsel is embellishing the witness testimony."

"Sustained. Do not add to the testimony, Mr. Choate."

Choate held up his hand in a now-familiar gesture of appeasement. "That will be all, Mr. Cooke."

Parker sat and leaned toward Emily, whispering,

"You are doing an excellent job of maintaining your composure." But inwardly, Emily seethed. Why was spending the day in Tampa so wrong? It was not as if Sarasota had anything worthwhile to offer. She had gone out of her way to be kind to Joe, even tipping him out of her own handbag after a long drive. Yet here he was, betraying her.

THE WORST DAY was when John himself, the man who had vowed to love her and cherish her until death, took the stand, playing the role of a sickly longsuffering husband who had no choice but to dissolve their marriage to survive. "This will be the most difficult testimony of all, Mrs. Ringling," Michael Parker had warned her ahead of time. "I'll be right next to you. Take strength from that and try not to show any emotion."

"I understand," Emily had responded in the attorney's office, but on the day of his testimony, with all eyes on her as she walked into the courtroom, she felt her resolve slipping. How could John turn against her so cruelly?

As they sat at their table, Parker patted her shoulder and whispered, "I know you can be strong." She glanced his way, then faced the judge's stand and steeled herself for what was to come.

John appeared in an ill-fitting suit, a dark gray wool, one that Emily recognized from when he had been more robust. *Always the quintessential showman!* John, consistently meticulous about the tailoring of his garments, must have chosen this one purposefully to accentuate his diminished girth. The jacket draped loosely from his shoulders and the pants pooled in untidy folds over his shoes. Here he was, as if in costume, trying to elicit some sympathy from the court for his declining health. Emily, irked that John would stoop to these theatrics, scribbled a note on the legal pad in front of her but knew that her attorney could hardly mention John's over-sized suit in his questioning.

Another of his attorneys, a Mr. Carson, dressed in an impeccably tailored pinstriped suit, his hair shiny with Brilliantine, interviewed John. As Carson adjusted his gold cufflinks and approached John in the witness stand, Emily speculated on the costs John was accumulating. Why not just give her what she rightfully deserved and save himself this expense?

Carson led John along with a range of questions that shined a spotlight on his success as a circus impresario, a businessman, and an art collector. John beamed as he boasted of his work to develop the city of Sarasota, his building of the causeway which he donated to the city, and the establishment of his museum. Straightening his red bow tie, he quipped, "Some might say that I've put Sarasota on the map."

Carson oozed admiration. "So, you and your late

wife built this art collection with the people of Sarasota the intended beneficiaries? My goodness! How generous. I applaud you, sir."

Emily struggled not to scoff and kept her face impassive. *How do I stand a chance against a man portrayed as the next Cornelius Vanderbilt? What if they knew that he was an unmitigated bigot? His museum was established only to shine the glow of public acclaim on him and Mable, not because he cared for the public one whit.* She itched to interject but held her tongue.

Eventually Carson turned the questioning to the marriage of John and Emily.

John began with a long sigh, and his voice softened. "Emily is shortening my life."

Parker stood once more. "Objection, your honor." Bu the judge dismissed him with a wave of his hand.

"How is that, sir?" Carson continued.

"Well, I've had my share of illness, and Emily's virulent rages, her attacks on me, are probably going to kill me."

"Please explain, sir." Carson folded his arms over his chest and tilted his head. "This must be difficult to recount, but we need to hear it all."

Several incidents come to mind," John began. "But mainly Emily is constantly haranguing me about money, money, money. She hates the museum, hates it. Once she said, 'Nobody but a—'" John paused and twisted his lips. "Don't like to use the Lord's name in vain myself, but she said, 'goddamn fool like you would put that money into pictures.'" He shook his head. "She has no appreciation for art. She wants me to sell all of the collection, turn it into cash. She bickers with me constantly."

Once again, Emily contradicted him silently. *You fool, John! You couldn't part with even the most inconsequential pieces because you were obsessed with getting your hands on more more. Even getting that El Greco could not loosen your grasp on the most mediocre pieces.* She stared at her lap, reliving John's and Lulu Bohler's horror at the mere suggestion he liquidate a couple of lackluster canvases.

"Unfortunate. What else has caused you distress?" Carson asked.

"A disregard for my property. She chopped up a rare Berlin rug with an ice pick, claiming moths had gotten into it. And, she had the gold-leafed Venetian columns in Ca d'Zan painted black. Without seeking my permission. she snuck behind my back to desecrate my home." John sneered.

How Emily strained not to stand up and shout a rebuttal. *That so-called rare rug was threadbare and motheaten! And those gold columns—the paint was chipped and they made the place look like a bordello!*

For just a moment, like a spark of electricity, her eyes connected with John's. Unbidden, that Dule Ellington tune, the one that had ribboned through their courtship, emerged from her memory.

"I fell in love with you the first time I looked into Them There Eyes."

Do you remember, John? Do you recall the way your eyes sought mine? The way you softly crooned these lyrics as we glided along so many dance floors? Do you remember?

As if to avoid her unspoken questions, John glanced away, breaking their momentary connection. He cleared his throat and continued his testimony. "Besides that, she's exceedingly rude to my nurse, threatening to fire her, and in spite of my illness, she insists on holding raucous parties in our home, disrupting my peace."

"And when you try to reason with her?" Carson continued.

John grimaced. "She's hit me on more than one occasion. Slapped my face, beat me about the chest." He rubbed his fingers across his forehead. "I could not believe she could be so volatile."

Carson raised his eyebrows. "And did you ever retaliate in kind?"

"Never. I am not the kind of man who would strike a woman."

Emily took a sip of water from the glass on the table as she tried to quell the tune wafting through her memory. *"My heart is jumpin', you've started somethin'…"* These words had once wooed her, but now they seemed saccharine, even bitter.

I was a fool to fall for this man. Who strikes with words, with actions. How many times has he belittled me? Ignored me? My only recourse was to strike back at him, and now he is portraying me as a hellcat.

As that November day wore on, Emily endured the dismantling of her reputation. Parker objected sparingly on her behalf, and, in Emily's eyes, his cross-examinations seemed tepid and weak, bordering on deferential. *Why wasn't he hammering away at John?* While waiting in a private office during a recess, she confronted him. "Why aren't you defending me? Why are you allowing John to say such terrible things about me?"

"Mrs. Ringling, it would not serve you well. John presents himself as a sympathetic character, as did Ina. Badgering them would only sour the judge against you."

"But they're lying! Or exaggerating!" Emily removed her hat and raked her fingers through her hair. "I'm being portrayed as a harridan, and you just sit there." Tears that she had held at bay during the proceedings suddenly broke through and she put her head on the table and wept.

Parker pulled his chair closer to hers and lay his hand on her shoulder. "I know it must seem that way, but we will have our moment to counter these ugly accusations.

You will have your turn."

She looked up at him, gulping away a final sob. "I don't know how much more I can take." She rubbed her cheeks with the back of her hand and sniffed. "It's nonsense, all of it. I'm the injured party here. I'm the one who should have filed for divorce, instead of succumbing to this humiliation."

Parker murmured soothing sounds, then added, "I admire your strength in the face of John Ringling. I know it's been difficult."

Emily straightened, bolstered by Parker's assurances. Despite all he'd heard, his loyalty to her appeared strong. Yes, it was what he was paid to do, but she read a kindness in his eyes that warmed her. "Now we have to return to the courtroom, and I look a fright."

He smiled at her and pulled a handkerchief from his pocket. "You don't look a fright. Just touch up your lipstick and you'll look as beautiful as ever, Mrs. Ringling." Reddening, he turned his head. "I'm sorry. That was an overstep on my part."

"No." Emily accepted his handkerchief and dabbed her cheeks. "You're truly kind, Michael. It's just been so grueling. And after all we've been through together, isn't it time for you to call me Emily? I insist."

The late afternoon session focused on the matter of Emily's loan to John before their marriage. John claimed that Emily agreed to accept paintings in lieu of a cash payment of fifty thousand dollars. Emily's anger hummed inside of her, and her head began to throb. *I don't want his paintings! I want my money!* Still, she listened, keeping a look of passivity on her face.

After the testimony concluded, Michael Parker saw to it, as he did each day, that she was whisked away out of reach from the cluster of reporters clamoring for her comments. On the day of John's final testimony, Michael joined Emily in the car he had arranged, and accompanied her to the Ringling Hotel, ensuring that no reporters would harass her.

"I advise that you avoid reading any press. It will only be upsetting," Michael said as they rode the elevator to her suite.

Emily nodded, not admitting that she had already seen some of what was being printed about the divorce.

At the door of her room, Parker grasped both her hands and squeezed them. "Try to let your apprehensions go."

But once Michael had left, she found herself wandering throughout the suite and on to the terrace, smoking cigarette after cigarette, unable to put her mind at rest. How she longed to escape to New York. She felt imprisoned in the hotel that bore John's name, stuck in his town of Sarasota. *Would these hearings never end?* She longed to be back in her apartment, located in the same Park Avenue building where she had resided with John.

It was furnished sparingly, but Emily had found comfort in being out from under the layers of Mable's accumulations and away from the public eye. But after listening to John's testimony, she was fraught with anxiety and anger. Thinking of her new apartment was a reminder that John had agreed to pay her expenses, but thus far his promises were unfulfilled. She paid the rent herself.

Telling herself that she needed to know what was being said about her no matter how cruel, Emily summoned a chambermaid, a local girl named Lilly who seemed starstruck in Emily's presence.

"Lilly, could you be a dear and see if you can find some New York newspapers? Perhaps Liggett's Drugs has some for sale if there are none in the hotel." Emily reached into her handbag. "And let's not tell anyone who these are for." She handed the girl a few dollars. "You may keep any change."

Lily curtsied as if Emily were royalty. "Yes, ma'am. Surely, ma'am."

In a matter of an hour, Lily returned with copies of the *Post*, the *Daily News*, the *Times,* and even the ridiculous *Broadway Tattler*.

"Wherever did you find these? Aren't you the cleverest girl?" Emily took the papers as Lily mumbled and blushed to the roots of her hair. Sending Lily on her way, Emily spent the evening pouring over every story, snide comment, and barbed insult.

"A tigress he could not tame!"

"Wife raged for hours, circus tycoon alleges!"

"Scorned wife brings Ringling to the brink of death!"

But the papers did not spare John either, Emily noted. One writer scoffed at John's assertion that Emily caused his blood pressure to rise. "Isn't that what all husbands hope for?" asked the newsman.

Other stories focused on John's diminishing fortunes. "What happened to the mogul John Ringling?" one story asked.

"Pay the girl back!" another writer proclaimed.

It was all so tawdry, so humiliating. She placed a long-distance call to Sophie. "How will I ever show my face again?"

"Emily, believe me when I say that this will pass. You're in the throes of the storm right now, but a calm shore lies ahead. Keep your head up. When all of this is behind you, you'll have a glorious new life to live."

"I can't imagine it." Emily's gaze drifted toward the sofa, barely visible under the newspapers she'd strewn there. Had her travails now become the evening entertainment for all of Sarasota, New York and beyond—a tabloid version of the soap opera *The Romance of Helen Trent*?

"This won't last forever, you'll see. And, just so you know, I'm hearing talk that favors your side in all of this. 'How could she bear that insufferable man?' is the running theme." Sophie paused, then chuckled. "Of course, I'm stoking those flames, Em, casually dropping thinly veiled innuendos here and there."

"Sophie, what would I do without you? I'm sorry to be so weak and whiny." A bit of the weight slid from Emily's shoulders. "I'll buck up. Thanks, my friend."

They made their goodbyes and Emily placed the phone onto the receiver. She scooped up the papers and bunched them into a ball for the waste bin. A tiny smile crossed her lips. She had to agree with one writer. Wasn't a rise in blood pressure what every man should want from his wife?

When the hearings continued in January, Parker brought forth witnesses who spoke on Emily's behalf.

Emily had often found Frank Tomlinson, employed as a chauffeur and household assistant, to be taciturn and cold, but his testimony shed a new light on Ina's testimony. "She asked me to buy the notebook for her at the drug store so that she could keep track of Mr. Ringling's pulse and such, and when I brought it to her, she thanked me. Then she said, 'This will get him his divorce.'"

Parker feigned surprise. "Really? And what did she mean by that?"

Choate barked, "Objection!" and Parker held up his hand in acquiescence. But a murmur spread through the gallery.

Emily suppressed her urge to applaud. *Thank you, Frank, showing everyone what a conniving little minx Ina is. And what a fool John is to have fallen for her act.*

Lena was summoned from New Jersey and spent several days at the Ringling Hotel in order to testify. On the day her sister Lena took the stand, Emily noted that she had dressed in a subdued tweed suit, a fashion unlike her usual style. Emily bit the insides of her cheeks to keep from smiling. She imagined Lena tactlessly approaching their dowdy younger sister Olga for a courtroom-appropriate garment, then, on court day, adding her own ruby red cloche adorned with a floppy black bow to her ensemble.

Parker led her through a testimony that depicted Emily as a loving and considerate wife, doing all she could for an infirmed husband.

"And what about Mrs. Ringling's relationship with Nurse Sanders?" Parker asked.

Lena sniffed and thrust out her chin. "Nurse Sanders seemed bent on keeping Emily away from John as much as possible. She would often tell Emily that John could not be disturbed, and then she would spend an inordinate amount of time with him, jolly, laughing, and joking, until Emily came along. Then Ina would be curt with her."

Parker continued. "And how did Mr. Ringling treat

Emily?"

Lena's eyes darted toward John, then she looked earnestly at Parker. "Not very well. He often rebuffed her. If Emily offered to help with something, he'd say 'Ina will do it.' And Ina was never dressed in nurse's garb, either. John bought her an entire wardrobe."

"And did you ever hear your sister and Mr. Ringling arguing?" Parker asked.

"Argue? Not exactly. But Emily would try to speak to John about matters, and he would brush her aside. And Emily would become frustrated."

"Can you describe the nature of these discussions?"

Lena nodded, causing her hat's bow to flutter. "Mostly about money. There was some issue with Bloomingdale's, I believe, and Emily thought that John should pay the bill. Emily was paying for the household expenses, but she felt that she should be repaid by John. I think that was what they agreed on when they were married."

"I see. Now you were with your sister when John first filed for a divorce in July of 1933, isn't that correct?"

"Yes."

Parker placed his hand on the railing of the witness stand. "Please describe for the court what ensued."

Lena took a moment to glare at John before she continued. "It was terrible. She was served right in Kress's, right in public. Then later, John insisted that we stay at Ca d'Zan. and I wanted to go back to New Jersey but thought I should stay by my sister's side."

"And what was occurring at Ca d'Zan? Did Mr. and Mrs. Ringling argue?"

Lena looked toward her sister and furrowed her brow. "Emily was distraught. She begged John not to divorce her. She told me that he said—"

John's lawyer Choate stood and called out, "Objection! This is hearsay!"

Lena startled, and the Judge turned to her. "Mrs. Kelley, you may only describe what you heard or saw yourself."

"I see. Well, I didn't exactly hear what John said, but Emily was very nervous and upset and fearful. But she finally agreed to sign some papers and the divorce was rescinded."

Now, AT LONG last, Emily herself would take the stand and reverse the injustice she had suffered.

Parker, seated next to her, whispered reassuringly. "Are you ready, Emily? Remember, just tell your story. I'll lead you through it all."

She barely tuned her head to respond. "I'm ready."

At the next table John sat flanked by his attorneys. At least she assumed he was there. She had not, would not look his way. Once she had thought she loved him, and that love turned sour when he treated her with indifference. Then as his health declined, she began to pity him. Now she despised him, loathing his duplicity, his determination to leech her own money from her, his willingness to be manipulated by those who fawned over him.

The gallery buzzed with spectators. Without glancing back, she could picture over-eager reporters bent on snagging a byline the front pages of their newspapers. To her, they were no better than vultures feasting on the carrion of her personal life. Today, she planned to toss them bits about John for them to chew on.

Sworn in by the bailiff, Emily seated herself in the witness stand, her spine rigid. Keeping her hands folded in her lap and her eyes focused on Michael Parker who spooned up questions that they had rehearsed, Emily told her tale. "I've always been a loving and indulgent wife to John. I've been solicitous of him through his illnesses. I've ensured that he received he best care." She described his hospitalizations in depth, his recuperations in New York and in Sarasota.

Parker, his voice soothing and solicitous, posed question after question. "In turn, how were you treated by your husband?"

Emily described John as fault-finding, neglectful, and cross, frequently using vile language towards her. As she and Parker and practiced, he asked her to recall specific incidents. Emily had several at the ready, each one illustrating the difficult life she'd been living as the wife of John Ringling.

"Tell me, Mrs. Ringling, how would you describe your relationship with your husband's nurse, Miss Sanders?"

"Ina was cold to me, and on many occasions tried to keep me away from my husband. I believe that she plotted against me, taking advantage of John's enfeebled state." Emily's voice faltered. "There was one particular evening that is difficult for me to describe."

"Please, Mrs. Ringling, please explain what occurred."

And Emily did. "One evening in Sarasota, Ina hurried me out of John's room, insisting that she had to give him a massage and prepare his bath. I returned to the room a bit later, and found Ina in her pajamas, sitting on the arm of John's chair, embracing him. On another occasion, I entered John's room in the morning to discover that Ina had remained in John's room overnight." Emily kept her gaze on Michael's face as the gallery rumbled. The judge rapped his gavel and threatened to clear the room and the noise subsided. *This should give them something to write about tonight.* Emily tamped down an urge to toss a smirk in John's direction and to maintain her demeanor of the wronged wife.

Michael continued with questions regarding finances: John's failure to pay household expenses, the threatening letters from Bloomingdale's and other retailers, his refusal to sell any art or to keep her apprised of the state of his investments, his capital, or any of his business dealings. As the day wore on, Emily sensed that the spectators were seeing her in a more positive light. *But they were just spectators. What was the judge thinking? How would he rule? That was all that mattered in the end.*

"AND THEN HE filed for a divorce in July of 1933 in Sarasota, isn't that correct?"

"Yes, he did." Emily felt her cheeks redden as she relived the day in Kress's. She could still feel the curious eyes of housewives whose mundane errands to buy thread or thimbles suddenly provided them with a salacious story to tell when the process server carried out his task.

She swallowed and continued. "I was taken completely unawares. Then John offered to rescind the divorce filing if I would agree to give up any dower rights. He badgered me constantly, telling me that Sarasota was under obligation to him, and that public sentiment was in his favor. He told me that Florida wanted the museum so they'd do whatever he wanted."

Parker nodded gravely and tilted his head. "And how did that affect you, Mrs. Ringling?"

Emily took a deep breath. "I was quite nervous, incapable of pursuing a course of action. John was quite forceful."

"And did he threaten you in any way?"

"Yes, he continued to press me, telling me he was in control of the courts and that I would be completely disgraced, the subject of a public scandal and devoid of any social contacts." She blinked, recalling one incident at Ca d'Zan.

DAYS AFTER SHE'D been issued the divorce filings in Kress's, she'd gone out on the terrace, pacing, and smoking a cigarette, mulling over John's ultimatum.

John approached her. "Have you made your decision to sign the papers I've asked for?"

She turned to him. "No, I have not." *Why was he haranguing her?* "You and I both know that your demands are grossly unfair to me, John." She stepped toward the water to end the conversation, but he reached for her arm.

When he spoke, his tone dripped with venom. "Don't be a fool, Emily. No lawyer will have anything to do with your case. You'll end up a laughingstock. And just wait until the press gets a hold of this. Ha!"

He hates me. Everything that has gone wrong in his life, he's attributed to me. She repeated his words in a mocking tone. "'Don't be a fool, Emily.' Had I only told myself that before I ever married you, John. Your treatment of me is despicable." She tossed her cigarette into the water. "You are a weak and pathetic man." She strode toward the house, her heart pounding. But lashing out at him would not solve her dilemma. What recourse did she truly have?

✧ ✧ ✧

Parker continued. "And on August 31 of that year you signed the papers John wanted you to sign, and he rescinded the divorce, is that correct?"

"Yes, it is." She bit her lower lip. She wanted to add *And a few months later, he did just what he had set out to do, toss me aside.* But Michael had warned her against being perceived as hysterical or shrill.

"And has your husband yet to repay you for the fifty thousand dollars you lent him on the days before your marriage in 1930?" Parker continued, looking askance at the table where John sat.

"No. He insisted that the loan be extended for four years. I had to agree or he would have gone through with the divorce at the time." Why had she given him the money in the first place? How foolish she had been, enthralled by the aura of John Ringling, the high-powered and charming man of the world. How many times since then had he tossed her vague, unkept promises, dismissing her as a nag who was never satisfied?

When Parker completed his questioning, John's lawyers interrogated her. Choate insinuated that she had abandoned her husband by not returning to Sarasota at

Christmas of '33. "Didn't you tell your husband that Sarasota was no fun, and you did not wish to go there?"

Emily was steadfast. "No. I begged John to allow me to accompany him. He told me to stay in New York."

Responding to her answer with a cold scowl, Choate continued peppering her with questions.

"Did you disregard the advice of your husband's physicians?"

"Isn't it true that you belittled his art collection?"

"Isn't it true that you disparaged him? Isn't it true that you refused to accompany him on the circus routes?"

Each question was crafted to show Emily as conniving and cruel, but Emily held fast. "I am not the woman you describe, Mr. Choate."

After the day on the stand, Emily felt battered. Who would the Judge choose to believe? Would justice prevail or would she leave the courtroom with little dignity and in diminished financial standing. She wanted her dower rights; she wanted her fifty thousand dollars; she wanted her standard of living to be maintained. But most of all, she wanted to be rid of John Ringling. She returned to New York to await the final decision of the judge.

IT WAS NOT until months later that the divorce was granted. In the judge's chambers, Emily ignored John, seated nearby, and sat rigidly as the judge read the decree in a monotone. "There is no evidence that Mrs. Ringling has been cruel to Mr. Ringling. On the contrary, there is evidence that she attempted to relieve his suffering by paying for his health care at times, and also bearing household expenses."

As Michael Parker had advised, she did not react. *But this was a good thing, wasn't it? The judge had seen through John's attempts to smear her reputation.* A glimmer of hope rose in her chest.

Then the judge continued. "But between September of 1933 and December of 1933, her actions may have been detrimental to her husband." *No!* She wanted to shout. *Not true! Not true!* She dug her fingernails into her palms to keep her hands from shaking.

John was required to pay all of Emily's legal expenses. And he was required to repay her the fifty thousand dollars he had borrowed from her. Yet, since his fortune had dissipated, she was awarded five paintings as collateral. However, the paintings were to remain in the Ringling Museum. They were hers, but not readily accessible to her. Hope was extinguished as the judge continued. There were no dower rights. Nothing.

After all of the wrangling, after all of the public humiliation and heartache, this was it. John Ringling had prevailed. A romance that had begun in a sparkling ballroom in Amsterdam had now, once and for all come to an end. She bit back anger words that rose within her.

This is not good enough. I cared for him in illness, I lent him money in good faith, and he callously humiliated me and tossed me aside. This is wrong. Wrong.

Silently, without expression, she signed the documents required, capped her fountain pen, and slid the papers across the table.

And then, as if shackles had been removed from her ankles, she felt lighter, almost weightless.

She was rid of him.

Epilogue

December 1936

EMILY HELD HER coffee cup with both hands to warm her fingers and peered out the window of her Park Avenue apartment, scanning the street below. Was it snowing? Moisture trickled down the windowpane and she could see that the pavement was wet, but as yet, no powdery snow had accumulated. She squinted to detect flurries, then watched the cars and taxis make their way down the street, their windshield wipers slapping back and forth. She spotted only a few pedestrians, and all were hunched forward, keeping the dampness and cold at bay. One woman in pumps minced along on the wet sidewalk, her arms reaching out at her sides, as tentative as a tightrope walker.

How tiresome! I may need to wear my galoshes later. But that's to be expected in December, and it will be delightful to once again wear my furs. Emily pulled her satin dressing gown tighter around her and headed for the dining room where a plate of fruit and an English muffin awaited her. She considered the day that lie ahead. First, a manicure. Her nail polish was beginning to chip, and she could hardly appear at the bridge table this afternoon with ragged cuticles. She spread a thin layer of butter on the muffin, then gave her fingernails and appraising look. *By noon my hands will look as good as new.*

Reaching for the *New York Times* that lay next to her placemat, she scanned the headlines on the first page—more dismal news about Hitler, a photograph of the bridge being built in San Francisco, and new details about King Edward VIII and his romance with the American divorcee. *Why couldn't the press leave that unfortunate woman alone? Could they not allow her to live her life in peace? One cannot help who one falls in love with.* Her eyes skimmed over the story, and she made a mental note to read it more thoroughly later.

Then she gasped and nearly dropped her cup. Droplets of coffee stained the placemat as she set her cup back on its saucer. "Dear God! Oh, my goodness!" She covered her mouth with her fist. *Had this really happened?* She lifted the newspaper again but could barely steady her hands to read it. "I can't believe it!"

She felt strong hands on her shoulders. "What can't you believe, my darling?"

"This!" She cried out and extended the paper to the man behind her, who took it and pulled out the chair next to her. She watched as he settled into his seat and frowned at the print in front of him.

"This business about the Simpson woman?" He looked up at her, the corners of his gray eyes crinkling with concern. "Darling, I know you feel some connection to this woman's situation, but you mustn't let this bother you."

"No! Not her! It's John!" Her voice trembled, her mind a roiling cauldron of emotions. *Just what am I feeling? Pity? Sympathy?*

The man continued to skim the page until he found the article that had upset her. He read aloud. "John Ringling dead at age seventy-one." Standing, he reached for Emily's hands and guided her to her feet, then embraced her. "There, there, dear. This is a shock." He kissed her forehead as she sank into his arms. "Unexpected, isn't it."

"Yes." She clung to his shoulders and breathed deeply, allowing his familiar scent of sandalwood and his freshly starched shirt to steady herself. She looked up into his eyes for reassurance. "Of course, his health has been poor, but I had no idea." Her voice trailed off. "No idea." But that wasn't quite true. Although she had not seen John in months, she'd witnessed his decline over the years. In the courtroom, not so long ago, she detected an increasing weakness and fragility under the pomposity he displayed. "I suppose seeing this headline just caught me off guard."

"A death is always troubling. It's never good to find out news like this in a newspaper." He smiled at her. "Seems like this man has made a practice of it where you are concerned. Not that we can blame him this time, though."

"What a thing to say!" But Emily could not stifle a smile as her initial pangs of distress diminished.

"And there have been so many reports of his financial ruin. That certainly would take its toll on any man."

"And especially on John. Always so filled up with bluster about his enterprises. It can't have been easy being in the public eye these days." A tiny spark of sympathy for her former husband flickered, then died. *Perhaps if he hadn't always assumed he knew everything. How many times did I try to suggest—* She shook her head. "Well. No sense in rehashing all of it."

She heard the phone ring in the other room, and then the soft voice of the housekeeper answering it. She sighed. "I suppose everyone will be hounding me for my reaction."

"If it's the press, I'll instruct Catherine to simply say 'No comment.' But tell me, how are you feeling?" He lifted her chin gently and studied her face.

She thought for a moment before answering. "I hesitate to admit that I'm relieved." She stroked a bit of salt-and-pepper hair above his ear and raised her eyebrows.

He chuckled softly. "My dear, I so love your candor."

He kissed her. "And I love your beautiful face. But now, I've got to get to the office, and you have a bridge engagement, don't you? Let's finish our breakfast and get on with our day."

Emily kissed him back. "Michael, you're so dear. How could I have known that the worst days of my life in that despicable courtroom would lead me to you." She dropped her arms from Michael's shoulders and returned to her chair. Spearing a banana slice with her fork, she sighed. "Just my luck to have a bridge engagement today. I'm sure I'll be fielding questions and won't be able to concentrate on my cards."

Michael stirred a teaspoon of sugar into his coffee. "May I suggest that you employ the tried and true 'no comment' there also. After all, you don't know the circumstances, only what the papers say."

"Yes, the less said, the better. After all, John and I have been apart for ages. What can I add?" She nibbled on the banana, then set the fork onto her plate. "Would it be terribly crass if I suggested we open a bottle of champagne this evening? Toast to our future?"

"Superb idea, my love."

Author's Notes

For many years, my husband and I have been able to escape the frigid Illinois winters and to make Sarasota, Florida our part-time home. There is much to love about Sarasota. Its white sand beaches, the balmy weather, its rich history, and a myriad of cultural activities put Sarasota on many of those "Best Cities" lists annually.

When in Sarasota, one soon learns that John Ringling, the circus magnate, and his wife Mable are much revered by Sarasotans. John Ringling can be credited for his efforts in the 1920's to make Sarasota a premier destination for Northerners seeking respite from cold winters. His presence is everywhere, from the John Ringling Causeway that spans the Sarasota Bay, to the statue of Mr. Ringling at St. Armand's Circle, a lively shopping and dining mecca that he developed, to the Ringling College of Art and Design. Perhaps Sarasota's largest claim to fame is simply known as the Ringling, home of the John and Mable Ringling Museum of Art, Mable's Rose Garden, the Historic Asolo Theater, the Ringling Circus Museum, and Ca d'Zan, the mansion along the bay built by John and Mable. Visiting the property is a must-do for tourists and locals alike.

I had visited the Ringling a couple of times and was agog at the lavish home of John and Mable, designed in a Venetian style and meticulously described by the docents who describe the couple's way of life, highlighting their attention to detail throughout the property.

And then I came across an article in the *Sarasota Herald-Tribune* written by Jeff LaHurd. It was entitled, "Ringling's Second Marriage a "'Three Ring Circus'". Filled with juicy details, the well-researched piece describes the demise of John Ringling's second marriage to Emily Haag Buck, whom John met about one year after the death of his beloved Mable.

A second Mrs. Ringling? Funny, no docent mentioned her on a tour of Ca d'Zan. On our next visit, when we took out-of-town friends to see the mansion, I asked about Emily. The docent gave me a steely look and replied, "We don't speak of the second Mrs. Ringling."

Hmmm. I was intrigued and wanted to know more. Just who was this Woman Who Shall Not Be Named? Details were scarce, but I begin to envision what it might have been like to be John Ringling's second wife in a city that seemed to worship his first.

And so, my novel was born.

Much of what I have written is based on fact. At the Sarasota County Historical Resources Center, I read the complete divorce proceedings of John and Emily that are filled with tawdry accusations from both sides, and scoured newspaper articles from the 1930's. I've read books about John Ringling, delved into the pieces on the website *Sarasota History Alive*, and hunted the internet for any information on Emily Haag Buck.

Much of what I've written is based on fact. John did live next door to his brother Charles' widow Edith, whose daughter Hester and her family also lived on the property. Sam Gumpertz was part of the Ringling organization, until he and Edith ousted John from his role in running the circus. Julius "Lulu" Bohler was the art dealer who helped John and Mable acquire the contents of their museum. And Ina Sanders was John Ringling's nurse.

But this is a work of fiction. Much of the story comes from my imagination as I pondered what *might* have happened, and not only what exactly happened. There is no Sophie, no Edward Appleton, no art dealer named Smythe. And although Emily's sister Lena was a frequent visitor to Ca d'Zan with her son, I've aged her son and named him Nicholas.

My goal was to peek inside what might have occurred in the marriage of John and Emily. Being married to an icon who was deeply mourning his first wife could not have been easy. And being married to John Ringling, thirty years her senior, whose vast fortunes along with his health and prominence withered away soon after their marriage, was certainly fraught with challenges.

And so, here is what I imagine was the life of Emily, the Second Mrs. Ringling.

Acknowledgements

It's often said that it takes a village to raise a child. In my case, it has taken a village to create my novel *The Second Mrs. Ringling.*

My village is populated with a talented and eclectic group of individuals whom I met in the Writers' Workshop at the Ringling College Osher Lifelong Learning Institute, known as OLLI. When COVID caused OLLI to close its doors to in-person classes, some of us workshop regulars formed a Thursday morning ZOOM group. It was then that I began my novel. Their encouragement, advice, suggestions, attention to nits and especially their modeling of what good writing looks like spurred me on week-by-week to keep going and write my story.

I cherish each one of you—Jo Schmidt, Ellen Marks, Meg Spinella, Bill Casale, Bob Fellman, Tom Smith, Harold Ellis, Seab Stanton, and the late Bill Andrews—and am forever grateful for your friendship.

My thanks also go to the staff of the Sarasota County Historical Resources who helped me with my research, and to Jeff LaHurd, who steered me in that direction.

And for those friends who occasionally asked me,

"How's Emily?", thank you for your interest in my project.

And a hearfelt thanks to my husband Michael who has encouraged me every step of the way.

About the Author

Ellen Brosnahan is a Chicago native and a lifelong educator. Spending many years as a middle school language arts teacher, she guided her students to "show, not tell." After leaving her own eighth grade classroom, she supervised a next generation of teachers at Illinois State University. Currently she as an instructor of a writers' workshop at the Ringling College Osher Lifelong Learning Institute in Sarasota, Florida. She has co-authored two books: *101 Things to Do in Naperville*, and *Guiding Students into Information Literacy*. In addition, she has written several novellas and has published a variety of pieces on her blog *Hello Lamppost*. Ellen and her husband Michael divide their time between their hometown of Naperville, Illinois and Sarasota, Florida.